THE LANTERN ON THE PLOW

George Agnew Chamberlain in his New York City apartment, 1924.

THE LANTERN
ON THE PLOW

George Agnew Chamberlain

South Jersey Culture & History Center

2023

THE LANTERN ON THE PLOW
By George Agnew Chamberlain

First published by Harper & Bros., New York and London, 1924
This edition published in 2023

Design, layout, and additional material Copyright © 2023 by
the South Jersey Culture & History Center at Stockton University
Critical Foreword Copyright © 2023 by Tom Kinsella
Biographical Foreword Copyright © 2023 by Jim Bergmann

Printed in the U.S.A.

stockton.edu/sjchc/

ISBN: 978-1-947889-19-4

Critical Foreword

Rattling Run Fields, the principal setting of *The Lantern on the Plow*, is a rambling, ramshackle, difficult property. The Sherborne family has held possession of the farm since the early eighteenth century, before the American Revolution, and each successive generation has sunk deep roots into the land. Author George Agnew Chamberlain picks up the family story at the start of the twentieth century, introducing readers to Warner and Eunice Sherborne and their two exceptional children, Drake and Io. At story's opening, they are wretchedly poor, trying to wrest a living from the seemingly unforgiving land. With demand for more work than can be readily done, Warner sometimes plows at night by lantern.

The story takes place in southern New Jersey: Greenwich, Bridgeton and Alloway Township play important roles, but none more important than the overlooked farm. Judge William Alder, intrigued by their attachment to the antagonistic land, befriends the family. Tryer Mattis, local entrepreneur and early adopter (he drives an automobile!) enters the story as well. Chamberlain skillfully delineates each character, furnishing realistic motivations and compelling reactions to the events of their lives. The story presents multiple love triangles which, at the conclusion, are resolved with surprising and touching satisfaction.

The story can be rambling and difficult, like Rattling Run Fields, but it is never poorly constructed. Chamberlain supplies provocative themes: humanity's struggle against an implacable world; aging and loneliness; growth and independence. A favorite topic is the impact of modernity, specifically the changeover from horse to automobile culture. The language of the text can be challenging as the thoughtful, but loquacious narrator attempts to present complex thoughts that the characters themselves are not quite able to articulate. Mother and daughter struggle to communicate, lovers as well. Characters attempt to explain with inadequate words what they feel but do not fully comprehend and as they do, they take part in an age-old storyline:

> You pass, and yet you do not pass. Spring cannot always reign. Flakes of snow, like great white tears, will drive against the panes, yet surely the branch will bud, the leaf sprout, and the vine send forth its shoots. Thus Rattling Run Fields across the measured cycles of the years; and thus you also may endure.

Throughout the novel, as the characters strive to understand and communicate, the story becomes a journey toward self-discovery. While the plot follows a generation in the life of these South Jersey natives, it is never turgid and often takes surprising turns. Chamberlain has written a very entertaining novel. Most satisfyingly, he makes us care for these characters. At the close of the story, we are left witnesses to ordinary people who have lived extraordinary lives.

Tom Kinsella

Biographical Foreword

George Agnew Chamberlain is a largely forgotten South Jersey author who lived and wrote during the first half of the twentieth century. Born to American missionaries in San Paulo, Brazil, in 1879, he came to America in 1891 to further his education, attending first Lawrenceville School in Mercer County, New Jersey, and then Princeton for two years. At both schools, he was involved in literary societies and wrote stories and poetry.

In 1902, he returned to Brazil to teach, sell religious books, and, finally, join the consular service. It was also at this time that he began to have stories accepted for publication. After returning to America for a short time, he returned to Brazil as the Consul General in Pernambuco. From Brazil he was assigned to Lourenco Marques in Portuguese East Africa and from there to Mexico City, Mexico. He resigned from the service in 1919 to write full time.

George Agnew Chamberlain was not living permanently in South Jersey when he wrote his first three Jersey novels: *Highboy Rings Down the Curtain* (1923), *The Lantern on the Plow* (1924), and *Man Alone* (1926). He had a mailing address at 99 West Commerce St. in Bridgeton, New Jersey, his mother's home, but still had apartments in New York City, Paris, and London. In an interview he told a reporter that he wrote his first three South Jersey stories while in Paris. What is remarkable is how accurately he portrayed the area in his novels. It would not be until 1927, when he bought Lloyd's Landing in Quinton, New Jersey, that he became part of what he lovingly described as the "Barrens." Chamberlain died in 1966.

The Lantern on the Plow was Chamberlain's first long novel about South Jersey. In an article that he wrote for *We Women* magazine (October 1945), he described the inspiration for the work.

7

The seed for the story was a short paragraph in the *Bridgeton Evening News* describing the arrest of a farmer for not sending his children to school. His defense was what got me: he stated that he had to plow all day and then by lantern light, to feed them.

Chamberlain went on to explain the local inspiration for the setting he chose. Speaking about the farm, he identified it as a stone house on the road from Deerfield Village to Alloway just past Bostwick Lake. The village is located in Upper Deerfield Township on Route 77. He noted in the *We Women* article that the house had been renovated and that it still existed to that day. He chose "Greenwich on account of its ancient and unspoiled charm . . . ." The house he described you see ". . . as you leave Greenwich on the way to what was then Head of Greenwich and has now been dubbed Othello." The village represented for Chamberlain the type of charm he would continue to write about in future stories. Chamberlain was taken by the quaint South Jersey architecture and questioned if the "taste that went into the construction of local patch-work houses prior to the Civil War, and most remarkably in Greenwich itself, has died from the land."

The Bridgeton that Chamberlain describes, "the principal town of the three counties . . . ," in some fashion still exists today. Myrtle Manor, a key location in the novel, is based on the still existing Ivy Hall. The edifice has lost its wooden appendages but the main building still stands on the northwest corner of Commerce St. and the entrance to the City Park in Bridgeton. Chamberlain's descriptions of the park are also still viable today. The raceway he described has been changed some by various flood events, but you can still canoe from the south end of the raceway near Ivy Hall to Sunset Lake if you have your own canoe, since there are none for rent today. There are still walking trails and bridges that make it possible to walk most of the 700-acre park; a bathing beach remains, relocated from the east side to the west side, and provides a place to swim.

Horseback riding in the park was permitted when Chamberlain wrote the novel. He would come to Bridgeton to see his mother and to ride in the park, hiring a horse from the stable that was behind the Hankin's lumber yard. One day the ten-year-old son of the lumber yard owner was at the stable checking on his pony. Chamberlain and a woman came to hire horses and the boy was asked whether he would like to ride with them. He accepted and that evening when he returned home his father asked whether he knew the people he went riding with. He did not. His father then told him that he rode with the author George Agnew Chamberlain and Amelia Earhart, a good friend of Chamberlain who visited him frequently in Bridgeton and later at his home in Quinton.

Prior to being published as a novel, *The Lantern on the Plow* appeared in the *Saturday Evening Post*. It was released as a serial in November and December 1923 and January 1924. Following its publication, the story generated letters to Chamberlain from readers who commented on ways that the story touched them. A woman from Cranberry, New Jersey, who was born and raised in Bridgeton, wrote that the story gave her the "keenest pleasure." She mentioned her acquaintance with Old Broad Street Church and the "all seeing eye of God." She was old enough to remember going to the "100 anniversary" celebration for the church in 1892 as a child. Chamberlain received this letter before the series in the *Post* was complete.

In a 1924 letter, a gentleman born in Woodstown, New Jersey, described his admiration for the story. He wrote that the literary license that required Chamberlain to import a rock ledge was "entirely understandable." The writer also recognized Chamberlain's references to Lawrenceville where Chamberlain attended Lawrenceville School from 1898 to 1900. At the end of the letter, the correspondent noted that the address where he sent the letter had previously belonged to a friend, Mrs. Cox. The details of Chamberlain's South Jersey setting, though fictionalized, rang true to community members who knew the area well.

Chamberlain also received a letter from the assistant to the president at the Atlas Portland Cement Company, who was struck by the industrial detail in *Lantern*. The letter writer had a "notation from our technical engineer, after having read your chapter thirty-seven, describing the operation of the mill . . . very clever—O.K." He went on to write, "I think you can be assured, therefore, that there is nothing in the description that anyone can find fault with."

This last letter reinforces that Chamberlain's descriptions were not just figments of his imagination but written from careful research of the subject. The description in the novel to which the "technical engineer" referred reads:

> . . . The one on the right was carrying clinker to the tube mills. The burned rock looked like ashes, dark gray, cool; and then, as each bucket struck its tipple, there was a flash of garnet red, sudden, unexpected, vicious; cool gray on top, raging heat beneath. . . .

Chamberlain wrote with this precision in all his works.

His penchant for realistic detail provides the setting in which readers readily immerse themselves, but it is the empathy with which he draws his characters, and the situations in which he places them, that make his novels a joy to read still. *The Lantern on the Plow* is a story about a battle of wills between young and old; it is a love story, a tragedy and the end of a dream. It also acquaints readers with a little-known part of the country and its contribution to the country as a whole.

Jim Bergmann
Deerfield Township 2023

THE LANTERN ON THE PLOW

"WARNER SHERBORNE" called the clerk of the court. A rawboned farmer of a type which was on the verge of extinction even at the close of the nineteenth century arose and stood hesitant in the back of the room. He wore a straggling sandy beard. His sleeves and trousers were too short by inches. From his hands, gnarled and startlingly freckled, dangled a tattered hat, which he rotated nervously in the proverbial gesture of awkwardness. His deep-set eyes were fixed unflinchingly on the judge, but there was no strength in their gaze. It was both baffled and baffling.

The clerk motioned toward a bench, and though Sherborne was not looking at him he evidently perceived the gesture, for he moved forward with the peculiar gait of one inured to walking in plowed ground and sat down. Behind him followed his two children: Drake, a boy of thirteen, and his sister Io, a child of seven. The boy appeared to have been stunted in his growth; the girl was so slight that it seemed a breath might blow her away. The clothes they wore were much mended, much stained, but freshly washed.

Superficially the children presented no striking resemblance to their father; but Judge William Alder, bending shrewd eyes upon the group of three, was troubled by an evasive likeness. There was some continuing factor so hauntingly elusive or so deeply buried that it could not be casually caught and pinned to the wall

11

for leisurely observation. Two things at least were apparent. The features of children and father were similarly overrefined, and the quality of the gaze of the boy and girl, enveloping the judge in a wide eyed stare, was the ageless replica of the baffling gaze of their parent.

Judge Alder was a veteran of the bench, though his years and appearance suggested nothing venerable. He was forty-six, bright-eyed, clean shaven, and his hair was at that eminently becoming shade of premature iron-gray which reminds one of rolled steel. His cheeks were faintly pink, smooth as satin under the expert manipulation of an old-fashioned razor. The countryside would have been inclined to think him something of a fop had it not known him to be every inch a man.

He ruffled the papers before him, looked at the strange trio and then back at the docket. What names! Warner—that would pass; but Drake and Io! From whence had come such fantastic appellations to settle on the sordid denizens of a buried South Jersey farm? He stared again at the farmer and his two children, only to be met by the baffled and baffling gaze which seemed a visual demonstration of an actual trinity. It was as though one person were looking at him through three sets of eyes. The judge was not accustomed to being baffled. With a gesture of impatience, he concentrated his attention on the father and spoke.

"I consider this an aggravated case," he began. "Your farm is located within reasonable walking distance of the schoolhouse. According to your own statement and the records, you are the possessor of two hundred and sixty acres of unencumbered land. You have been thrice warned as to the consequences of persisting in absenting your children from school and forcing them to give their time to manual tasks far beyond their strength and years. If they were sturdy youngsters there might be some excuse. They are not sturdy. You are robbing them of more than opportunity; you are sapping their vitality. The law of this state mercifully no longer permits that sort of thing to parents. Have you anything to say for yourself before I pass sentence?"

For an instant the farmer's eyes flickered with light. The hat dangling in his hands stopped twirling. The strange pallor of his thin-featured face turned to a brick red. His lips opened as if to speak, strained for a moment, as though striving to form an initial word, weakly gave up the effort and closed. His gaze returned to meet the judge's eyes, but it was no longer wholly unreadable. It possessed a suggestion of the smoldering fire of rebellion which gleams in the eyes of all inarticulate animals when hard pressed.

During the pause the clerk of the court arose, hastily gathered up some papers as an excuse for approaching the bench, and addressed the judge in a whispered unofficial aside:

"Say, Bill, he's the feller that plows by lantern light."

Only a long intimacy could justify such interference with the course of cut-and-dried justice, and, as a matter of fact, clerk and judge had puddled together barefooted in the dusty lanes of a bygone day, stripped for the honor of the first icy plunge into deceptive spring waters, stolen the seductive Astrachan of June and meddled with the flue of a four-corners schoolhouse in a companionship and rivalry so remote as to savor of another existence. The clerk knew the boy and man upon the bench well enough to say enough and not a word too much.

Judge Alder drew slowly erect in his seat and regarded the farmer, with an interest suddenly intensified.

"Are you the man of the lantern on the plow?" he asked.

"Yes," replied the farmer, with suppressed vehemence and none of the hesitancy displayed in the previous futile effort he had made toward self-expression.

"Sentence suspended for investigation," declared the judge. "Court adjourned." He turned to the clerk and added informally, "Before you let him go, Harry, get me a clear bill of way to his farm."

Chapter 2

In spite of the sudden reversal of the intent to pass a severe sentence, the judge was not a man of impulses. Two weeks elapsed before the day arrived which he had deliberately chosen for his inspection in person. It was the thirtieth of May of 1901. He attended the ceremonies of Memorial Day, but immediately thereafter drove his smart hickory buggy, drawn by a sturdy little Morgan mare, out along the highway to the south. Gypsy, a handful at any time of the year, was more than feeling her oats; she was full of the sap and urge of the new grass. She slapped hoof to the springy ground with a vigor that demoralized into a frenzy of impatience when the judge was forced to draw her up at the tollgate.

Once that bar was passed, he gave her her head for two miles of straight going, by which time she was content to abandon foolishness and settle down, still eager and reaching, to a businesslike trot. He turned at a point marked by a famous lone oak and presently came to an unusual division in the form of a three-pronged fork. He knew well the gravel roads which swept at an increasing angle to the left and to the right. The one traversed a billowing region already renowned for its peach orchards; the other descended to the lush bottoms which fringe the flats of the Cohansey River. But the road in the center he could not remember ever before having noticed.

It was such a road as the driver of any vehicle might easily discard subconsciously. It opened with a narrow, rickety bridge which contrasted unfavorably with the strong culverts of the more traveled ways that flanked it. Its ruts were half overgrown with weeds and rose toward a sudden ramp in a series of humps which suggested effort and discomfort. Even the judge, intent as he was on his mission, felt a definite annoyance at having to slow down the willing mare; but once he passed the rise which had served as a blind to what was beyond, his spirits were immediately soothed.

From that point the narrow way descended smoothly toward the damp shadows of a thick growth of trees which bordered the little creek of Rattling Run. So refreshing was the sudden coolness of the shade that he would have been tempted to linger had not Gypsy caught sight of another sharp rise beyond. She flung herself at it with characteristic energy, and he was still soothing her with cries of "So, now! Easy, girl! Easy does it," when his attention was diverted to a house standing at a short distance from the road.

Instinctively he drew aside and brought the mare to a full stop. Few knew better than he the wealth of ancient structures that give interest to the myriad byways of South Jersey, of the three counties of Cumberland, Salem and Gloucester. The brick-floored church at Bridgeton, with the eye of God staring in its century gaze from the white plaster above the perilously high pulpit; the hamlet of Greenwich, wrapped in dead dreams of a rivalry of the port of Philadelphia; the stately red-brick homes of Salem, to which decades are as a day, were not curiosities to him. They were the background of his boyhood and the pride of his mature appreciation.

But even this remembered setting of very old landmarks seemed a quick growth in comparison with the unmistakable air of age, stark and unadorned, which marked the house he was now gazing upon. The building itself was made of roughly hewed blocks of red Jersey stone, surmounted by a sagging gabled roof of shingles. The steps which led to the high, narrow doors, and a lean-to of

16

wood, built against the rear, had warped away from the main edifice, leaving an unbroken moatlike chasm around the sheer walls. This effect gave the square stone tower of two stories an appearance of isolation which was negatived only by the many evidences of occupancy.

Dimity curtains, frayed from too frequent washing, gleamed in the small square windows and the door to the large kitchen was half open, permitting a glimpse of pots and pans. On the top step of the approach to the main doorway a drowsing dog lay in momentary danger of falling into the gaping interval between the stair and the threshold. A bucket stood beside the high well box and clothes were hung to dry on the long sweep. Most significant of all, the ground around the house was worn bare of grass.

One feature in the general aspect of the old place tantalized the judge, and he sat quite still until he had puzzled it out. It was that everything in sight—the bushes, the cedars, the timbers of the well box and outhouses, the dog, the chicken coops and the fowls themselves—all had an appearance of being twisted and gnarled as though growth and even mere permanence in those surroundings entailed a hard struggle.

He hitched the mare, blanketed her and approached the open kitchen door. The dog thumped lazily with his tail but did not get up. The house was empty. No sound came from it in answer to the judge's knock save the simmering of a kettle on the stove. He walked around toward the barn, found a path, and followed it through an ancient orchard to a fallen snake fence and a screen of trees, beyond which stretched a broken series of cultivated fields.

A glance at those fields told a tale. A small acreage of potatoes, just budding into leaf; a larger patch of Indian corn, and, beyond it, a billowing rise blanketed with the tender green grain in first growth formed an index from which one might deduce a volume. Somewhere there would be a pigsty, an annual sacrificial calf and the butter and eggs which are the small money, the ready cash, of the self-contained farm.

17

Judge Alder knew what that meant. He stood still for some time, studying the meager soil and his surroundings. With all the world to choose from, why should anyone have settled on this particular patch of ground? It formed one of the rare escarpments which thrust their low heads above the billowing flats of the South Jersey country. The place was irregular in contour as well as in shape; it was commanding and yet hidden; it was hard, awkward to handle. He was conscious of an increased feeling of exasperation against the farmer who found it necessary to plow by lantern light; but gradually his mood passed through a subtle change. Apparently against reason, he felt the mixed thrill of envy and admiration which seizes upon any one of us when we divine in a fellow creature something unconquerable.

Then something sinister struck through to his inner consciousness—something almost as unseizable and yet as definite as a chilling blast of air wandering across a balmy day. As by a passing flash of illumination he perceived this farm, this hard bit of land, as an actual entity with its own inexorable life to live; a dragon, if you like, armed with claws to wound and tentacles wherewith to bind and absorb. In that instant it bristled, and seemed to say to him as to all men, "Touch me at your peril!" He shrugged his shoulders, and laughed shamefacedly at his fancy.

Even so, he was still far from solving the problem of Warner Sherborne, but he had his feelers out and they were in contact. Already he sensed a battlefield where some obscure element of the soul fought tenaciously against the material elements of Nature. He was glad of a chance to watch the man of the lantern on the plow at work. In the wake of a lanky team, Sherborne was cultivating the cornfield. Far in arrears labored his wife with a hoe, and the two children, stooped over, weeding with their hands. The judge waited patiently while the farmer approached him along the full length of the field; then he hailed him.

"Rest your horses. I've come out for a talk with you."

The man glanced up without surprise, continued methodically to the end of the row, dropped the reins reluctantly and cast a look, almost eager in its keen calculation, at the sun and then toward the portion of the field still to be cultivated. He turned with a sudden droop of his shoulders and crossed over to where the judge awaited him.

Conversation does not open easily with the occasional recluse of South Jersey, and in this case it could be expected to present special difficulties; but Judge Alder had been in his day too shrewd a cross-examiner to miss the significance of the unhesitating reply given to the single question subject to a direct answer which he had propounded in the court room. This strange man might be inarticulate when it came to giving expression to the ideas which rumbled within the cavernous emptiness of his mental existence; but he was neither shy nor a fool in the face of an issue set squarely between the boundaries of yes and no.

"Sit down for a minute," said the judge, indicating the other end of the log upon which he had rested himself. "Do you smoke?"

"Naw," answered Sherborne. He paused, and then, with a jerky gesture which seemed to arraign the whole farm and its atmosphere of struggle before a higher court than any over which the judge had previously presided, he added, "I don't smoke ner chew ner drink ner shave."

The judge nodded understandingly.

"It's hard work," he said, "making a living out of a farm like this."

He waited, but in vain. Evidently the farmer had no conversation; at least, he was not yet launched.

"Have you never had a chance to sell out?" asked the judge presently.

"Ye-ah," answered the man, his deeply set eyes narrowing. "Twice."

"How much?"

It was a different question, deliberately put.

"The party had no call to make an offer," replied the farmer. "That's all the further it went. I warned him off at the outset."

"Why?" persisted the judge.

19

Instantly he perceived that he had overstepped the bounds of yes and no. Warner Sherborne was nonplussed. It was not that he was offended. One could see and almost share the distress of his struggle to answer. He gave up the attempt; but his wavering eyes, guided as though by an ingrained magnetic pull, wandered to fix themselves blankly on the gleam of red, seamed with mortar, which marked the location of the ancient and unlovely house.

"Been here long?" asked the judge quickly.

"Going on one hundred and seventy-four year," answered Sherborne promptly from the depths of his abstraction.

"That's a long time," said the judge after another understanding pause. "Seven generations is a long time in any country." His eyes swept the broken acres and fallen fences, only to return to fix themselves on the face of the living enigma before him. "It's a hard place to work and a hard place to love; but perhaps you do love it."

In answer to the half question the gaunt man gave him a swift look, as eloquent as it was astonishing in its portent.

"Ha!" exclaimed Judge Alder, half rising to his feet, and then settling back again.

This speechless relic of seven generations wasn't submerged, dead; not by a long shot. He was as sensitive, alive and ominous as a rattlesnake on a hot day. If he could not chatter; at least he could hate. The man was human, and the judge began to like him.

Chapter 3

"No," said Judge Alder, nodding his head, and with a whimsical twist to his expressive clean-shaven lips, "you don't love it. You hate it like Billy-be-damned. Why?" He frowned in the effort of concentration and then answered his own question. "Because you haven't fed on it; because the shoe is on the other foot; because this farm has fed on you and your wife and children and on your people for over a century and a half. That's why you hate it."

The words produced a slow awakening in the face of the farmer, as though his intelligence moved forward to grasp a central motive his unaccustomed tongue could never have articulated, but which his heart had long harbored. The judge was not slow to press home his advantage. His eyes grew more shrewdly penetrating, as if he sought to enter and dwell within the mind of this man who could not speak for himself.

"But you could not go," he murmured. "None of your people could go; least of all you. I'll tell you why—since you can't tell me. One can't break away lightly from the soil of a hundred and seventy-odd years. Habit; custom; most of all, roots. To you, all the world apart from this hard spot is a place of terror. You wouldn't dare move. You simply wouldn't know how or where. Listen! A grown oak can't be moved and live."

21

For the first time the farmer disclosed himself utterly. His body suddenly relaxed, came to rest. He gave the judge a look of trust and surrender, a look which seemed to say, "Here is one who understands the unintelligible, who collects the battle of a lifetime in a cupped handful of words, who lends form and a voice to the hidden soul!"

"I know how you feel, Warner," continued Judge Alder in the same low tone. "Your fight isn't against the world or even poverty; it's against this place. You have to choke food out of it, and fire, and a certain amount of clothing. Your wife belongs in the light on your side; your children inherited their share just because they were born here where you and six generations before you were born. You aren't feeding on your children. You don't drink, chew or smoke; you even plow by lantern light. No; it's the place that's feeding on them."

The farmer gulped and nodded his head violently. The judge frowned.

"It isn't right," he concluded. "They ought to have a chance—a different chance—these kids of yours. There must be some way to give them their schooling. We'll have to think it out—that's all. I'll have to think it out. Call them over here."

Sherborne stood erect, uttered a hoarse cry, raised his arm and let it fall. The woman dropped her hoe and started toward him slowly; the children came more swiftly. The boy was in the lead, but as they approached, the girl made a determined spurt and caught him by the arm. The judge could hear her gasp, "No, Drake; no!" The boy seemed to understand what she wished. He slowed down and took her hand. Together they came to a stop before their father.

The judge studied them with a kindlier curiosity than he had employed in the court room. Something was behind these young-sters—something that made them different. He did not like dirty children, but these were stained with soil alone. Somehow that made it all right with him. Behind their broken and blackened finger nails, their roughened hands, tattered clothing and clumsy

22

footwear shone a sort of intrinsic cleanliness. It was absurd to think of it that way, but he couldn't help it. There wasn't anything else to call it.

"Drake is your name, sonny, isn't it?" he asked. "And yours," he added, looking at the girl, "is Io?"

As he spoke, perhaps letting a little of the irony of his thoughts in the court room over those names creep into his voice, the woman drew near. She heard him. She stopped, still three paces away, so abruptly that he cast a quick glance at her. She was thin, built on delicate small bones; but nevertheless, at this fleeting glimpse, she did not give an impression of womanhood so much as of something inanimate, like a bit of tough harness. She was dressed in earth-colored gingham, belted at the waist, and wore a deep sunbonnet of the same material.

The judge knew she had heard him; or else, why had she stopped so suddenly? What had there been in what he said, anyway, to make her stop? He looked for an answer into her eyes. They had widened; now they shrank into themselves with a sudden veiling, a withdrawal, a fugitive look of seeking to hide, of running for cover. Her lips trembled and set in a straight line. She glanced inquiringly at her husband, turned and walked away, more swiftly than she had come. What! Was this woman also human? Was there something almost but not quite dead within her? Or was it that it was he who was seeing fanciful things under the influence of the burgeoning summer air? He turned back to the children.

"Come now," he said, "where did you get those names? Do you know?"

The children were not shy. They heard him, they stared at him steadily, comprehendingly, but did not answer. He could not find in the calm expression of their faces even the glimmering of an intention to answer. Still holding hands, they turned, as had their mother a moment before, and trotted off. The judge's eyes followed them, but he was not seeing their backs. Strangely enough, what he was still looking at intently was their faces—the firm set of the

23

boy's chin, for all the fineness of his features; the straight line of his nose, the unusual shade of his eyes. It was difficult to say whether they were blue or a dark gray, like slate.

The girl was more easily defined. Her hair and eyes were brown, with a glint of red fire in them. Where had he seen that glint before? Only once, for it was very rare. He could remember its rarity, but not the time or the place or the object which had disclosed the unusual gleam. Anyway, she was distinctly a brunette, olive skin and all. A mere wisp of a thing. Ah, he had it now—the smoky gleam within her eyes! It was like the dark red fire in the depths of an alexandrite; rare gem, once seen, never forgotten.

The children were running, leaping the corn hills. The girl let go the boy's hand. Had he been right in thinking her a mere wisp? What carried her? What lifted her, stride for stride, with the boy? The wind? Her spirit? Well, anything but muscle. While he watched the children Warner Sherborne looked wistfully at the idle horses and cultivator; but when his leisurely visitor finally arose he motioned to the farmer to follow him. Judge Alder was not to be hurried in a decision, nor would he accept a dismissal, however mute and pleading. On the way to the road where he had left his rig he paused for a moment and then turned aside for a closer inspection of the old house.

Walking around it slowly, he now perceived that the section containing the kitchen was half a story lower than the rest of the structure, and that within the high gable thus formed was placed a blackish gray stone which bore the inscription "1727." He read the eroded figures absently, and was about to move on when he was arrested by the sharp contrast between the stone upon which the date was graven and the rest of the iron-red wall.

"Was all the rock for the house quarried from the farm?" he asked presently.

"All on it," replied Sherborne.

"How do you know?"

"For one thing, the old folks told me; and for another, I know the spot it come from."

24

"What about that gray stone," persisted the judge—"the one with the date written on it?"

"It was the last stun they took out," asserted the man, with a quick gesture toward a distant elevation which marked the verge of the escarpment of the farm.

"Bring me a ladder," said Judge Alder, coming to a sudden decision. "I want to climb on the kitchen roof."

A few minutes later he had clambered on hands and knees over the sagging shingles to the ridgepole and was subjecting the stone which had aroused his curiosity to a minute inspection. All his life he had dabbled in mineralogy, but he scarcely needed to draw on the knowledge so acquired to determine that the object of his study was a block of cement rock, the raw material from which Portland cement is most easily recovered. It was badly weather-worn and the date would have disappeared long since had not the figures been cut large and deep. One corner was split so that with little effort he could pry off a triangular fragment, which he slipped into his pocket. He climbed down, dusted his hands and trousers and stood waiting for the inevitable question: but it did not come.

Warner Sherborne stood courteously beside him, dignified by silence. The judge was puzzled and then touched. He began to realize that he had been accepted once for all as a friend. He started to speak, changed his mind and crossed the road to where Gypsy stood with ears pricked and head turned toward him. Sherborne helped strip the blanket from her and undid the hitching rope. The judge gathered up the reins and threw up one hand in farewell as the mare made a smart turn and broke immediately into a furious trot. The farmer stood watching the disappearing buggy. He seemed to have forgotten for an instant his own idle horses; but suddenly he turned and hurried back to the field where team and cultivator awaited him.

The Lantern on the Plow

Chapter 4

Gypsy was in a hurry to get home, and so was the judge. He wanted to think, and to him there was no place for it like the friendly room where he had acquired the habit of thought. As he swung into the highway he was visualizing his littered flat-topped desk and the worn swivel chair which could turn him toward the sun-bathed garden, the scraps of ore and curious rock which formed his amateur mineral collection, or toward restful shadows backed by shelf upon shelf of musty books.

But the farm he had known for so short a time refused to be left behind. He could feel it gripping him, riding him. He gave his mental shoulders a shrug, but it hung on with a sort of sullen violence so that he had the illusion of his body rushing away while his mind was being dragged back. To what? To an exceptionally unattractive and insignificant bit of land? No; he couldn't honestly call it that—not while its memory reached out so easily to keep step with Gypsy's flying feet.

By nature as well as by profession, the judge was analytical, and it bothered him not to be able to reduce a sensation to its basic parts. He knew that because of certain obscure causes he was in the grip of something big which moment by moment grew bigger. What the devil was it? It couldn't be merely a parcel of

27

fields remarkable for their barrenness in a district famous for the richness of its soil; and yet it was. Just that—with something added.

He was astonished at the clearness with which recollection seemed to picture every stick, mound and stone of the Sherborne heritage. If he had been an artist with his easel before him, he could have drawn the whole scene to scale—the irregular road, the broken fences, the warped out houses, the tortured shrubs and trees; most eloquent of all, the stone tower of the house itself, looking like an excrescence of the hard earth, as if it had writhed upward into birth through interminable pain. He could have drawn all that, and still left out the kernel of his puzzle—the dominating power the place laid like a spell upon those who came even casually within its reach.

He had said to Warner Sherborne that a hundred and seventy-four years is a long time. Well, in a way, it was—a damned long time. Long enough, for instance, to have looked with equanimity upon this region as a pocket perquisite of the Lord Protector of the Salem Tenth; long enough to have woven legends not only around that pompous name, but around an epoch all too dimly remembered by a generation careless of the traditions of its simple sources. Long enough to embrace both the birth and the consummation of a stalwart nation.

Probably—almost inevitably—from that stone home of the Sherbornes men had marched forth against the Indians, and later to the tea-burning on the market place across the street from the Dan Bowen house at Greenwich. Ha! Boston might be the hub of the universe but it wasn't the whole earth!

Now wait a minute. What about that strange Revolutionary tale of the farmer who had recruited a daughter because he had no son? Dumb and dazed before the jibes of his comrades, he had offered to match her against any fighting man of the command. Hadn't that been a Sherborne, or Sherbourn—Isaiah Hancock Sherborne? Yes, by Cricky! Just as stolidly must the breed have penetrated to the battlefields of the Mexican war and of the Rebellion. Warner himself must have gone as a matter of course to the aid of Cuba.

Why, the house was already at its half century mark when Washington wintered at Valley Forge not much over fifty miles away! A hundred years had settled on its roof before a Sherborne went to war to avenge the massacre of the Alamo; and when Union fought Secession, five generations had already called it home.

All these ventures—the struggle of sparse settlers against hordes of savages, the fight for liberty of a handful of colonists, the victory of an absurdly small army on the far field of Chapultepec, the death grapple of brother against brother for an idea, the bestowal of freedom on an alien isle—were such enterprises as loom mighty big in the human mind. Yes, sir. Conquest, liberty, empire, union and freedom were mouth-filling worlds, and a hundred and seventy-four years was undoubtedly a very long time.

With that thought the judge's mind was about to sink drowsily into complacent coma when something happened. He seemed to hear a peal of reverberating laughter. Instantly the farm arose to reassert itself within his vision. He could see it jeering not only at years, and men, and their important ways, but at all those notions we have labeled immortal. Conquest? It was already small. Livery? Just another name for a changing face. Empire? A familiar myth. Union? Freedom? Yes; they were eternal—as the unstable tide is eternal! But what laughed at them all? What stayed? What endured? The land, by God!

"Whoa, Gypsy! Steady, girl."

Yes, sir—the land. It wasn't even remotely concerned with what we called events, rolling big words like revolt and the dawn of liberty on our short-lived tongues. No, sir. What mattered to the land was something hard to grasp, limitless and unfathomable, and yet strangely confined to a single mysterious bond—the bond with which it shackles those who brag of possessions of the soil!

There you were. Here was a little piece of it watching Sherborne farmers come and go endlessly and hearing each one of them say in his short day, "You are mine." Had the land—Warner Sherborne's holding—any answer to that? You bet it had. The judge could see it looming, dark as a towering cloud, hard as rock. He

29

could almost hear it rumble to the latest of the Sherborne tribe, "Well, we'll see. Look at these twisted trees, these gnarled shrubs. Now: are you sure? Am I yours, or are you mine? Listen. I'll give what you can take; not another inch—not another grain!"

"Whoa, Gypsy!" cried the judge and pulled on the lines uncertainly. So impressed had he been by his own musings that he felt a restless temptation to head the mare back in order that he might correct his perspective in full view of the miserable farm that had given it such a jolt. But the next instant he had his eyes, hands and ears full of something else. The sound of a staccato throb reached him from down the road, and simultaneously Gypsy was on her hind legs, quivering, ducking her raised head to right and left in a frenzy of terror, pawing wildly at the air with her forefeet.

"Hi!" yelled the judge, rising to balance himself against the dashboard. "Stop that engine, you scatterbrained road hog!"

His words were unheard, but the sight of the frightened mare had been enough for the motorist. He steered the little one-lunged car he was driving well to the side of the highway and throttled down his engine. Nothing but the shafts kept Gypsy from coming over backward. The judge leaned out, put one hand on her back and pushed. She was so delicately balanced that she actually toppled forward, and, once she felt the grip of the ground, shot down the road at a twenty-mile clip. This was something more to her master's taste. He braced his heels, wrapped the reins on his forearms and gave her his weight in a pull that lifted her head from between her knees.

All went well until she came abreast of the motor, which chose that instant to give a last dying gasp. The mare swerved so sharply from the terrifying sound that a shaft snapped under the strain. Swearing under his breath, talking to her softly between expletives, but mostly applying all his strength and skill in the conquering of rebellious horseflesh, the judge swung her into the soft loam at the side of the road, brought her to a stop, leaped out and ran to her head. She was quivering as with an ague and asking him one question after another out of wide, outraged eyes. It was as though she shouted, "Now tell me, judge, what the devil was that?"

In the automobile was a big sandy-haired man and a sandy-haired boy, the exact replica in miniature of his father. The man leaped out and went to Judge Alder's assistance. Together, but in a silence—ominous on the part of the judge, at least—they unharnessed the mare, tied her to a fence post with the strong hitching rope and then turned to face each other. The habitual healthy pink of the judge's cheeks had turned to a deep red. His neck looked swollen, as if it were choked full of words his long training in self-control was scarcely able to keep from pouring out in an overwhelming torrent.

"Tryer," he asked finally through white lips, "has it ever occurred to you that women and children have been driving around these roads since before your grandmother was born?"

"Aw, come now, judge," said Tryer Mattis with a propitiating smile, "I ain't no murderer. You didn't read my notice in the paper, did you, telling which way I was going today?"

"Notice in the paper!" exclaimed the judge under his breath. "I can't pretend not to know the law," he continued in a louder tone. "I know, of course, that you don't even have to give notice of your intention to hog the entire highway for the benefit of your rattletybang contraption. But the day will come———"

"No it won't," broke in Mattis, who, for all his deprecating manner, took browbeating from no man. "The day was when the law said a horseless vehicle had to have a man walk in front of it with a red flag, but it won't never come again, Bill. No, sir; just the other way round. You and me will live to see the day when the law will make all the rattletrap buggies that's left hang a red light to keep automobiles from running over them."

The discussion as to how to pronounce automobile was at its height, and Tryer happened to be of the persuasion that stressed the third syllable with great emphasis. The judge turned from him to stare at Gypsy, so vibrant, so full of a number of things besides power—life, willfulness, affection. He stared also at his smart red-

31

wheeled hickory buggy with its broken shaft, and as he looked, his impetuous indignation faded away and left him thoughtful, almost sad.

"I wonder," he murmured.

"Sure," said Mattis, his face brightening. "You and me will live to count a hundred automobiles for every horse and rig."

"Hardly that," said the judge with a shrug of dismissal of the subject.

Mattis was famous for his exaggerations. It was from a species of inborn exaggeration that he had got his nickname of Tryer. Years ago it had been I-Can-Try Mattis; but folks had found that too long, and shortened it to Tryer Mattis. Man and boy, Judge Alder could not remember the day when Mattis' voice, drawling "Well, I can try," had not been a familiar and maddening sound. He turned to give his attention to the broken shaft.

"Can you lend me a hand with this?" he asked perfunctorily.

"Well, I can try," replied Mattis promptly. "Wait a minute and leave it to me. I'll show you."

He went off toward the motor car, where his son was already holding out a roll of stout copper wire in one hand and a hank of clothesline in the other. Mattis was a big man, and full of a restless energy. He was always in a sort of suspended hurry, as if he waged eternal war with the present. Watching the thrust of his stride, the judge reflected that this exuberant contractor was overdrawn at three banks. He had a way with banks—and women.

At that tag end to his thought the color mounted again in the judge's cheeks and his lungs swelled to a sharp intake of breath. He was reflecting without bitterness that he would have been twenty years a married man if it had not been for Tryer's way with women. A vision of Elizabeth Banning as she had been on the occasion when last he had talked with her arose before his eyes. They had been betrothed for three years while he struggled to establish a law practice, and then like a bolt from the blue had come the news of her marriage to Mattis. No word from her, no breaking of the engagement; just a swift sentence from a friend and playmate of his boyhood: "Say, Bill, Betty Banning was married to Tryer Mattis yesterday afternoon."

He had taken a rig from the livery stable, driven furiously to Mattis' new house, leaped from the buggy and thrown open the front door without knocking. Strangely enough, and in contradiction to the usage of the countryside, Tryer and his bride were sitting in the parlor, one on each side of the central round table. Never would the judge forget Elizabeth's expression as she looked up and saw him. Her face was like an empty pitcher, as if someone had poured all the life out of her features. Her lips had trembled violently as she cried out no more than his name in a choked voice, "Will!"

"Why did you do it?" he demanded, paying no heed to Mattis. "Just tell me that one thing! Why?"

She dropped her head and murmured almost inaudibly, "I don't know."

Mattis, shock-headed, blue-eyed, large in frame, had been sitting with his hands in his pockets and his legs extended. He neither moved nor spoke, but a smile gleamed in his eyes, passed down to his lips and began to spread slowly over his face. It was a maddening smile, and, seeing it, the judge—young Bill Alder then had taken a stride forward, then stopped suddenly, stunned by the strangeness of the answer Elizabeth had given him.

"Bill," Tryer had remarked coolly, "I see you got your fists all balled, and if you really want to hit me I'll get up. That way Betty will have a chance to find out if she married the better man."

He made no move to rise, however; and after staring at him blankly for a moment, the judge had turned and gone as abruptly as he had come. So short had been the interview that the livery horse was still blown from the fast trip out and was allowed to jog-trot all the way home, not from pity but because the young lawyer was so dazed from collision with that sphinx which dwells in every woman, often hidden even from herself. He had put a question which was to wait twenty years, and over, for an answer.

As far as love in the sense of heartache was concerned, the judge had long since recovered from the loss of Elizabeth Banning. The wife of Tryer Mattis became genuinely uninteresting to the judge, bore children, grew slatternly and had recently died, without trespassing on his imagination. Like many another man, once the pangs of passion and outraged pride had passed, he did not regret her individually so much as he regretted that for which she might have stood. Even so, she was and would ever remain the most important single event in his life; but only as an inanimate rock which turns the course of a stream is important. Everything he was he owed to the fact that she had chosen to marry Mattis rather than himself.

There was no sentimental old maid or matron throughout the length and breadth of the three counties who did not ascribe the two decades of his celibacy to an undying devotion to the blighted romance of his youth, and worship him accordingly. As a matter of cold truth, however, the judge's single estate was due to the fact that he had rebounded from the collision with the inexplicable in Elizabeth Banning to a position of safety and equilibrium well outside the range of every and any woman within his experience. Thenceforth he had become an observer, and nothing could be more dispassionate than his attitude toward femininity in the mass.

As a consequence, the dislike which he felt toward Mattis had grown to have little to do with the person of Elizabeth. Except for the feeling of outraged pride, he would have felt exactly as he did toward Tryer if Elizabeth Banning had never lived, for the two men were congenitally combative and antipathetic. However, neither despised the other. They called each other by their first names, and though holding consistently to a personal aloofness, they were not awkward in their occasional contacts.

Tryer had a way with women, reflected the judge; but it was nothing to the way he had with banks. Those were the days of overdrafts and entries in red ink on the wrong side of the ledger, and it was a matter of common knowledge that at least at two institutions, separated by the length of the three counties, Mattis was in so deep that his indebtedness actually became an asset to himself. The banks dared not let him fail, and he knew it. They were obliged to feed him more whenever his multifarious enterprises grew hungry. Take the Cedarton cement plant; certainly out of Tryer's legitimate—— The judge's thoughts stopped as suddenly as if they had run into a wall. He put a hand in his pocket and felt of the fragment of stone he had taken from the Sherborne house.

Chapter 5

In the meantime Tryer had returned, bringing the roll of copper wire, and was making an expert job of wrapping the broken shaft.

"I don't give them this often," he said loudly, in the tone of one who makes excuses for himself. "Costs too much. Even clothesline you can't get for nothing. And take that notice in the papers. Do you think I don't have to pay for that?"

"Why do you bother?" asked the judge. "However we may feel about having our horses scared out of a year's growth, we know you are within your rights."

"Oh, well," answered Mattis good-naturedly as he put the finishing touches on the splice; "I was tired of having folks send around to know if I was going out with the automobile, and which way, so as they could give me a miss. There you are, judge. All we got to do now is to hitch her up."

"Thanks, Tryer," said Judge Alder. "By the way, do you mind telling me what the Cedarton plant cost you?"

Mattis straightened, surprised at the question, and his eyes began to narrow.

"The Cedarton plant? Why, no; I don't mind. I don't mind telling anything. That is, I wouldn't mind telling you, judge. Why?"

The judge smiled.

"Oh, well, keep it to yourself, Tryer. People have been wondering why you bought it. They say it's turning into a junk pile. What would you take for it in cash, just as it stands? Would you cut your losses at 10 per cent of what it cost you?"

Mattis' eyes contracted to two pin points of blue light.

"The Cedarton plant never stood me for a loss," he said, "and it never will. When I get ready it will pay for itself twice over. That's why it ain't for sale." His tone changed. "Judge, I seen where you turned onto the pike. You know something. Spit it out and trust me for a fair answer."

"Tryer," replied the judge, still smiling, "you know something— you do, indeed! I believe you know the same thing I do."

He turned and began hitching the mare preparatory to a start. Mattis followed and helped him mechanically. His thoughts were not on what he was doing; they were very busy elsewhere. When the judge actually put his foot on the step Tryer laid a detaining band on his arm.

"Did you find out," he asked, "that that dumb fool Sherborne won't talk prices—won't even listen? But I'll get him yet. I'll have him fined and jailed on one count and another until his scarecrow of a farm leaks out of his wife's eyes. Rattling Run Fields—what a name for a farm anyway! Why, it's a hundred years since all the other folks around here quit calling their holdings fields! It isn't as if I hadn't been willing to play and to pay fair. No mortgage, confound him! There ain't even a mortgage!"

The judge whirled.

"If you make one more move of that kind against Sherborne you'll have me on your back, at your throat, over you and under you. We'll find out, once for all, which is the bigger man."

"Judge," protested Mattis, "I wasn't, trying to rile you. What I said just bust out of me. When you've had a thing like that cooped up in you for a mortal age and then find that someone else has bumped into it before you could close—why, you're not yourself, that's all."

The judge freed himself and climbed into the buggy. Restraining the mare, he leaned over for a parting word.

"The trouble with you, Tryer, is that you only know one way to try. If you want to do business come to my house tonight at nine and I'll show you how."

On the very next morning Judge Alder was making his second trip to Rattling Run Fields. In his pocket he carried a certified check for a considerable sum of money and a document of far greater importance. He frowned as he went over in his mind, step by step, his long tussle with Tryer Mattis, who, having read the lease which would empower him to exploit the cement rock on the Sherborne farm, described it as a legal straitjacket. The original draft had placed the term for ten years, called for a flat annuity of three thousand dollars, and stipulated a fixed royalty of two cents on every barrel of cement produced.

There were certain safeguarding clauses which justified Tryer's descriptive phrase, and the judge had smiled with appreciation not so much for the shrewd perception displayed by Mattis as for the power of expression which could cram everything there was to say in the way of criticism of a lengthy and important agreement into three words: a legal straitjacket. Tryer had a mind like a set steel trap—always wide open, that its jaws might close with a swifter snap. What made the judge frown was wonder as to why the contractor had refused point-blank to don the straightjacket for ten years, but had readily accepted it for fifteen. So painstakingly had he drafted the document that he could recite it from end to end. He did so now, decided once for all that it was without a flaw, and promptly dismissed care from his brow.

He was happy—extraordinarily happy. Never had man a better right to feel like Santa Claus than himself on this excursion. But soon he was frowning again, confronted by an absorbing speculation. What was going to happen to those children, Drake and Io? He remembered them as he had seen them in court and again when they had been called from their work in the field, soiled and yet uncoarsened. What was he bringing them? And the woman with the strange shrinking in her eyes—what was he bringing her? As for the man——

When he thought of Warner Sherborne the judge was conscious of a break in the course of his thoughts, a sort of mental gasp. What was going to happen to this strange, silent product of the soil, this farmer who did not know how to quit, this half-animate man who dared to measure himself against Nature and the farm he hated? How would he take the news that out of its entrails was to be torn a weapon which would give him at a single stroke the victory in a lifelong combat?

The judge slowed down the mare. He was a bit frightened, and took time to ask himself if he was anything more than a meddler. Had he been rushed off his feet in the last twenty-four hours—carried along at a pace wholly foreign to his nature and to his years of training in deliberation? If so, whatever power had performed the miracle now dragged him on relentlessly. Arrived at the field he summoned Sherborne and, with a jerk of the head toward the house, led the way back in silence, and entered the kitchen. He sat down at a much scoured deal table and motioned to the farmer to seat himself opposite.

"Warner," he began, "do you trust me?"

"Yes," said Sherborne, a slow fire lighting in his eyes.

"You feel that there is nothing on earth that would lead me to deceive you?"

"Yes," replied the farmer without hesitation or curiosity.

The judge took from his pocket the check and the lease.

"There is something on this farm," he continued, "which is as legitimate a product as potatoes or hay or milk. You can sell it for money without selling your land. It is a deposit of cement rock. I haven't had an opportunity to find out how extensive it is, or how valuable; but evidently someone else has had the chance, and taken it. Here is a check made out to you for three thousand dollars, and here is a lease by which you engage to permit cement to be made from the materials on your place for a period of fifteen years. On each barrel produced you will receive two cents, in addition to the flat annual rental of three thousand dollars. Trust what I'm telling you. Sign the paper and you will never have to work again."

For a long moment Warner seemed not to have heard; at least, the fact of sudden wealth appeared not to have moved him. But as his brain, steady for all its agonized diffidence in expression, began to seize doggedly on one implication after another, his face grew more and more set and his gaze increasingly staring and vacant. Two spots of color began to show vividly on the points of his cheek bones. Finally he turned upon the judge strange eyes, suffused with a suppressed glow, faintly, almost imperceptibly ardent.

"I got no call to work?" he murmured.

"No more than you want to," replied the judge cautiously.

A weird spasm passed across Warner's face, more of a contortion than a smile. He arose, fetched pen and ink, signed the lease laboriously, his knuckles showing white, so tightly did he hold the pen, and handed the document to the judge.

Chapter 6

Up to the event of his pitiful attempt at a smile, Warner Sherborne's mind might have been likened to a fog—deep, broad, translucent, yet impenetrable except through immersion. But now it had become suddenly concreted. To find a symbol one would have to fall back on some such simple, efficient implement as a plowshare or an ax. His mind now knew what it wanted. It walked alone. It cleaved its way forward along a single groove to a single end.

Words dropped from his lips in slow but methodical sequence, and when he had finished speaking the judge found himself formulating the last will and testament of one Warner Sherborne, who bequeathed the products of the property known as Rattling Run Fields in equal parts to his wife and two children, the title to the land to rest in the boy. It was further provided that Judge Alder should be sole executor and trustee. When the document was completed the farmer took the paper upon which his wishes had been set out in legal phraseology and toiled through it, checking off each line with his soiled thumbs.

"That's it, jedge," he said finally.

An hour later he went to bed, never again to arise. At the end of ten days Judge Alder got the doctor to run out as a matter of form.

43

"I know what's the matter with him, doc. It's just as well, though, you should see him. Besides, I want you to witness his signature on a paper or two."

After a thorough examination the doctor turned from the bed with something of the same exasperation the judge had shown on his first contact with the man who plowed by lantern light.

"Well," he said privately to the judge, "if you know what's the matter with him you know more than I do. Physically, there's nothing wrong—but he'll be dead inside of a week."

"Exactly," replied the judge. "Resting himself to death and glad of it. Medically, you can't admit the diagnosis; but you've seen it done before—more than once."

Without committing himself the doctor went on to patients more amenable to treatment; but the judge stayed. Had he had time to think of surface matters during these days he would have been amazed at the number and frequency of the hours he found it possible to devote to the affairs of Rattling Run Fields and its inmates. But such trivialities as the passing hour and its occupations did not even enter into his thoughts. Without knowing it he had stopped thinking except as a minor accompaniment to a tremendous innovation. He had begun to live. Strangely enough, he did not make the discovery in regard to himself at that time. To him it seemed that it was those about him who had begun to live.

This family, which only by flashes had escaped remaining a pale, composite blotch against a sinister background, now stepped forth. It was as though the figures in a faded tapestry had suddenly come forward into life. How had it happened? The judge did not know. Here is the scene: He himself sitting in a stout chair of bent hickory at the pivotal center of the spacious kitchen. Across the two windows at the back, Warner Shcrborne, lying on the bed which the judge, with the doctor's assistance, had carried from a cheerless bedroom. The children in new store clothes, clean, starchy, odorous with soap, very quiet. Startled, they looked— startled into happiness. Like butterflies just born, with moist, untried and shining wings.

How gently they moved! And yet was it not written that soon mischief would dawn in their eyes and the itch of energy creep into their legs? Would they smile, laugh, talk and leap? Would Drake shout for the love of noise and Io call out, full-throated as the treble of a bobolink, her gasping "No, Drake! No!"—the only words the judge had yet heard her speak? Extraordinary children! Was he going to see something happen? The uncurling of petal, leaf and bloom? Had he stumbled at forty-six into the mysteries of the garden of the soul?

There is nothing lovelier in its assumed shyness or more delicate in its touch upon the heartstrings than the budding friendship of children for a grown man. Here is the gossamer of all human emotions, lighter than air and as silently gay as thistledown on a playful breeze. This all but imperceptible web the judge felt settling down upon him, binding his strength to the chair upon which he sat with Lilliputian threads, each laid with amazing deliberation.

What troubled him was not that he could not move at will, but that he could not wish to move. Long before he had any circumstantial evidence, valid in court, he perceived that these children knew and accepted him for their friend. The boy was the first to make an open advance. He approached, touched the judge, leaned for an instant against his knee.

"Drake was the first all-round Englishman," he said, his whole thin face twitching to an unaccustomed smile. "He went around the world."

The judge was dazed. Before he could realize that he was receiving the answer to the question he had put many days before, the boy was gone. But his smile remained, for it was such a smile as can die from a face but never from the eyes which have seen it.

"No, Drake! No!"

It was Io's treble voice, cutting across the placid silence of the room. The judge felt like jumping out of his skin, but he never moved so much as an eyelid. He knew that he must not move. Io drew near, not evenly, but by little advances and poised withdrawals. It was as if two impulses were at war within her tiny body—the

45

instinct of reserve against the urge never to be left behind. At last she stood before him, the hem of her fresh cotton frock caught up between nervous hands. Her dark eyes were very wide open, challenging, yet ready to turn.

"Some folks say," she whispered breathlessly, "that Io was a heifer, a milk-white heifer; and some she was the baby moon."

She also fled. If the judge had felt bound before, he was now imprisoned. His eyes were fixed like agates in his head. His lungs filled up with air and forgot to let it go. His blood bulged in his veins as if it had stopped flowing. Extraordinary elf! Amazing words! Mystery heaped on enigma! Io! Io, the crescent moon, wandering in the starry heavens, watched over by Argus of the hundred eyes. And—Io in the kitchen of buried Jersey farm! Into what pool of oblivion had his meddling dropped him? Was there no one to drag him out, wake him, and set him free?

"Now, children, don't bother the judge."

Immediately his eyes were released. He turned them and perceived the woman, Eunice Sherborne, to whom in his blindness he had ascribed no more volition than to a bit of useful harness. What miracle had happened while his senses slept? None. Was it that she had discarded her sunbonnet, washed her hair and put on a flimsy dress of an ancient pattern? Quite evidently that frock was a resurrection, for no leg-of-mutton sleeves outraged the lines of her slim shoulders. Was it that she was unmanacled, freed to the content of legitimate household cares? It was none of these things. It was her eyes, calm, unafraid. Her placid gaze enveloped him casually; accepted him, ingulfed him! It was as though someone, unseen and unfelt, had wrapped him in a soft shawl.

He swallowed hard and cautiously let go a long breath. More entanglement. Here was something else entrapping him, something less elusive than the friendliness of children, but with which his strong hands and highly specialized mind lacked the experience to grapple. He turned his eyes warily toward the bed, appealing mutely for aid from one of his kind—and the help came. The sight of the still face upon the pillow, almost translucent in its emaciation, lifted him swiftly up and away from thoughts of himself, for most astounding of all was the flowering which had come to Warner Sherborne.

The gaunt man was alive; nearer death, yet more alive than ever before. He had deliberately come out of the dross of himself into the spirit. It was not that he had passed from poverty to ease or from labor into rest. It was something bigger than that—much bigger. He had traversed a lonely waste, a wilderness, a parched desert, and found a friend. At the end of an arid and monotonous existence, loneliness had come upon the tenderly resolute plant of friendship and was holding its breath at the miracle. Trust and understanding were the pillars of his awakened mind.

In these misty regions the judge had not only become the stable pivot of his fellow creature's universe, but without words was made to know it. What mattered even the outcome of the Herculean struggle, a frail body the battleground, between tradition and the bulldog grip of a sullen soil? They two were no longer judge and farmer, tossed by chance into collision; they were friends, deeply, inexplicably indebted to each other. Why? Because each had delivered and assumed a burden. Strange reason, but the taproot of all human devotion. The judge had given and Sherborne had received allegiance, stripped forever of distrust. The farmer had sloughed a load sustained to the superhuman limit; but what was it the judge had received? A burden? He didn't know; he was only beginning to find out.

Profoundly moved by his own partial perception, he leaned toward the bed and tried to speak. To his amazement he, in his turn, had become inarticulate. It was Sherborne who spoke, his voice coming from far away, faint yet clear.

"A grown oak can't be moved and live."

For a moment no one stirred. His words, the first he had spoken in many days, fell one by one into the silence of the room, sank and were drowned. But the voice had stilled the restlessness of the children and drawn them toward a fixed point, a refuge. Seemingly by a common impulse, they moved toward Judge Alder.

47

Io leaned against his shoulder; Drake climbed confidently to sit upon his knee. The shyness which lately had been theirs now took possession of the judge, and he learned with an inward start that it was the bold shyness of the sprouting leaf.

What tingling sensations were these? What the mischief had happened to him—was still happening? Had children never touched him before? On an impulse of bravado he passed his arms around boy and girl and drew them close, so closed that his heart heard a double echo. He was appalled by the choking in his throat which the pressure of their warm bodies had induced. If before he had been snared, entrapped, imprisoned, now he was totally lost.

Sherborne raised himself by a spasmodic effort on one elbow and called, "Come here, son."

Drake clambered from the judge's knee and approached his father fearlessly. Facing each other, the two seemed gradually to merge and become one. Each was ageless, each belonged equally within the scope of generations, each knew what no man learns singly or alone. The voice spoke again, but with a rasping yet resonant intonation, as if the dying man, on the verge of translation, were expelling by a deliberate effort the last breath of life from the swept cavern of his body.

"He'p the jedge look after sis and momma, son. The land's yours. You ain't got no call to sell it."

He fell back upon the pillow, lifeless.

Chapter 7

Drake whirled with a startled gasp. His mother dropped her work, turned, stared for an instant, and then her eyes lit suddenly with something more than comprehension. She crossed the room swiftly, picking up Io as she passed. The boy ran to meet her. She took his hand and led him into the darkened, unused parlor. The judge sat on, alone with Warner Sherborne, gazing absorbently at the calm face where so lately the light of the lantern on the plow had flickered and gone out.

Gradually he perceived that it was not in any sense as comforter that he had held and still held his place in this household, for no comforter was needed. Here forces far beyond his depth and comprehension had been in movement, and mysterious planets in conjunction. Here on this bed within the empty husk of a man, happiness and the kindly shadow of death had found it possible to dwell for a time side by side, lingering on the brink of a glad embrace.

Just there the judge asked himself a question: Had he been posing as erudite among the ignorant? Had he? In answer he dropped his chin upon his breast. He felt humbled, almost abased. Only now did he begin truly to perceive the stature of his friend, Warner Sherborne, and to measure the extent of the legacy he had received at his hands. Only now, for death, above all other

49

transitions, lends distance to perspective. In life Warner had been a miserable farmer, uninteresting to the casual eye, unkempt, sordid, eking out a meager, stingy existence from a hard and vindictive soil. But in death he was radiantly disclosed as the harborer of those qualities which shame the trivially weighted human heart—tenacity, abnegation, supernal patience and an unconquerable spirit.

Those attributes of the fiber of his peculiar being the man could not pass on to any not of his own blood. Yet he had left a legacy to the judge—a distinct legacy. What was it?

The events of days which already seemed like years swept by in mental review. First of all had come the baffled and baffling gaze of the farmer and his children, explained as the concentrated gaze of generations; baffling no more. Next among outstanding impressions was the startling revelation of the hatred of Sherborne for the land which had devoured and still fed on so many Sherbornes—humanizing touch! The visualization of a titanic struggle between a barren locality known as Rattling Run Fields and a puny individual named Warner Sherborne had been slow to take definite shape; now it was blazoned large in the terms of an epic. But illimitably above and beyond these high lights of revelation, the judge paid homage to the masterly generalship which, having won the victory, could lie down and inexorably die.

Was the legacy any of these things? No; it was quite another. It was what had happened to the judge when Drake Sherborne's face had broken into a first mischievous, heart-wringing smile. It was what had happened to him when a little girl, poised on her toes as on the tips of the wings of flight, had declaimed with caught breath, "Some folks say that Io was a heifer, a milk-white heifer; and some she was the baby moon." It was what had happened to him when a woman's calm, unasking glance had made him feel as though he had been wrapped in a soft warm shawl. In short, what Warner Sherborne had bequeathed to Judge Alder was something commonly received only at the hands of God; it was the gift of life.

50

With that question definitely settled, he could once more turn his thoughts away from himself. Something else remained unanswered, something specific. Whence had come those fanciful names, Drake and Io? Whence the assured glace that was like the wrapping of a soft warm shawl? These were the light questions of idling curiosity, but behind them lurked a veritable cavern of mystery. Why had Warner Sherborne, surrounded by his family, been lonely with loneliness so great that death became a guerdon and a boon?

A strange sound, coming from the neighboring room shivered across the silence. It was unmistakable. It was the sound of splintering glass. The judge arose, took up a lamp and pushed open the intervening door which Eunice, Sherborne's wife, had left ajar. He looked in. She was seated, half kneeling, at a central table, the frightened children crouched beside her with faces hidden against her skirts.

The judge moved forward. On the table, laid flat on its back, was a grimy glazed frame. Upon it the woman had dropped head and arms, breaking the glass. Glancing over her thin shoulders, which were quivering, though she remained soundless, he saw Latin words, boldly engrossed on stained parchment. "Curatores," he could read, and part of the name of a famous college. And then, in vivid black letters, "Eunice Teller." Below, "Baccalaureæ Artibus," and the date, June, 1886.

He stood profoundly still, but the lamp quivered in his upheld hand as he stared at the diploma. So here it was—the hidden source of those names, the covered well, the moss-grown neglected stone of the builders! Even in the face of the evidence so pompously engrossed, he could not immediately accept this soil-smirched woman as Eunice Teller, for he was occupied with a revealing light shining from the lamp of memory within himself. More like a twin echo than a light, insisting to be heard, it came to him, faint, deadened now, as though through the muffling wall, not of days but of years.

"Drake was the first all-around Englishman; he went around the world."

51

"Some folks say that Io was a heifer, a milk-white heifer; and some she was the baby moon."

So much for the names; so much for idle curiosity, thought the judge as he drew back cautiously into the kitchen and noiselessly closed the door. With narrowed eyes he gazed long at the body of Warner Sherborne, Eunice's husband, actually more articulate in death than he had been in life; then he replaced the lamp on the table and sat down to resume his vigil.

Here was food for thought with a vengeance, and abundant time to think.

"Eunice Teller," he murmured to himself from time to time, and with each repetition the frown on his brow deepened. Eunice did not sound right. What was it they had called her so many years ago—ten, twelve—no, eighteen years? He had it! Vic! They used to call her Vic Teller. A sort of girl prodigy of learning; a flash in the pan that had lit up the ancient hamlet of Greenwich, making it visible for a day, and then had died. She had been like a torch, one moment held aloft; the next, plunged into a puddle—out of sight into the mud; out of mind, forgotten.

"Greenwich!" He formed the word with his lips, and a smile drew the corners of his eyes.

Who does not know New Jersey, Brooklyn among the states, bedroom of the city of New York? Who has not ridden on its ferries, tunneled to and from its shores, used it for a causeway, surveyed the communal beauty of its conglomerate lawns, smelled the stench of its flats and the ozone of its board walks? What state is better known? All; all are better known. From ocean to ocean and from the Canadian border to the Gulf of Mexico, there is no state in the Union so little known as Jersey.

Bridgeton is old; but in its youth, under the name of Cohansey Bridge—even at its birth, in fact—two generations had come and gone in Greenwich. Before the first baby born of a Pilgrim Mother had reached the half-century mark, John Fenwick, younger son of Sir William Fenwick, Baronet of Northumberland, roundhead captain under Cromwell, later Quaker, and eventually lord proprietor of the Salem Tenth, had founded the hamlet of Greenwich.

Let not this premier settlement of Cumberland County be confused, however, with that township of the same state, name and age across the Gloucester line on the banks of the Delaware, where two hundred years ago there was a custom which decreed that the widow of a bankrupt, wishing to remarry, had to go out from her house in nothing but her shift to meet her bridegroom, who must hand her some clothes, saying, "I lend you these." Why? So that he might not be sued for the dead husband's debts. Equitable and picturesque law, where are you now? Gone, sopped up along with the Swedish blood that gave you birth. But Fenwick's Greenwich still remains; in a somnolent and lovely manner, it still lives.

Look at it. Stand at the northern end of its one great way, a mile long and a hundred feet wide, and you can see the sap of centuries still alive in the vast fronded arch of elm, maple and buttonwood trees and in the permanence of the houses which align it. They are of an entrancing variety both in construction and composition. Here is one of warm red brick and chaste white trimmings, there another of broad clapboards; beyond, one of blocks of stone imported in sailing vessels, and, to cap the lot, one of all three—brick, frame and stone—each addition marking a separate century. And yet there is no Old World atmosphere about the setting. It is intimately American in the most delicate shading of the phrase. It is at one and the same time the American antithesis to the Middle West and slumberous nadir to Hoboken's blatant zenith.

Midway of this embowered avenue stands a dwelling of peculiar conformation. Its central portion is of two stories, roofed with a sharp gable, facing the street. On each side is a wing, one having a smaller gable at right angles to the main house, and the other being roofed in a single slope like a lean-to. Over the main door is a fanlight ornamented with four bull's-eyes of blue glass.

This feature, added to the bulk of the assembled edifice, would have made it pretentious in its day were it not for the fact that the walls of stone had insets of brick, and those of brick had been eked

53

out with stone. These patches were as evident and unashamed as those on the seat of the trousers of Abraham Teller, cobbler by inheritance and profession, who owned the house at the close of the Civil War. Owing to clubfoot, which troubled him not at all, he had not been drafted. He married rather late in life a woman almost as mature as himself, who died in childbirth, leaving behind her a baby girl.

"Abe, where are you? Name her Eunice, will you? Please, Abe."

It was the first and last request Abraham Teller's wife had ever made of him, and she seemed by a determined effort to have regained consciousness for a moment in order to make it. He complied with some reluctance. Eunice as the name for his only child appeared to him fanciful to the verge of foolishness. There was no genealogical justification as far as he knew, and the Biblical reference to Timothy's mother was lacking in weight. If his wife had had it in mind to denote faith, why could she not have come out with it straightforwardly and asked that the child be called Faith? He would have preferred some such downright name as that, or Jane or Mary. When he delved into the Attic derivation the thin lips of his wide mouth drew into a sardonic smile. In later years he had been wont to call the girl Vic, which he explained to her, always with the same smile, as his abbreviation of Happily Victorious, the Greek equivalent for Eunice.

It will be perceived that Abraham Teller harbored the peculiar demon of erudition which once inhibited every true exponent of the trade of cobbler. Let those who doubt that a guild, in the days when guilds were guilds, possessed a continuity of spirit which pervaded its devotees, and even warped their characters to a uniform mold, glance at Lamb's essay on the melancholy of tailors. It opens with the following words: "That there is a professional melancholy, if I may so express myself, incident to the occupation of tailor, is a fact which I think very few will venture to dispute."

In similar mood I would say: "Point me out a cobbler of the old school who is not a skeptic with a wallop behind his skepticism, who has not dipped into the sources of knowledge and retained

54

his delvings, who does not look askance at all other possessions and incidentally at most living men, who recognizes any master save the master of the mind, who accepts any belief other than the eternal right to speculation; lastly, who will have a job done on time—and I will take my boots elsewhere, for he is no true cobbler." Alas! Point me out a cobbler—any old cobbler!

If there is one feature which stands out head and shoulders above all others as a drawback on the benefits of progress in the shape of creature comforts, it is that which marks the passing of individual industry as the forcing house of character. Who will venture to dispute that the brothers Wright were infinitely greater in their own bicycle shop than is the Wright Company in the annals of the world? Henry Ford perfecting his engine than Henry Ford spawning motor cars? The humblest independent tinker than the standardized workman turning out a single standardized part by the million? The erudite Abraham Teller at his ineffectual bench than the combined manufacturers of Lynn, Massachusetts? Many will dispute it; but let the accusation stand.

Abraham Teller had character in the sense that his faults and his virtues stood out on him like the tusks on a wart hog. He was slow with an exasperating deliberation; no urgency and no man could hurry him. He was uncouth in appearance, ironic as to tongue, careless of obligations and derisive of the accomplishments of others. Equally, he was proud of his expert workmanship, charitable under a rough exterior, brilliant in monologue, unwavering in his devotion to knowledge as the sole end of all being, and patient in its limited dissemination. As a result, his daughter Eunice, at the age of sixteen, knew more than all the other girls of all ages in the village put together.

Because her father called her Vic, everyone else came to do the same but to none but herself had the old man ever divulged the derivation the nickname; nor did she. Even in the face of certain remarks overheard to the effect that Abe had granted his wife's dying request at the baptismal font only to snatch it back in characteristic fashion at the cobbler's bench, Eunice would merely toss her head and presently smile to herself. She did not mind her father's irony; it did not even affect her secret joy in having been christened Happily Victorious; for to her the name was not a misfit. It was at once an omen and the single thread upon which she hung all her love for the mother she had never known.

Towns are proverbially proud of a prodigy, and advertise it; villages are equally proud of such a possession, but keep their mouths tightly closed about it—at least within hearing of the prodigy. To all intents and purposes Vic Teller's fame as a scholar was more notorious in Salem, Fairton or Bridgeton, even at the ancient settlement of Sheppard's Mills, only two miles away, than it was in Greenwich. Wasn't old Abe hard enough to live with as things stood? All of which served Eunice well rather than ill. Her isolation made of her a lonely figure, but it did her good.

It is comparatively easy to look back from the year 1924 through the long telescope of four decades and see Eunice as she was at sixteen, when the judge had caught his first glimpse of her, never dreaming that the fleeting vision was to gather cobwebs for eighteen years and still live. Children then, as now, wore straight-hanging smocks; girls of sixteen, one-piece frocks, modestly yoked; and women went about not unbecomingly clothed in high-necked dresses fitted closely to shoulders and arms. Jackets were in vogue for those who fancied them, and poke-shaped hats.

What the judge had seen was a swift figure, vivid as a golden shaft of sunlight, a young girl, slight, but by no means frail. Hair wavy, and so light that it suggested a breeze even though the air was still. A saddle of freckles across her nose and freckles of a darker shade floating in her hazel eyes. An expressive mouth, inherited from her acidulous father, only that it wore a smile easily and more sweetly than ever could his. Her appearance had not struck the youthful visiting lawyer as remarkable in any particular, but as a whole it had lived in memory so that, after all the years which had intervened, the judge could conjure a picture of symmetrical and eager youth, crowned with the eternal allure of springtime—a lasting vision of the subtle essence of loveliness.

Everyone knew of her prowess as a scholar and of her consuming ambition to go to college. There were reasons why this aspiration was absurd, but that did not preclude her being pointed out with smug satisfaction as one who was expecting an important communication, nothing less than a report on her entrance examinations, which would prove that is was not for lack of learning she could not go.

The mail was in. You could be sure of it when you saw her like that, darting out hatless in swirling organdie frock to run to the little post office. Alive she was, from the feet up. Not only her brain—all of her.

Chapter 8

Sitting in the kitchen at Rattling Run Fields, with head bowed and eyes fastened on that vibrant vision of the past, the judge could hear Eunice Sherborne moving about, sending Drake and putting Io to bed, climbing up the stairs at their call to say a last good night, descending again, pausing in the parlor; and then he heard no more. Instead, he felt her presence. As she pushed open the door, passed swiftly to a chair and sat down, it was as though some vital essence had been injected into the air he breathed. She was silent, but she was alive. He did not look up. He could feel her, sitting there, hands clasped, eyes wide, waiting. Waiting for what? For him to speak?

"I saw you once before," he murmured. "It was in Greenwich, the day you got your letter——"

"Did you know my father?" she interrupted in a low voice.

"As everybody knew him," replied the judge.

"As everybody knew him," she repeated, her eyes staring backward down the years. "The day I got the letter."

At her tone the judge could not help but look up. He had returned to the chair placed midway of the kitchen for the convenience of the children, whose quiet games had centered about his knee. On his left was the still form of Warner Sherborne; in front of him and a little to the right was the cooking stove; still

59

farther to the right, beside a window which looked out down the road by day but was now black with night, sat Eunice Sherborne. Her chair was turned from him; but, at the moment of speaking, she had twisted her body and folded her arms on its back. None but a supple woman could have taken that pose and held it. The light of the lamp, set on a table just behind the judge, left her in half shadow, so that when he glanced at her he was startled at the sudden girlishness of her appearance.

"I didn't know him as everybody knew him," he continued. "He and I were friends."

Remembering the sardonic smile habitually worn by the cobbler and his caustic reputation, the judge could not help but wonder but he did not question aloud. He watched, listened, waited. The trained instinct of the bench warned him that this woman who had abruptly sunk from sight so many years ago, and whose incipient resurrection he had witnessed, was on the point of revealing hidden things, secret things which demanded release as importunately as a planted seed. He fastened his eyes on her face. Presently he felt like one who watches a play in an unknown language. What did she see?

Eunice Sherborne was watching herself as a young girl with a letter pressed to her heart, flying to tell the great news to her father—the father who had sometimes postponed but never refused a request; the father who, short of mortgaging the house, provided he could find a mortgage, could not have paid even her railway fare to college and yet had never told her so. With what a bitter look he had read the letter; but that was nothing only himself. How he had evaded her, taking perverse pleasure in forestalling every attempt to broach the all-important subject! Vic—his girl Vic—who wanted, and expected to go to college! Within him his heart shrank into a hard little knot. Then he had arisen, stumped off to bed, and, just at the top of the steep, straight flight of stairs which led from the upper structure of the house down to the workshop in the lean-to, he had fallen dead and pitched headlong, to bring up with a crash against his cobbler's bench.

Eunice Sherborne's eyes grew fixed, almost glassy. She saw herself, young Vic Teller, spring to her feet at the terrifying sound and then stop, her body all of a tremble. How suddenly empty the house, with such an emptiness as it had never before known! The girl, swaying to the blow of premonition, reaching down to steady herself with shaking fingers, wishing to cry out over the lump in her throat, swallowing spasmodically, calling, at first hoarsely inaudible, and then clear, full-throated, "Father! Father, what is it?"

Silence. Not even an echo. Frightened eyes bent on the double reading lamp, too heavy to carry. Courage! A candle, tremulously lit, held high as she followed the course her father had taken. How palpable the stillness! How vast the emptiness! Here his footsteps had ceased, quite suddenly; here the rattle and rumble had begun. She peered down the slanting pit of the stairway to the shop and stopped to call again:

"Father! Wha—what is it?"

Ashamed of the break and tremor in her voice, she crept down the steps, one by one, pausing, waiting for she knew not what, going on again, until at last she reached the bottom of the stairs. She held the candle high above her head and the gloom seemed to open with a majestic slowness. There in the light, with his back to the cobbler's bench he had faced for a lifetime, legs extended and limp, sat Abraham Teller, his head fallen as though in profound thought. On his face was fixed the deep, sardonic smile, giving the lie even after death to the heart that had stopped beating rather than let him tell his daughter, so happily victorious, that she could not go to college.

"The day the letter came," said Eunice aloud. "The day——"

"The day your father dropped dead," supplemented the judge to his own astonishment.

She tossed her head in the characteristic gesture of her girlhood and stared at him, but there was no youthful surprise in her eyes at his having read her face.

"Yes," she said gravely; and presently continued, "She had to get away—she had to."

It was altogether natural to the judge that she should speak of herself in the third person, as though Vic Teller were quite divided from Eunice Sherborne, mother of Drake and Io. A peculiar atmosphere had entered the room, an air to which he was thoroughly inured. It seemed to him that himself, Warner Sherborne and Eunice were three judges, gathered together to weigh evidence against a prisoner unseen but vitally present, and that that prisoner's name was Vic Teller.

Chapter 9

"All Vic possessed," began Eunice, giving actual entity to the prisoner at the bar, "was the house, and nobody wanted it—nobody. The bankers of Salem and Bridgeton gasped when she asked for sixteen hundred dollars on mortgage. You see, she needed sixteen hundred to see her clear of debts and through college. Her guardian and the merchants whom her father owed, when she asked them, threw back their heads and laughed. All of them said one thing—almost in the same words. This is what they said: "Why, Miss Vic, Tryer Mattis himself couldn't raise sixteen hundred on that house!' She had heard of Tryer Mattis, a Salem man, but had never seen him. She looked him up to ask him how to borrow money. As it turned out, he did not teach her how to borrow money—he loaned her what she needed."

"Tryer Mattis!" exclaimed the judge with a sudden contraction of his hands. He leaned forward and fastened shrewd eyes upon her.

"That man," she whispered.

She spoke almost inaudibly, but her lips formed the words so deliberately that they seemed to resound, magnified. The Judge was puzzled by her bearing, for it appeared to be presenting contradictory evidence. Her eyes, not fixed on him, were very wide open and her head was erect; but he caught the shadow of a deepening flush in her cheeks. So, he thought, the youth which had been Vic Teller had been caught in that old, old trap of loaned money—of a mortgage and threats of foreclosure! Suddenly her eyes turned, met his, and read them.

"That is what Vic thought," said Eunice, "when she learned he was a married man."

"What do you mean?" demanded the judge.

"You know. You think he wanted the mortgage as a club over her. She thought so too."

Judge Alder could not at once surrender his deduction, knowing Tryer Mattis. He remembered the swift look with which the man had been wont from the beginning of his career to examine a job when everything hung on the making of a shrewd snap estimate— the same look with which he appraised women.

Even in the presence of men who were his rivals in business or in love, that look never lingered long enough to be measured. The judge could picture it passing over Vic Teller at sixteen so swiftly that she might never have noticed it, let alone taken it for a cynical calculation.

At the thought Mattis came vividly to mind. The word "cynical" did not fit and the judge withdrew it. The passing years had brought scarcely a change to Tryer's blond virility; he had always been an easy man to talk to, large-framed, open-faced, hearty in appearance and manner, a professional enthusiast rather than a cynic. Everything about him was turbulently static—everything but his eyes. When they were open they were round and seemed large; when they were narrowed they looked like two points of polished steel. As he was today, so had he been yesterday, so would he be tomorrow.

Eunice had been watching the judge's face, but now let her eyes fall and rested her chin lightly on her hands, folded on the back of the chair.

"Vic went to college, and it was Warner Sherborne," she stated, "who drove her, fresh from graduation, out to where Mattis was overseeing a job."

She stopped speaking and closed her eyes. For a moment she reëntered the body of her youth and she could hear Tryer's great voice as though he were in the room.

"Well, now," he had cried heartily as he helped her down from the buggy, "if it ain't the college graduate! Don't have to ask how are you, Miss Vic. Pretty as April dogwood and sound a winter apple!"

There had been something in the grasp of his hand and in the bold caress of his words, startlingly imaginative, that had sent the blood leaping through Vic Teller's veins in little skips and pauses. When Warner Sherborne tried to make love he was nothing but a dumb misery; when Tryer Mattis, a comparative stranger in spite of his benefaction, merely took her hand in friendly greeting and told the world at large how she looked, she felt drenched in his vitality and wanted to gasp as though at the impact of a bucket of cold, invigorating water. She had laughed in his face for the very joy of laughter, even while she wondered why she did it. Then he had led her out of sight of Warner into the construction shack, only to state that that was no place to arrange their business affairs.

"Look at it!" he had shouted. "Nothing! No paper and pen! No desk! Nothing but shovels and picks and two cases of dynamite —one in the corner yonder, and the other is me."

"You a case of dynamite, Mr. Mattis?" she had laughed, responsive to the gayety in his words.

"Sure ma'am," Tryer had replied, smiling broadly. "Slow to burn, but the devil to blow up. Show me a rock. Perhaps I can't split it, but I can try." Then his expression had changed suddenly and his voice had fallen to a lower key. "Tell me now, what are you traipsing around the country for behind a team that ought to be plowing this very minute? Why, that Warner Sherborne ain't nothing but a lump of marl. He ought to be mashed up and spread on his own worn-out fields. Why don't you go buggy riding with a fence post and be done with it?"

"Tryer Mattis," said Eunice aloud, "called Warner a lump of marl and a fence post."

"He would!" exclaimed the judge, and waited.

65

He knew that there was more to come, that she had scarcely begun to tell her story. So absorbed was he in watching her face and rare gestures of hand and body that he did not realize how seldom she spoke.

"That very day," she continued in a hoarse whisper, "on the way home, Warner said, 'Vic, I want you should marry me. I ain't got much, but what I got don't include a wife and two children.'"

She was silent for a long while, remembering the shock of thus learning that Mattis was a married man—had been a married man since before she first met him. When he came that evening Vic Teller had been ready for him. He did not drive up to the house, but there was nothing surreptitious in the manner of his approach from the tavern where he had left his team. He entered her gate boldly, paused to plunge his face into a bush of pungent clipped box, walked up the steps and knocked. She opened the door and led him into the parlor, a formal room, never used. She had had to search long for the key with which to unlock it.

Tryer was a man of quick perceptions. He had greeted her with a hearty word and a broad smile but as soon as he had perceived her cold face and the stilted room into which he was shown his demeanor changed with a single swift gradation, as the color of a chameleon changes to accord with its background. With cool deliberation he had picked the strongest chair and settled into it his spare yet massive frame.

"You got two good pieces in this room," he remarked. "The mullioned desk, that's San Domingo mahogany; you can tell it a mile by the black hefty look of it. And the table is Sheraton— genuine."

He pronounced "genuine" to rime with "columbine," but that was not what had startled Vic Teller, nor even the surprising content of his words. What startled her was the fact that she had not seen him cast a single glance around the room, and yet she knew positively that he had never before entered it. Strange, she had thought, that such a man should bother or stoop to lay the old, old trap of a mortgage!

66

Just there Eunice Sherborne, sitting in the kitchen of Rattling Run Fields, heard across the years the echo of Mattis' shouting voice and threw up her hands as if to shut out the sound: "You little bit of pretty nothing, so proud of yourself and what you thought out about me, do you want me to read the inside of your head out loud? You think because a man's married he's got no call to see, hear or feel no more. That's nothing. Why shouldn't you think it along of all the wooden people in the world? But this here, this other thing! You think that I'm the kind that has to buy a mortgage to get a woman. Me? Tryer Mattis? Why, if I had the damned paper here I'd tear it up and throw it in your face!" Suddenly he had leaned forward and his hands gripped hard. "Stand up!" he had commanded.

Scarcely knowing what she did or why she did it, Vic Teller had arisen, and the next instant staggered like an untried ship launched into deep water. What was the matter? What was happening? What right had Mattis—any man—to speak to her like that? Why had she obeyed? He, too, was on his feet, masterful, unsmiling, striding toward her. He caught her in his arms, lifted her up, crushed his mouth to hers, dropped her and was gone. From the door he had called back heartily. "I'll bring that paper tomorrow night."

Eunice raised her eyes and turned their troubled gaze upon the judge.

"She thought what you're thinking about the mortgage until he said, 'Why, if I had the damned paper here I'd tear it up and throw it in your face.' Then he caught her up, kissed her, dropped her and walked out. She—she didn't scream. She let him do it."

Judge Alder nodded his head violently, but Eunice did not see him. Her eyes were away again, watching Vic Teller, only half reassured by the light of day, riding with Warner Sherborne, at whose advances she had consistently jeered, and thinking: A lump of marl? Well, marl had its uses; it enriched dead soil. A fence post? Yes, Warner was like a fence post, inarticulate, submissive, fixed; but more like an anchor post than the rank and file. A man easy to handle, whom one would always know where to find. Not

67

like Tryer Mattis, a married man, a philanderer. How absurd to be afraid of him—she, a college graduate! Why, even if he were free—ten times free—would she want him? Never!

True to his word, Mattis had come back the following night, and Vic, grown secure in the accumulated calm of the day, led him through the hall into the familiar sitting room, where she and her father had passed so many placid evenings in unplacid and daring speculations. She did it on an impulse; it was an instinctive appeal for the presence at the interview of the spirit of the old man, all his life steadfastly ironic to outer seeming, yet so charitable within. Were he alive, the girl had thought, he alone in the whole world could never misjudge her.

She had not looked at Mattis; she had merely opened the door when he knocked, left him to close it or not as he saw fit, and walked before him into the sitting room. Arrived there, he had spoken in his lightest manner:

"Well, aren't we going to shake hands?"

At the sound of his voice, casual and apparently unremembering, a tremor went through her frame. She paused for an instant, controlled the tremor, turned and gave him her hand. He held it; his fingers closed on hers steadily as though forcing her, daring her, to look up. Fire shot along her arm and into the blood of her body.

Instantly her hard-earned calm had been shattered into fragments, struck by lightning, falling with a deafening internal crash of thunder. Within her was whirlpool, tempest, a conflagration. She dared not look up for very shame; but all else she had dared. Ah, God! Arms about his neck, clinging to him desperately; face pressed passionately against his rough coat; she herself sobbing as though her heart would break.

"Vic, honey, don't you cry now," Mattis had murmured, his voice steady, but his eyes round and startled. "It's all right. Leave off your crying and smile, for I'm telling you it's all right. I'll find a way. I don't know how, but I can try. Don't you be afraid, Vic. Leave it to Tryer Mattis."

For all answer she had clung to him more desperately, her sobs, one after the other, shivering through her slight body as though they would shake it apart. He had gathered her in his arms as one picks up a feather pillow. To hear her weep had been agony, but to feel her weep was terrifying. How small she was! How light, yet firm! How her warm flesh quivered and writhed beneath his touch! He felt that he was treading on something alive, crushing the life out of it.

"Vic," he had cried roughly, "come out o' that! I mean it! You come out o' that!"

Then, without moving, she had spoken—the words so muffled that he could not hear what she said.

"What's that now? Say it again." He shook her. "Say it again."

She did; again and again, each repetition ending in a trailing, fading, heart-rending sob.

Suddenly Eunice Sherborne's body, not Vic Teller's by many years, collapsed against the back of the chair, face buried, head fallen on doubled arm. There came from her crumpled body a terrible hoarse sound, repeated again and again each repetition ending in a heart-rending sob.

"Go away! Go away! Go away! Go away!"

Judge Alder sprang to his feet and stood with clenched hands, staring first at the woman and then casting a desperate glance of appeal toward the peaceful presence on the bed. Not for an instant did he mistake that raucous cry as addressed to himself. No! Let Tryer Mattis carry that burden. But he—Judge Alder—what was he doing here? What had he to do with the all but translucent body of Warner Sherborne, lingering like the pale reflection of a flame? Or with this hoarse woman, scorching him with the memory of her ancient moment of despair?

As though in answer to his question, she raised her head and showed him her face. He drew back from its revelation with a strange tremor and a feeling that he had been standing on holy ground, too near the burning bush. The realization swept over him that she whom he had taken for a withered bit of human harness

69

had once been a torchbearer of the divine fire, foolishly, supremely ardent. Even today—— His thought broke with the abruptness of the snapping of a pipestem. He could think of neither youth nor age as he gazed upon Eunice Sherborne's face, stained with tears, illumined from within, ageless as an unwritten page, and yet alive, quivering.

"Did he go?" he murmured, and, suddenly remembering the presence on the bed, trembled for the answer. What if Warner was dead? What right had he, Judge Alder, to sit in inquisition on his wife? How had he dared ask that question? He need not have feared, save for the lapse of his own intelligence, for this woman had nothing to hide. Something big had riven her wide open. She was disclosed. A glimmering reached his brain that there were depths in Eunice Sherborne still unsounded.

"Yes," she answered simply and without hesitation. "He went away; but he had to unloose her fingers one by one and force her arms from around his neck."

Chapter 10

The judge sank into his chair and sat with bowed head. He was not visioning Tryer Mattis frightened, escaping from that passionate embrace, nor thinking of the nobility which abasement can assume on the lips of a woman in love. His thoughts were upon that which had happened to him through this same man so many years ago, long before Mattis had crossed Vic Teller's path, and he was wondering if only today he had come upon the key to that disaster. Was this what had come to Elizabeth Banning whom himself, young Alder, had loved? Had she been swept away from him by some such inner storm as this? Had she? Long was the road behind that question, and while he traveled it Eunice sank bodily into memory.

She was back at nineteen years old, wilting before Tryer's gasping acquiescence:

"Go away? All right, Vic. I heard you now. You don't have to say it any more. Don't! Do you hear me, Vic? For God's sake, don't! I tell you I heard you! I'll go; but I'll come back."

The dress Vic had worn that night was a filmy, simple frock; not a new one, but still a favorite. It was white, with a modest round yoke and a ruffle of lawn from which her slim throat rose like a pillar, crowned above with the airy lightness of her disordered hair. She had chosen it deliberately because she had hoped it would make

71

her appear girlish, unsmirched; for even in her calm security she had felt the need of the support of an atmosphere of purity. Fully an hour after Tryer's departure she had gone upstairs. Arrived in front of the mirror in her room, flooded with moonlight, she had fastened scornful eyes on her reflection, and before their merciless inspection her body seemed to begin gradually to shrivel. In the glass had been the youth of Vic Teller; in the withering glance of the eyes was the age, and the accusation, of generations.

What had happened to her? She did not know; she did not even dare to ask. Whatever the power that had ripped her pride sobbing from her body, to her it was vile. Of a generation still held in absolute subjection to the ogres of the mind, she accepted the overwhelming tyranny of passion as wholly vile. Behind was all the massed tradition of suppression; before her, held in the grip of overmastering desire, she saw only an abysmal brink. Tryer Mattis had not had what he would of her through no virtue of her own, but only because he had been frightened by the violence of her surrender. All the more was she defiled.

What a sight was Vic at nineteen, slim, upright and smooth as a young hickory! See her face turn white and her full lips set in a straight line. See her shudder, draw nearer to the glass, and, with her eyes buried in their own level reflection, catch her dress at the shoulder between thumb and finger and begin tearing it off in strips. The flimsy material tears easily and it is not long before she stands in her plain, high-bodiced chemise within a snow-white, feathery circle of tatters and raveled lint. She gleams for a moment in the moonlight like a marble shaft; then crumples at the knees, sinking to the floor, to sit cross-legged, with her head buried in her arms, and weep not as she had sobbed against Tryer's rough coat, but unashamed, as a young girl cries for sorrow alone.

"Mother! Mother! A married man!"

To some Vic Teller in a little heap on the floor, whiter than the white moonlight, telling her trouble to a mother she had never known, will seem a pathetic figure; to others she will appear merely an unbalanced young woman at the end of a neurotic fit.

But in truth she was neither of these things; she was something more than both of them put together. She was the human heart in direct action, before anyone had thought of an index file for impulses.

She was miserably unhappy, terrified; but under her unhappiness and terror immeasurable forces which today are already half forgotten were at work. The traditions of her race and church were the least of these influences, while the greatest of them were certain obsolete traits of the pioneer; an assured cleavage between right and wrong, for instance. Add fortitude in abnegation, and, above all, a cruel power of self-elimination for the protection of the tender plant of the secret soul.

That exposition may sound like Greek to the sentimentalist or to the impatient; nevertheless, it contains the solid girders of the platform from which she was about to launch herself into life. It is not a question of what any girl would have done in like circumstances and under the whip of similar traditions, for though the equation of impulses may or may not conform to the mathematical rule of the doctrine of complexes, one truth is written large in the annals of the throbbing heart, and that is that the equation of character never does. Its attitude ever has been and ever shall be, "Complexes be damned."

It was this illusive and indefinable attribute which we term character that led Vic to issue from her night of torment a straight-lipped, cool and determined woman. In a manner of speaking, she was stripped—stripped of more than the symbolic frock, stripped of youth, of college education, of all those corollaries and frills which individual habit adds to the stark stem of what we are. She had discovered her own metal; but having discovered it, she did not knuckle down under the whip of tradition—far from it. She and tradition marched as equals, hand in hand. She waited with folded hands and fatalistic assurance for the coming of Warner Sherborne. He did not fail her either in the hour of his arrival or in the steadfastness of his purpose. They drove to Salem and were married.

73

Eunice looked up to find the judge's eyes fastened on her with deepening intensity.

"So," she said, interlacing her fingers and dragging on them nervously, "she married Warner. She—she had to. She was frightened. But Warner knew she did not love him."

Once more the judge nodded violently. He was afraid of her words; he wanted her to know that the brief signposts she gave him from time to time were enough to point the way and enable his thoughts to follow. Never again did he wish to hear a woman say of her girlhood: "He had to unloose her fingers one by one and force her arms from around his neck." That the words should have been uttered at all had been his fault; he had asked a question; he would ask no more.

The marriage, which to Vic Teller had been merely an impregnable wall raised between herself and her own weakness, to Tryer Mattis had been a bombshell. He was like a madman, a maniac so caged within the straitjacket of circumstances that he could move neither hand nor foot. None could value more accurately than he the finality of the step she had taken. So absolute did he know her sudden security to be, intrenched behind marriage, added to tradition, that it seemed to his distorted perception the result of a shrewd and malicious move. He became infuriated, and, for lack of any other outlet to his rage, had foreclosed on the Teller homestead and its contents. When all obligations were met and fees paid, Eunice Sherborne received the sum of twelve dollars.

"Then Tryer Mattis foreclosed," she said aloud. She raised her hand to her bodice and drew out a folded packet, wrapped in paper, incredibly flat as are only the packets left folded for many years. "Here," she added, "is the twelve dollars I received—the same twelve dollars."

Knowing the stark poverty of Rattling Run Fields, and sensing the terrific long-drawn-out struggle to which this woman had been subjected, each of those identical notes became to the judge an eloquent tongue. In the face of innumerable temptations she must have clung to this insignificant sum because, to her, it was not insignificant, but vital as the spar to which a drowning sailor clings in the midst of a limitless sea.

The Lantern on the Plow

Chapter 11

Eunice arose, went to the stove where a pot of black coffee was brewing, and filled a large cup for the judge, but poured none for herself. Then she turned and looked steadfastly toward the still figure on the bed. The fine features showed up sharply, like a cameo in silhouette. They did not appear to be lifeless, except in the sense that marble is lifeless, though perpetuated by the sculptor's skill in an undying image of life. A suggestion of such permanence lingered in the empty shell of Warner Sherborne; something endured which made his widow's throat contract and her eyes harden as she looked at him.

Watching her face, the judge was startled; not that it showed hate, for it did not, but because its expression was eloquent and yet absolutely unreadable according to the catalogue of known emotions. It had the calm of apathy, but none of the indifference which apathy implies; it had passion, but passion as frigid as the grandeur of a glacier. If it were possible for the human countenance to make concrete to the eye so abstract a thing as a definition he would have said that the expression on Eunice Sherborne's face symbolized a monumental division. For the first time she seemed totally unconscious of him, and as she resumed her seat without taking her eyes from the figure on the bed, the judge knew that the trend of her thoughts, at least for the moment, had evaded him.

She was, in fact, retraveling a dull road. She was remembering how with her framed diploma, her scant personal possessions packed in the trunk she had bought to go to college, and a single case of books, she had driven with Warner to this house at Rattling Run Fields which for six generations before him had harbored the Sherborne lineage. No description can picture the bleakness of its prospect at the time, or the sordidness of its interior; but by a paradox these very features had been invested to her with the quality of mercy. It fitted in with her mood that her material place of refuge should be as shriveled as the hope within her.

She had hung the diploma in the darkened parlor and set about her duties mechanically, but with an expert thoroughness. Warner had inherited what was virtually already rack and ruin, all but the house itself, built of the red native stone of New Jersey which grows more flintlike in its texture with each passing century. His dumb courtship of her had so consumed his time and attention that he had neglected even the common decencies of the chores of daily life, to say nothing of the crying needs of the farm. The suddenness with which he had won his bride had given him no chance for preparation. As a result, the young couple were plunged from the heights of two dreams, strongly diversified, straight into the welter of the lowest forms of toil. Eunice in the house and chicken run, Warner in the barns and pigpen, started in to get rid of filth. Fences to mend was the order of their days.

It is difficult to say just when she began to discover that Warner Sherborne had other qualities than the inanimate anchorage and submission of a fence post. True to his generation and environment, it never entered his head to make love to his wife in the sense of courting after marriage. To him, as to millions of others of his time, marriage was not yet a beginning so much as a terminating period. Like the rites of accretion to certain African tribes, it marked the slamming of the door on freedom. It was a culminating act beyond which two people entered, not upon initiation but into a fixed condition. With this attitude Eunice had had no quarrel whatsoever; she gloried in it. To have had Warner suing for her favors or appealing to that intimate tenderness which is the immortal crown on human affection would have driven her mad.

Her slow discoveries as to his character were quite other than this. At first the bodies of both of them were so completely drained of vitality by each day's unadorned labor that the mind had no chance either for thought or expression. Warner was innately unselfish. He did everything possible to lighten her burden so automatically that his unselfishness lost the meaning it might otherwise have carried and passed virtually unnoticed. That it should have done so is natural, for it lacked the personal touch of an intentional gift. In addition to helping her in little ways, generally after dark, he worked daily from the rising to the setting of the sun with a perseverance that was uncanny. He even plowed occasionally by lantern light.

This faculty for unremitting labor had begun to wear on her in spite of the fact that she worked almost as continuously as he. What? Never sit down at ease? Never linger to watch a sunset? Never save enough strength for five minutes of leisurely talk before banking the fire and putting out the light? Never read? Bury the mind for ever beneath the rubble of incessant occupation? The conviction, gradually attained, that unceasing labor was a constituent element in Warner's make-up formed the first of her series of discoveries as to his character. And the second illumination was allied unto it; for all Warner's automatic thoughtfulness, he took it for granted that Eunice should work her slim fingers to the bone.

As time wore on she suffered a reaction; her mentality clamored for an appeal to intelligence. What if she wasn't a school-teacher? Was there any law against Warner Sherborne's wife using her brain? In the dead Sherbornes' sparse library she found an old book on the treatment of the soil and a few bulletins of later date. She read them avidly and emerged with only one gleam of comfort: marl was a revivifier of the soil. She had known that before; had not Tryer Mattis likened Warner to a lump of marl? A wan flush spread over her face; it was actually the first time she had thought of Mattis since her marriage. But even before his advent the opened-faced marl quarries of neighboring creeks had been familiar to her childhood. Marl in that region was not expensive to those who would haul it for themselves; it could be had almost for the asking.

She approached Warner and made her suggestion. He gave her a look she would never forget, and yet it was well-nigh indescribable. It was the look of a dog on a treadmill, waiting for the refilling of the churn. It neither enthused nor denied. Without a word he got the warped wagon and hauled load after load of marl to spread upon the fields of the farm. He hauled marl and hauled marl until Eunice, hindered in her work by standing in the window against her will to watch for the heads of the straining horses to appear over the rise from the hollow of Rattling Run, dashed out hatless with outstretched hand to cry, "Stop, Warner, I can't stand it! Don't bring any more marl! Don't!"

Any other farmer would have thrown a clod at her head, thinking that she was joking or bad gone crazy; but not so Warner. He knew what was happening to her; he did not understand, but knew. She was beginning to learn the meaning of his look, of the look of the dog on a treadmill—a meaning which he could never hope to put into words. Work and Rattling Run Fields were not allies. Rattling Run Fields ate work, devoured work. Rattling Run Fields produced in return only one harvest—the harvest of more work. Here barren labor by some extraordinary contortion of hidden forces became its own end.

When Eunice began to catch a glimmering of this amazing truth she gasped, and then almost laughed aloud. Work was meant to pay in cash; even the Bible had recorded the right of a laborer to his hire. It was inconceivable that such efforts as she and Warner were daily putting forth should not produce, almost anywhere else, more than a living wage. Promptly she went to him with her second suggestion:

"Warner, this place will never pay. Even the marl doesn't seem to be doing much good. We have had just one thing of Rattling Run Fields—it has taught us how to work. Let's try working somewhere where it will pay. Advertise the place; sell it."

Within the next half hour, the next year, the next decade she made the discovery in regard to Warner Sherborne which was destined to blind her forever to any other faults or virtues he might possess. She did not uncover it all at once, because it was too huge, too inconceivable, too overpowering for immediate absorption. It was the discovery that he was not a submissive fence post, but a rock embedded for all time in the very bowels of the soil. At first it astonished her that she could not shake him. Later she was to laugh at herself derisively, not aloud, but deep within where laughter hurts, for having thought she could shake that which such elemental forces as poverty, hunger, death of one's own flesh and blood, and the loss of love and companionship could not budge so much as an inch.

"Advertise the place," she repeated. "Sell it." Warner's eyes met her for a startled instant, and then wandered vaguely. By the movement of his Adam's apple, prominent because his frame had grown so gaunt, she could see that he swallowed twice before he answered.

"We ain't got no call, Vic, to sell the land."

There was something in his tone which made it different from any speech he had ever before uttered. She puzzled over it, and for the moment let the matter drop. But the time was to come when, after several repetitions, that quiet announcement, "We ain't got no call, Vic, to sell the land," was to assume in her ears terrifying proportions, more ponderous, more ominous, than are the anathema and excommunication of the infallible pope to the faithful.

In the meantime day followed day on the swift wings which only routine can lend to time. The first toiling week of married life, seen over the shoulder, became a speck in recollection; the first month a shrunken moment. Almost a year went by before an event occurred which raised an unforgettable landmark amid the even flood of hours; she became aware that she was going to bear a child. Her first feeling was one of anger and shame, for what cause let those who know answer. But there followed days less emotional, when a sober elation, unconnected with the love

81

of man for woman, took root within her and grew apace. Weeks went by, and months, without her saying a word to Warner; but finally he could not help but know.

He would steal a few moments between supper and bed to watch her flying fingers fashion some tiny garment out of the materials of some of her former wardrobe, long since laid aside for the coarsest gingham. Three and four times a day he would pass through the house and his eyes would follow her about, not anxiously, but as if they were looking for something he might do to help her, something out of the ordinary. On one such occasion he found her strangely perturbed, her face white and her lips blue. He flushed and gave her a questioning look.

"Tryer Mattis is here," she had said shortly. "He is out looking for you."

Once or twice in the last few weeks she had thought she recognized Tryer's trim runabout with its fast team of horses taking a shortcut from the highway to the lower road. She had wondered vaguely what he might be up to, for the only part of her that at that time was afraid to meet him face to face was her pride. This day he had taken the road to the house itself, had come to the kitchen window, and called out that he wished to see Warner. Without opening the door, she had sent him to the upper field, not because she thought Warner was there, but because it was the farthest away.

At her statement that Mattis was about, Warner had gone out, and when he came back she asked listlessly, "What did he want?"

Sherborne did not hesitate.

"He wanted I should sell the place."

For a moment Eunice was absorbed by wonder as to the motive behind Tryer's action. Was it pity? Did he know the straits they were in? She had not pictured him as a forgiving man. Then the significance of the sheer fact that there had been a tentative bid struck her with its full force. She threw up her head and asked, "How much?"

"He had no call to make an offer," answered Warner, his eyes aglow. "I put him off at the outset."

To most farmers winter brings a time of idleness; but winter or summer, Rattling Run Fields gave no man a holiday. With two fires burning wood all day long and most of the night with the stock to feed single-handed and the cows to milk, with a long path to keep clear of snow between the house, the barn and the scattered out-houses and with endless patching of all sorts to do, whatever way he turned, Warner had little occasion for idling. But as the evenings lengthened and Eunice grew less capable of attending to her duties he found the time to assure them one by one.

In her ignorance, due to youth and a healthy body, of all med-icines and medical men, and most especially of the caliber of the country practitioner, she had been wondering hour after hour and day after day as to whether any doctor would come to Rattling Run Fields for twelve dollars. In the event, as it happened, no doctor reached the secluded farm. Instead came the most terrible blizzard in the memory of living man, the blizzard of the month of March, 1888.

Draw a torn veil across what happened at Rattling Run Fields during that three days' storm—and after. Through the veil only glimpse what no outsider has the right to see fully. Two people, trapped behind mountainous drifts, mastering the terror in their inmost souls and rising triumphantly to the pinnacle of human woe and courage. Eunice, blue-lipped, silent, abandoning her body to the agony of immolation; Warner, equally silent, a tower of tender strength grown great in the supreme acceptance of the term tran-scended in his wife's eyes, for the first and last time, to kinship with Godhood itself.

In that tremendous grappling between the forces of life and death, where they two, man and woman, were the trampled field of battle, it mattered not that he was inarticulate. Wordless, he himself had become expression—an expression of incarnate tenderness, valor and strength, moving with humbleness and majesty amid the mists of her pain. For a moment she loved him. Make no mistake. There is such a thing as momentary love, rare visitant, phœnix of the white fires of the heart, poising unseen on strong pinions—for an instant inviting capture; but unseized, gone forever.

Chapter 12

Suddenly the glacial stiffness melted from Eunice Sherborne's body. She left off staring at the body of her husband and her forehead fell forward against the back of the chair in which she sat, with a rap loud enough to arouse the judge, who had fallen to drowsing in the prolonged silence. An instant later and he was more achingly awake than ever before in his life.

"The snow!" moaned Eunice with a wailing cry that brought winter into the room. "Oh, Warner, my dear! The snow! Its flakes are like great white tears heaped in a bank against the window. Only they do not melt; none of them melts. I shall die and you will have to bury me in white tears!"

The judge leaped to his feet. He was terrified; not as a man is afraid of danger, but as one who hears the voice of resurrection calling across the years. Instinctively he turned his eyes toward the figure on the bed, for none needed to tell him that it was not the Eunice Sherborne whom he knew who was uttering that single lonely cry of love for her mate. What he was hearing was echo— exact, measure for measure with a sound long dead, but empty. Empty! He started to flee, but the very force which had frightened him drew him back. He felt for his chair with a groping hand, sat down, folded his arms and settled his chin on his chest.

Quite five minutes passed before Eunice lifted absent eyes to his intent gaze and murmured, "It was not she but the child who died."

Oh, tragic hour! Warner laying away the child in a vault, cut deep in the white wall of the snow. Warner waiting many days and then going out to fight the still-frozen earth with pick and crowbar. Warner, single-handed and without benefit of clergy, burying his first-born under a spreading, bare-limbed apple tree and closing the wound in the ground with a slab of rock torn from the foundations of the bridge across Rattling Run. Warner watching and waiting for his wife to come back to earth from those regions of surcease where her frantic mind had dragged her; and when, at last, she could ask him for her baby, Warner finding his stumbling tongue to tell her all.

Alas! Courage and dignity forsake her. See her claw her way to the foot of the bed to get nearer to him; seize the rail and pound on it with tightly closed fists. Hear her scream "Sell the place! Sell the place!" See Warner, giving her the look of a whipped dog, knowing that a momentous issue is at stake, though he cannot formulate it even to himself. While he tended her, she had called him "My dear" just once. The issue is related in some manner to this trifling, tremendous fact. To hear those words again—that tone in an unknown tongue—he would gladly pawn his immortal soul. His brow clouds; he opens his mouth, but the words that issue are quite other than he had intended: "Why, Vic, what would be the sense of that? We got no call to sell the land."

"No call! No call!" laughed Eunice wildly aloud, swept from all consciousness of the presence of the judge and striking the back of the chair with her fist. "No call to sell the land! Ha! Unconsecrated! Unhallowed ground!"

Her head dropped and the judge arose uncertainly, as if to go to her. He was profoundly moved, for her words conjured no uncertain vision. It was as though the throb of her body held a mirror to the past so that he could feel and see her throw herself back on the pillows and read the full meaning of her cry. No call to sell the land after what had happened in that stormbound house?

No call, with the child of her first travail buried in a casual grave, hidden away, hidden from the very knowledge of the world?

What the judge could neither read nor hear was the shout which had come from Warner Sherborne in answer to her cry—Warner Sherborne emerged for a single instance from the habitual fog of his own mind. Some thought of the days of terror through which he and his wife had passed—above and beyond that, some cyclopean memory of wind, snow, ice, the iron ground and a cold, rigid baby held close to his sweating breast—had dashed in to strike lightning from the flint within him. For once he had become articulate, even though only with borrowed words.

"Unconsecrated!" he shouted hoarsely. "Unhallowed!"

On those words he had turned, stridden furiously toward the door; and then stopped, quite suddenly, and with hanging head walked out softly.

She did not hear him, for one part of her had died, and already there had begun that apathy which was no apathy, that passion which was a frozen contradiction, that attitude of mind which was like an elusive definition of a monumental division. And yet a boy was born to her a year later; a lapse of six years more and there came a girl. She roused herself to demand that the boy be named Drake; equally insistent, she decreed that the girl be called Io. Why? Was it that for some obscure reason she looked upon these children as belonging to herself alone? Or was it that no agony of mind or body could erase the indelible impression of the symbolic name which had shone and died in her own youth?

Sir Francis Drake, unchained free wanderer over the surface of the earth, trampler on all men's lands, emblem of conquest and defiance, all-round man in the face of law and God; Io the crescent moon, two-horned laughing, serene above all turmoil in the illimitable heavens, mischievous, waiting to play hide and seek with the evening star! In bestowing those incongruous names upon her children had Eunice been merely ridiculous, or did she demonstrate that there are no depths of poverty or disillusion where a mother may not find a gift for those whom she loves?

Women sleep less than men; even though they spend more time in bed, they sleep less. Many were the hours that Eunice had lain awake, unconscious of all her surroundings save her children. With no right to hope, she still hoped in them. When she looked upon their tattered misery, when she touched their little bodies, her breast ached with a stabbing pain; but on the bed, in the dark, it was different. She was drugged. In that hazy region of the mind just this side of sleeping she could watch herself striding, happily victorious, through Elysian fields, a tiny hand in each of hers. Oh, quivering dream of the drowsy heart!

During the practical light of day there were two hours, one in the morning and the other just before the fall of evening, which belonged at first to Drake alone; and later, to Drake and Io together. When those hours struck, Eunice dropped whatever else she was doing to draw her children aside and plant in their minds the first seeds of a garden plot. Strange flowers for such starved soil; imagery, personal pride, aspiration! She told them over and over again the original Drake; and the world became familiar and, for the first time, round. She whispered all the myths of Io; and gods became playmates, the starry heavens a playground. The boy absorbed fearlessness almost from the days of her breast; Io, who patterned herself upon his ways with a sort of breathless emulation, lacked the very mechanism through which fear is felt.

Twice in the year, at planting and harvest time, Eunice had neglected her household duties to work in the fields. One day she leaned on the handle of her hoe, bowed her head on her hands and tried to remember just when she had begun to do this. She could not. She had not noticed when Drake joined her there, except to feel the mute gratitude of a straining beast for a helping shoulder at the mired wheel. But when Io toddled out of her own accord and Sherborne accepted as a matter of course her elflike aid—ah, that was different! That was too much! Io, newborn crescent moon, thistledown against the sky, on the way to wrinkles too? No! Never!

A torrent of words, too long restrained, had ripped and torn its way from her laboring breast; first to the children, hoarsely, "Go away! Run to the barn and gather eggs! Run faster!" And then to Sherborne, "Warner, you———"

But no. The acrimony which springs up between two people, each honest, each following an appointed way, each tragically unseen of the other—the acrimony which sears the passionate throat that gives it utterance and lays a branding iron on the fiber of the receiving soul—has no place in this record. Its textual narration could not add stature to Warner Sherborne or lessen by a jot the heaped measure of his wife's courage and endurance. Better to vision them thus—immobile man and ardent woman, fatally discordant, in bondage beneath the inflexible yoke of Rattling Run Fields. Flown beyond all recapture momentary love, the phœnix of the heart's white fire. Behold Warner, henceforth entombed in loneliness; and Eunice, ashes, still aglow.

She had cast her eyes about her wildly and then dropped them to the meager soil.

"Farmers cannot quite starve to death. What a pity!"

Chapter 13

In that midafternoon Eunice took the two children and plodded three miles to the railroad station. From her bodice she drew a small package wrapped in paper, held it tightly, and asked for a time-table. She stared at it and passed her free hand across her brow. Something was wrong; there were no prices. No prices? What? Was she so far sunk into the numbed regions of the suffering mind that she could confuse a time-table with a menu card? Oh, cowardly brain! How puerile and how terrifying!

She turned to the ticket agent and asked with frightened eyes, "How far can we three go for twelve dollars?"

He stared at her in amazement; then he recognized her. She was that woman from Rattling Run Fields, a little madder than usual. His eyes slowly narrowed, and as though in compensation his jaws worked more rapidly on his chewing gum. Several seconds passed before he spoke:

"You better go along home."

So that is how she looked—a man could speak to her like that! Her head drooped; she put the packet of money away, took the children's hands and wearily they had plodded all the way back.

In later years Eunice was to look upon that futile pilgrimage as the lowest level of the sunken pit of misery into which her willful fate had cast her. From that day things, exterior things, had begun to happen. Because Warner stubbornly ignored the school law, the hand of authority reached out for him, a hand that could not be brushed aside. Warner haled to court! Good! Good! Let him learn! No, she would not go; she would not help him. Let him pay, him and his land! Let the rock of generations crumble and the heavens fall, so that Drake and Io might go to school! When he gained a reprieve she was angry. How had he done it? Was justice, indeed, blind?

For hours after he and the children returned from the county seat she did not speak; then she asked dully, "Why did they let you off?"

Warner frowned, a vague smoldering in his deeply set eyes.

"Because," he had said finally, "I plow by lantern light."

At those words she had shrunk into herself, shriveled before a terrifying thought. Was Rattling Run Fields greater than the law? On the heels of that terror, which lingered through many days, had come Judge Alder. One moment the world had been a vast gray emptiness, an overcoming void; the next it was a mere setting for a man—a man well groomed, placid in his self-respect, sitting at ease upon a log as though it were a seat of honor. The voice of authority hailed Warner, and Warner obeyed its summons. An interim, and then had come Warner's gesture and hoarse commanding cry. The children went to him and she had followed, on what impulse she did not know. But when she heard the judge speak, when she heard his faintly ironic words, "Drake is your name, sonny, isn't it? And yours is Io?" she knew why she fled. She fled for very fear that he might look at her as the station master had looked—and add pity to the injury of his irony.

Followed event climbing breathlessly upon the shoulders of event. The judge's curiosity—discovery of a block of cement rock—inquiry—a contract with Tryer Mattis, of all men! Tryer, who all along had known of the hidden wealth of the farm, ever since the day he had called to her through the kitchen window. Warner, taking to his bed irrevocably at the news that he need no longer labor, calmly continuing his raid on Omnipotence, setting his own hour for entering upon eternal rest. The judge, herself, the children, coming slowly to life in the warmth of a transcendent peace, each unfolding to the perennial miracle of the sprouting leaf. Rattling Run Fields, prostrate for a time at least, waiting to nurture those upon whom it had fed.

These occurrences, heaped upon each other with a breathless rapidity after so many years of dragging monotony, formed a mounting sequence which implied a climax. In their light it would seem that she, no less than the judge and her husband, should have seen clearly as the gods see, with the measuring eye of an aloof justice.

But it is blindness above all other qualities which stamps humanity on men and women, and the habit of years may not be sloughed in a moment, nor in a tragic hour. To Eunice, the emaciated figure on the bed set in the spacious kitchen, abiding steadfastly by a deliberate summons to friendly death, was invested with none of the glory that swells the sources of affection. The shock of her discovery of the immutable within that plain gaunt frame still reverberated too loudly in memory for her to measure the full portent of a lifetime of tenacity in silence.

Nevertheless, she was neither so deaf nor so blind as not to know that in the consummation of Warner's victory, astonishing in the scope of its fulfillment, she was not shut out from a share in his triumph. The balm of peace that had fallen upon him was not his alone; it was vast enough to embrace her also, though not big enough to make her forget that between love and a colossal permanence he had chosen permanence. No; never big enough to obliterate that treacherous denial of herself for allegiance to the soil. Never! When she remembered his last words, she almost laughed aloud:

"Son, the land's yourn. You ain't got no call to sell it."

Each syllable had fallen like the blow of a hammer, striking the chains of the past from her body and spirit. No time to waste on hatred now; no breath for recrimination; no thought save for the feeling of unbounded release in the face of that final unpardonable

93

reiteration of the rock-like tenet that had stood between her and love. Free! Unyoked! No wonder she could move swiftly to catch up Io from the judge's knee and meet Drake as he turned, startled, from the sudden rush and emptiness of death.

Quick! Into the darkened parlor. Grope along the walls. Find the grimy frame, the stained parchment which proclaimed Eunice Teller a bachelor of arts. Lay it face up upon the table. Clutch it! Believe in it! Cling to it—or drown! A shuddering sob. A caving of the knees. A single choking cry. Outthrown arms, fallen head, splintering glass.

How had she come to reënter the kitchen? Where were the children? Indeed, where was she? Warner on the bed, she by the window, and between them a judge. Were they merely three people, and one of them dead? Or were they three forces, three elements, three symbols of the eternal pageant of man's pilgrimage? No; nothing so grand as that. She was a culprit without a feeling of guilt. She had been pleading her case desperately. Judge Alder had been weighing all her life in the balance against Warner's, and perhaps finding her wanting. For the first time she looked at him consciously, curiously, and noted the black shadows the night-long vigil had stamped beneath his steady eyes. Instinctively she perceived that here was one who neither judged nor condemned—no jurist, but a friend.

The short summer night had all but passed when the judge, becoming aware of an unusual sound on the stairway which led from the kitchen to the upper story of the house, reached back and unlatched the door. Before he could save her Io tumbled headlong down the steps, followed by Drake. She did not cry from her fall, as almost any other child would have done; and when the judge picked her up and started to pet her she repulsed him, to run to her mother.

Eunice neither questioned nor reproved the children; she took Io upon her lap and drew Drake to her side. From the shoulders down, owing to their nondescript night clothes, they seemed formless and colorless bundles; but from their necks up they shone with

94

a species of self-contained iridescence. The dew of sleep, which makes children most kissable when newly awakened, still lay upon their lips, on their cheeks and in their eyes. They were illumined, beautiful, intrinsically adorable, as are candles upon an altar, and gradually their radiance seemed to envelop their mother.

The judge did not trouble to note that the gray light of dawn in the window had brightened to gold; his eyes were too intent on the transfiguration of Eunice Sherborne. She seemed miraculously enlarged from the spare woman he had first seen begrimed with labor and looking like a stain on the very soil. So complete was the change within and about her that memory flatly denied itself. This woman a bit of human harness? Never! How weigh her? Had she been more than right and wrong as all of us are right and wrong? Yes; she had earned the privilege to stand above all averages, for she had traveled her path with such intensity that with a dozen broken speeches, scattered through the long hours of a night, she could flash her whole life upon the vision of another and, unashamed, make vivid the secret places of her heart. She was alive, by heaven! Right or wrong, she was alive, and by that token lovable!

She arose and stood hand in hand with each of her children, and, as it chanced, in the path of the level sun. Immediately a blinding effulgence seemed to spring from her body, dimming the paling lamp, dissolving the very walls. She took a single step, and it was as though she strode, attended, through open fields. She looked down into Drake's eyes, gray by day, but when in shadow dark as powdered slate; then she turned slowly to Io. A smile lit up her face, such a smile as the children had never before seen. They answered it by casting themselves against her body with a movement of joy astonishingly unrestrained, and eager. Still looking down, she said quietly to the judge, "You may have forgotten the Greek derivation of Eunice." Her eyes lifted to give him a share in the smile which swept over him like a revivifying essence, like a warm flood that recognizes no fixed channel. "Happily victorious," she murmured almost inaudibly.

Chapter 14

To all outward appearance no more commonplace group can be imagined than that which gathered to lay away Warner Sherborne under the same spreading apple tree where, single-handed, he had buried his first-born. There was nothing surprising to those present about the choice of location, for small clusters of tombstones are not an unusual feature on the private holdings of the three counties, nor was the occasion noteworthy because it consecrated a double interment. It was remarkable from quite another cause.

Only too often people gathered together for a funeral are intent on the fit of their clothes, on the impression on others of their grief; or, ill at ease, they are taken up with thoughts of discomfort, or of money, or with longings to have the matter over and done with. But on this occasion three adults were absorbed, to the exclusion of every other consideration, in the manifestations of their own vitality mysteriously released by Warner's death; and four children were equally enthralled by their individual affairs. The four children were Drake and Io, staring fixedly at Jimmy Mattis, a blue-eyed, sandy-haired, freckled boy of ten, and at his sister Lessie, four years older, pale and thin, with peculiar eyes, shaped like almonds. The three grown persons were Eunice Sherborne, Judge William Alder and Tryer Mattis.

Have you ever watched gas-filled toy balloons, escaped into the air? They leap from insignificance into significance, and then what becomes of them? How high and far do they fly, and where and when and how do they land? If anyone had told Eunice, Tryer and the judge that with the breaking of Warner Sherborne's thread of life they three had become toy balloons at the mercy of the breeze, they would have stared uncomprehendingly. Looking at one another's stolid flesh, they would have felt assured that their informant lied.

Aside from the group of seven, so ordinary to look at, yet so vibrant under the touch of the past and the spur of the future, there were present no neighbors; only an officiating clergyman and a funeral director accompanied by his assistants. Each of these attended to his specific duty with a singleness of purpose which looked neither to right nor left. Priest, pallbearers, and even the gravedigger, did with dignity and dispatch the proper thing to do, and did it correctly, thereby becoming a setting as flat as the mat in a picture frame to the seven beings who were humanly alive.

Midway between the two groups, both in spirit and fact, stood a man who belonged with neither and yet to both. He was short of stature, huge in girth, wore a full gray beard and was possessed of twinkling eyes under bushy brows. None called him by his full name of Thomas Bodley and few had ever heard it, for on every byway between the Delaware and the sea he was known as Connecticut Tom; or Tom the Whip Man; or, more familiarly still, merely as Tom.

Tryer Mattis had arrived at the funeral by accident, which he promptly made to appear as intent; but Tom had been brought. The very fact that Rattling Run Fields stood on the steepest elevation of the countryside precluded his coming there by chance, for it was to avoid the hills of his native state that he had abandoned Connecticut and taken to the myriad gravel roads of a fertile and gently billowing region.

Looking back a bare score of years, it is impossible to conceive of a more vivid symbol of a day that is gone than was comprised

in Thomas Bodley, his fat horse and his carriage, the last a cross
between a victoria, a barouchet and a chaise—in short, a phaëton
without the driver's box. It was four-wheeled, slung close to the
ground on leather straps, had a calash top and a very low dash
surmounted by a nickeled rein rod, scrolled at the ends. Its shafts
were deeply curved for art's sake rather than utility; nevertheless,
it was built throughout to endure beyond the usual span of life
of horse or man. The keynote of the quaint outfit, however, has
been omitted. It was sounded by a bundle—nay, a great sheaf—of
whips, straight, limber and tapering, each tipped with an eight-inch
snapper of red, yellow or blue.

When boys saw those whips their mouths watered, their fingers itched and they longed achingly for the price of the cheapest.
When the boy in any man driving along behind a horse looked at
them, having the price, he promptly stopped to buy of the best.
And yet, strange to say, Tom's equipage was not provided with
a socket, nor had his sleek fat horse, Alexander, felt the cut of a
whip since the day he was foaled. It may be added that though
the cheapest as well as the most expensive of the whips were a
lovely sight standing straight from the dashboard or held across a
proud driver's front, not one of them but would have snapped in
two at a sharp blow or fallen to pieces in the hands of rage. Even
so, the fact that Thomas Bodley, gentlest of men, should have
been a dealer in whips shows to what pranks the serious business
of living can stoop.

While on level ground or a down grade it was his custom to
sink back in the one broad seat of the small carriage and whistle
by the hour; but no sooner did the traces tighten than Alexander
would halt to permit his friend and master to dismount. Horse and
man would then walk up the rise side by side. There were times,
however, when Alexander would stop far afield out of sheer inertia
or through having fallen into reverie. On such occasions Tom would
talk to him, argue with him, plead with him, call him Alexander,
and finally loose all the brutality in his make-up in the two sharp
syllables, "Aleck!" At that call the horse would invariably move on,

while Tom mopped sweat from his brow, wondering desperately what he would do once this last resort should fail. He happened to be in such a speculative mood when Judge Alder, on the way to Warner's funeral, chanced upon him and paused to make his annual purchase.

"Tom," he said as he turned to lay the new whip away, "you're a great fraud, almost as big a fraud as your whips. You know I never use them. Here! Take this one back. I don't want it, after all."

"I can't do that now, judge," said Tom sadly. "A superstition, like when a black cat crosses your road. I'll tell you why. According to what you say, and a lot of other folks, the life of one of my whips is about ten minutes; so you've owned that one for one-tenth of its natural life already. No; I can't take it back; but for a quarter more I'll tell you the name of the manufacturer."

"Some other member of the Society for the Prevention of Speed, I suppose," laughed the judge, and then changed to another theme. "What do you think about these automobiles, Tom? You drive around the country a lot; do you think they are getting thicker?"

"You mean them horseless kerridges," replied Tom gloomily, "that needs a horse to pull them home. If they ever get so they can go and come of themselves——"

He stopped and the cloud on his face deepened. The judge completed the unfinished sentence:

"——there'll be no more market for whips, eh? Well, I wouldn't worry about that, Tom."

He in turn stopped speaking suddenly, as though he had been interrupted, and studied Bodley's outfit with a new interest. Horse, shay and master were getting old. For years they had appeared in Jersey, coming from the south along with the flickers, oven-birds and warblers about dogwood time and staying until the sweet gums turned purple in the fall and the holly berries began to ripen. Whence Tom came and whither he went in winter no one knew. The judge was now curious about the matter for the first time and for a definite reason.

100

For weeks he had been living a double life, attending to his official duties and law practice automatically, almost impatiently, and, immediately he was released, turning to immerse himself in the affairs of the Sherborne family with an avidity which he himself could not explain except in terms of the wordless impulses of the heart. All he knew was that he had a hunger to be with the denizens of Rattling Run Fields, and that where their welfare was concerned all his senses were sharpened. Without having spoken of the matter with Eunice, he knew that the intention was forming in her mind to abandon the farm at the earliest possible moment, and it was due to this premonition that he took an interest in the winter quarters of Tom the Whip Man. It was no part of the judge's plan to see the house on Rattling Run actually vacated.

"Tom," he asked, "where do you go in winter?"

Bodley stared at him and a vacant look crept into his eyes. "Across the ferry," he replied, and gathered up the reins as though to escape. But Alexander was of different mind; he ignored the hint.

"Listen," said Judge Alder, reining in the impatient Gypsy. She had sensed departure in every fiber of her tense body and seemed to cast a look of scorn at the lethargic Alexander. "You know I'm your friend, Tom. There's just a chance of comfortable winter quarters for you and the horse off the road a bit at Rattling Run Fields. I don't have to tell you Alexander is getting pretty old and mighty fat for a long journey. Do you remember Warner Sherborne?"

"I remember his dad well enough," answered Tom promptly; "but Warner never bought only one whip off me, and that was fifteen summers ago."

"Must have been when he was courting," remarked the judge. "Well, he's dead and we're burying him today. Come along for the sake of that one whip. Warner was a good man."

Thus it happened that Tom Bodley stood at the grave side halfway between the group which was doing its formal automatic duty and that which represented the forces of emotion released or in suspension. He was more than a spectator; he was a link, as if his daily contacts on a thousand highways had made him a sort of

101

solvent as between comatose beings in the rut and those definitely out of it. Somehow he had learned that the human family, after all, is not a conglomeration; there is a line of division between the rushing quick and the walking dead; and, strangely enough, this line is not marked by the grave, nor is it impossible for any one of us to cross it twice in the same day, being dead one moment and alive the next.

Tom had possessed himself of this truth and his wise eyes lingered on the judge, on Tryer Mattis, but longest on Eunice and her children. Then they went back with a sort of involuntary snap to Lessie Mattis, standing aloof by inches only, as if merely to mark a division between herself and her father. None knew the countryside gossip better than Tom or kept a closer mouth about it; but he remembered. He remembered now that they said of this awkward girl of fourteen with the strange long eyes that she was the only female within a range of fifty miles who was more than a match for Tryer.

Only Tom among those present knew how unusual it was for father and daughter to be seen together; only he, also, knew that since Lessie was with Tryer, it was by her own choice; that Tryer was afraid of her and practiced blotting her from mind to such an extent that he never spoke of her when mentioning his children unless forced by a direct question to do so. Tom knew, too, from the lips of her own mother how she had come by her peculiar name. He could hear Elizabeth's plaintive voice narrating the event.

"We wanted to call her Lassie and I begged him to let me say it to the preacher. But he wouldn't. He said he'd hold her and he'd tell the preacher how to name her. And when the time came he said Lessie for Lassie, like he always does. I coughed and whispered, out there in front of everybody, and tried to explain, but they named her Lessie between them, for all I could do."

When the ceremony of Warner's burial was concluded and the clergyman with the paid attendants had departed, the remaining persons, all but Tom, seemed suddenly incited to action. They moved forward and assumed rôles like characters in a play. Drake and Io advanced on Jimmy and Lessie, bringing up the guns of their eyes into closer range in a last attempt to stare the strange children out of countenance; Tryer Mattis, hand extended, strode toward Eunice with definite intent, and she and the judge drew impulsively together, shoulder to shoulder, as if to meet an attack.

"Well, Vic," cried Tryer heartily, "aren't we going to shake hands?"

Eunice regarded him steadily, but kept her arms folded across her bosom. She wondered if he knew that his words were an exact echo, and if he had made them so intentionally, wishing to bring back to her mind the most poignant of all the memories of her girlhood. Also, she wondered if he had come deliberately to Warner's funeral, or if mere chance had brought him past Rattling Run Fields at the moment when its friendless master's body was being carried from the house.

She knew intuitively that Tryer was incapable of giving a frank answer to either of these questions had she put them to him; but even as that thought passed through her mind she became aware that she knew even better than himself his motives and intent. Whatever force had once blinded her so that she could see him not at all with her eyes and only by the feel of her clinging hands no longer obtruded between them. She saw him now, inside and out, as clearly as though he had been cut open and mapped, and, strange to say, he was a bigger man than she had ever before believed him to be.

There are some men who are tortuous of soul, evasive in verbal expression, uncertain of standards, and yet frank by nature. Seldom small in physical stature, they stride through life like walking contradictions, building massively with one free hand what they destroy with the other. They are splendid material gone partly to waste through some congenital flaw, or weakness in upbringing, or handicap of environment, or merely through lack of that major education which establishes values in true proportion. The very structure of their rugged virtues and devastating faults makes them magnetic to women.

103

Mattis was such a man. He had the flashing imagery which could call out to Vic Teller at twenty, "Pretty as April dogwood and sound as a winter apple"; and the astuteness which could feel good furniture, apparently without looking, and name it. The boldness of his eternal phrase, "I can try," would have been meaningless if it had not been linked to phenomenal foresight. He had not only the flair to cry out, "If I had the damned paper here I would tear it up and throw it in your face," but the daring to follow up the assertion by a lesson in how to sweep a woman from her feet. Most treacherous of all, he possessed the sheer beauty of sensuality which could lead him to pause on the way to a tryst long enough to plunge his face into the crisp pungency of clipped box. And yet——

He was a liar—a casual, inconsequent liar. Why pretend that he had come on purpose for Warner's funeral? What difference would the truth have made? None. Furthermore, he was cruel in his desire. Why had he married Elizabeth Banning? Because he loved her any more than any one of a half a dozen other women? No; only because she was betrothed to another, to a man he admired and envied, a man who would have made her a far better husband. Never had it occurred to him to apply to himself the building standards which he employed on the jobs, some of them big in conception and admirable in execution, in which he took a legitimate pride. In short, in all physical things he was a giant; in all morality he was unsound; and right or wrong, he was likable.

Chapter 15

No blow is equal to the insult of the refusal of an extended hand. Perceiving that Eunice kept her arms folded and believing that she meant to keep them so, a flush of shame rose to Tryer's face which changed suddenly to the red of anger.

"So you hold a grudge for fifteen years, do you?" he exploded. "And what a grudge! Tell me what harm I ever done you! What have I ever had of you? Was I unkind? Did I ever do aught you didn't want I should do? Did I?"

The judge thrust himself forward.

"I'd go easy if I were you, Tryer," he said, glancing at the three younger children, who had gathered around Tom as a neutral. He saw that already they were safely absorbed in their own interests to the exclusion of the wordy affairs of their elders, and that Lessie had withdrawn to her father's automobile, ignoring Drake, her elder only by a matter of months, and scorning to play with those beneath her age.

Mattis paid no heed to the judge, nor did his eyes swerve from Eunice Sherborne's untroubled face.

"Don't you know that me and you are going to be partners?" he continued, without giving her a chance to answer his torrent of questions. "Haven't I paid you good money and ain't I going

105

to pay you more? What's the sense of treating me like dirt? I left you alone while Warner was alive, didn't I?"

"Why shouldn't you leave her alone, then and now?" demanded the judge sharply. "Look here, Tryer! You'd better listen to me! She isn't your partner and she never will be. Until Drake becomes of age I'm the only partner you're going to have on this deal, and the sooner you realize it the better."

"I have a good mind to tear up the damned contract and throw it in all your faces!" cried Mattis, whirling on the judge with a toss of his leonine head.

At his words the fullness of Eunice's lips twisted slowly to a mocking, whimsical curve, even while her eyes remained maddeningly steady. Why must men repeat their grand gestures? What fatality leads them back even across fifteen years to a once successful ten-strike? How often had Mattis used these dashing words since that far-away day when they had so impressed her? How childish, how lost all men look, especially the big ones, when they are angry! She was sorry for him.

"Read it over carefully before you tear it up," she heard the judge say. "I wrote it, Tryer. It's the kind that doesn't tear easily or cheaply. It's a———"

"Don't tell me!" shouted Mattis, raising both fists in the gesture of a despairing Samson. "Didn't I name it? Didn't I call it a legal straitjacket? But by the eternal, I'll———"

It was Eunice who brought his shouting to a sudden break. Pushing by the judge, she stood squarely before Mattis and held out her hand in such a manner that he had abruptly stopped speaking.

"What are you making all the fuss about, Tryer?" she asked. "There's my hand if you want it. I wasn't going to refuse to shake hands with you; I was only thinking it over, just as you are now about mine. Do you want it, or don't you?"

"Want it? Sure, I want it," replied Mattis, recovering from his surprise no less than from his rage, for he was as responsive to atmosphere as a barometer.

The instant he took Eunice's cool hand in his hot one he became jovial, expansive, friendly with all the world. Being no sentimentalist, he released her promptly to turn to the judge.

"Well, Bill," he said, as though eager to get on a friendly footing all around, "we've started moving the plant, and that ain't all. It takes money, big money, to make cement, and I've found it. Now money costs money. Anybody can throw it into a hole fast, but it has to crawl out on its own feet. That's what I want to talk to you about, judge. Fifteen years doesn't give me a chance. I want it should be twenty."

"It seems to me, Tryer," said the judge, his eyes narrowing, "that you're getting fonder and fonder of the idea of wearing a straitjacket for life. What's the reason? What are you keeping back?"

"Well, it's this way," said Tryer, making a genuine effort toward frankness, "I most wish the contract didn't begin running till five years from now."

"Why?" demanded the judge.

"On account of automobiles," replied Tryer in a voice which for him was unusually humble.

"Automobiles!" scoffed the judge. "What have they got to do with it? You have automobiles on the brain."

"Lots of people have," commented Tryer mildly. Then he flashed a full-eyed glance all around. "Before we die," he predicted boldly, "this state will have a thousand miles of roads made out of solid concrete, all on account of thousands of automobiles."

"I wonder," said the judge. "I wonder if there'll ever be a thousand of those things." His eyes wandered to the spot where Tryer's single cylinder car, with Lessie in it, was drawn up off the road; then passed to Gypsy, hitched to a stout cedar; and finally to Tom Bodley's outlandish outfit, with the fat Alexander slumbering between the grotesquely curved shafts. The boys and Io, having discovered the whips, had promptly abandoned all other interests and were gathered as near to Aleck's heels as they dared go, for he was a selfish rascal, distinctly unfriendly to children either by

107

training or disposition. He humped his hind quarters whenever Drake set foot upon the low steps of the carriage, or Jimmy, from a safe distance, so much as pointed at a coveted whip.

"Hard roads are bad for horses' feet," called Tom Bodley from near by.

It was his first contribution to the talk, and it drew Eunice's eyes to look at him perceivingly. Of course, she had seen him before; but it is astonishing how often we meet people and talk to them without actually becoming conscious of their presence. Now she noted more than Tom's great girth and his eyes, very small, but widely spaced under a fine forehead. He had a gentle manner and kindness radiated from him. She liked him.

Tryer Mattis, having planted a seed of suggestion in the judge's mind, departed for his car with characteristic suddenness, taking his son with him. When he started the engine Gypsy quivered violently and sagged backward in a desperate attempt to hang herself on the hitching rope, and even Alexander pricked up his ears and snorted, but did not deign to lift any one of his four heavy feet. Nevertheless, Tom went and soothed him as if he were a restless charger.

"How much does a whip cost?" asked Drake from the very depths of inquiring ignorance in such matters.

"There's some as cost fifty cents and some as high as a dollar and a half," replied Tom.

"What do you want of a whip? What would you do with one of them whips if you had it?"

"Play with it," said Drake fervently.

Tom pawed over the bundle until he found a whip broken near the end, pulled it out and offered it to Drake. The boy's eyes glistened and a flush rose to his cheeks, but he put his hands behind his back.

"What's the matter?" demanded Tom. "Don't you want it?"

Drake shook his head in denial, and Io, standing close beside him, looked the Whip Man squarely in the eyes and said, "He doesn't want it because it is broken."

"Broken!" shouted Tom. "I give him a brand-new whip for nothing, only a little bit broken at the end, and it isn't good enough for him. Huh!"

"It isn't that," protested Drake, in his turn drawing the eyes of the Whip Man. "It's because it isn't straight. When I grow up I'll buy a straight one. I can wait."

"So you're willing to wait till you grow up just to have a straight one, eh?" inquired Tom.

Already these children had laid their spell upon him. It seemed that though they were so short, their eyes were on a level with his; and that though they were so young, they lived in his world. He liked them, and trying to think how he might best crown their friendship with honor, he placed Io in the deep seat of the chaise, urged Drake to get in beside her, and taking the reins proceeded to drive Alexander along the level section of the road away from the dip to Rattling Run.

As the judge and Eunice drew near the house he looked around at its bare surroundings and then turned to her.

"It is so warm, it's too bad there's no place to sit out here," he said. "Only the old front steps, and they look as though they would cave in."

"No," said Eunice, "nothing about this place ever caves in; it only warps."

She went to the narrow steps and they sat down rather close together. The judge was puzzled both at her and at himself. Why had she moved toward Tryer so frankly after an initial hesitation, and why had she given him her hand? Did she not know what that meant? Tryer would make it his business to pass the house going to and from the new plant every day, twice a day. But what the devil had he, Judge Alder, to do with all that? Why shouldn't she take Tryer's hand? What was this feeling that had crept over him? Let him meet it frankly—was it love for Eunice?

No, not that; but an impulse of protection for her and for all that pertained to her—protection against harm, against desecration, against intrusion. That was it. He was on the right track at last—

against intrusion. No man could go through such an experience as he had had with her on the night of Sherborne's death without feeling a subtle sense of possession, of guardianship before a shrine. Was it credible that she could ever again tell the story of herself as she had told it in the august presence of Warner Sherborne's symbolic shell?

The temple of what we truly are is the most mysterious edifice known to man; none holds the key, not even ourselves. Only a triple conjunction between elemental forces, the vital hour and a God-sent opportunity can ever swing open the door of self and grant the freedom of the hidden heart to another. The judge knew that he had been admitted to the profound depths of Eunice Sherborne's soul in a manner that precluded retraction on her part or on his. In an involuntary sense they belonged to each other, for that night had laid its chains upon them without so much as a by your leave. No, he told himself, he did not love her; but when she stirred so that her arm brushed his sleeve a tingling shock of infinitesimal vibrations raced up and down his spine.

"Of what are you thinking?" he asked in self defense.

"Of the terrible hard beauty of this place," replied Eunice after a pause; "of how I hate it because it does not yield, will never yield—to me. I was thinking, too, of the fact that there is no seat out here, has never been a seat out here in fifteen years, in ten times fifteen years! I was thinking that I shall go away and never come back—never."

In his turn the judge paused; then he said, "I can understand everything but your discovery of beauty. It's here, of course; beaten down, suppressed, aged and flavored like old wine; not easily discerned; not—not easily abandoned. Go away, by all means; but keep some sort of grip on this place. To gut it and shut it up would be brutal. It would be like putting out a perpetual vestal fire."

"Brutal!—I, brutal to Rattling Run Fields!" cried Eunice, leaping to her feet. She threw back her head and laughed quite freely, not bitterly as he had expected; then she turned and smiled at his dubious expression. "You have said something funny," she went on. "You have made me laugh. I wonder if you could often make me laugh."

"Not by such poor means as that, I hope," replied the judge easily, as he, too, arose and turned to watch the approaching of a quaint cortege. The children had persuaded Tom to drop the calash top so that they might ride standing, as if in a chariot. Drake embraced the bundle of whips as if it were a sheaf of spears, while Io held to the rein bar on the dash, shouting "Go! Go!" to the all but somnolent Alexander, and even leaned forward to strike his glossy rump with an imperious hand, thereby incurring Tom's displeasure. He told her to leave off beating the horse, and when she ignored the command, he stopped Alexander, lifted her to the ground and started the carriage without her.

"No, Drake, no!" she screamed with a vehemence that startled even Alexander into a faster walk.

She rushed forward, hurled herself recklessly at the step, missed it, caught the spokes of the revolving back wheel in desperately clinging hands and was dragged up under the leather mud splash before Tom, amazed and terrified, could again check the horse. He dropped the reins, released her body, quivering with the frenzy of her determination, set her on her feet within the carriage and stared at her.

"What were you trying to do?" he demanded. "Pull my old kerridge to pieces?"

"Yes," said Io very clearly.

She was surprised that this bearded stranger should have guessed her exact intention and decided to smile at him. Her smiles were rare, and more seldom still were they bestowed on any particular person. The effect of this one on the stout Tom Bodley was little short of a devastation. His eyes watered, his jaw dropped, he gulped, forgot to breathe, and as a consequence turned purple. He did not know why he did any of these things; he only knew that he had met the captain of his soul. He stooped laboriously, picked up the fallen reins, placed them in Io's hands and actually stood by while she slapped them and cried "Go! Go!" to the indifferent Alexander.

Chapter 16

From watching that scene the judge turned to Eunice. "When you do go," he said, "why not leave Tom in charge here for the winter? You could get rid of the stock, of course; but Tom would keep the place alive. Since you can't sell it, you shouldn't let it turn sour."

"We might burn it down," said Eunice absently, "but I suppose it wouldn't burn." Then she threw up her head and added, "That was a small thing to say, wasn't it? It sounded petty to you, I am sure, and yet——" She laid her hand on her breast and the judge noted its agitated rise and fall. "You understand a great deal," she continued, "but even you could not understand that if I were offered happiness in this place I would choose to be unhappy elsewhere. You can't conceive of that, can you?"

The judge did not answer directly; finally he said, "My mother's house is very large and mostly empty. Why don't you come there with the children until you decide where you wish to go? Why don't you leave Tom in charge of everything here just as it stands and come with me now? Drake could sit in the back of the buggy and Io in your lap. Why not?"

A smile crept into Eunice's eyes and into the corners of her mouth, distinguished by lips which had never lost their fullness. She laid her hand on his arm in a gesture startlingly out of place

113

against so stark a background, an easy, finished gesture of trust, companionship, almost of affection. However, she did not say anything. She did not accept his impulsive invitation, nor did she thank him for the many things he had done for her; and yet in that one touch of her fingers she repaid him.

He left her and a week passed before his neglected affairs permitted him again to drive out to Rattling Run Fields, only to see, as he drew near, Tryer's automobile standing at some distance from the house, almost in the middle of the road. It was as though Mattis had left it there deliberately as a warning and a signal that he was in attendance. The judge took genuine pleasure in the horsemanship necessary to coax Gypsy past the stalled car and a moment later brought her up with a smart turn at the cedar to which he was accustomed to hitch her. While he was tying the rope in an expert knot he heard Tryer's voice issuing loudly from the house.

"What's the use of you and me playing at hypocrites, Vic? You ain't sorry Warner's dead; you're glad. Nor I ain't sorry Elizabeth died five years ago, leaving me with one boy out of the three I had of her, and him the youngest. I ain't sorry, I say; and I wasn't sorry at the time. But you, Vic! Why, you're my woman! Why, if you was to die——"

Judge Alder did not wait to hear more. He walked out past the barn, through the orchard and into the crescent-shaped patch of standing timber which Warner had guarded to the last as a screen to the low bottoms, half pond and half swamp, in which Rattling Run found its source. This wood was a place of quiet charm at almost any season of the year. In winter its concave slope cupped the snow and held it as a dazzling background to waxy-leafed holly trees decked in gay red berries, standing around like sentinels beneath the taller growth of oak, sycamore, hickory and gum. In spring the holly gave way to a vast sheet of dogwood bloom, billowing and white as the foam of a comber creaming across a reef. To the same month of May belonged things sweeter though less spectacular—the last of the trailing arbutus, resplendent banks of bird's-foot violets, the wild azalea in contrasted pinks, and a dozen lesser flowers ushering in the tremendous chord of the glory of the laurel. Just now the wood was sombrous under the full foliage of summer, which gave to it a restful, cathedral stillness.

But even this peace failed to comfort the judge. He was heavy-hearted for no reason that he could name, and walked quietly with head bowed, wondering how that speech had ended and what had been Eunice's answer. One half of him asked why he had not waited to find out; the other half demanded what business it was of his. Presently he became aware of the sounds of splashing and shrill voices. He left the path and peered through the veiling branches of a thicket of laurel and caught sight of such a scene as made him forget Eunice for a moment in Eunice's children disporting themselves in a deep pool set close to the steep bank.

Never before had he seen such darting, slithering bodies; they were active and vigorous as tadpoles. When Drake plunged across the pool, Io would hurl herself after him, scurrying over rather than through the water. Again the judge was amazed at the driving power of her tiny limbs. He remembered the day when he had thought her a mere wisp, and, watching her leap the corn hills, had asked himself what carried her, what lifted her stride for stride with Drake. The wind? Her spirit?

"Well," he had decided, "anything but muscle." He looked at her naked body now, so small of wrist and ankle, so elflike, apparently so fragile, and yet so incredibly swift in movement, and gave up the problem as to just what was the motive force within her. From far away came Tryer's bull-like voice, shouting for his son.

"Jimmy!"

To the judge's utter amazement, Jimmy crept out from the laurel thicket some paces away, gained the path on his hands and knees, then stood up and ran swiftly toward the house. Following the course of his flight, the judge saw him all but collide with Eunice as she entered the wood. What had brought her out so quickly? He wondered, and waited for her to draw near. She was wearing a deep sunbonnet, such a sunbonnet as she had worn when first he had seen her; and for an instant he thought she would pass by

115

without noticing him; but she did not. She came to him, stood beside him and watched the children as he had been doing.

"Did you come here to find me?" he asked presently in a low voice.

"Yes," she answered.

"How did you know I was here?"

"I saw you pass while Tryer was talking. I watched you, saw which way you came. Why?"

Why indeed! The judge was nonplussed for an answer. Why should he ask her such things and in such a tone? The color mounted to his smooth cheeks as he turned his eyes to hers and said, "To tell you the truth, I don't know why I asked you those questions. Do you?"

In a way it was a challenge, and it was on the tip of Eunice's tongue, pretending that she misunderstood him, to ask, "Do I what?" But she refrained. She had come from the presence of a man who was, in a way, turgid and tortuous, directly into that of one who was clear-cut and limpid as crystal; she would give each his due.

"Yes," she said frankly, "I know why you asked them. It's because you are nervous about Tryer Mattis. You don't want me, but you do not wish him to have me."

She spoke so calmly that the judge could scarcely believe his ears.

"How do you know I don't want you?" he demanded. "And just how do you mean? What—what are we talking about, anyway? How did we ever—What do you—" He turned red with anger and embarrassment.

She glanced at him, surprised; then a tolerant, amused smile curved her lips, such a smile as she might have bestowed upon Drake. It made him turn still redder with exasperation. Before he could collect his wits for a more dignified attack on her equanimity she had raised her voice and called to the children. When they answered she turned to walk slowly toward the house with Judge Alder at her side, and only after they had gone some distance in silence did she begin to talk rapidly.

116

"Tryer Mattis has been here every day. He comes in the morning when I'm giving the children lessons to leave his boy Jimmy, and again about this time to take him away. He even asked to board him here, but the girl never comes; never once since that day. Tom Bodley has been here too. I've talked to him about staying the winter. Last night he fixed himself a bed in the old harness room and today he's gone to town to buy some things for me, just as if he were a hired man. He helped Drake with the chores too. I have written to three places about schools. As soon as the summer is over I'll take the children and live with them near a good school."

She spoke rather breathlessly, as though she had been waiting for a chance to confide and feared the opportunity might pass; but now she stopped in the path, faced him and asked in a low tone, almost of accusation, "Where have you been all these days?"

"I couldn't come," replied the judge, feeling again the strange, pleasant thrill up and down his spine. "I wanted to, but I couldn't; not until late at night, and, somehow, that wouldn't seem right without Warner around."

Eunice glanced at him with a queer, restrained look, as if she were about to laugh again, and then sobered and stared at the ground unseeingly.

"It's a strange thing," she said. "I didn't love Warner, just as Tryer says. I can't be sorry that he's dead, nor would he expect it of me. All Warner ever expected was what he got—hard work from himself, from me and the children. But now that he's gone, and when the children are safe in bed, there's a terrible emptiness about the place. I get lonely, frightened. Not afraid of things like thieves or beasts. Not that way; only afraid of emptiness. Something has happened to me. I'm not like the woman I was the dawn after Warner died, full to the brim, happy. My feet float. They don't touch anything. That's why I've got to go away soon."

"Tryer's boy was hidden in the bushes watching the children," stated the judge with apparent irrelevance. "I thought you ought to know."

117

"I did know," said Eunice, rousing herself from her abstraction. "I saw it in his scared face when he almost ran into me. Perhaps you were surprised, too—at the children, I mean. You see, no one taught them how to swim. Drake learned of himself and Io must have just thrown herself after him in a way she has. I didn't know anything about it until they both could swim, and then what was there to say? Until now they have always been alone. I don't know what to do. It sounds so easy to say 'Keep Io at home'; but to do that means keeping Drake too. Io is unusual. Perhaps you've noticed sometimes I'm afraid of her-afraid, I mean, of what she might do."

"The works are started on the other side of the ridge," suggested the judge, "so why don't you tear a leaf out of Tryer's book and send Drake and Io to spend the day with Jimmy? Have Tom take them around half an hour before Mattis is accustomed to turning up here. Give them a holiday."

Eunice smiled.

"I knew you would help me," she said. "I will let them take their lunch as if they were going to school or to a picnic, and Tom can stay with them to fetch them home. I'll let them go every day for a week."

"It isn't Jimmy you are trying to rid yourself of," thought the judge, "but his father. You are still afraid of Tryer." Aloud he said, "Why don't you do as I said—come to my mother's place? She is an invalid, quite old, and never comes downstairs. She would not mind the children, and you could be a help if you wished. Why don't you come?"

She laid her hand on his arm and turned so that the light struck into the deep bonnet, dispelling the shadows.

"Why do you wish me to come?" she started to ask, and suddenly stopped, perceiving that the children were close by. They rushed forward at the sight of the judge, and, regardless of their damp garments, hastily assumed over wet bodies, hurled themselves upon him.

"Have you been on a journey?" shouted Drake, swinging from one of his hands while Io, hanging to the other, cried, "A long journey—a journey around the world?"

118

The judge was pleased; it was good to feel that he had been missed. Finding that Tom Bodley had come back from town, unhitched Gypsy and put her in the barn for a feed, he agreed to stay for supper. After it he and Tom, with the two youngsters, invented one game after another while Eunice attended to the dishes and put the kitchen to rights. She did it with incredible swiftness, as though spurred by an impulse of rebellion; and immediately the dishcloth was washed and wrung she threw open the screen door and passed out. The judge wished to follow her, but it was half an hour before the children permitted him to escape.

He found her sitting on the warped steps to the main entrance of the house, a door which had been opened only twice in the memory of living man—once to give exit to the body of Warner Sherborne and once to that of his father, the same steps on which he had sat with her on the evening of Warner's funeral. The afterglow was still resplendent in the sky, and Eunice was sitting with hands locked round her knees, head thrown back and face upturned as though to leave it in the tender light. When the judge came near she drew to one side and permitted him to sit down.

After a moment, she said, "In fifteen years Warner and I never sat here once. I have been wondering whether it was my fault or if it was just that these steps were not built for a bench."

Tom Bodley, accompanied by the two children, issued from the house and stood hand in hand with them before the kitchen door. All three raised their eyes to the pink bowl of heaven and to the evening star, showing abnormally large in its isolation.

"There's things about sunsets and stars," rumbled the bearded hogshead of a man, "that you don't need ever to know about—things like why they are, what they are made of, where they came from and how long it took them to get here. I've known those things most all my life, and they've never done me any good. Drake, look at the sky, boy. How curly pink, eh? Miles and miles. Io, look at the evening star. Ain't it near? Look at it close, my dear, for you shall have it when you grow up. I myself, Connecticut Tom, Tom the Whip Man—Listen: Tom will give it to you to wear, on your finger or in your hair."

119

As they passed around the corner of the house on the way to say good night to Alexander, Io's treble voice and Drake's huskier one floated back, chanting the irresistible rhythm:

> *"Tom will give it to you to wear,*
> *On your finger or in your hair."*

"Both," said the judge, answering Eunice. "Partly your fault; partly because these steps were not meant for a bench."

"No," said Eunice presently, "you have not answered. I—I still wonder. Sometimes I think no two people ever meet except for the sudden pressure of a hand in the dark."

"What do you mean?" demanded the judge, his attention seized.

"Yes," continued Eunice as if he had not spoken, "even when we are nearest, when we are best understood, one of the other, it is only a handclasp in the dark. No one knows me, myself. Not even you—that night—when we touched hands in the dark. For a moment you heard my voice, not as it sounds to all the world, as it sounds now, as it will sound for others until I die, but as it is. You heard it, and perhaps not even I will ever hear it again—as it is."

"I don't quite know what you're talking about," murmured the judge.

"Neither do I," said Eunice. Her upturned face was infinitely aloof, white, like a pool of moonlight. "But," she added, "I wish you could have understood me and told me what I mean."

As the judge drove home that night he was tormented by the thought that he had lied, not through intention but through stunned stupidity, when he said he did not know quite what she was talking about. What he might truly have said was that his senses refused to grasp that which his soul felt and shared. He, too, knew the loneliness which had seized upon Eunice, a loneliness which never before had he dreamed could be described in words; and yet she had done it; she had expressed the inexpressible.

How? By not talking sense; by letting her heart beat out loud. Suddenly he drew Gypsy to a walk. Was it not conceivable that again he had been hearing her voice, as it is, and had not recognized it?

What possible hold could Tryer Mattis have on such a woman? Surely she was more spirit than flesh, more subject to the gossamer traps of the mind than to the heel of the conqueror. Why, she was like some fiddle, fashioned by a master, lightly delicate yet resonant, attuned to sublime chords never yet struck. She was like that, never yet played upon, a reservoir of sounds, of phrases, of music, awaiting the touch of the knowing hand. And if Mattis ever seized her he would crush her into splinters, kill the music forever! At the thought of Tryer the blood rushed to the judge's head so that he felt giddy.

Very early the next morning he drove out by way of the flats to where three scoop shovels, with their heavy teams, the pride of Mattis' heart, were already at work, leveling the approach to the long low cliff and stripping the rock of loam, laying bare the hoarded wealth of Rattling Run Fields. The shape of the farm was unusual. It began with an acute angle between two well-traveled diverging highways and widened in proportion as they spread. The rutted track which sprang from the center of the acute angle, to run past the homestead, was a private road, and almost exactly bifurcated the entire property. To its left were fields, more or less level; to its right, the house, the orchard, the wood, the swamp and pool, a sloping pasture, and, finally, at the widest portion of the Sherborne holding and practically at right angles to the dividing road, the elevation containing the deposit of cement rock.

From the energy with which Mattis was driving forward his attack it was evident that he had taken many soundings and knew not only the extent of the buried lode, but the point from which it could best be exploited. He had chosen a site, staked out the location for the plant itself, and, in spite of the early hour, the judge overtook teams hauling material and found a gang already at work on the foundations. Here, on the job, Mattis had nothing to hide and was at his best. His eye was everywhere at once, his strong hand was ever ready for a lift where it was really needed, and his bull voice had the clarion ring which inspirits men without angering them. He waved to the judge with a broad, friendly gesture of greeting; then his thoughts leaping to his daily visit to Eunice, he drew out his watch with an impatient movement, forgot his work, and immediately seemed to shrivel into something small.

At that moment Tom Bodley's odd rig, preceded rather than drawn by the sleek Alexander, appeared from around the corner of the low cliff. Tom walked beside the carriage, and within it, deep in the shadow of the raised top, were Drake, Io and their mother. At seeing Eunice, the judge felt an extraordinary contraction of the muscles of his chest. So she couldn't even stay away! She had to come too. He tautened the reins as a signal to the ever-willing Gypsy; she turned widely and dashed homeward at a pace that he urged rather than restrained.

Chapter 17

That flight was one of the most boyish if not the most childish action of the judge's life. As the mare turned he had heard quite distinctly Tryer's loud cry of "Bill, I got to see you," but he had pretended not to hear. All the way to town his mind was occupied with what Eunice had thought. Had she believed that he had come out on purpose to spy on her? Had she—and was it true? What was Mattis to her anyway? By the time he got home he had reached a resolve. Never again would he stand in the way, since she wished to see Tryer enough to go to where he worked. In the meantime the contractor had regained all his aplomb upon discovering Eunice in the carriage.

"Like old times," he shouted as he strode toward her. "Here's the works, construction shack and all; cases of dynamite; me, too, and you driving up in a rig, pretty as April dog——"

"Stop!" interrupted Eunice sharply. "Haven't you the sense—" she began, then broke off abruptly, having changed her mind. "I brought the children around to play with Jimmy today. They have quit lessons for the present."

"Oh, all right, Vic," said Mattis with instant comprehension and a shrug of his broad shoulders as he helped her out of the carriage and turned in such a manner as to shut her off from Tom and the children. "Have it your own way," he continued in a lowered tone. "Ride your high horse anywhere you like; but just remember that in the end you got to come back to me—to Tryer Mattis—because you and me was made that way."

"What I started to say," replied Eunice coolly, "was this: Haven't you the sense to see that I have grown up? I am not the girl you knew, nor are you half the man you were. Not to me, I mean."

Mattis flushed a bright red, cast a quick glance back at the carriage, already some steps away, and saw that the children were running off in search of Jimmy.

"I don't know what you mean," he said in a low, pulsing voice, "and what you mean don't matter. What I got to say is this: It's all right for you to talk that way when you got folks around; but if ever you and me is alone for five minutes I'll show you if I'm half the man I was. I'll pick the dead coal of Vic Teller off the ash heap and blow her into life. I'll——"

"Don't," said Eunice quietly, and to his own amazement he stopped in the full flight of what he had to say. She eyed him up and down deliberately. "Women have done you no good," she continued, standing very erect. "It's too bad, Tryer. You were meant to be a big man—a great man, I mean. As it is, you're only a sort of physical extravagance, an attractive waste of everything decent."

"That's enough highfalutin' language from you," rumbled Mattis ominously. "You're just crazy, that's all. Say another word like that and I'll kiss you like I done once before, only in front of Tom there, in front of the work gang and your children and my boy Jimmy. I'll kiss you till your arms go around——"

Again he stopped in the midst of what he was going to say, halted not by a spoken protest but by a single glance of scorn which Eunice cast at him as she turned her back and started away. He followed her, talking rapidly:

"Don't be angry, Vic. Don't be angry at what I said. Can't you see it's different now? I'm free to marry, and if you want I should marry you I'll gladly do it. It ain't like it was, Vic. I tell you it's love—real love."

She stopped and faced him, her cheeks aflame, her eyes suddenly ablaze.

"Love!" she whispered. "How dare you say that—to me? Stay where you are! Keep away from me! Keep away from the house, and keep your boy away, unless you wish to drive us out of it."

"Vic!" stammered Mattis, staring at her with round eyes as she left him. "Vic!"

He was frightened, like that time when she had clung to him and sobbed "Go away!" Only this was different; this was crazier. That other he could understand in a way; but not this. What had he done? What had he said to make any woman fly off the handle? Keep away from her! He liked that! Why had she come around bothering him? Why didn't she keep away from him?

All these questions, in slightly different form, Eunice was asking herself as she walked swiftly along a cow track which led upward toward the pasture. Drake and Io called to her, but she answered only with a wave of her hand. She was trying to face herself. Where was she and whither was she bound? What had led her to talk as she had to the judge on the night before, and what had just made her fly into a rage at Mattis? When he had said "It's love—real love," a terrible emptiness had seized her; and then fury, unreasoning fury. What was the matter with her? What had come over her? At Warner's death she had felt a great release. It was as though she had been unchained from a barren peak and hurled into the air on strong wings. That's how she had felt—soaring, free. But now—feet floating, just above the ground! Was it possible that one cannot be truly free alone?

She stopped at the split-rail fence which bounded the pasture and pounded on it with her clenched fist. She bit her underlip until tears came to her eyes. Why—oh, why hadn't she gone away at once and forever, immediately after the funeral, as she had planned while Warner lay dying? What had she wanted more in all her life than to be free? What was freedom? Had she deceived herself into thinking that it was merely the difference between twelve dollars and three thousand? She thought of the judge. Their hands had

125

touched in the dark that night when she had lived over bit by bit all the course of what seemed to her a colorless life. Was that freedom—touching a passing hand in the dark of oneself? If it was, would she ever find it again? Why had she felt a paroxysm of rage over those words, "It's love—real love?"

She was like the toy balloon, descended to earth, bumping along; but she did not know it. She gripped the fence and stared before her at a vision of Mattis. No longer could he sting her into life with a flick of unexpected imagery. To her sharpened senses he was merely a great oaf, rough, untutored, in a way repellent. When he worked he was a man, a big man, admirable; but when he talked or attempted to make love he was like an awkward, well-meaning, overgrown puppy. And yet he had once swept her off her feet. What if she shut her eyes tightly and gave him a chance? Could he perhaps do it again? Did she wish him to? No; she was not even curious as to whether he could. Why, then, had she gone near him? She thought of the judge again. How extraordinary that he should have driven away the moment he saw her, without speaking, without even greeting the children!

She climbed the fence and started across the pasture, but stopped halfway to look around. In all her years at Rattling Run Fields her feet had never trod that spot, and it was with a sort of jarring astonishment that she discovered the prospect to possess a gentle beauty all its own. The slope slanted up from where she stood to the edge of the ridge at whose base Mattis and his men were at work. All the pasture was clothed in short-cropped turf, as evenly laid as a carpet. In the angles of the snake fence and dotted over the field itself were black-green upland cedars of every size and age, formal as the cypresses of an Italian garden and apparently far more at home. They had a stately but friendly look.

Eunice walked on toward the house, threading them, sometimes touching their sandy roughness as she passed. She went beyond the barn, then stopped, turned, entered it impulsively and proceeded to hitch the plow horses to the old buggy, the same buggy—so seldom had it been used since—in which Warner had courted her and had driven her out on a memorable day to where Mattis was at work.

Fifteen years ago! "Pretty as April dogwood and sound as a winter apple!" Was it on purpose that he repeated himself so, she wondered yet again as she had wondered twice before of this identical trick, or was it merely that men use the same bait over and over again until it drops off the hook, worn out, nibbled to pieces? The horses harnessed, she drove to the county seat, learned that the court term had ended on the preceding day, sought out the judge's house, descended, walked up the long paved path and drew the bell pull. He opened to her himself. Quickly recovering from the surprise he did not attempt to hide, he let her in and started to usher her into the parlor. But Eunice, drawing a long breath, stood spellbound for a time in the hallway itself, which was exceptionally wide and deep.

At its farther end a box staircase with slim fluted balusters rose airily in three right-angle turns to the floor above. Through a door opening to the left she glimpsed the set parlor, whose windows must be wide open, since the curtains, stately in their old-fashioned length, were stirring. From her right, through another open door, came a smell of books and musty leather, which brought quick tears to her eyes. With a pleading look to the judge, she passed into the library and stood quite still, her head up and turned slightly to one side as if she were listening.

It was a peculiar pose to take in the presence of books, but it seemed to the judge to dovetail into the mood she had been in when last he had talked with her. What more fanciful than to talk of one's voice not as it is heard but as it is! What more whimsical and yet plaintive than the cry, "I wish you could have understood me and told me what I mean"! What more fitting than that such a nature, lost for the time being amid the spaces of an unaccustomed liberty, should quirk a head, birdlike, to listen for the voices of books, the most familiar note of her childhood! Lest she feel that he was spying upon her again or delving into her motive for coming, he passed to the rear of the room, where two windows

127

opened on an inner garden filled with such a wealth of trellised verdure that it seemed to drip with shade. Presently he was aware that she was standing close beside him.

"This," she said, "is the first fresh air I have breathed since I was a girl."

He turned to look at her, expecting to find a quizzical look on her face; but never had he seen it more grave. As her eyes met his he had a feeling that they were years younger than the rest of her body, quite detached from it, as if they had stepped back into that period when knowledge has not yet clouded the bright gleam of the questing lamp of youth. They made her seem not only sexless but virginal; and the judge, forgetting her age and the hard years she had caused him to live over with her, saw only the gold-brown freckles which swam deep in her eyes like sunfish seen within the shadowed curve of a billow.

"I take that back," she murmured, their eyes still interlocked. "If I'm not more careful of what I say you, too, will think I'm crazy."

"I could never think that, for a very simple reason," said the judge easily, as if the training of years constrained him to control an overemotional moment. He was looking exceptionally handsome on that summer morning. Custom had not yet sanctioned white trousers for country wear; but he wore a white alpaca coat cut with wide lapels like a smoking jacket and thrown open to show an expanse of snowy pleated linen. His smooth neck rose like a column from the very low collar, threaded with a black string tie, and the faint pink of his clean-shaven cheeks seemed to be allied in some manner with the ardor of his brilliant eyes. His hair, carefully parted and brushed, though already iron gray, was very thick. To Eunice he seemed virile, strong, young—younger than herself.

"What reason?" she asked.

"Because for weeks," he replied, "my heart has been going to Rattling Run Fields to school. It learned a lot from Warner, something from Drake and Io; and it is only beginning now to learn from you."

"Are—are you teasing me?"

128

"No."

"Why did I come here? Can you tell me that?"

"I can."

"Then tell me."

"Are you sure you want me to? Think a minute. Don't you know, yourself?"

"Tell me."

"You came here because this morning you went to see Tryer Mattis. If you hadn't gone there, and if I hadn't seen you, you would never have thought of coming here."

Eunice flushed and threw up her head.

"I didn't!" she exclaimed hotly. "Oh, I didn't! I didn't go on purpose to see Tryer, nor did my going there have anything to do with my coming here."

She knew as soon as the words were out of her mouth that they were untrue, and so did the judge. He looked at her steadily until her eyes dropped; but when she turned to rush from the room he started forward to bar her way. She attempted to force by him and for an instant he held her. No sooner was he aware of the violent quivering of her body, however, than he let her go and leaned against the doorpost for support. So impetuous had been the rush of blood to his head because of the fleeting contact that he felt stunned as from a blow. He covered his eyes with his hand, pressed his forehead against the jamb and tried to remember that only a few weeks before he had taken this woman for a dried-out bit of human harness.

The Lantern on the Plow

Chapter 18

Eunice dated resurrection from the moment the judge had led her to see herself as the emotional shuttlecock between two battle-dores. Never would she forget that drive back alone from town in the noontide heat of the day, with the reflected sun scorching her from without and shame searing her from within. Before she got home, however, the incandescence had passed, leaving her burned clear of slag. Scales fell from her eyes, so that she saw herself not only with distinctness but in proportion to the people and things about her. Only now did she realize the extent of the vague oppression under which she had labored since Warner's death.

In what that oppression had consisted she did not know; but as the horses paused of their own accord in the deep shade which embowered Rattling Run it seemed that the coolness entered actively into her body, sought out her fevered soul and appeased it with a thoroughness which made the doctrines of conversion and of love at first sight seem suddenly quite natural consummations. The woman who drove out of the dip of Rattling Run was not the woman who had driven into it moments before.

There is no more persistent illusion than the belief in abrupt reversals of the intricate mechanism of spirit and body which goes to make up oneself. As a matter of truth, the course of a life may turn upon an event as definitely as a stream splits upon a rock; but that unnamed thing within us which endures before and after flesh, as a single link in an endless chain, does not turn or change except by the gradations of the evolution of the individual soul. Thus with Eunice. Nothing cataclysmic had occurred to her from without; but the current of her being had swerved radically, though to her imperceptibly, on the event of Warner's death. With his passing a simple but momentous thing had happened: The forces of passion, which unbeknownst to her formed the keynote of her being, had become released. Through their workings she had approached the moment of transformation in the dip of Rattling Run as normally as a bud arrives at the miracle of a sudden blooming, and her rebirth was none the less real because neither she nor those about her could perceive what was transpiring.

All rebirth presupposes youth; and though youth had not come back to her in all its outward manifestations, it was stirring, it was on its way, and the mere starting of its sap had been enough to unseat her own serenity as well as that of William Alder, even while, for some involved reason, it seemed to have sidetracked Tryer Mattis and left him, for the time being, in the lurch. Why? Eunice did not know, for the mind that turns a corner and attains to clarity of vision is seldom interested retrospectively in how it got there; it is too busy. Arrived at the house, she stared at the abode which had harbored her for nearly half her life as if she had never before seen it.

The thing that struck her as most astounding was the fact that she had permitted the front room to remain hermetically closed for fifteen years, in accordance with the custom of the country. How had it happened that she had submerged from a college graduate into a kitchen-bedroom dweller without even realizing her descent? She looked back to the day of her coming to Rattling Run Fields, to the first week, the first month, the first year, and immediately all her course became clear, understandable, inevitable. She had done what she had done by no volition, but in obedience to an inexorable demand. She had succumbed not to permanency and tradition alone, but to these factors backed by an overwhelming burden of unlovely labor. Well, that day was gone. She drove in, stabled the horses in a frenzy of haste and actually ran to the house.

Even with the aid of a heavy hammer it took her half an hour to open all the windows, raise them and prop them up before she could give her attention to the front door. It creaked, but swung so easily on its hinges that she almost stumbled out into the chasm between the threshold and the warped flight of wooden steps. Old Ben, the half-blind dog the judge had found lying there weeks before, was there again today. As on that other occasion of disturbance, he did not move except to thump his tail.

Yielding to a sudden impulse, Eunice knelt on the floor, leaned out and patted his head. For a surprised instant his tail suspended its beat while his cold nose investigated; then the thumping began again, but with a clumsy rapidity which had breaks in it as if choking on the expression of too much joy. Eunice laughed, and it was quite a new laugh, one that she had not heard for years.

The children, returning with Tom, found disorder without the house and chaos within; but when they heard the laugh, which Eunice herself had not heard for years, ringing out to meet the dazed surprise in their faces, and then their mother's voice, a strangely changed yet familiar voice, calling to them to come and help, they rushed to her with an impetuosity out of all proportion to an occasion of mere house cleaning. Even Tom was affected. He hastened to care for Alexander and do his chores so that he also might surrender to the unfailing magnet of the light heart. Sensing that Rattling Run Fields was entering upon a new epoch, he said in a solemn aside to his friends, Drake and Io, "There's days when sunrise happens along toward evening."

The proof that Eunice had passed through a transition, and not merely entered a mood, accumulated as days and weeks passed, each bringing with it some new venture into life as a happy pilgrimage. In agreement with the judge, she sold stock and equipment until there remained only the minimum of farm paraphernalia. She let out the harvesting on shares and promptly forgot the fields. She made a definite arrangement with Tom Bodley which established him as a factotum between her and all trouble outside the four walls of the house. She bought a new cookbook and a new sewing machine, bolts of material and a sheaf of patterns. Never had her days been more busy; but with a difference as sheer as the division between darkness and light. Now she was doing those things which she loved to do. The burdens of housekeeping became amazingly light through the passing of the crushing need for parsimony, and none but the starved can measure the elation with which she turned from more homely duties to the fashioning of soft fabrics or to leisurely twilight hours with Drake at her side and Io on her knee.

After the children went to bed she had hours to herself which developed astonishing tendencies. Never would she forget the night when, with shutters closed and curtains drawn, she was performing her ablutions and noticed the fine texture of the skin in the hollow of her arm. Whose arm was it? Her very own? It looked like Vic Teller's; could it be Eunice Sherborne's, too? Almost like Io's— smooth as satin, with shadowy blue veins beneath the protected surface. She had read somewhere that joy does extraordinary things to the body. Was it true? Could happiness, mere content, perhaps set one's pores to breathing and lend brilliance to a fading eye?

So occupied was she at this time with her intimate and household affairs that she scarcely noticed the apparent deflection of Tryer Mattis or the less noticeable aloofness of the judge. The latter still came to Rattling Run Fields with great frequency; but only in the role of observer, guardian, general companion to the family and particular playmate to the children. Had she taken the trouble to study him as interestedly as she had been viewing herself she would have discovered that he was in a continual state of controlled excitement due to the fact that he knew what had come over Tryer Mattis.

On the night of the very day when Eunice had entered Judge Alder's house upon an obscure impulse, and rushed from it burning with shame at the self-revelation she had brought upon her own head, Tryer had gone there in a highly nervous state and forced an

134

entrance. It was natural that the judge should have connected the visit with that of Eunice, and he braced himself for an ugly scene as Tryer brushed by the housekeeper-nurse and burst into the library. It was some moments before he could readjust his mind to the fact that the man who stood before him was not Tryer Mattis, jealous breaker of women's hearts, but Tryer Mattis, contractor pure and simple, from the soles of his feet to the crown of his shock of hair.

"Bill," he began, "it's no use my trying to play double with you on this Rattling Run deal and I'm not going to. One reason is that I couldn't if I wanted to. Every time I read over that blasted contract you got my name to I know all over again that your head was set in this new-fangled reënforced-concrete foundation before the process was invented. You got me cold, fixed up to the knees, and the only way I can pull out big and pull everybody else out big with me is for you and me to be friends."

"Tryer," interrupted the judge, "I don't know what you're talking about. Sit down. Take a cigar and start from the beginning. What has happened?"

"Sit down!" cried Mattis, throwing his hat on a chair. "I don't want to sit down. I feel as if I wasn't never going to have time to sit down again. Bill, you know Jake Werten as well as I do. Queer bird. Sort of a cross between a ferret and a clam. He made a chemical analysis for me some time back, and I thought perhaps he was just trying to please me, and perhaps his foot slipped. But this noon, by the morning mail, I get figures the same as Jake's, only from the city laboratory. Even at that, I couldn't believe it; so this afternoon I made Jake do it all over again with me standing over his shoulder. Not that I'm a chemist; but somehow I had to see. Well, we just finished, and I come straight here without my supper, because if I haven't got time to sit down I haven't time to eat."

He threw out one big hand in a backward gesture toward Rattling Run Fields.

"That out there—I took samples from the face of the cliff, three on 'em, sixty feet apart, and they show 75 per cent carbonate of lime."

He paused climatically.

"Well," asked the judge presently, "what about it?"

"What about it?" shouted Tryer.

He calmed himself by an effort, swept his hat to the floor, sat down and began to talk to the judge as if he were addressing a primer class.

"Listen!" he said. "Seventy-five per cent is just about perfect for cement. If there was 3 per cent more we'd have to throw in our strippings to pull it down. If there was 5 per cent less we'd have to import lime rock. As it is, it's perfect; do you get that? Why, even the strippings are going to be so thin they won't much more than fill a hat, and I can use enough on our gradings to bare all the rock we can chew up in three years! Now listen, judge! We ain't found a deposit of cement stone so much as a gold mine. All we got to do is to blast off the face of the cliff, grind it, burn it and sell it a lot faster than we can get it ready. There's two or three pits up in Warren County has what he got here; but nobody has nothing better than what we have inside a thousand miles, and just as soon as the railway puts in a spur——"

"Wait a minute," interrupted the judge again. "You're traveling too fast for me, Tryer. Long before we get to the railroad end I'd like to know what you want from me."

"I want so much from you," said Tryer, making a movement as if he were fighting off bees, "that I don't know rightly where to begin. I want a twenty-year lease, with a renewal clause. I want two hundred thousand dollars more than what I've got borrowed already, and I want you to make the dicker. I want you for counsel on a retainer to handle others the way you done me. Them's some of the things I want, Bill."

"Two hundred thousand!" exclaimed the judge, and asked ironically, "Do you think you could pull through on that?"

Mattis considered for a moment.

"No, I don't," he answered; "not by half; but I figure that by the time that is spent we'll have plenty to show on to borrow more. That part of it will be easy."

The judge ceased to jeer; he saw that Tryer was in dead earnest; and Tryer in earnest was never ridiculous, nor even far-fetched.

"Why so much money?" he asked.

"It's funny," said Mattis after a thoughtful pause, "how important you lawyer folks think money is. In a way, you're right; and then again you ain't. Making cement, making most anything, even at a loss, is cleaner and bigger than the average run of money. But let that ride. The first reason I got to have a lot of money is I want to scrap the whole Cedarton plant. Judge, did you ever know the rights of that deal?"

"No."

"Well, the Cedarton people started out just like you think I ought to, with a couple of hundred thousand too little. Even at that, they would of pulled through if they had been able to show enough rock. They weren't. They failed, and, knowing what I did about Warner's place, I bought the whole outfit at a sheriff's sale when no one was looking, and at scrap-iron prices. I didn't pay a tenth, nor a twentieth, of what the plant cost; and listen! I wouldn't of paid that if it hadn't been all new stuff, erected only two to three years ago. Do you know what that means?"

"No," said the judge again.

"Well," continued Tryer commiseratingly, "it means the difference between heaven and hell, sea and land, night and day; the difference between set kills and rotary kills."

"Do you mean kilns?" asked the judge.

Tryer eyed him impatiently and then shrugged his broad shoulders.

"If I was writing, I'd put it like you say; but I ain't writing. I'm talking, one man to another; and when men talk, kilns is kills," declared Tryer, sticking doggedly though perhaps unknowingly, to the more correct pronunciation of the word. "I'm trying to tell you that I can move the Cedarton plant if I have to, and turn out three hundred and seventy-five to four hundred barrels of cement a day, crushing one hundred and twenty tons of rock; but you listen to this: It's a holy shame not to give the very best there is to what we got handed to us by God in the way of a quarry. Why, judge——"

He broke off and let his hands fall as if he despaired of making another see that which was so overwhelmingly plain and important to his own eyes.

"But I can't do it without two things," he continued fervently. "I got to have an extension on the lease or an option for renewal. That's the first thing before I sink into one hole all I've got and all of me, and all I can squeeze out of the banks and any others with money to lend. The other thing is this: I got to have you for a partner instead of a watchdog keeping just one jump behind the seat of my pants."

Some men in the judge's place would have thought that they were being offered a bribe, but he made no such miscalculation.

He knew that he was looking upon Tryer at his very best, a sublimated Tryer who was of one mind, of one powerful body, and as direct as is every expression of the creative force in action. This was Tryer the builder, in the grip of a clear vision, as big a man in himself alone as one could hope to find in a long day's march. The judge felt more kindly toward him than ever before; but even under the expansive impulse he realized that he divided Mattis the man of business sharply from Mattis the man of pleasure.

"Tryer," he said presently, "don't go off half cocked at what I'm going to say. Hear me through and listen with your brains as well as your ears. There isn't going to be any extension of the lease until Drake Sherborne can sign it, so just drop that out of mind. On the other hand, the last thing I want to do is to fight you. The interests of the Sherborne family are your interests, and, just so we'll all be in the same boat, I'm going to make them mine. I mean I'm going in with all my cash and a good deal of my time as soon as I've checked up on what you say. Now, are you ready to take in my first bit of advice?"

Tryer nodded and flipped one hand in a noncommittal and unenthusiastic gesture.

138

"It's this," continued the judge: "We'd better borrow money at a high rate, in any form we can pay off, than get it for nothing at the expense or even the threat of outside control."

"Just so," said Tryer, his eyes narrowing; "and will you tell me who is going to lend it against a short-term lease, as such things go?"

"Leave that side of it for a minute," said the judge, unruffled. "I believe with all my head and heart in starting small to end big. The itch for perfect equipment is a praiseworthy ambition. It looks fine and it is fine. But here's a funny thing, Tryer: In all my experience I've found that perfect equipment has ruined five factories to every one that lost out through the lack of the latest gadgets. In other words, any plant that can't take care of the business offered to it is in a normal and healthy condition. Be honest. Am I right?"

"I'll say it looks that way," admitted Mattis grudgingly; "but it oughtn't to be. What I mean is, everything that's proved ought to go in on a new plant. It's the knowing of what's proved and what ain't proved in machinery and money that fools the best of us. And even that ain't what I'm trying to say."

"I know what you mean, though," put in the judge. "You mean that everything hangs on reading right the balance of money and machinery, on sinking a little less in effort, money, plant and raw stuff than you take out in net cash; on figuring twenty lines of profit and loss back to one central point so you can face any point of the compass of a business and know where you stand. One man is a crack at finance and a sucker at production; another reverses the order. To make a business successful, take one of each and join them up on an eccentric."

"That's it!" ejaculated Mattis, his eyes brightening. "You've said it now, Bill! You picked my mind!"

"I'm going to pick it some more," said the judge. "If I should say to you, 'Tryer, forget to dream. Double all your gangs. Put two on stripping, two more on foundations and grading, two more on moving the Cedarton plant, just as it is, in double-quick order. Put three shifts on construction, beginning with hoist and crusher; but before you do anything else, persuade the railroad to start in with

139

a spur. Don't think about money; just wipe it from mind and go to work.' If I could say all that, and mean it, how would you feel?"

"Drunk," said Mattis, rising to his full height, holding out his open hands and staring down into them.

"Roaring, happy drunk!"

For an instant the judge was swept out of himself by the imagery and symbolism of the unconscious gesture. Those great hands held at the level of the big contractor's hips became instantly a source of power, of labor and of conquest by the sweat of other men's brows—a profound pool, twin reservoirs of dreams in terms of stone, iron, coal and concrete.

"How long between now and production?" he asked.

Tryer's staring eyes promptly narrowed to the two slits through which he was accustomed to make his famous snap estimates of men, costs, time and women.

"Seventy days, with or without luck."

"And with luck?"

There was a rush of color to Tryer's already florid face as he swung toward the judge.

"Don't ask that," he snapped. "Leave me show you."

"All right," agreed Judge Alder, also rising. "I mean it, Tryer. Hit the line hard. Swing in with all you've got in the way of a punch. By a week from now, if your figures check right, I'll show you an agreement between Bill Alder and Tryer Mattis that will make us walk the same plank; and I don't have to tell you it will leave the Sherborne interest solid at the rental of three thousand flat and two cents a barrel on sales. There'll be room enough for you and me outside of that, if all you say is true."

"There will," agreed Mattis.

He stooped with surprising suppleness for a man of his bulk, picked up his hat, turned and held out his hand. They shook, not as friends, but as men who sealed a bargain. Tryer started toward the door, only to be halted by the judge's parting admonition:

"Set your foundations so we can double the plant at the drop of a hat."

"Still picking my mind," muttered Tryer as he walked out."

The Lantern on the Plow

Chapter 19

Scarcely four weeks passed before Mattis issued a formal invitation to Eunice through the judge to witness the first blasting. In all that time she had not once seen him. At first she thought that his absence was due entirely to her sharp command to stay away from the house and keep his boy Jimmy away too. But as day followed day, and Jimmy came occasionally to play with the children as though nothing had happened, and more frequently to persuade them to cross the fields and the pasture to the edge of the quarry, without his father ever appearing, she began to wonder. It was not like Mattis to pay much heed to a woman's denial.

Except for a vast increase in the number of men at work on the site of the new plant, the group was exactly the same as had gathered there fortuitously on the eventful day when Eunice had doubled a corner and found herself. Instead of driving to the quarry by the main road, which paralleled the spur from the railway already in process of construction, the judge went first to the house. Eunice had not yet completed her work, and, quite innocently, he suggested to Tom that he go ahead with the impatient children. Thus it happened that Tryer Mattis, turning from giving last orders to his foreman and the quarry manager, looked up to see Eunice arriving alone with the judge. They had passed the lethargic Alexander, who was only now turning the point of the low hill.

A look shot through Tryer's eyes and face as if there had been a quivering of the muscles answering some commotion beneath the surface of the flesh; but it passed so swiftly that it left doubt in the mind of Eunice as to whether her imagination had not tricked her. She perceived that a change had come over Mattis since last she had seen him. Although still bulky, he looked like an athlete at the top of his form. He was one of those florid persons who do not tan; but the color in his cheeks and on the back of his neck had deepened to the stain of wine; health radiated from all his hardened frame. Today he seemed not so much a spider at the center of the web of other men's endeavors as a giant with hundreds of tentacles, each endowed with a brain subject to his brain.

They climbed to the platform at the top of the hoist. Tryer stood in the forward corner of the rough railing, with Eunice and the judge at his side; behind him were the children, with Tom Bodley, puffing heavily, on guard. He had his hands full, for Drake was by nature, training and name an explorer, an adventurer, an inquirer, prehensile as a monkey and elusive as an eel. Whatever he did or attempted, Io was sure to be at his heels with her breathless cry, of "No, Drake, no!"

It was just her way of asking him to wait for her; but, often as he heard it, old Tom was never to get over the impression that she was calling on her brother to abandon some temerous enterprise. Never was man more consistently deceived, and many were the times Tom found himself too late to arrest Drake and in a quandary as to what to do with Io, turned suddenly into a writhing spitfire in his restraining arms.

At such moments, if Eunice was present, she would say calmly, "Let her go, Tom. It's better she should break her neck than strangle."

Tom would obey, his deep-set eyes grown round and his lips murmuring fuzzily through his beard, "The strength of her, ma'am, and she no weight at all! The heat in her little body! Burns you! Burns my hands and inside my chest. There's something there that can't be stopped. Bigger than me and you, bigger than any-

144

one, bigger than her." Then he would frown darkly and rumble, "There's fillies that will never wear a bridle," even while his eyes followed Io's darting form with a mild wistfulness that took the sting from his prognostication.

No perturbation ever came to him through Jimmy Mattis, whose boldness was limited to teasing Io by nudging her, pulling her hair and daring to lay hold of her skirts while Tom was embracing her writhing form, and suffering agonies from her toes and heels, beating a devil's tattoo on his shins. As to recklessness of other sorts, Jimmy followed Drake only at a distance and displayed much shrewdness in finding a way around hazards. Nevertheless, he was no coward; what his father told him to do he would attempt without a whimper.

To any one who knew the Rattling Run Cement Company, makers of the Rattler Brand, as it appeared in 1916, taking fourteen blast holes, each five inches in diameter and a hundred and fifty feet deep, along the length of its towering face, and flinging forward sixty-five thousand tons of rock at a single shot, it is almost impossible to reconstruct the puny scene which made Tryer appear a giant in his own estimation and in the eyes of those about him. How go back from the roaring thunder of roll crushers; of a battery of six kilns nine feet deep and a hundred and forty feet long; of another battery of six Bentley Goliath mills, three for the raw stone and three for the clinker; of still another of twenty tube mills, divided eight and twelve; to say nothing of the rattle and bang of giant coolers, of T & S conveyors and of a dozen other adjuncts of an output of five thousand barrels a day?

How go back from all that to Tryer, standing on a homemade hoist with his back to a picayune gyratory crusher, waiting to give the word for a blast of six two-inch holes, none of them over sixteen feet deep, which, owing to the irregular edge of the quarry, could not be expected to throw out over three hundred tons of rock? Or to Tryer, taking immense pride in his half-erected power plant of an engine, two boilers and a small generator? Or to Tryer, figuring with a frenzied brain on the capacity of his two sixty-foot rotary kilns backed by four balls and four tube mills, two dryers, a Tupper mill to grind his coal and a modest compressor?

It was the difference between the prospect of a hundred and sixty thousand barrels of cement for the entire season of 1902 and of two hundred thousand in the single month of April in 1916. And yet it is confidently asserted that Tryer Mattis was a greater man when he raised his arm in signal for the first of a thousand blasts than he had ever been before, and perhaps then he would ever be again, with the possible exception of a single hour, far in the future. No one in the group about him was competent to measure the magnitude of what he had achieved since the night he and the judge had struck a bargain, the night Mattis had declared he felt he would never again have time to sit down or to eat.

Some things the judge knew. He could not help but be informed, for instance, of the development of an almost maniacal regard for economy on the part of the big contractor, once he had become reconciled to making use of the Cedarton plant. He seemed to be holding his mania for new inventions in abeyance by sheer will power, as though he were shrewdly laying the foundations for a claim against every cent he saved to back his demands in the future. He would show the judge, he would show himself! By the great Lord Harry and the blazing Zenith, he would show the world, and Vic—Vic Teller! He sublet every contract he had and camped on the job at Rattling Run. He dug plans, specifications and future requirements out of unsuspecting experts and adjusted them to his own needs. By absorption, he was an architect, builder, contractor, quarry manager, gang boss, foreman, carpenter and bricklayer rolled into one. He was the avenging angel and the hosts of the mighty of an ancient tradition; he was atomic energy before it had been discovered or named, let loose in a time when bricks cost three dollars a thousand and a laborer was glad to get a dollar and ten cents for a ten-hour day.

Chapter 20

To the ignorant in matters pertaining to cement and construction in general, chaos reigned supreme about the tower of
the crusher chute; but an expert would have traced the trail of
a powerful hand of genius in every direction. All disorder was
moving hectically toward centralization and eventual order. The
stripped but untouched stone, the cleverly placed hoist, the waiting
jaws of the crusher, the mill in process of assembling, and even
the railway spur, striding in to link the plant with materials and
market at an appointed hour—all were climbing steadily toward
a single apex of completion.

The hoist was erected on level ground not three hundred feet
from the foot of the low cliff toward which a narrow-gauge track
had already been laid. The deposit of cement rock had been
stripped for a short distance, and to a fixed line, of the thin layer
of loam and gravel which had covered it. Perforce, the fixed line
was waved. At some points it rose only three or four and at others
sixteen feet from the flat floor. Above it was the clean cut of the
stripping; below was the irregular low mound of the barred rock,
blackish gray, and looking in the sunlight as if it would be soapy
to the touch. Tryer's lifted arm drew the attention, not only of
the judge and Eunice, but of the children. There was a moment
of silence and suspense. The arm fell. A dull roar. Two hundred

tons of rock heaved outward and shot forward fanwise, leaving behind a great square hole, as smooth at the sides and back as if it had been cut with a monster knife.

"No, Drake, no!" shrilled Io's voice; but before the words were out of her mouth Drake had slipped under the rail and leaped from the platform to a heap of sand twenty feet below. She tried to follow, but her cry had given warning. Tom, throwing himself on his stomach, was just in time to seize her by one ankle, while Jimmy, true to habit, clutched her skirts. She dangled in air for a moment, and then was dragged ignominiously back. In the meantime Drake was running, stumbling and staggering, toward the quarry.

"Hey, you! Drake!" roared Mattis. "Come out of that! Come back!"

Drake kept on, and Mattis first made a move as if to leap from the platform himself, then turned with quick decision to the skip, which had been drawn to the top of the hoist for safety. He uncoupled it, gave it a push, leaped in and went hurtling down the incline. By good fortune the car kept the track, and before it lost its impetus was well ahead of the blindly stumbling boy. Tryer jumped out, seized him, and instantly was attacked with unbelievable strength and fury.

"Leave go!" cried Drake so hoarsely that his voice sounded like that of a grown man.

"You little fool!" gasped Tryer, dragging the struggling body closer to his own and striving to imprison arms and ankles as well as to protect himself from Drake's teeth. "You can't go over there! There's maybe another shot——"

While the warning was still in his mouth there came a lesser dull roar. He threw himself forward with Drake under him. Splinters of rock flew over their heads and heavier pieces rolled almost to their feet. When the commotion ceased, Tryer arose and gladly released his prisoner.

"What come over you?" he demanded, mopping his bleeding cheek with a great silk handkerchief, none too clean. "Wanted to get yourself killed, eh?"

Drake's small chest was heaving, but he regarded Mattis with a steady, wide-eyed stare. Eunice came hurrying, holding Io by the hand and closely followed by the judge and Jimmy; but not by Tom, whose barrel-like figure atop the hoist looked like a water tank against the sky. The group gathered around Drake.

"Speak up now, you little bobcat!" Tryer was saying. "What come over you?"

The boy stared at his mother and at the judge, then turned his eyes toward the quarry where the great hole had been widened by the blast which had hung fire. His face was immobile, like a mask; but his body quivered through all its length with almost imperceptible vibrations. Suddenly his fixed expression broke; his eyes fell and a vivid flush mounted to his cheeks.

"I don't know," he murmured, ran to Eunice and hid his face against her breast. The heart of a child, when most eloquent in emotion, is least articulate in expression. How could Drake put into words what he had felt at seeing a great wound torn in the side of Rattling Run Fields?

The Lantern on the Plow

Chapter 21

Apparently the incident of his comprehensible behavior on the occasion of the first blasting passed rapidly from Drake's memory; but the seed it had planted in three minds was not destined to die. From the day Tom Bodley had wrapped up his whips in waterproof paper and stowed the bundle away, Eunice's children had absorbed him to a ridiculous extent; he was become an old woman, a spineless nurse, and secretly gloried in his downfall. He was one of the three who pondered over Drake's strange outburst, though he had seen it only from afar. The two others were Judge Alder and Eunice Sherborne, each of whom had better sources from which to draw their deductions than had the ex Whip Man.

Tom was merely curious, the judge was interested in what appeared to be evidence of occult phenomena; but Eunice, remembering Warner Sherborne's adamant allegiance to the soil, was subtly alarmed, and hurried Drake away from the quarry. During the progress to Tom's carriage her awakened sensibilities noted another intriguing development. The great demand for labor at the new plant had brought not only a horde of outsiders to Rattling Run but had called forth an unusual proportion of natives.

Many of those who had never spoken to Eunice as a neighbor now twitched their hat brims as she walked by, and addressed playful words to the children.

151

Within a week half a dozen women stopped at the house on one excuse or another to see her. They were at some pains to make their visits appear even more casual than the ordinary run of such country calls; but so hidden was the location of Rattling Run Fields that Eunice knew they could not have happened alone without definite intent. As the first of them drove away she was conscious merely of surprise; but with the coming of the second, and then of the third, she allowed herself moments of bitter reflection, which soon readjusted itself to a sane measure of the sincere motive behind the awkward and nervously brusque advances. These women were not snobbish, nor were they unkind; furthermore, they had never meant to be unkind.

She looked back over the fifteen years of their neglect and found ample justification for it; first in the position of the farm, neighborless, on a rough and little-traveled road; then in the crushing poverty amid more fortunate landholders, a poverty so drastic that she had never once cared to raise her eyes from it to give a chance for a friendly nod from any passer-by. No; she had not wished friendship, companionship or intercourse of any kind. During all the dragging supplice of her life with Warner she would have resented passionately any intrusion, and these women had merely had the sense to know it.

They were not like that man, that station agent, whose eyes had plainly called her mad.

Church! Why hadn't she gone to church, taken the children to Sunday school? She had—once. She remembered the occasion now; and at the recollection, even after two years, a vivid blush stained her cheeks; then her eyes crinkled at the corners and she laughed clearly, ringingly. The children abandoned their play and rushed to her side.

"Mother, what is it? What made you laugh?"

"Tell us, mother. Please! Please!"

"Nothing," she answered; "nothing that you would understand just now; but I'll tell you, Io, on your thirteenth birthday. Don't forget to ask."

They were satisfied, never pausing to sum up the long list of things which they were to have explained when Io should be thirteen. Not every inconvenient question was thus sidetracked, however; for Eunice believed that what she failed to answer would eventually be asked elsewhere, and perhaps from a less able guide. Incidentally, it was a question of Io's that had precipitated the visit to Sunday school.

"Mother," she had asked, with the eternally surprising precociousness of many a girl of five, "what is it when there are no more days?"

How explain infinity in less than a lifetime? How better start than with a religion, with the symbolic church, or even with a Sunday-school lesson? Eunice had patched the children's clothing, scrubbed it and them, and then led them in due course to the portal of the old stone meeting house almost three miles away. An attempt was made to separate Io from her brother, but without avail.

"Well, for today only," the superintendent had finally conceded in an embarrassed whisper, casting a look at Eunice which made her wish she had not come. "You see, they haven't even learned their verse."

She lingered in the backmost seat, watching the children and worrying over the fact that Drake was murmuring incessantly in his sister's ear and Io as constantly was nodding her head solemnly in assent.

"Let us pray," declared the superintendent from a stand beneath the pulpit, closed his eyes and waited almost tyrannically for the total subsidence of every sound. The pause lengthened and lengthened, as though the empty seconds were piling up to add importance to the speaker and portent to his words. Eunice felt the weight of their injunction and bowed her head. Had she not done so, she would have seen Drake nudge his sister and Io arise, fluff out her skirts, and——

> *"I may not throw up on the floor.*
> *The crust I will not eat,*

153

*For many hungry little ones
Would find it quite a treat."*

In the stillness the treble voice had the peculiar penetrative powers of a corkscrew; it twisted through the unexpectant ear with a revolving stab which reached every lobe of the brain. Io, bravely declaring the only verse she had ever learned, wrecked the laboriously prepared silence far more effectively than if she had exploded a bomb. In fact, the superintendent's eyes and face flew open with an action absurdly like the bursting of an overbaked potato.

Io, poor Io, so single-hearted, so unafraid, so confiding and so treacherously deceived by him whom she most trusted and loved! Violent hands seizing her fluffed skirts and pulling her to a seat with a bump! Dismay! Gasps! Drake choking with laughter; biting his fists. The rush and flurry of her mother coming down the aisle! A snicker! A chuckle! A single loud guffaw from the back of the room. Her hand seized, Drake's hand seized! Ignominious retreat, with toes touching the floor every three yards! Outside, in the middle of the highway, sudden shame, burning tears, and then overwhelming rage, with little feet stamping the devil's own tattoo in the soft deep dust!

After two years Eunice could laugh. After two years! But she knew that it was not the passage of time that had accomplished the restitution of humor. She considered that she was a different woman, and smiled. She remembered Drake, leaping from the hoist, and frowned.

She thought of the women callers, and reflected that she was not ready for them. Summing up these diverse ponderings, she packed what was necessary and with the children abandoned Rattling Run Fields, leaving the care of the homestead to a disconsolate Tom Bodley, and consigning the upper reaches of the farm to the judge and Tryer Mattis, backed by his alien hordes, his scoop shovels, blasting powders and the iron jaws of the thunderous mills.

Chapter 22

It is an incontrovertible fact that men do their best work for women; but they do it when the women are not around. The construction of the cement plant progressed to completion with tremendous strides, and on a much smaller scale the immediate environs of the homestead began to take on a new air for, Connecticut Tom was one of those bachelors who abhor disorder, even though they can put up indefinitely with unwashed windows. He collected rubbish and burned it; trued the fences which abutted on the road; did an extraordinary amount of clever tinkering; stole bricks when the night watchman at the plant was asleep, and with them built new broad, shallow steps, pyramided to meet the narrow thresholds of the three doors of the house. By the coming of winter he had the place in better order than it had known for a hundred years; by winter, also, twenty-two thousand barrels of Rattler Brand cement had been launched on a rising market.

Compared with figures of only a decade later, the output of that first abbreviated fall season seems a mere bagatelle; but it was, in fact, a most notable performance. With cement selling at one dollar and twenty cents when the dollar was worth three times its present value and when labor was costing one-third as much as it does today, it can be seen that the actual returns were proportionately greater than the mill was ever to know again. The judge contributed in no small measure to this success, and by the time operations were suspended for the annual shutdown and general repairs, he and Mattis knew beyond a doubt that the Rattling Run Cement Company was on the highroad to success, and they with it. Neither Tom, Tryer, nor the judge ever spoke of Eunice except to inquire or report as to her whereabouts and welfare; yet Eunice, in the last resort, was the driving power behind all their endeavors.

She wrote seldom, and when summer came, contrary to natural expectation, she gave the farm a wide berth and took the children to the seaside, even avoiding the Jersey shore. This defection pleased Tryer and surprised the judge; but it deeply wounded Tom Bodley. He gave notice to find another caretaker, unwrapped his bundle of whips, washed, greased, and polished the chaise, rubbed Alexander's sleek hide until it shone, led him forth, hitched him up, climbed into the deep seat, took up the reins and clucked.

The horse did not move. Tom clucked again and again, and said "Gid-ap!" over and over; dismounted, pretending he had forgotten something, returned briskly, jumped in and clucked again, all to no avail. He took out his bandanna to mop sweat from his brow and neck, called Alexander by name, talked to him, implored him, reasoned with him; but was held back by a sinking of the heart, coupled with a premonition of mutiny, from uttering the cabalistic cry of "Aleck!" So genuine was his fear that he sat within the somber shadow of the calash top for two hours rather than dare the ultimate test. Finally the sound of approaching rapid hoof beats forced his hand. He gathered up the reins and cried out sharply, "Aleck!"

Alexander threw his rump two inches into the air in the absurd and insulting gesture which heretofore he had used only against strangers, and promptly settled down on all four feet as stolidly as though he were made of varnished wood. Tom gasped and his cheeks showed bright pink through his gray beard as the judge whirled in behind Gypsy, drew up, and presently began to laugh.

"Tom," he begged, "let me give him one genuine cut with a real whip."

"No," said Tom hoarsely.

"Just one lash under the belly where it won't show," persisted the judge.

"No!" groaned Tom, with a shrinking quiver of his own round paunch.

"He's the most colossal fraud I've ever known," continued the judge; "the only horse my fingers have ever itched to lick for the mere sake of licking, and by hickory, he's been asking for it all his life! Every time I see him I look around for a litter of pigs. If you should try out the lard from his carcass there wouldn't be anything left but hide—not a bone, a muscle or a single pound of honest flesh."

At the sight of the moisture which suddenly rose to Tom's kindly eyes the judge felt ashamed of himself. "Well," he concluded, "as I was saying, he's a fine horse, only a trifle too fat for my taste."

"I can't deny," admitted Tom, "that Alexander is a bit fat; but I like them fat. Then there's this about him: He isn't bunchy; he's fat all over—neck, withers, legs, barrel and rump; so that, just standing there, he cuts a fine figure. Give him his due for that, judge; but I do wish he could talk."

"Why?" demanded the judge.

"Well," said Tom, "I'd like to ask him if he's ever known an unhappy day."

The Lantern on the Plow

Chapter 23

The judge drove on, feeling a first touch of gratitude toward Alexander for saving him the trouble of installing a new caretaker. There was a smile in his eyes as he remembered the group he had left behind, standing like an exhibit awaiting shipment to a museum—the great sulking black horse, glistening as if grease had exuded on his well-rubbed hide; the antiquated chaise, hung in the graceful lines of a bygone day; the sheaf of whips, according to Tryer Mattis, approaching an equal symbolism. Finally his thought rested on Tom himself, Tom as an urbane skinful of gentleness, reservoir of the philosophy of an unhurried age and of character, hand in hand with avoirdupois.

To turn from such a personality and enter the presence of Tryer Mattis was almost the equivalent of a physical collision. Tryer represented all those things which Tom denied. During these days he was the dynamic principle incarnated, driving himself and others to the verge of collapse; spurning the weak and battening upon the strong; loosing his fulminating thunderbolts within the entrails of the rock, and dominating the ponderous machinery to grind slowly and exceeding fine, as though he had commandeered the mills of the gods to do his bidding. No wonder he was glad of Eunice's absence; the longer she stayed away, the more he would have accomplished and the better would he be able to domineer.

Achievement was giving him weight in his own eyes day by day; why not in those of another?

But when the second winter arrived, bringing with it a certain amount of enforced idleness, he sang a different tune. He grew restless, and envied the judge his magisterial duties, his love of books and his power of living within himself. He even envied Tom, and got out a cutter sleigh to plow through deep drifts to Rattling Run Fields for an occasional chat. When the snow began to melt he resurrected his discarded buggy, hitched up two draft horses and went wallowing through the mud on the same errand. Occasionally the judge would happen along, too, and the men would sit in Eunice's kitchen by the hour, sometimes talking, but often absorbed each in his own thoughts. Later, seated at the much scoured deal table where Warner Sherborne had signed lease and will, Tryer and the judge would talk shop, covering sheets of paper with calculations, while Tom cooked supper for three and discoursed on the great folly of crossing now the bridges of the future or of counting one's chickens before they were hatched.

"Talk less and cook more, you old grayback!" roared Mattis, leaping up to stride the full breadth of the spacious kitchen and back again. "Who ever got anywhere without crossing bridges before they come to 'em? Who ever done anything with out counting their chickens long afore they was hatched? The difference between you and me, Tom, is that you died day before yesterday and I live day after tomorrow. Burn your silly old whips or you'll have to tag 'em so folks will know what they was for. Talk less and cook more, I say, for the judge and me is hungry."

During the following week, the last in March, Tryer disappeared from his usual haunts. The last of the snow was thawing fast, though the ground was still frostbound beneath the slippery surface of the earth. There was a smell in the air of coming warmth, and it warned Mattis that soon he would have no time for any thought unconnected with the plant. He took train for Camden, changed there to another which let him off at Trenton, and an hour later was in the village of Lawrenceville where he knew Eunice to be living.

160

As he strode along the single street, sparsely aligned with houses for a distance of over a mile, he tried to persuade himself that it reminded him of the hamlet of Greenwich, made unfamiliar, however, by the bleak prospect of the naked trees. To this unfamiliarity he attributed a faint uneasiness that had seized upon him since leaving Trenton; but the truth was quite other than that. With the capital of the state he had had frequent contact through past connections with public works. When he went there, in a manner of speaking, he projected his own atmosphere with him—the atmosphere of the three counties where the name of Tryer Mattis was like a pennant flying at the front of battle, where there was not a man but nodded when he passed, not a boy but knew him, and scarcely a woman who did not feel his presence as one feels the more active elements sun, wind, invigorating rain. It was because he was aware of a sudden absence of background that he strove to connect this strange village with something he knew, and he felt uneasy because he failed.

He entered the general store, took refuge behind one of the encumbered windows and stared across the street. Through gaps between houses and the trunks of trees he could see the buildings of the great school, which held itself aloof in a closed circle. Buildings of brick, of sandstone, and one old one of granite were warmly splotched with matted patches of English ivy.

A bell clanged. Doors opened. Boys poured out in streams that opened fanwise and scattered. Out of the throng of hundreds only half a dozen individuals sought the village proper. Among them was the erect figure of Drake Sherborne.

Tryer watched the direction taken by the boy and followed him at a safe distance. He saw him turn in at the gate of a very small house of broad white clapboards, dignified only by its age, and hurried forward as if to join him, but at the last moment slipped behind the bole of a large elm. Drake whistled; Io threw open the door and flew out to meet him; Eunice came to stand for a moment on the narrow stoop.

At sight of her, Tryer caught his breath and gulped. She was

161

Vic Teller in the flesh, and yet not the Vic Teller he had known. No; not that. He had it! She was what Vic Teller had promised to be before her youth had felt the blighting power of his hands, before he had driven her into the barren refuge of Warner Sherborne's arms and of the bleak emptiness of Rattling Run Fields. She was fresh of skin, renewed, lovely. He looked down at his hands now, at his heavy muddied boots, at his bagged trousers, and finally at the deep wrinkles which had pulled his sleeves high, disclosing soiled shirt cuffs and hairy wrists. Up went his eyes again to that trim high-headed vision on the narrow stoop.

He turned and slouched heavily away. What was he doing here? Who knew him? Who was there to whisper, "There goes Tryer Mattis," with never a look or a thought for his baggy clothes? The shrewdness that had made him a figure to reckon with throughout the length and breath of the three counties dawned in his face and eyes. Not here; or now. He would not come to her like a fish on land, gasping for its natural element. He returned to Trenton and walked the streets for an hour, waiting for a train to Camden.

Five weeks later a breath-taking transformation had swept across the fertile rolling country which centered upon Rattling Run. The startling pink flush of the flowering peach orchards had come and gone, giving way to sprouting leaf; but sweet-scented pear trees were still in full bloom, masses of white amid young foliage of bronzed amber. Bird's-foot violets covered the banks along the roads with a riot of vivid blue. Within the woods, buried beneath blanketing dead leaves, lay hidden the shy yet shamelessly prolific blossom known variously as Mayflower, trailing arbutus or hope of heaven, source of an ineffable perfume, throbbing, as it were, with the pain and joy of hearts in love.

Long ere this Tom had discovered that Alexander's refusal to draw the chaise applied only to the chaise with the sheaf of whips aboard. Were it left behind as an earnest of a return by nighttime to the sloth and epicurean luxuries of Rattling Run Fields, fat as he was, Alexander would consent to trundle the

162

insignificant load of the small carriage up and down dale, and his master in it when grades happened to be propitious. Beholding the wonders of the newborn earth, Tom hitched up and drove into town to see the judge, whom he caught in the act of tearing open a telegram.

"Judge, you got to come out to the farm. It's so lovely to look at, my eyes can't eat it all. I need help; someone to see things at the same time I do. Ever feel like that?"

"Yes, I have," said the judge with a smile as he unfolded the slip of paper in his hands. "It's one of the decentest things about us menfolks, Tom, that we can't stand looking at anything beautiful alone. One of two things: We've got to talk about it or else we've got to have somebody around to love. That's the way it hits me."

"Me, too," agreed Tom fervently. "Will you come out?"

"One minute," said the judge. As he spoke the smile died from his lips, leaving them set and purposeful. "Listen to this," he added after a pause, and read the telegram:

Drake disappeared last night. Search shows he took the trolley to Trenton. Come at once or wire me what to do.

The two men looked at each other for a long moment of silence, broken finally by Tom.

"How old is the boy, judge?"

"Fifteen."

"Fifteen and hard as nails, but not hard enough to hold back from the pull of the stingy earth where he was born! Well, walking won't hurt him. You go to Mrs. Sherborne and fetch her to Rattling Run Fields. I'm going to borrow something out of your shed."

"Wait a bit," said the judge, having kept pace with the thought in Tom's mind. "The boy has got to go back."

Tom's kindly eyes hardened.

"Not afore he sees the place he's headed for," he declared as he' started around the house, presently to reappear, carrying the judge's best whip—a genuine implement of authority made up of slender hickory stock and rawhide lash.

"Why don't you take Gypsy?" asked the judge.

163

Tom pivoted, suggesting more than ever a barrel on end.

"I don't take Gypsy," he said, "because I'm afraid of her; and also because all I got to do with Alexander is to head him up the pike and say Elmer, Glassboro, Woodbury, Haddonfield, Bordentown, and he'll go to them places in the order named. Besides, lean him against an apple tree at night and he thinks he's in a stall."

"All right, Tom," agreed the judge. "But if the boy walked most of the night, he's already pulled out of Bordentown. What with a little money, lifts, and one thing and another, you ought to meet him somewhere around Glassboro—always providing Alexander doesn't run away."

Tom paid no heed to the taunt. He went to his chaise, lowered the calash top, uncurled the whip lash, took his seat, picked up the reins, held out the whip awkwardly at arm's length, and without further preliminaries whispered hoarsely, "Aleck!"

Aleck cast one amazed glance backward from the corner of his eye and plunged forward so violently that his master's head snapped back and his hat flew off. The judge rushed forward, picked it up and started at a run after the carriage; but from the first it was a hopeless chase. He stopped, leaned against a tree, and in his astonishment forgot to laugh. All he could hear was a thunderous, elephantine trot; all he could see was the glint of a shining black hide shot across with streamers of Tom's flying gray hair and beard. Then a cloud of dust blotted out the astounding vision.

Chapter 24

It was too late for the judge to make a connection at Camden on that day; but early the next morning he was off, and by noon was saying to Eunice, "Don't worry about Drake; we haven't found him yet, but I feel sure he will reach Rattling Run Fields just about the time we get there."

"Rattling Run Fields?" repeated Eunice vaguely, and then threw up her head to stare unseeingly into the garden. "So," she added, "you think that's where he's gone?" The judge looked at her and realized that he had not yet seen her. For an instant Drake, Rattling Run Fields and the whole Sherborne family, as he had known it, were wiped from mind. It was as though he had stepped back into a day before he had met Warner, before Drake and Io were born, a day of his own youth, when beneath a high arch of buttonwood, maple and elm he had seen a swift figure, vivid as a shaft of sunlight, dart out hatless in a swirling organdie frock to run to the little post office of Greenwich Street. He stared at Eunice. Alive she was, from the feet up. Not only her brain—all of her!

"Don't worry," he stammered, at a loss for anything else to say.

"I won't," said Eunice. "Not at present—not about Drake, I mean. But come in. Please come with me."

She led him through the tiny hall to a corner bedroom, opened the door and stood aside to let him pass. "Like that, every so often," she whispered; "all day yesterday; all last night, even in her sleep. For hours she kept calling out, 'No, Drake, no!' as she always does when she wishes him to wait for her. But today she hasn't spoken."

The judge crossed the room and discovered Io, stretched face downward, feet close together, arms out thrown, and weeping faintly, with a whimpering flutter of the breath. She lay on top of the bed and was clothed only in a nightgown of sheer muslin whose folds molded her figure into a bas-relief in marble, all except her bare arms and legs, which shone with a subdued, alabastrine glow. Once again the judge was struck by the astonishing slimness of her limbs. She reminded him of something. Always she had suggested elusively an impression, never before quite seized. Now he had it. She was like an arrow—slender, fleet, direct. Today—a fallen arrow.

He leaned over, touched her, spoke to her and, when she did not move or answer, gathered her up in his arms. She turned to him without lifting her wilted head. Her slim hands crept blindly around his neck. With her face fallen against his breast, she continued to weep softly, steadily, each sob sending a tremor through her elflike frame. He started to walk up and down, comforting her, nursing her as if she were a baby. Suddenly he stopped, and a look of dismay dawned in his eyes. Her body, so still without, was riotous within. It was hot, like fire. Through the soft cambric muslin, it burned his hands and drove daggers into his heart. Oh, quivering weeping flesh of childhood, stupendous reservoir of love and pain, fleet vessel of hope along the treacherous coasts of disillusion! Oh, maiden voyage and the rock of first betrayal!

Judge Alder trembled and his hands tightened. At that moment the morsel of human woe in his arms leaped the bounds of conception and became tremendous, immeasurable, infinitely more important than the breath of his own life. For Io he would have done anything, renounced salvation itself with a laugh. Love swirled through his veins with the purity of a leaping flame, consumed him, destroyed him, leaving behind only love—love in its most limpid manifestation, shorn of all seeking desire.

166

Oh, Io, hidden child, creeping out from that vast penumbra of persons seen but unknown, breathlessly announcing her advent with an unforgettable sparkle of dark eyes, wide open, challenging, yet ready to run! "Some folks say that Io was a heifer, a milk-white heifer; and some she was the baby moon." And Io, wilted, quivering, burning; strangling his heart with her enlacing arms! Never more reverent in all his life, he swore:

"By God Almighty," he muttered, "I can't stand it! Here, take her! Put clothes on her! Hurry!"

Strange, silent journey Eunice sitting very still, with her hands folded in her lap and eyes far away; the judge, frowning, pondering; and Io at his side, sunk into the curve of his arm, quiet as death itself, weeping no longer, unless tears can fall within, showing no sign and giving forth no sound. They went first to the judge's house. He carried Io up to his own room and laid her on the great old-fashioned bed, four-posted, but testerless. From the door he turned back, took up her limp hand and pressed it until she opened her eyes.

"Listen," he promised, "if you'll go to sleep—sound asleep—we'll take you to Drake when you wake up. Will you try?"

She nodded listlessly and turned her face away. Eunice went to the windows, lowered the shades and drew the curtains.

Ten minutes later the judge was sending Gypsy along the highway at a terrific pace. When he reached Rattling Run Fields he felt its abandonment even before he threw open the door, which had been left unlocked. Old Ben got up, came snuffling at his heels, whining with distress. Realizing that he was half starved, the judge went into the cellar, fetched a great bowl of soured milk and put it down before the dog; then he hurried out to the barn.

Fortunately the two horses and the one cow, which, with the chickens, now comprised the entire livestock of the farm, had been turned out to pasture. Taking a pail, he went to look for the cow, found her waiting with neck stretched across the bars and stripped her leaking udder. How many years since he had last milked? Well, a great many; more than he wished to count. He was surprised

167

and pleased that his hands had not lost their cunning. He drove home slowly, his eyes straining in vain at every turn and every crossroads for a sight of the unique Alexander and Tom's no less unmistakable barouchet.

Late that same afternoon he stood with Eunice, admiring the new brick steps which had replaced the ancient warped ones of wood, while Io climbed to the room she had shared with Drake since long before she could remember. They had warned her that he had not yet come, but she paid no heed. Eunice went into the kitchen, started to go through the house, changed her mind, and approached the window, the same window through which she had watched and watched, against her will, for the spaced comings of Warner, hauling marl. Presently she exclaimed, "There!"

The judge looked out. Alexander's head was just thrusting into view from the dip of Rattling Run; then followed his great fat body, no longer sleek, alas, but sadly ruffled and streaked with sweat. In the shadow of the top of the chaise, now raised, could be descried Tom's vast hatless bulk, eased forward to the edge of the seat, with Drake beside him, sound asleep; altogether a weary and bedraggled cortege. Tom alighted heavily and prodded Drake. He awoke, stumbled from the low carriage and stood dazed, rubbing his eyes, while Alexander plodded stolidly toward the barn.

Drake had grown in the year and a half since the judge had seen him; but, unlike most boys of fifteen, he was compact and lithe, though slender. His features were finely cut and he had his mother's light-brown hair; but for all his delicacy, he gave no impression of effeminacy. His eyes saved him from that. They were widely placed, steady, and both by their color and expression suggested the quality of steel. He used them now as he studied the old house; the familiar, tumbledown out-buildings, the gnarled shrubs and cedars and a single lovely flowering bush, a japonica, drenched in vivid coral bloom. At the sight of it he stood spellbound, as if for this, and for this alone, he had dared rebellion and ventured so long a journey. Answering a hail from the judge, he went to the kitchen door and entered. He seemed narcotized, for the presence

168

of his mother appeared not to startle him. She was sitting at the old deal table and made no move to greet him as he dragged off his cap, crossed the room and stood before her.

"Did Tom tell you we would be here?" asked the judge curiously.

"No," said Drake, never taking his eyes from his mother's face.

"Go up to your room," said Eunice quietly.

"Don't come down until you have made Io laugh."

The boy started to say something, and stopped. His eyes fell before Eunice's inscrutable gaze. He turned, opened the door behind the judge and climbed the steep stairs, down which, almost two years ago, Io had tumbled at the break of a memorable dawn. Moments passed, lengthening into a quarter of an hour. The judge became alarmed, but Eunice never wavered.

"Today is Saturday," she said, breaking a long silence. "I wish you would talk to him—persuade him that we must go back tomorrow, on his account. You realize that, don't you? He must go back."

The judge nodded, turned in his chair, and as on that morning of long ago, suddenly reached back and opened the door to the stairs. Drake was standing there, alone. His face was flushed and there were tears in his eyes; but whether they were tears of contrition or rage it was difficult to say.

"Did you make her laugh?" asked Eunice evenly.

"No," said Drake; then he burst out, stammering,

"Mother, I—I couldn't help it. I had to—"

"Go back upstairs," interrupted Eunice.

"No," said Drake, throwing up his head in the gesture so characteristic of Eunice.

A rebellious look lighted a tiny flame in his slate-gray eyes. He crossed the kitchen, pushed open the screen door and passed out. His mother did not call to him; she gripped the edges of the table until her knuckles turned white—almost as white as her face. The judge arose to follow Drake.

"There's more in this than shows on the surface," he said to Eunice. "You were right not to try to stop him. Go up to Io while I find Drake and talk to him."

169

Eunice did as he suggested. When she reached the top of the stairs she started to speak, but arrested her words at the sight of Io. Drake had done more wisely than to make her laugh; he had got her to lie down and put her soundly to sleep, with a happy smile curving her lips. Eunice drew up a chair and sat down close to the bed. She felt contrite at having ordered Drake to do an unreasonable thing. It did not occur to her that he should have told her frankly that Io was not laughing, but asleep. He had had something else to say—something to him far more vital—and she had stopped him.

"Mother, I—I couldn't help it. I had to come." Yes, that is what he had been going to say. "I had to come here to Rattling Run Fields." That was the thing that had been holding his thoughts above Io's grief and above his mother's command. Never before had he disobeyed a major command. She thought of Warner and a tremor ran through her body. Why had she ordered Drake to go back upstairs? Why had she not guessed that he would not and held her tongue? Had she lost him, or was there yet time—— The specter of Warner Sherborne rose before her. Her eyes widened. Never again! No! Never would she fight her son! No ogre of the land should ever come between them. He could do and be what he would. Only one thing mattered—only one thing in the whole world—that she should love and be loved.

At that thought her head flew up as if she were listening. Tryer's voice came to her in recollection, "I tell you it's love—real love," and her own, in echo, "Love! How dare you say that to me?" She remembered the terrible emptiness, and then the fury, the unreasoning fury, which had seized her. Had she found, now, the answer to those days of blind emotion and futile questioning? Was love something above and beyond the tragic power of man over woman and sex over man? Fresh from the morning of that very day, a vision came to her of the judge holding Io's warm, sobbing body in his arms. She heard again his fervent words—"By God Almighty, I can't stand it!"

Her eyes turned to the bed and filled with tears. The tears began to trickle down her cheeks; but her eyes remained wide

170

open, fastened on Io—Io with her blot of dark, tangled hair, cupping the white pool of her face, curling caressingly against her pale cheeks with their dusky stain of color glowing deep beneath the petal surface of the skin. Eunice saw things she had never consciously seen before—the infinitesimal vibrations of her girl's nostrils; the tiny twitchings of her lips, curved to a happy smile; the thumping beat of the pulse at the side of her slender throat, and the shuddering rise and fall of her breast, too slight to hold so great a heart.

Evening was falling. In the kitchen Tom was anxiously preparing supper, a love feast of many eggs, a few rashers of bacon and a huge batch of hot biscuit. Out amid the shining apple trees the judge was pacing up and down with Drake, and Drake was repeating doggedly, "I can't tell you, sir. All I know is I had to come. It's no use saying I'm sorry, because I'm not. You see, I had to. I'm glad I did it; I'm glad I'm here. Anybody else can come or not, just as they like, but I had to. I guess mother doesn't understand how it is."

They left the faint scent of the budding orchard and passed on into the redolent woods. High above was the sheen of the new leaves; beneath their feet, the brown earth. Midway of tree tops and ground was spread the milky way of the last of the dogwood, floating like a billowing sheet of fallen stars. Far down the slope glimmered the black mirror of the swimming hole. All was silence, save for the deep reverberating voice of a lone bullfrog, coming from far out in the swamp, proclaiming with incredible hoarseness, "Water, here's water! Water here's water!"

Drake drew near to a towering tree and laid his hand against it.

"Judge," he asked, "did you ever get the feel of a hickory?"

"Many's the time, Drake," answered Judge Alder.

He, too, laid his hand against the bole. He passed his fingers lightly up and down the bark.

How smooth, hard, upright; how tight with life—fixed, yet aspiring.

"If I wasn't me," said Drake in defiance of his schooling, "I think I'd like to be a hickory."

171

"Drake," said the judge, "let's find a log. I want to talk to you and I want you to talk to me. Don't be afraid. I was your father's friend, and I'm a friend to your mother and to Io and to you. You know that, don't you?"

"Yes, sir," said Drake, and led the way through the gathering gloom to a fallen tree.

"You may not think it," continued the judge when they were seated, "but I can give you something today which perhaps no one else could give you, something that may never be offered to you again. I'll put it this way: If someone had told Tryer Mattis when he was fifteen what I am going to tell you, and made him listen, he would be a great man today. I mean he would have grown up into a hickory, and a big one. As it is, he's a buttonwood—bigger than any hickory, but spotted. There are places so soft in him that you could shove your thumbs in up to the knuckles. You see, I'm trusting you, I'm talking just to you. I pick out Tryer because he's somebody you know, and are going to know a lot better. The closer you get to him the greater—and smaller—you'll find him to be. Tryer was handed all the tools of life, without the knowledge to use them; all the locks in the world without the master key. I'll tell you its name presently, but not just yet. I want to ask you a question or two first. What's the matter with your school?"

"Nothing," said Drake. "I guess the school's all right."

"Do you like it?"

"No."

"Why?"

For a moment Drake was silent; then he spoke slowly:

"For one thing, it's too far away from here. That's the worst. Then I'm a day boy, something from the village. Somehow, I'm— well, I'm outside. The last thing is, I don't mind fighting; but I can't stop them from calling me Mary."

"Mary!" cried the judge, laying a hand on the boy's knee. "Why, Drake, where did they get that? What does it come from?"

"You won't tell?"

"Never!"

"From Io following me around. They call her Mary's lamb."

The judge's fingers tightened.

"We'll fix that," he muttered. "You and I will clean that up between us. Tryer Mattis hit on a truer name for you when he called you a bobcat, and before we get through———" He stopped, loosed his hold on Drake's knee and controlled his voice. "Do you think you could listen now if I were to tell you the name of the master key?"

"Yes, sir," answered Drake more warmly than he yet had spoken.

"It's just one word—'schooling.' I don't mean merely learning your book lessons. I mean so much more than that that I haven't enough schooling of my own to say it all. Your dad, Drake, was a hickory, blown to pieces by the lightning of circumstances, so that all that was left was a straight stump and roots to the very bottom of Rattling Run Fields. He never had a chance at the kind of schooling I mean; but because he held on like a bulldog to the one thing he knew, you have all the chance that fortune can give one boy. You don't have to learn to earn money; what you've got to learn is how to live. Listen, Drake; listen to this! We all want you to do exactly what you want to do. Have you got that?"

"Yes—no, sir," stammered Drake.

"There you are! You see, you can't believe it; but it's true. Here's the rest of it: Take a thousand grown men, hand-pick them. Listen! Out of that thousand you'll find only one who wasn't too lazy as a boy, or too blind, to learn how to do what he wanted to do. Now do you get it?"

"Yes, sir, I think I do."

"Drake," said the judge, after a pause, "I'm going to tell you what you're going to do, beginning with tomorrow. Don't answer me now; just think it over, tuck it under your pillow and sleep on it. You're going back with your mother and Io to school as a day scholar for the rest of this term. But you're going all alone as a boarder next year, with permission to come to Rattling Run Fields for a week-end every month or so besides your holidays. Now, here's the last thing you're going to do, and you'll only have to do it once: The first time a boy bigger than you calls you Mary, you're going to light into him with feet, finger nails and teeth—wildcat rules. If necessary, you're going to get a joint off one of his thumbs, or perhaps his ear, and eat it. By the living Harry, you're going to mark him for life with the brand of the bobcat!"

"I don't have to think it over," blubbered Drake, quivering with excitement and surrendering with a passionate allegiance to the understandingness of his friend the judge. "I've thought it over already. I'll do it all—especially that last."

Chapter 25

After supper Tom suffered a moment of embarrassment. He had long since moved, with the judge's permission, from temporary quarters in the old harness shed to what had been Warner's and Eunice's bedroom. He had had no time to prepare the room for Eunice; and although he was in many ways as neat as an old maid, he was remembering one thing after another that he would have liked to attend to or put away before admitting her. The children went to bed; Eunice, the judge and Tom sat in the kitchen, talking only at long intervals, and then of insignificant matters. Tom had a guilty feeling that he should be upstairs, but sat on, as a man is apt to do when at a loss just how to tackle a task—above all, just where to begin. Suddenly he grunted. Sheets! There were no fresh sheets! His face turned pink beneath his beard as he turned to Eunice.

"I been living in your room. There ain't any clean sheets."

Eunice said nothing; the judge moved slowly in his chair.

"That's easily arranged," he said to her. "You can come with me and share the nurse's room. There are two beds in it, and she seldom uses either."

Eunice did not reply directly; she spoke to Tom of the new steps, congratulating him on their appearance.

"Everything about the place," she added, "is in beautiful order, Tom. It's high time you had a raise in wages."

175

"If I had my way," replied Tom after a pause, "you'd pay me for every week the children is away from Rattling Run, and I'd pay you back for every day they are here—one week's pay for each day."

Eunice smiled.

"You like them, don't you? They'll be here all summer, Tom, so we won't make your kind of arrangement until the fall."

She arose and started to put on her hat. The judge hurried out to fetch his rig. Five minutes later, with Eunice at his side, he was driving through the warm spring night, drenched with the odors of leaping sap in young grass, new leaves, in swelling bud and flaring bloom. His heart was beating fast, faster than the rattling catabibazon of Gypsy's hoofs. He pulled her down to a walk and kept her there. Neither he nor Eunice had spoken since leaving Rattling Run Fields, nor did they speak. The judge's eyes were fascinated by her hand, lying white against the dark material of her traveling dress. Since she dared to share so long a silence, he was emboldened to lay his free hand over hers. He felt it tremble violently and then suddenly grow still, controlled, self mastered. Her fingers turned and folded around his with a touch that was light and cool, indescribably friendly and yet unyielding. At his house she waited in the library while he put up the mare. She heard him enter, go up the stairs and speak to the nurse. Presently he came into the room.

"I want to tell you that it's all right with Drake," he began; "only I've made him certain promises. We—well, we exchanged promises. He will go back tomorrow with you and Io, and stick out the term. He will return in the fall, but on condition that he is to go alone and to be a full-fledged boarder, with one week-end every month or so at Rattling Run Fields if he asks for it, and all his holidays. Is that right with you?"

"Yes," said Eunice, "quite all right. I thank you."

"He's a fine upstanding boy," continued the judge. "He said he didn't think you understood what had happened to him, that he had——"

"Don't," interrupted Eunice. "Do you think," she added bitterly, "anyone need explain to me what the grip of the farm can do?" She arose.

"Will you show me where I am to sleep?"

"No; not yet," said the judge, moving toward her. He waited, forcing her to meet his eyes. "You know well enough what I want to say to you," he continued in a low voice. "I want to tell you that I love you, and to persuade you that you love me. It will take hours to tell all that has come over me. When I touch Io, I touch you; when I talk to Drake, I talk to you. When I'm alone, you are with me most. In a way, you have created me. I am yours, whether you take me or not. I love you."

She looked at him steadily; her lips opened, but she did not speak. He strode forward and put his arms around her firmly, and yet not as Tryer would have done. Even so, all her body began to tremble, her hands crept up over his shoulders and she dropped her face against his breast. Like Io, thought the judge. It was as though he held again the warm, quivering form of Io.

"Eunice," he whispered, trying to make her look up. "Please."

She shook her head in denial, without lifting her face, but clung more closely to him. Presently she spoke.

"I will not tell you tonight, because I'm too tired to think. Let me go to bed, Will. Tomorrow I'll know. Tomorrow I'll tell you."

He stood quite still until she stirred restlessly in his arms; then he released her and led her into the hallway.

"The second door on the right from the top of the stairs," he directed her. "You will find your bag there."

For all her exhaustion, Eunice did not immediately fall asleep. She lay awake thinking, wondering whether she loved Judge Alder. How may a woman know whether she loves? She remembered her own girlhood, swept from the pedestal of an immemorial tradition by Tryer Mattis and saved from shame only by the alarming violence of her surrender. Then there was Warner, with whom she had lived for fifteen years. She did not think of the fifteen years, but of a single moment in all their course, the moment when she

177

had moaned, "The snow! Oh, Warner, my dear, its flakes are like great white tears, heaped in a bank against the window." Now the judge—less, and more, than both the other men put together. How direct had been his declaration; how upright; how like himself; how his words had hewed to the line, and left it clean! Oh, why had he not taken her? Why had he consented to wait—left it to her to decide?

In the morning, while they waited for Tom to bring in the children, the judge did not trouble her with words; but his eyes followed her around and besought her answer. "Not now," she stammered finally. "I mean—in the fall, when Drake goes back to school."

"You will marry me then," he asked, "and come here with Io to live? Is that what you meant?"

She flushed. It annoyed her that he should not have taken full advantage of her ambiguity. "I mean," she said quickly, "that I shall tell you then."

He caught the swift flicker of resentment in her eyes, and for a single instant the shrewd magistrate within him gained the ascendancy over the unseeing lover.

"No," he said, stepping forward and seizing her by the elbows; "you will tell me now."

"What do you wish?" whispered Eunice, the blood rushing from her face, and even from her lips, leaving them cold and colorless.

"Say that you love me and will marry me in the fall."

"You will tell no one until then?"

"No one."

"I will marry you."

"The rest—say the rest," he ordered, tightening his hold on her arms.

His eyes met hers, held them, burned them.

Her hands fluttered toward him as though they were blinded and lost, but still he gripped her firmly, constraining her to face him.

"Say it!"

"I love you," whispered Eunice, so low that he scarcely heard the words; then her head fell slowly to one side and the weight of her whole body dragged on his hands. Emotion welling to a flood within her, and finding no commensurate outlet, struck her down. She sank in a wilted heap upon the floor.

The Lantern on the Plow

180

Chapter 26

The summer of 1903 was momentous in both the lives and material activities which centered around Rattling Run Fields. With cement selling at a high figure, Mattis and the judge had decided to plunge. With all their profits of the previous season they first met their carrying charges, and then went out to borrow to the full extent of their resources. Their object was the doubling of the capacity of the plant. In furtherance of their plans, equipment had been pouring in all through the winter; and as soon as the frost was out of the ground, work had been started on the new foundations. By the middle of June, Portland cement of the Rattler Brand was being turned out at the rate of eight hundred barrels for every twenty-four hours, which meant that each weekly blast had to show over fifteen hundred tons of raw rock torn from the low cliff.

Tryer was more productively active, and consequently happier, than ever before in his life. He was constantly on the scene in person; in fact, it might be said without exaggeration that he lived only while within hearing of the rumble, crash and grind of the monstrous machinery which first pulverized the virgin rock, then burned it to a clinker, only to powder it once again into the softest yet most valiant dust of commerce.

Gradually he was collecting about him certain of those personalities who form the backbone of any long-lived industry; men

181

who baby their work, who acquire the maternal instinct toward dynamite, crusher or kiln, and often end by adopting an entire enterprise as though it were an orphan. Such was Jake Werten, who had abandoned a long-neglected second-rate drug shop to become chemist to the Rattler plant; such another was Mazaro, the long-nosed Neapolitan, who had risen in a year from ditch digger to quarry master. To these and many more like them, a strike was only another name for treachery. They held their jobs the year around and lorded it over the floating labor that was rushed in each spring to carry the peak load of production and rushed out each fall to lower the overhead.

Tryer's attitude toward Eunice during these crowded months is most difficult to define, because, even could one have picked his brain, no indication of his plans or intention would have been discovered. He had no plans and was only nebulously aware of any intention. Somewhere amid the complexity of detail of his individual cosmos lingered the conviction that she was ultimately to be his. Had he not served notice on her, staked his claim? In that vague thought was set forth both his greatness and his naive immaturity; his tremendous power of acquisition through faith, against his limitations of habit and the oft-trodden rut. He was scarcely conscious of the frequency of Judge Alder's visits to Rattling Run Fields, in spite of the fact that his new car often passed Gypsy, going or coming on the roads to town; and even had he surmised that his partner was his rival, it is doubtful whether he would have stolen an hour from his labors to strengthen the fences which he deemed secure.

In the meantime life at the homestead had assumed an idyllic temper, troubled faintly by the distant rumble of the mills only when the wind blew strongly from the west. Never before had Eunice considered Rattling Run Fields as emblematic of peace or of fruition. During the fifteen years of her life with Warner it had stood for struggle, disaster and an unbending sterility.

Now its atmosphere seemed to be changing to that of a nest set securely within a crotch of the living earth, with fledglings pruning

182

untried wings for flight. She remembered almost with dismay the bitter words she had spoken to the judge:

"If I were offered happiness in this place, I would choose to be unhappy elsewhere."

How had she come so near to blasphemy? She went over in her mind once more those poignant events which had scarred her very soul, and in a moment her face grew hard, old. Thinking of Drake leaping from the hoist to rush toward the wound in the land from which he had sprung no less than from her womb, and of his mutinous flight from school, she held in the end to her aversion. No creeping beauty should win her; she was glad that she was going to marry the judge and move away at last.

The children were wholly unconscious of this feeling and given over to a quiet yet greedy orgy of enjoyment. The item which had first seized Drake's attention was the effect of the new steps Tom had built to the three doors of the old house. He had been clever in not following the lines of the old ones of wood. The wide flare of the new steps, narrowing as they ascended, had made the awkward tower of the ancient homestead almost a thing of grace. Drake sat on the warm bricks, patted them with his feet and hands, and felt foolish when Io asked him what he was doing. But Tom, coming from the harness shed, where he had once more taken up his abode, did not have to ask.

"Say, Drake, get your mother's permission to tear down the old corn crib and the lean-to at the back of the house. There's plenty room in the barn now for all them things. Let's build a new chicken run with the best of the lumber and make the place look a bit shipshape."

Drake flew in search of Eunice, and in the days of feverish demolition and construction that ensued Io grew more and more disillusioned, waiting to see Rattling Run Fields assume the form of a vessel, high poop and bow, masts, bowsprit and perhaps a pennant flying at the taffrail. When she learned that Tom's romantic word "shipshape" implied nothing more than spring house cleaning, applied to out of doors, she made her initial approach to boredom in following all of her brother's leads. This first defection was fostered intentionally by Eunice and the judge. Looking backward to the paroxysm of weeping brought on by Drake's abandonment of her on the occasion of his escape from school, and forward to an inevitable separation, they made plans and joined forces in keeping the children apart for as many hours as possible in each day.

This could be done only by giving them separate interests, and the project was greatly aided by two factors—the frequent presence of Jimmy Mattis, too lazy to work; and the aversion of Drake to approaching the cement plant, much less the quarry. Io, on the other hand, was fascinated by the activities beyond the brow of the far-away ridge, and Jimmy was ever ready to lead her to where she could watch them. He was a strange mixture of a boy, much like his father, except that he was less promiscuous in his affections. Ordinarily he never looked at any but the bigger of the girls among his schoolmates, and then only to tease them; but from the day Io came back to the farm he seemed to drop his usual habits and followed her around sheepishly as if she were the bell mare and he one of a herd of ponies.

On days when there was no blasting the two would watch Drake and Tom hammer and nail as long as idle flesh could stand the strain, and then go off to lie for hours on the very edge of the quarry beneath the blot of shade of some cedar, doomed to imminent destruction. From such a point of vantage they would watch the men immediately beneath them, some breaking up the larger blocks of rock, others with ten-pronged forks loading the broken stone into the skips, and still others standing by to couple up the laden cars with the snakelike cable running from the hoist.

As each load went up the incline they would hold their breath, waiting for the sounds of tipple, roar and crunch. Like a background was the ponderous low drone of the battery of mills.

There came a day when Jimmy gained permission from his father to bring Io to the plant. Men stopped their work as she drew near, so slight was she, and with great a presence. Rightly had the judge named her the arrow. Incredibly slender, moved by some

184

unseen power, she seemed to be here and there at one and the same time, without fuss or effort. Her dark curly hair was clustered about her head like a crown, and from beneath its disordered thatch her brown eyes, with their buried flashes of smoky fire, challenged the world, giving warning that she stood ready to take all dares. When she smiled—ah, when she smiled, that which was hardest in the breast of any man turned to water, and that which was tenderest choked and almost strangled on itself.

Jimmy led her to the floor of the quarry and Tony Mazaro himself took them in an empty skip to the top of the hoist. Unheard of sacrifice of time, complete and unsurpassable homage! He even remained to hold Io up so that she could lean over the guard rail and watch the next car hit the tipple and rumble its load of rock into the insatiable maws of the crusher. So fascinated was she by this sight and the amazing hunger and capacity of the grinding jaws of iron, that she refused point-blank to go farther. In vain did Jimmy recount the wonders of the ball and tube mills, and even of the blinding blaze of the fiery kilns; in vain did Mazaro assert with naive, tender-sounding profanity that he had to go back to his work. Io clung to the rail, and, restrained by the feudal traditions of the Old World, he dared not cross her, much less pull her away. In desperation he sent for Mattis.

Tryer came swearing and stayed to laugh long and loud at the swarthy quarry master's predicament. Gradually he sobered as his eyes made swift estimate of his boy Jimmy, sandy-haired, blue-eyed, large for his age, and moderately well formed, and of Io's delicate figure, stirruped in Mazzaro's hands and doubled as clean as a jackknife at the hips to permit her to lean far out over the crusher.

"Here, I'll take her," he said, stepping forward and encircling Io's waist with his powerful fingers.

Instantly she threw herself backward, writhed, twisted, slipped from his hands like an eel and darted away along the rickety platform. Tryer, Mazaro and Jimmy all dived for her flying skirts, and missed. Tryer was the first to recover his presence of mind;

185

he bellowed to the man at the skip head, who was just in time to hold out his arms and deflect her flight down the narrow stairway which led to the ground. Jimmy followed, and presently caught up with her.

"What's the matter, Io?" he asked. "Why did you run away from dad?"

"He caught hold of me," stated Io, apparently unperturbed. "He—he touched me."

Jimmy looked at her, saw that she was not at all angry, and wondered. She started to run up the ascent to the pasture, and though he was her elder and a boy, he was far more blown than her by the time they reached the top of the low hill. "Io," he panted presently, "it's a real hot day. Let's you and me go swimming."

She stopped and stared at him.

"No," she said, in the same untroubled tone in which she had stated her reason for running away from Tryer Mattis.

Chapter 27

So important had grown the affairs of the Rattling Run Company that the judge had resigned from the bench and returned to a
desultory law practice which made him the master of his own time.
Owing to the heavy carrying charges, the income he received from
the plant was not large, but he was content to leave all his eggs in
the one basket. He was shrewd enough to perceive that whether
Tryer's fantastic dream of concrete roads ever came true or not,
the future of the enterprise in which they were jointly and almost
equally interested was assured. He gave legal consultations in the
mornings and in the afternoons could be seen invariably taking
the road to Rattling Run Fields.

His connection with the plant was so well known, and the
house of the Sherbornes was so hidden, that his daily visits to the
homestead passed almost unremarked. Indeed, even if the most
avid gossips had followed him and watched his meetings with
Eunice they would have got little reward for their pains; because
the judge had learned his lesson. Never would he forget Eunice's
head, drooping slowly to one side, and the full weight of her body
dragging his hands to the floor. That had been no ordinary collapse,
but the sheer victory of a suppressed emotion over flesh too sorely
tried. When, yet again, he remembered that this was the woman
whom he had once likened in his mind to a bit of useful harness

he felt small in his own eyes, and frightened. He was different from Mattis in that it was not in him to play with fire for the mere sake of the game.

He spent hours with Eunice and her children; but even after Io, and then Drake, had gone to bed, he never risked more than a quick contact of hands as he said good night to Eunice. That restraint, however, did not apply to his eyes or to his tongue. He would follow every movement she made, and when they were alone he would make love to her with words that kept her from ever doubting his ardor and which sometimes swept over her almost with the effect of a lingering caress. Only when the summer was drawing to a close did he remind her of her promise and ask to know her wishes. Where would she like to be married, and when, and did she want the children to attend?

"No," said Eunice, answering his last question first. Then, after a pause, "The day before Drake goes back to school; quietly very quietly."

"Do you wish to go away afterward?"

"Yes; a long journey," she answered. Her eyes remained grave, but a mischievous smile played with the corners of her full lips as she added, "A journey in your library. Nowhere else."

On the appointed day she changed her decision in part. Drake, with Tom's aid, was so absorbed in putting the finishing touches to some last embellishment that it seemed cruel to leave Io behind. Besides, how better could the blow of separation from her brother be softened than by giving her a new and divided sense of importance, a privilege in which he had no share? Drawn by Gypsy, the three set out on the long drive to a neighboring county seat, not the one of the judge's residence. There, before a justice of the peace and Io's wide-open, wandering eyes, William Alder and Eunice Sherborne were married. One would have thought that the parallel of this procedure with that of her former marriage would have reminded her of Warner, but it did not. She had lived too profoundly to attach much importance to a similarity in mere externals. The mood in which she faced union with the judge had

188

nothing whatever in common with her flight from Mattis into Warner's arms. Then she had plunged into a material penance; now she moved sensitively and in a subdued exaltation toward a spiritual fulfillment. If she was afraid, it was the fear of humility before her own limitations, real or imagined.

The judge's long restraint had made its marked impression. During the four months which had passed since she admitted her love for him this man had seen her constantly, known that she was his by right of conquest, and yet had stood steadfastly by some law which to him ranked higher than the achievement of a merely intrinsic possession. Little did he know how much he had gained by this exhibition of a strength to which she had been a stranger. Day by day she had felt growing within her the power to love above and beyond the implications of physical surrender—that power whose first stirrings had made her turn on Mattis with unreasoning fury and ask him how he dared to speak to her of love.

As they were driving homeward the judge chanced to glance at Eunice just as she threw up her head, shaking it free from fear and doubts. Io, tired by the long drive, was sitting in her lap, with head fallen against her shoulder, and though Eunice was not looking at the child, there had stolen into her face the self same effulgence which he had seen once before at the end of the nightlong vigil beside Warner's body, an effulgence which had seemed to dim the paling lamp and dissolve the very walls of the room in which she stood. Holding her children hand in hand, she had taken a single step, and it had been as though she strode, attended, through open fields. So now did her face appear.

When they reached Rattling Run Fields Tom was in the kitchen preparing supper, with Drake following him around, talking purposefully of what they two would do when another summer should have at long last come around.

"Drake!" cried Io excitedly, and cast a pleading look at her mother.

"No, Io," said Eunice. "Wait a moment, dear." The judge came in from hitching the mare. "Drake," called Eunice, "come here.

I have something to tell you." Drake turned and met her smiling eyes. "The judge and I were married today. Drake, are you glad or sorry?"

Drake drew erect and studied his mother's illumined face. Her smiles, so rare in the first days of their childhood, had an extraordinary ascendancy over the moods of her children. Now it was as though she took an unfair advantage in smiling at her son. He felt like flinging himself into her arms, and yet drew back, struggling with a new-found sense of individuality. He and his mother, who had once been one, were suddenly no longer one, even though love remained. It was puzzling; it made him awkward, but he held his ground.

"I don't know," he answered. "Will I have to call him father?"

"No, Drake," interposed Judge Alder. "Why should you? Yesterday I was the judge to you; today I am the same man, only happier—a lot happier. And you are still Drake Sherborne, the son of your father, Warner Sherborne, and of Rattling Run Fields. Nothing can change those two things."

Drake's troubled face broke into a whimsical smile.

"I know now, judge," he said. "I'm glad, almost as glad as mother."

No one had noticed the red flush which had glowed for a moment on Tom's cheek bones, or the water that had risen to his eyes, making him for an instant a pitiable object. He recovered himself, came forward and wished Eunice happiness with a finished courtliness that made the children stare and the judge wonder; but there was little time for speculation as to where Tom had learned his manners. There was supper to eat and packing to do, for Drake was to spend this last night of his holiday in the judge's house, where Eunice and Io were to take up their abode, leaving Tom, as before, in possession of Rattling Run Fields.

The judge, with Eunice, drove ahead, and the children in Tom's old chaise followed at a far more leisurely pace behind Alexander, once more astonishingly fat and incredibly sleek. During the ride, with Io standing at the dash and Drake sitting at his side, Tom grew gloomier and gloomier, finally giving vent to the following aspiration: "I wish I was a bear."

"Why, Tom?"

"Because," replied Tom, "the bear is a hibernating animal."

"Is he?" asked Io vaguely. "And is that something nice, Tom?"

"Very nice. It means he is an animal that will have no truck with winters, not on any account whatsoever. As soon as ever it gets cold and lonely he fills his belly, makes himself comfortable in a deep hole, and goes to sleep until the spring."

"Gee!" exclaimed Drake fervently. "I wish I was a bear too."

"But you won't be lonely, Tom," said Io after a moment's thought, "because I am going to have a pony and I'll come to see you every day."

"Who told you you were going to have a pony?" asked Drake.

"Nobody," replied Io calmly. "I told myself. I just thought of it."

At the moment when they were thus chatting, the judge was leading Eunice into the bedroom of his mother. She was very old and an invalid, but there was something in the frame of her face, made evident under the tightly drawn and almost transparent skin, which proclaimed her the source of the strength in her son.

"Mother," said the judge, "this is Eunice, of whom I have told you so much. We were married today."

"Let me look at you," said Mrs. Alder, reaching out. Eunice took the extended hand and knelt beside the bed. The old lady peered into her face. "Don't be frightened," she said presently. "I give you a good son."

Chapter 28

On the following morning the judge accompanied Drake to the station while Eunice went to enroll Io in a local school. Io kissed her brother good-by with a set face, but without a tear. Thanks to the preparation of the summer, or to some far deeper influence within herself, she did not look upon this separation as she had regarded Drake's treacherous flight. The impulse to follow him in all things was not necessarily dead, but it was under control, to remain henceforth a possession, not a master.

Just as the judge returned, he heard a low call from across the street. It was Eunice. He waited, and together they entered and went to the library. With the children gone the house was strangely still, and yet not empty or deadened, for each room in it seemed to have a subtle power of self-assertion, of animate life. Too little attention has been paid to the individuality of houses and rooms. Who ever thinks of a room as a mold to body and mind? And yet all men reflect in their souls the rooms in which they have lived; all men bend here and bulge there, little or much, according to the material horizons that have hemmed them in or hurled them to the peaks which transcend all walls.

Sitting in the library, with the judge before her, Eunice stared at the spot where she had sunk to the floor, overcome by that within her which had been permitted to find expression through no other channel save collapse.

The drone of summer called her eyes through the open windows to the inner garden—that garden so filled with trellised verdure that it seemed to drip with shade, sifting the brazen light of day, toning it to a soft radiance before it entered to the company of the somber yet friendly books. She turned and looked within. She perceived presently that the room knew no divisions. Here were not serried volumes on shelves, cool shadows, worn chairs and the judge's glowing eyes against a background of right-angled walls, each set apart from the other. No; all were one, an expression of a single whole. Gradually she possessed the truth that peace can be an element in which we may live by intention. She leaned back in her chair with a sense of immersion in a slow-moving flood of content, a suppliant for inclusion within its unity. How still everything was, and yet alive. How very still.

There came the jangling of a bell, a furious knocking, the front door flung open to crash and jar against the wall, the heavy steps of a man blundering into the parlor, returning to the hall, entering at the far end of the library. Mattis stood there for a moment, hatless, glaring, his hands hanging low at his sides. He came toward them, and as the light from the windows struck his face his bloodshot eyes showed red as garnets.

A rumbling was issuing from his throat which became distinguishable as hoarse words when he drew nearer. He was speaking to Eunice.

"Why did you do it?" he demanded. "Just tell me that! Why?"

The judge had arisen and sprung forward, but at Tryer's words, the exact repetition of those he himself had cried out to Elizabeth Banning years ago, he stopped suddenly, threw back his head and laughed. Eunice stared at him, wondering. Even Mattis was startled for an instant into a puzzled, vacuous expression.

"Oh, that!" he roared at the judge with abrupt understanding. "I ain't asking you why you done it. I know well enough. You done it to get even; but you've taken that which bears my mark, the mark you never put on a woman in all your born days."

The judge sobered, his face turned white and his eyes blazed.

194

"Stop! Another word of that and I'll hit you with anything I can reach!"

Tryer threw up his hands and waved them about in his gesture of a man fighting off bees. He did not wish to hear the judge, nor to fight him; his momentous business was with Eunice alone. She had not left her chair, and his great head sank between his shoulders as he thrust his face toward her. Sweat was trickling across his forehead and down his bronzed neck; his chest heaved like a bellows, and his words came out in gasps.

"Vic, you're my woman. Didn't you sign and seal it with your arms around my neck? 'Go away!' you says. 'Go away!' and like a fool I went, but I said I'd come back, and I did come back, as soon as ever Warner was under the ground. Didn't I tell you then you was my woman? Couldn't you wait? What I been doing all these months but standing by, working my head off for you and your kids, feeding you and them, making you into a lady and giving them their school? I was there, and you knew it. You're my woman. I put my mark on you afore you was growed, and it's a mark that never comes out. Get up, come out of that chair and away. To the devil with your marriage lines and the Judas judge."

"Eunice," said the judge rapidly, "when I go for him leave the room—lock yourself in somewhere—stay there."

"Stop, Will," said Eunice, without rising.

"Stand back!"

So quietly did she speak that he obeyed, confused by her calm into thinking he had been alarmed without reason. The two men yielded subconsciously to an arresting pause, but a pause of expectancy. They waited, their eyes fastened on Eunice.

"Stand where you are, Tryer."

She arose and placed herself directly before him. Her gaze met his bloodshot eyes squarely. He knew a wild instant of hope, and then a swift sinking of the heart. Her eyes, her face, all her erect body, were like a fixed wall of denial. Seconds passed, lengthening into moments. She did not move or speak. She could have been cruel had she permitted her eyes to wander over his person, but

195

she was content to remain completely impassive; and Tryer, ever as sensitive to atmosphere as a chameleon to color, needed no dagger to tell him where he stood.

His eyes broke away from her steady gaze and flickered up and down her figure, so securely poised, so fresh in its reacquired youth, so convincingly unattainable. From her they leaped to pass swiftly about the room, discovering it for the first time. Presently they dropped. As on that day when he had watched her from behind the elm, he stared down at his hands, at his heavy muddied boots, at his soiled shirt cuffs and hairy wrists. His shoulders slouched and the expression of bold audacity so habitual to his face suddenly broke and began to disintegrate. It was a terrible thing to see. Eunice's eyes became suffused. She turned quickly, picked up a book from the table beside her and left the room. To avoid looking at Mattis, the judge watched her go, and even after she had passed out he kept his gaze fixed on the door.

"Bill, I take back the Judas."

The judge looked around to find Tryer standing beside him with extended hand—a changed Tryer. Wisps of his shock of hair, usually standing at every rebellious angle, were fallen and plastered to his brow with drying sweat. In his eyes, his lips, in his whole face, was a peculiar unnamable suggestion of nakedness, a shameless yet innocent revealment of the stripped body of the soul. It was as though the vessel of his strength had been shattered by a blow and quickly emptied. He was like a giant tree with the heart riven out of it by lightning and when the judge saw that this crumbling wreckage of a tower of self-esteem was trying to smile, a lump rose in his throat and he felt such a surge of compassion as he had never before known. He seized the extended hand and held to it, though it remained limp in his grip.

"Tryer," he said, "brace your shoulders."

"My shoulders," repeated Mattis apathetically, but made no effort to comply. What strength he had he was pouring into the endeavor to make his lips smile. "I can't," he added presently.

"You can try, can't you?" demanded the judge.

"I can try," said Mattis, giving utterance to the fighting phrase which had nicknamed him, but in such a tone that the words seemed a denial of themselves, as if they, too, had become suddenly emptied. They accomplished one thing, however.

"I-Can-Try-Mattis-Tryer Mattis," he said, and smiled.

He freed his hand and turned to go, but the judge followed, praying for an inspiration; and it came before they reached the front door.

"Got your automobile here, Tryer?"

"Yes."

"I wish you'd drive me out to the works. Have you thought out a way to run in the new conveyor without a shutdown?"

For a moment Tryer's face remained vacant, then he frowned and the muscles of his jaws began to tighten.

"We can do it in three sections," he began, and went on, while they stood on the sidewalk beside the car, slowly gathering his thoughts, outlining his plans, making his points with increasing emphasis.

"Take me out to the plant," repeated the judge. "I want to go over that and some other things with you on the spot—all the things you've been growling to me about."

He entered an automobile for the first time in his life. For a swift mile he kept silence, absorbed with trying to measure the new sensation; then, finding himself at ease, he turned his head, looked at Tryer's gathered brows and took comfort.

"Tryer," he said presently, "I'm beginning to see things. I'm just learning to know that when you are right I am dead wrong. There's no halfway about it. We ought to put up a plant at Rattling Run that will make all the bricks in the world water at the mouth for our cement." Tryer drew a long, quivering breath and his shoulders slowly straightened.

The Lantern on the Plow

Chapter 29

There opened for Eunice a remarkable period of her life, and yet one which does not lend itself easily to narration because its flow was so even. She became for a time that rare thing—a secure woman. Mattis had long been merely a looming figure on the horizon of her past; now he had fallen below all her horizons as a harbinger of storm. In that role he would come no more. Io was in school by day, and new occupations and contacts made of her a very sleepy person by nightfall. Drake was away. Eunice could sit still for a little and look out at life. As the months passed she smiled more and more often, sometimes with only her eyes or only her lips, but on rare occasions with a glowing illumination of all her features. Certain events transpired, of course, to break this calm, one of which was of indisputable importance. But as for the rest, with what yardstick shall one measure the interest in mere happenings? Such, for instance, as the almost simultaneous passing of the judge's mother and Tom's ancient horse, Alexander, in the spring of 1904.

Here are two occurrences of a striking disparity. Is there a doubt as to which was the more important? There is—according to the point of view. The judge grieved genuinely for his mother, but to Io at ten and Drake at sixteen, her death meant nothing at all, occupying as it did but an infinitesimal point in their private histories as they sat spellbound on the steps of Rattling Run Fields and listened to Tom.

"Yes, sir," he asseverated, a solemn expression on his bearded face as of one who contemplates in recollection something prodigious, "no other horse ever did it before him. You see, it was this way: He grew fatter and fatter—solid. When you rubbed him down, press as hard as you might, you couldn't make a dent in him anywhere. I tried cutting down his feed, and he ate the manger and grew fatter than ever on that. One night he must of just gone up to the fence and pushed it down with settling his weight to it. Then is when he did the thing I'm telling you. He picked out the apple tree with the most blooms on it. Like a great bouquet it was, round and fat as himself, only sweeter smelling. He leaned up against the trunk of that tree, fixed his legs just so and died standing up. Stiff as a grand piano when I found him—yes, sir—standing up!"

Tom stared wide-eyed at the children and they wide-eyed at him. What was Mrs. Alder's death to Io? Nothing. But the picture of her supercilious friend Alexander, mountainously fat, sleek as a mirror, jet-black, miraculously upright in death, unique to the last as he leaned stiff-legged against the stem of a mighty, sweet-scented bouquet of sheltering apple blossoms—that picture would live as long as she; perhaps pass down to her children and her children's children.

This was the summer of Drake's return from his first year at school as a boarder; and owing to an exceptional circumstance, he proceeded, not to the judge's house but directly to Rattling Run Fields. With him went Io in charge of Nora, a maid who had been long in attendance on the late Mrs. Alder, but who was now delivered hand and foot to a sort of gaping allegiance to her new charge. She did not so much minister to Io as stand by and gasp.

The exceptional circumstance and the event of indisputable importance previously mentioned were one and the same, and are summed up in the advent of William Alder, Jr., as son and heir to the judge. Presumably all babies create a commotion upon arrival, but the effect of the coming of this particular infant seems to present some unusual features. Let it be conceded that Drake took only one look, turned his back and dismissed the newcomer with the statement that he was too red; that the judge, troubled by what seemed a first close contact with the miraculous, went to war in his mind with the fact that in spite of his sensations millions of other men were also fathers; that Io, filled with a devouring curiosity, asked all those questions which have stumped and convulsed endless generations. Concede all that, and then look at Eunice, regarding her latest born as something phenomenal, in some subtle manner disconnected from her own or anybody else's past.

Here was a child who arrived out of a cerulean sky into an untroubled bourn; who came more to assuage than to demand, completing the empty gift of peaceful hours. Nothing to do but attend upon his needs; bathe him, clothe him and, with caught breath and a gasping prayer, watch him grow. "Not too fast; be a baby; stay just as a baby for a while!" There had been an element of fierceness, almost primitive, in her possession of Drake and Io, but not a vestige of it tinged her attitude now. She shared this wonder, this animated plaything—and playmate. She was one of an admiring circle who regarded him with spellbound eyes, and at his cry she would look around with a quizzical uncertainty before snatching him up, as if she needed to be reassured that he was hers. Behold Io and her mother alone with the baby.

"Mother, when I'm thirteen will you tell me where you got him?"

Eunice, a puzzled look in her eyes: "Why, I'd tell you now if I knew. I'm not quite sure he's mine. What do you think?"

"I think he's my half brother, and so does Nora. If he is, then he belongs half to me, doesn't he?"

"No," said Eunice solemnly. "He belongs, I suppose, half to the judge and half to me. Out of my half, you and Drake get each a third, and a third of a half is one-sixth of a whole. So when he gets to be sixty you will own ten years of him."

"If you don't mind," said Io with her most winsome smile, "I'll take the first ten years."

"Oh, no!" cried Eunice, gathering up William Alder, Jr., taking both his crinkly feet in one of her hands and staring into his unfathomless eyes.

"Not the first ten!"

Strange complexities are women; they feel the truth and talk nonsense.

Enough has been said to indicate that the judge's home was a happy one, in rare accordance with its aspect from without. To see him pass up the walk from the maple-fronded street, pause halfway and bare his head, was to perceive a man in an unconscious act of reverence to which halting tongue could never have given expression. A big square house with lowered wings, looking like a hen covering her brood. Never had looked to him like that before. High white pilasters flanking the door, giving it the dignity and strength of a portal. Spaced upon the lawn, two great blobs of box, round as the terrestrial sphere in which their immemorial roots were set. Such were the stately adjuncts of an unobtrusive peace like unto that which reigned in Judge Alder's face.

There is a cruelty in contrasts which transcends the odiousness of comparisons, and it is more than unkind to leap from contemplation of the haven which had given Eunice refuge to a glance at the latest of the residences of Tryer Mattis, for he permitted neither box nor grass to grow beneath his feet. He built to sell—there was nothing he would not sell; and upon looking at some of the monstrosities of cement and gewgaws of which he disposed at a profit, one is tempted to add that there was nothing he could not sell. Here was the contradiction of the man at its worst. He who could tell the period of a bit of airy furniture with his eyes shut, put up half a dozen houses hideous to behold by reason of the very factor which made them attractive to himself and to certain others—namely, their reenforced strength. Ivy cannot hide them; they will never rot nor bow to anything short of dynamite.

In one of these unlovely settings Tryer lived with his two children and a maid of all work. His bearing toward Jimmy was that of any father toward a rather colorless son of twelve, but not so his attitude toward his daughter Lessie. How explain that this hulk of a man, who vaguely perceived in his daughter the' struggling embodiment of all the undeveloped qualities of greatness which he himself contained, had been goaded into detesting the sight of her? Who had goaded him? Lessie.

By a not unusual twist of inherited blood she had certain man-like attributes, among them a sense of elemental justice which led her to take uncompromising sides with her mother. Unfortunately, she had been old enough to understand the indiscreet and pitifully ineffectual rantings of Elizabeth against Tryer's casual infidelities; and where he was apt to behold himself in the light of a conquering hero, as she grew older she saw only the talk of the town to whom all skirts were alike. Deeper, however, than this clear-sighted scorn was embedded another dominating motive—she knew that she was the daughter of an unloved wife. Precocious? Yes. Well, given the necessary environment, all girls are precocious. But there was more to Lessie than the premature development of the faculties of perception. She was Tryer Mattis' own daughter, and she despised and hated him.

Starting with that premise, studying her strong, well-formed nose, her almond-shaped eyes and her mobile mouth, it takes little effort to imagine with what slicing words she managed to unflesh him in his own estimation or with what barbed darts it was her wont to arouse him to impotent fury. Afraid of him? Not since babyhood; certainly not since she had shrewdly instilled in his equally shrewd mind the belief that her ambition was to drive him to the point of doing her a permanent physical injury, thus placing in her hands an everlasting two-edged sword. One hesitates to state that both she and Tryer found morbid enjoyment in these bitter conflicts, not because the assertion is untrue but because such psychological phenomena are not easily explained even when understood.

The fact remains that when Tryer, after the shock of losing Eunice, recovered through the avenue of hard work successfully accomplished to an empty physical well-being, and plunged into an orgy of ignoble conquests to salve his self-esteem, Lessie was stirred to such a white heat of anger that she advanced on him, tore open his coat, and, before he realized her purpose, snatched out his well-filled wallet. With trembling hands which he dared not seize she opened it, pulled out a wad of papers—memoranda, notes written in illiterate hands, souvenirs, railway passes—and scattered them scornfully on the floor. She sorted out all the money, flung the empty case in his face and walked out of the door, never again to reënter it. She was seventeen years old.

Drake, returning from graduation and the passing with honors of his entrance examinations to college, stopped for a chat with his mother and Io, and then proceeded as a matter of course to Rattling Run Fields, where the preceding summer, owing to the fortuitous advent of William Alder, Jr., had definitely established him. Eunice watched him go with a little twist to her lips and an unreadable gleam in her eyes. She was wondering if, baby or no baby, things would have been any different—if she would have dared give battle to Rattling Run Fields in any case.

"Drake," said Io as she drove him out to the farm in her pony cart, "do you remember Lessie Mattis?"

"No—yes," said Drake. "Yes, I remember her. Long nose and yellow hair."

"Well," said Io, "she's run away from her father. I guess they quarreled awfully, and perhaps she didn't like him."

Drake smiled.

"Perhaps she didn't," he agreed.

An hour later he was in conference with Tom Bodley.

"Well, Tom, what's the news? What's happened?"

"Nothing," replied Tom, out of a subdued glow of content. "Nothing around here to mention. All folks has got to talk about when they ain't working is that Tryer Mattis fought once too often with that girl of his and she run off."

"Yes, I heard about that," said Drake indifferently.

"Well, it's anybody's secret," commented Tom. "I'll say that for her. She's got so little to hide she does all her talking to him by wire, and he sends the money by return post. Thinking back, I guess he's downright glad to be shut of her. Queer girl. You can't rightly talk to girls; they don't know how; but I would of liked to of talked to her more than to her mother or even Tryer at his best."

Drake's interest was aroused.

"Why?" he asked wonderingly.

"Because she's queer," said Tom placidly. "Never pass up a chance to talk to anyone that's queer—queer being the vernacular for original."

"What do you know about the vernacular, you old wine barrel? Come on out. Let's go over the place—every inch of it."

They came upon Io conversing with the annual calf, which she promptly abandoned to follow them. Presently she thrust her hand into Drake's and left it there when his fingers closed lightly upon it. The three wandered from point to point, Tom showing what he had done in the way of cleaning things up, and Drake busy with speculation as to just where and how he might best apply the savings from his slender allowance.

"Drake," said Io, breaking into his reverie, stirring her hand and gripping his fingers with all her strength.

"What is it?"

"I want to stay here all day and all night. Please, Drake; please. Perhaps tomorrow too."

While his senses had been apparently unconscious of her, the small hand in his had been doing its work. He looked down at her eager face and found there a note which rang true to the predominant chord in his own heart.

"This is your home and mine, Io. Don't ever forget it. I guess you can stay here whenever you like later on, but I don't know about tonight—not without mother saying so. So you trot along back."

A few hours later Tom, as he prepared supper, remarked that Io must have taken a snack before she went. At nine o'clock, when he and Drake were seated on the front steps laying plans for the morrow, the judge, with Eunice beside him, drove up and came to a halt before them.

"Where's Io, Drake?" asked Eunice in a low voice.

"Io!" cried Drake, springing to his feet.

"Why, she went back hours ago!"

"Are you sure?"

"No; I'm only sure I sent her. Tom——"

Tom was already on his way to the barn and acknowledged Drake's call only with a grunt over his shoulder. Presently he returned.

"Cart's in the barn," he said; "pony watered, fed and bedded, and I guess Io is too. I told Drake I seen signs of her having took a snack."

With Drake leading the way, Eunice and the judge entered the house and went upstairs. The moon was striking at a long slant into the room which had been the children's and now was Drake's. On a chair were Io's little dress, petticoat and stockings, neatly folded; beneath it her shoes. On the big bed, lost and yet not lost in its midst, was Io herself, one bare arm outthrown, the other doubled beneath the dark blot of her disheveled hair. She was asleep, immersed, profoundly still.

There was a long silence. No one moved, but Eunice's eyes took on a startled look as they wandered along the walls from bed to window, from window to low ceiling and door. How strange was everything, and yet how poignantly familiar, embedded and rooted in recollection! Take a trunk and pack into it old clothes, things you don't mind mussing; it becomes bottomless, miraculously capacious. This house was like that, packed with memories, old memories; for Drake and Io all the memories since the world began; for her—— By a visible effort she broke the current of her thought just short of that other room and Warner, and of the flakes of snow like great white tears. She turned to Drake.

"Where will you sleep?" she asked quietly.

"Oh, Tom will fix me up," replied Drake, never taking his eyes from Io. "I can bunk anywhere."

On the way home Eunice said half to herself, half to the judge, "Is it possible that both of them love a place more than their mother?"

He frowned and did not hurry to answer.

"That isn't right, Eunice," he said finally; "you've missed something. Just think a minute. When they are in that house those children don't feel as if they were away from you. They—well, they can't."

"That's so," said Eunice slowly, accepting the new point of view with an effort. "To them, it's home; to me it's just the prison from which I've escaped. No; not a prison—something equally terrible, but alive. Now I'm talking nonsense again—like long ago."

The judge touched her hand, but said nothing more.

Chapter 30

If the attitudes of a thousand assorted mothers toward their daughters between the age of thirteen and the day of marriage could be run through a clarifier and exposed to the mind's naked eye, a curious world would gasp at the variegated exhibit, and decide that "mother," after all, is not a generic term. The experiences of boys under maternal observation run, for the most part, along fixed parallel lines; but those of their sisters present a crisscross design amazing in its diversity. The reason is not far to seek.

Grant that men are readable and women unreadable, even to each other—is that the answer?

Only part of it. Behind that generality lies a morass of complexities out of which we may pick the tendency of every mother to assume that her daughter's girlhood is one with her own; that the same fears, questions, impulses and dangers which beset the path of her own youth attend the adolescence and budding into womanhood of her girl. The assumption is just true enough to add bewilderment to confusion. The truth remains that a mother may know all the ins and outs of all her boys, while in some one girl, any girl, there persists an inner circle of deportment utterly beyond comprehension, even though it remain within the reach of love.

"Jane, Mary, or Alice, how could you do such a thing? I don't understand. Why, if I had ever——"

209

They have said it always; they will say eternally, oblivious of the fact that the greatest revolutions pass unperceived by the very divisions of the human family which effect them—those people who change their mode of life, adopt new methods, accept inventions, discard internal motives in the face of the exterior pressure of material progress, hand a new world every so often to a new generation, and only then pause to gasp at the result.

Along these lines, it is true that the factors which were to make Io what she was at nineteen and Drake what he was at twenty-five were not the same as the influences which made Eunice what she was to be at forty-six, even though the space of the intervening years was identical, for Io and Drake had not helped blindly to form the new order; they were of it. Look back at that decade, the years between 1903 and 1913. No equal period in the course of Puritanism, or possibly in the history of the world, was ever more crammed with the innovations which form the warp and woof of spiritual and physical revolt.

But as regards the relations between Io and her mother, both were fortunate, owing to the very circumstances which had given to Vic Teller, and later to Eunice Sherborne, an inner life of storm, placed in a hard and ungracious setting. No mortal can pass through genuine tribulation without being a gainer, at least in character; and when suffering is supported through a period of years, attaining to the plane of abnegation, a broad liberality toward conduct is an almost inevitable result. Such people are most apt to have the steadfast vision which draws the line between what you do and what you are, without ever confusing the issue.

While Eunice was still engaged in wonder over the possession of William Alder, Jr., she awoke to the fact that another budding development was demanding her attention, storming the citadel of her dreamy-eyed security. Io, the ebullient, small seat of an astonishing amount of daring, stepped forth from the chrysalis of childhood and set her pointed foot upon a threshold. Here was a matter that called for immediate concentration of all the powers of love and understanding on the part of Eunice. Life as a blissful monotone ceased quite suddenly, leaving her with a dual preoccupation.

She remembered the day when the judge had come upon the children in the swimming hole of Rattling Run, and the echo of the words she had spoken to him then came back to her now:

"Io is unusual. Perhaps you've noticed sometimes I'm afraid for her—afraid, I mean, of what she might do."

That was the fear she was feeling afresh; but never for a moment did it occur to her to waver in her allegiance to what Io herself was. She appealed to the judge again when they were alone at night in the library.

"Will, Io is fourteen."

"Bless my soul! Is she?"

They were silent for a time, summoning her before them, not in person but in presence—a thing easy to do, though the resulting vision was by no means easy to comprehend. For the presentation in thought or words of Io's stride from a child into girlhood could be but an elusive grasping at things forever unseized, an exposition by flashes of a vivid portrait, unseen of itself, and veiled from others by trailing mists and moving shadows. Body and mind, she was the dwelling place of an eternal question; and thus, nebulously, they saw her.

"I don't wish her to go to college," continued Eunice presently, "unless she demands it later; but in the meantime she needs something we can't give her here. I don't know just how to say it—launching, perhaps. She's got to learn things, get acquainted with what is usual, tame what nobody else can tame for her, perhaps hurt herself a little. Oh, can't you tell me what I'm trying to say?"

"Certainly I can," replied the judge after a thoughtful pause. "You mean that this present world is the one she has to live in and the sooner she gets acquainted with it the better. Why not send her away to boarding school and see what that does?"

"I'm afraid," said Eunice. "There are so many roads she might take without my knowing anything about it until it's too late."

The judge eyed her quizzically. It was on his tongue to say that Io would turn to untraveled and unimagined paths in any case, but he refrained.

"Well," he suggested, "there's Myrtle Manor only ten miles away; one of those finishing schools. It can hardly be classified as an institution of learning; but it draws a fine class of girls. Under Miss Drew it has climbed to a rather high standard. Why not try that?"

Thus it was arranged, and a twelvemonth later another problem thrust its head above the even flow of events: Drake became of age in the July subsequent to the completion of his junior year at college. On the day of his majority the judge piled certain ledgers into the back of his buggy and drove out to the homestead, where he found its young master ruefully regarding the insignificant improvements he had been able to initiate. The judge made the appropriate greetings heartily, but with a certain solemnity, and then suggested that they repair to the sturdy deal table in the kitchen of so many momentous associations.

"Drake," he began, "with the exception of that little talk we had years ago on schooling as the master key, I've never said a word to you as to what you were going to be or to do with yourself. Do you want to know why?"

"Yes," said Drake.

"Because," said the judge, with a half-rueful smile, "you seemed to be so all-fired sure about it. I've never seen even a question in your eye. Now this isn't helpfulness or anything like that—it's plain curiosity, and you needn't answer if you don't feel like it; but what are you going to do?"

"Do?" repeated Drake, gazing at him with the trapped expression of one who is at a loss for words, and yet knows exactly what he would like to say. "Why, judge, don't you know? There's never been any secret about it, or any fussing in my mind, and I don't suppose it will amount to much with you, but I'm just going to be around here." He made an awkward gesture with one arm toward outdoors.

"It sounds kind of small when we're talking careers and things like that, I expect, but it's the only plan I've got. I can't explain why, but I just don't feel the need of any other at present."

The judge nodded with his understanding air of accepting another man's viewpoint at face value.

"Well," he said, "there's no hurry one way or the other, owing to a big enterprise in which you are vitally concerned but in which you have never shown the slightest interest. I mean the cement works."

Drake's face flushed slightly, and he frowned, not in exasperation, but as if he himself were puzzled to know the sources of his antipathy to the only exploitation of the farm which had ever brought in cash in appreciable quantities.

"As a matter of fact," continued the judge, "there's no reason why you should take an active interest in the Rattling Run Cement Company. That's an extraordinary statement under the circumstances, and it calls for proof. Grit your teeth, boy. I'm going to bother you for the whole of this morning, and then steal you for dinner tonight. Now listen! Every man has an obligation to himself and toward others to know where he stands in money matters. First of all, here's the proof that it makes no difference whether you concern yourself with the Rattling Run Company or not. Read the thing through twice before you speak."

Drake took the paper which the judge handed him and read it; the first time solemnly, the second with a deepening smile in his eyes and on his lips. While he perused the famous contract with Tryer Mattis the judge studied him, and was content. The boy was good to look at—clean, supple and strong as a whiplash. The features which on that long-ago day in the court room had seemed overrefined had lost their starved look. They were still clear-cut and startlingly reminiscent of Warner Sherborne; but of a Warner Sherborne who ate well, slept better and never by any chance found the day so short that he had to plow by lantern light. Drake looked up and laughed silently into the judge's eyes.

"It is one of the most remarkable documents I have ever read," he said. "Tryer must have been gagged and strapped to a keg of powder when you handed him the pen and pointed to the dotted line with a lighted match."

"Well, he wasn't gagged," asserted the judge, smiling. "He called it what he has called it ever since—a legal straitjacket. Now, Drake, we're coming to the meat of this interview. The court assigned the three thousand dollars flat to your mother for the support of you children. As far as you are concerned that arrangement comes to an end today. The proceeds from royalties have been divided in three equal parts from the beginning, and in these ledgers you will find just what has been done with your share.

"Roughly speaking, you can draw your check in five figures and have it honored. Some of your dividends have gone for education, of course; but you'll find all that properly set down; also you will learn that your income for this year will be something over four thousand dollars. The company is only now recovering from what the panic of 1907 did to it—but not to you Sherbornes, thanks to the fact that whether cement is selling at seventy cents or at its present price of a dollar-twenty, your royalty is fixed at two cents on every barrel produced. With luck, we should have the new plant in operation by a year from now, and it's to be a humdinger. It will triple our output and your income. Now get at the books."

"Not me," said Drake, whose eyes were already dreamy with thinking of what he could do to Rattling Run Fields with ten thousand dollars. "I'll take your word for everything you've said."

"You will not I" cried the judge, bringing his fist down with a crash. "You think that's a compliment and I call it a colossal impertinence—worse than that. It's the vapid sort of thing that makes every honest man shrink from the trap of guardianship. You'll give me your word that you'll go over every transaction in these books which concerns you and your mother and sister, or you'll find another trustee tomorrow."

Drake stared at him, first with amazement and then with comprehension. His cheeks flushed, but his eyes remained steady.

"I never thought of that side of it, sir. I apologize for being a blockhead and I give you my word to start in now and go through the books to the bitter end."

"Fine!" said the judge as he arose. "You know, of course, that I was yelling only to wake you up. I'll go out and hang around for a bit in case there's anything you want to ask."

Chapter 31

The judge had been sitting with his back to the kitchen entrance. He turned, started to go out, and stopped stock-still. Tipped against the wall beside the open door, in one of the familiar hickory chairs, sat a young man, hands in the pockets of flannel trousers, soft shirt wide open at the throat, and wearing on his face a nonchalant expression which was negatived by the sparkle in his eyes. He seemed considerably older than Drake, more by reason of his poise than of any evidence of age. As a matter of fact, measured in days, the difference could be no more than two years. His hair was dark and of that crisp variety which clings closely to the head, requiring only infrequent visits to the barber; but his eyes were gray and his complexion fair under the tan of the summer sun and the weathering of wind and rain.

The judge cast a backward questioning glance, but Drake was already absorbed in his task; then he looked once more at the stranger, who, catching his eye, nodded sideways, dropped the chair noisily forward, arose, stretched, and then led the way into the garden.

Arrived there, he said, "You mustn't think it's Drake who is queer. You see, I'm insisting on making all my own introductions this season, just like some girls insist on choosing their own frocks. I feel that some people aren't becoming to me."

"Is it permissible to ask who you are?" inquired the judge with mock solemnity.

"Oh, yes," replied the stranger quite frankly. "I'm Robert Colter, and you're the man I've been hanging around here to see."

"I trust I don't disappoint you, Mr. Colter," said the judge. At different times he had met a variety of Drake's friends from school or college enjoying the haphazard hospitality of Rattling Run Fields; but he was sure he had never before chanced on this young man, who was of a type not easily forgotten.

"You are one of Drake's classmates, I presume," he ventured.

"Not his classmate," said Colter, taking careful aim with his toe at a green apple lying on the baked clay of the yard. "Not by two years." He kicked, shooting the apple straight forward and causing it to splatter against the house. He looked around at the judge with a pleased smile. "I've been wanting to do that ever since last summer."

They walked away from the house, the judge now in the lead.

Presently he asked, "And why did you wish to see me?"

"Well, I'll tell you," said Colter. "Because I was so unfortunate as to be the first to call Drake Mary after you told him what to do about it."

"I see." The judge's lips twitched. "And what happened actually made you like him?"

"What happened," said Colter, flushing and smiling at the same time, "was that he practically undressed me with his teeth. Didn't bite me, mind you; only tore off my clothes. It was funny. They had to bring out a blanket." His face sobered, and he added, "Yes, it made me like him."

"Come this way," said the judge as they entered the wood. "Here—this is the very log we were sitting on when I gave him that advice."

They sat down, Colter on the ground with his shoulders braced against the log so that his eyes were thrown up into the inviting yet impenetrable foliage.

"There's something about him," he said, without troubling to mention Drake by name; "something evident and unreadable. I get the same fun out of watching him think as I do out of watching an oak grow."

The judge glanced at his face dubiously and found it grave.

"Slow fun, I should say," he ventured.

"Sometimes," admitted Colter; "but it all depends how you look at a tree. Why, I've had an oak reach a limb around the world and push me off just such a log as this before I knew what was happening. The humor of even a friendly oak is a bit heavy."

The judge was pleased with his company; he stretched out his legs and made himself comfortable.

"Well, what did you do about it?"

"Nothing. Lost my head completely, and found it again. Learned when not to sit on a log. But what I really wanted to tell you about this Drake business is that probably no one in all the school felt what I felt, watching him and his kid sister. I'm sure I saw things that nobody else saw. Can't tell you exactly, but it was like this: I would have done anything for either one of the pair—anything. And yet—— There you are. We're funny things, all of us. Really wanting to be friends with him, the best I could think of was to call him Mary the first time we met face to face, and get pushed off a log for my pains."

"I know what you mean," said the judge after a pause, "by feeling ready to do anything for that pair. I have felt that way more than once myself. The strange part of it is, they seem about as little in need of guidance or assistance as any couple on earth. What do you make of them? Begin with Drake."

"Well," complied Colter, "I'd say he's the only boy I ever knew who hasn't any questions in him. He learns the next thing and does the next thing in front of him with exactly the same air. Something says to him, 'It's there; attend to it.' He never was as young as I am; but he'll always be younger. Chew on that; I don't know what it means. All of him—each corpuscle in his blood—knows exactly where it's going. But get this, judge: Drake couldn't tell you where he's headed; he only knows he is headed. Not like the rest of us."

"Now Io."

"Io," breathed Colter, his eyes brightening, and at the same time taking on a distant focus.

"What a name, eh? Makes you look for stars and green meadows. If Drake has no questions, Io is all question, from head to toe and back again. That's where they've got me, those two: Drake like a permanent oak and his kid sister like an arrow overshooting all marks. She can't come to earth because there isn't enough earth."

"Finally we come to you," said the judge with the smiling directness which had won many a confidence. "What are you doing and where are you going? Do you know?"

"More or less," replied Colter. "Nothing like Drake, you understand; because he's never had to think anything out. At present I'm taking a post-graduate course in a combination of the arts and the humanities. My own recipe."

"Are you going to teach?" prompted the judge.

"Hardly; nothing like that. I'm going to breed a double strain of Morgans and Percherons."

The judge straightened to those words, and then relaxed.

"I advise you," he said, "to talk to Tryer Mattis on what the motor car is doing to the horse."

"I have," said Colter laconically. "That's why."

The judge frowned.

"You startled me into forgetting the arts and the humanities. May I ask wherein they are going to aid you in the fulfillment of your ambition?"

"You may," replied Colter, "but I'm surprised that you should. Schooling, judge, is bigger than anything between book covers. It is the master key to happiness. Out of a thousand men, only one boy took the trouble to get it in time."

"Yes, yes," said the judge, smiling broadly. "Go on."

"Well, to be happy on a stock farm I've got to have something to think about besides spavins and spalling hoofs. I'm laying in a mind cellar, and why the devil I should tell you about all these things, never having mentioned them to anybody else, is beyond me."

"Beyond you, perhaps," said the judge, rising, "but safe."

He decided that he liked Colter and invited him to the dinner in honor of Drake's coming of age.

"I'm truly sorry," said Colter, "but these clothes and a tooth-brush are all I have with me."

"I'm not above wearing the same outfit at a strictly family dinner," countered the judge, "nor is Drake; so that's settled. Only don't forget to make your own introductions."

Occasionally life throws into one's path some person through whose eyes one can see more clearly than through one's own. The judge had this feeling in regard to Robert Colter. Perhaps it was because they were in agreement, though they reached conclusions along different lines of deduction. However that may be, the events which transpired at Rattling Run Fields subsequent to Drake's receipt of the liquid portion of his patrimony frequently were made clear through Colter's casual comments.

Drake plunged into an activity which almost wrecked his senior year at college. He managed to get his degree by a narrow margin, and returned home on the same day. He could scarcely have given an intelligible outline of what he was doing, but each inception was to the imaginative vision of Colter a revelation.

"Something," he said darkly to the judge, "is growing on Rattling Run Fields."

The judge answered half absently and fully as enigmatically. "Perhaps it's Rattling Run Fields itself that's stirring."

Ten thousand dollars, spent judiciously and at comfortable intervals so that each morsel of improvement could be rolled on the tongue of appreciation, were working marvels in and about the homestead. The original tower of the house which faced due south eventually became an angle with a long low wing parallel-ing the road to the westward and another low wing running east, overlooking the gully of Rattling Run. The first of these additions was Drake's own haunt—an unbroken, heavily raftered hall of leisure and entertainment, with a huge fireplace at one end and a hidden narrow stairway running up to his bedroom at the other; the second comprised a suite of small rooms tacitly assigned to Io.

It was characteristic of Drake that he never said, "Io, these are your rooms. I have put up the walls and the roof and there's going to be hot and cold water; as for the rest, you may do what you like." That was not his way. He had left it to her to realize her acquisition and take possession of it piecemeal, much as he had attained to his own broad freedom.

As for the beaten plot which surrounded the house, it was plowed, cultivated and manured with an extravagance such as never had been lavished on the surrounding fields. Then it was cut up into plots and used as a testing ground for every variety of grass seed on the market. A selection having been made, Tom had to plow it all up again in the spring and sow it for a lawn. During this process not a single one of the gnarled trees or stunted shrubs was harmed or moved.

Noting that the healthiest bush on the place was a small clump of box, Drake said, "Tom, we'll have to grow a hedge of that from nursery stock. Straight along the road for a hundred yards, measuring from the bridge in the dip, then turn it at a right angle for fifty yards north. Everything inside of that will be the homestead garden—roses, shrubs, grass, the old cedars, of course. Can't you see it, with Rattling Run shutting us off on the east and the whole place banking up on the orchard and the wood?"

Tom stared at him.

"No, I can't; and what's more, you won't, either. Are you crazy, Drake? How much of a box hedge do you think you'll have in fifty years' time?"

Drake in his turn stared at Tom.

"Well, what's the matter with you?" he asked gravely. "What's fifty years?"

"Tom," said Colter, who happened to be present, "look out! You're sitting on a log!"

Chapter 32

Throughout ancient and modern times so much stress has been laid on the sweetness of girls of sixteen in general that it becomes necessary to limn a picture of Io at that age with especial care. How paint her? How shout in print that she was not sweet in the accepted sense of the overworked word, and yet leave, even with those who run and read, an impression of allure, fresh and clean as the first beam of light that streaks the dawn?

Still the arrow, still the embodiment of a slender, straight shaft from head to heel, she nevertheless presented a flexible contour so delicate that could some master of the etcher's needle have drawn her, the art within him would have cried out for a single line, thin as a hair, adumbrating her rounded head, cutting the sharp sweep of her low brow, the piquant turn of her chin, the lift of her shoulder, the pointed curve of her adolescent breasts and swiftly diminishing descent of her rounded limbs. Bald words. There are times when they will not bend to the expression of a curve; there are times when one would wish that they could throw shadows and leave them behind, providing thus a pigment wherewith one might attain to the lightness of vision itself, and echo the glimmering beauty of things seen, yet forever unsnared by pen or brush. Only thus might one hope to translate the image of Io at sixteen—pastel, silhouette, cameo—from its place against the misty wall of memory.

223

And yet, in her no less than in Drake, there was a hidden strength; something established, immovable; something which formed the basis upon which were cut the scintillating facets of her presence. Swift were the movements of her feet and hands, and no less swift the reactions of her mind, lifting to the silent echo in her eyes. One saw there that what others dared she might dare if she would, but behind what would have seemed to Eunice and the judge, for all their leniency, reckless extravagancies of deportment, there remained the foundation of all daring, the courage for instant and adamantine refusal.

To take so fantastical a gem and set it against the heavy foil of Jimmy Mattis was to throw it into startling relief. At this time Jimmy was nineteen, and to those who knew his father, it seemed that the youth of Tryer Mattis must be walking the world anew. As far as physical appearance was concerned, Jimmy was Tryer all over again—blue eyes, round in moments of astonishment and narrowing to calculation, sandy hair rising in a rebellious shock, long limbs and heavy bones, clumsy at times and surprisingly agile at others. One difference persisted—Tryer's youth had been promiscuous in its affections, Tryer's boyhood had known no Io.

Jimmy had left school and gone to work for the Rattling Run Cement Company. His father would have liked to make him a salesman, one of that Rattler pack of trained bloodhounds of commerce who, once put upon the scent of a ringed raccoon in the shape of a contract, never let up until they had treed it or so torn it that it was of little use to a rival.

But Jimmy had rebelled for two reasons. In the first place, even his heavy limbs were far more supple than his tongue, and he knew it. The other reason lay in the fact that he would put up with no employment which carried him out of easy reach of Myrtle Manor and Io Sherborne.

Myrtle Manor as a select finishing school exists no more; but at that time it occupied a corner of peculiar formation in the principal town of the three counties, and a building which was a chaste example of what the Colonial artificer could do with nothing but blood-red brick, shutters of solid wood and white trimmings for his material. On its easterly exposure, this edifice stood four stories high; but on the southern side, owing to a sharp rise in the level of the ground, the stories diminished to three, and then to two, and finally to one. In addition, to accommodate the rush of prosperous years, a two-storied wing had been thrown out to the north which reached to the edge of a wood whose shadows descended to meet and mix with those of trees that interlaced their tops above an abandoned raceway.

Within the triangle thus formed at the back of the building was a hanging garden, hidden from the public eye because it lay at the level of the top of the high sustaining wall which coincided with the line of the street. Here the trailing periwinkle which gave its name to Myrtle Manor ran riot, leaped the wall in a wave and hung in festoons which played tricks with the hats of passers-by. Within the garden proper a single Judas tree raised in springtime the vivid column of its pink reproach above a tangle of ornamental shrubs which had escaped the pruner's shears to mingle with rambling rose and grapevine. The fragrant thicket thus composed swept northward until it met the barrier of a mass of rhododendrons.

Io's room was located at the end of the upper story of the low wing which looked toward the wood and the raceway. Any casual observer would have judged the distance from the ground a sufficient barrier to escapades, even after noting the long level branch of a maple which stretched across within easy reach of her window. But to Io that limb spelled temptation. The very thought of casting herself upon it and then clambering out along its supple length to the end, which hung above the center of the patch of rhododendrons, seemed to demand the venture. It was she who told Jimmy Mattis of the branch, and then, angered by the slowness of wit which could not read all her implication, commanded him to a tryst in the garden as soon as he should hear the striking of the gong which spelled lights out for the school.

Jimmy came, waited, and finally supplied himself with a pocketful of acorns wherewith he began a discreet bombardment of

Io's open window. At last the dark nimbus of her hair appeared beneath the raised sash. A white hand came out of the dark as if either to sustain or detain her. She struck it aside. Once she had taken her decision, she did not pause. An instant more and she stood upon the window sill, slender arms outthrown, her fingers touching lightly the brick walls on either side of her.

She could have climbed out cautiously, but catching sight of the blot of Jimmy's face, strained, white and staring, she yielded to an impulse of mischief, pretended to fall, and threw her body across the limb with such violence as to produce an alarming rustle of all its leafy branches. Jimmy gasped, started to groan, but stopped. Io was laughing softly, a mere wisp of sound. Presently she whispered to him.

"Jimmy, can you reach the end of the limb?"

He went to its extremity, put up his hands, but dared not leap in the dark for fear of making a noise. Undaunted, Io crept down the limb, breathing in little gasps and chuckling as she went. At last he could seize the branch. She dropped to the ground. They stood and looked at each other. Afraid to talk so near the house lest they be heard, and yet not wishing to go away, doubtful as to whether the return to the room would be made as easily as the escape, they said nothing. After standing for a long time in an aimless silence Io turned, raised her hands, and whispered "Lift me up."

He stooped, threw his arm around her stiffened knees and lifted her high. She caught the limb, and at once was aware that this was no laughing matter. She swarmed along it slowly, resting from time to time until she came opposite the window. Reaching out as she lay jackknifed over the branch, she found she could touch the sill, but to no purpose.

"Jennie," she whispered, "are you awake? Give me your hand."

"I can't," quavered a tremulous voice on the verge of nervous tears. "I'm afraid. Oh, oh, Io!"

"Hush!" breathed Io.

Holding to a thin branch, she stood up, balanced for a moment and then took the short step to the sill. She caught the sash, jumped

226

into the room and disappeared from sight without so much as a good-by or even a wave of the hand to Jimmy.

Once performed, the feat became easy. Because she knew Jimmy so well; because it was so easy for her to see him during the summer months, her conscience troubled her much less than if these secret trysts had been with a stranger; but even with the commonplace Jimmy, she soon found that there was excitement in creeping through the blackness of the rhododendron thicket down over the brow of the hill to where they could watch the raceway and still be out of hearing both of the house and of the water. Here they could talk in murmuring voices, giving vent to those monosyllabic utterances which were even then beginning to characterize the conversation of the first of the generations of revolution.

Not every night of the spring did Io take it into her head to meet Jimmy, but scarcely an evening passed that he did not climb into the garden and give her some signal of his presence—the squawk of a catbird disturbed, a tossed acorn, or a peculiar whistle which he had been at great pains to teach her. It would have been easy for Io to return his signal in some manner, indicating her intention to come or not to come, but from the very first she never took the trouble. Poor Jimmy would stand for long minutes, lengthening sometimes into an hour, wondering if she were in her darkened room or if perhaps she were paying some surreptitious visit within the house.

Even when she condescended to meet him he never knew what might be her mood. There were times when her long silence made his heart beat fast, when he felt as though she included him, carrying him with her on the flights of her fancy, as she lay flat on her back, her eyes wide open, staring up into the blotched tracery of the leaves against the sky. There were other times when her silence seemed to whip him with small stinging lashes, an effect which she produced without so much as looking at him. On these occasions he shrank into himself as though he had been caught out on a night of sleet and rain. He grew miserable and more miserable, until Io would turn on him, accuse him of spoiling everything and desert him while the evening was still young.

He was not a particularly brilliant boy, but such intelligence as he possessed was of that shrewd brand which lies on the border between cleverness and instinct. He knew only vaguely what he wished to do. To have Io to himself, to draw her farther afield from the house and from her untroubled self-control were impulses embedded throughout his childhood in his nature. He could not have named them. They led him, however, to approach her along all those avenues, unsatisfying to the middle-aged, but which mean so much to the young.

To win a fleeting grasp of her tapering fingers, to touch her knee by accident, or even to have her trample on his foot, gave him the sensation of rising swiftly into rarefied air. He dreamed of a single fleeting kiss with the fervency with which a follower of the Prophet dreams of a vale crowded with houris. Io, on the other hand, seemed scarcely aware of the sensations which her mere presence induced.

It was she who had summoned Jimmy on the occasion of her first descent into the garden; but it was Jimmy who, by description of the joys of canoeing in the dark, aroused in her the primal desire which lies in us all for exploration. The raceway, with its mile of embowered narrow water opening at last on the lake, had no mysteries for her by daytime. He told her of its beauties at night, but his powers of depiction fell so far short of his intention that she was left unmoved. Suddenly his eyes narrowed in the half light to that shrewd look for which his father was so famous. He hinted that there were dangers besides mysteries, and the trick was done.

Standing beneath the trees, looking down toward the boathouse, they laid their plans. Io was to slip along the path on the southern side to well above the landing stage, keeping hidden behind the shrubbery. Jimmy was to get out his canoe and pick her up just around the first point.

As on the occasion of the first escape from her window, they were both nervous; but as far as Io was concerned this feeling soon

228

passed. She lay at half length in the middle of the canoe, the back rest slanted so that her eyes were lifted at an angle which left Jimmy, though he faced her, completely below her field of vision. There was no moon, which made the stars shine more sharply and seem nearer to earth than on a brighter night. Looking up through the branches which, reaching from either bank, barely touched their tips, it seemed that the spangled stars had descended to form an elongated Milky Way for her special benefit. She drew her breath long and deep, playing a game of her own, striving to fill herself so full of the air of heaven that she might become bodiless and float. Jimmy's voice awoke her, dragged her down.

"Io, do you dast go out on the lake?"

She nodded her head without speaking. Coming out into the open water, he was more afraid of observation and discovery. He drove his paddle deep and sent the light craft along at top speed until they were well past a long sharp point which thrust its shallow tongue far out into the lake. Then he turned toward shore and presently was coasting along within the deep shadow cast by looming trees. The shadow darkened suddenly into blackness. Io, startled, lifted her head and looked around. They had darted into the velvety gloom of the overhanging gumberries, famous rendezvous of generations of lovers. Io was awed.

"Where are we?" she whispered.

"Under the gumberries," replied Jimmy in a low voice, "and we're lucky to find it empty. Now all we got to do is to cough or light a match if we hear anyone coming, and they got to stay away."

"Why have they?" asked Io.

"Because," said Jimmy. "That's the way it is."

He tied the painter to a worn limb. Saying that he was tired, he crept cautiously to a seat beside her. She was so slight that there was ample room even for his bulky figure.

For a long time neither of them spoke. Io was in one of her more kindly moods of silence. She was dreaming, drifting, indifferent to his presence, and yet not unkindly. Her barriers were neither up nor down. Sensing her mood, he was content, more ineffably happy than he had ever been before in his life. He moved his arm so that he could throw his hand over the back rest and, without her knowing it, touched a wisp of her fine-spun hair.

As though it were something sentient, it curled around his finger, giving him a little shock, infinitesimal and yet dumfounding. For an instant he felt that she must know what had happened. Startled and afraid, he held his breath, then turned his eyes slowly until they caught the profile of her face. It was expressionless, totally lost, happy. He summoned all his courage.

"Io," he whispered hoarsely, "I touched your hair."

"Did you?" she asked from far away. "Well, don't do it again."

After a moment he spoke again.

"I would like to come here every night and be just like this with you."

"I would like to come here every night, too," said Io.

"Shall we? Will you come tomorrow?"

She did not answer. Sitting suddenly erect, she stared fixedly into the shadows. Her eyes had become dilated. Things, little things, crept out of the darkness toward her. Lily pads a closed lily bud, thrusting up its pointed nose. The climbing iridescent bubbles from some tadpole turning over in his bed of mud. A floating twig, with a leaf set for a sail, bound on some Lilliputian voyage at the mercy of minute unfelt drafts of air. Her eyes left all else to follow its fortunes. She imagined it manned by a crew of midgets, tiny, invisible to the naked eye, rushing about briskly and shouting profane orders in such powdered specks of sound that they fell miles short of her listening ears. Unconsciously she laid her hand on Jimmy's knee. It trembled, then grew steady, tense, as if there are times when a boy's leg can hold its breath.

"Io," he murmured presently, "what you thinking about?"

His voice startled her, reverberating tremendously in her ears which were straining to hear something less than sound. She threw back her head and shook her hair from about her face.

"I'm thinking," she said, "that it's high time to go home."

"Why did I speak?" cried Jimmy, deep within his own breast.

230

"Why? Why?"

When she returned to her room that night and began to slip off her clothes in the dark she heard a faint whimpering coming from her roommate. She knelt beside the girl's bed.

"Jennie," she said, "what's up? Why are you crying?"

Jennie flung her arms around her neck and tightened them convulsively.

"Oh, Io!" she sobbed between chattering teeth. "I'm frightened! I'm so cold!"

"What has happened?" asked Io. "Why are you scared?"

"Miss Drew came to the door," gasped Jennie. "She opened it and looked in."

Io cast a glance over her shoulder to her own bed, where she had skillfully arranged the bolster beneath the covers.

"Well," she asked, "did she come in? Did she say anything?"

"No-o-o-o," said Jennie, and began to sob aloud. "But, oh! Io, how can you!"

Io stared at her with uncomprehending eyes.

Chapter 33

There is nothing easier in life than to forget. We banish pains readily; pleasures lose their sharp contours more slowly; but they lose them. Favors and offenses fade from mind. Moving friends go out with the tide and come back only if they return to take the house next door; only the visual and the present endure. Stay around if you would be remembered. Even the stranger of what we are forgets the stranger of what we were. "I believed—wore—said—thought—that——— How funny!" Thus also do we forget the almost simultaneous arrival of two factors in a nation-wide contortion. To make the statement pertinent to this chronicle, let it be recorded that in the year when Io and her classmates graduated from Myrtle Manor they abandoned square dances for round—and Jimmy Mattis became the owner of an automobile.

These two developments find their prototypes in the Boston Tea Party and the Battle of Gettysburg; in certain respects they are more significant in the annals of the emancipation of woman than the name of Susan B. Anthony or the once familiar figure of Dr. Mary Walker. Already we have half forgotten what the motor car, by putting distance and seclusion with their opportunities and dangers at the beck and call of anyone with the price of gasoline, did to the qualified privacy of the home sitting room and to the chaperon as an institution. The effect of a few millions of automobiles on the century-old customs of a people is too evident to demand comment or to lend itself to misinterpretation. Not so, however, with those dances which, taking their rise from the dives of the Barbary Coast, swept eastward like a conflagration on an apparent mission to make the whole world one; the influence of these, as well as their effect, is frequently misjudged.

Make no mistake. The young girls whose lot it was to be the first to turn from the exhilaration of the Boston to the close contacts of the turkey trot, and from the turkey trot to the bunny hug—names already strange, dead before their teens—were a revolutionary army. They were back of that; they were pioneers, explorers not by intention but by inheritance and the circumstance of when they happened to be born.

Some were marked for moral death on the field of battle; some for total disablement; others for casualties; and some for wounds so slight as to be easily treated on the spot; but every one of them was a discoverer; every one of them took part in laying the foundations of the new order which is not branded today one-tenth as deeply by the superficial badges of bobbed hair, rouged lips and rolled stockings as it is by a truth, old as the hills, breaking out in slightly changed attire—the truth that the human body, put to any conceivable strain, develops its own amazing resistances.

These are the same girls our grandmothers were, the very same, the eternal feminine descendance. Yes; by all means, let us admit it. But do they garb their souls or their bodies in red flannels from neck to ankle, from Thanksgiving to May Day, as did those grandmothers? Do they wear anything inside or out that itches? As mothers, are they going to suffer the sickening sinkings of the heart, the bewilderments and gasping revivals of Eunice Alder, putting her girlhood to her eyes as if Vic Teller were an opera glass, and striving to bring Io into focus? And yet Io still had all her hair; still wore diminutive corsets, corset covers, suspenders and filmy petticoats. Nevertheless, she was of the advance guard.

Is it difficult to imagine with what misgivings the woman who had once caught fire at mere contact with Tryer Mattis' magnetism beheld her daughter's astonishing familiarity with his son? Eunice neither liked nor disliked Jimmy; she considered him a nonentity, lacking not only in education and superficial finish but more especially in all those fundamental attributes which make for breeding; and yet there were days when distraction drove her to praying that Io might marry him. Later her own indomitable nature would take her to task, accusing her of cowardly surrender to a traditional instinct to play safe in the eye of the world regardless of spiritual cost.

Under the urge of such moments of reaction she would seek a chance to be alone with Io, and would battle blindly against the most insidious enemy to the peace of mind of mothers, driving her head against the stone wall which marks the division between succeeding generations. She and her girl were friends in the deepest significance of the term; they loved each other dearly, shared confidences and a great mutual faith; and yet there were times when each spoke in a language which was Greek to the other.

When vague rumors reached her of Io's escapades at Myrtle Manor, coupled with insinuations that only graduation had saved her from being refused admittance to the school for another term, Eunice felt a tremor of alarm. She assured herself stubbornly that Io could not have done such a thing as this or that, and forced the matter from her mind. But she did not go to Miss Drew or to the judge. Piled upon this unacknowledged fear came the dismay aroused by the breathtaking intimacies of the new dances.

Nothing clandestine; not only Io and her friends, but Drake and his also. Matter of fact. That was what made it so bewildering. Late hours, too, and the needless risks of automobiling alone so far with any boy, even with Jimmy Mattis. Eunice was not weak, but some instinct prompted her to avoid recourse to arbitrary authority and its dictum—you shall not. Something of her attitude toward Drake since the day of his single mutiny crept into her intercourse with Io. If only she could love her enough and make her feel it, all would yet be well.

Hands tightly interlocked, and with luminous eyes and halting tongue, she talked to her of a woman's body as a domain, a walled

235

garden subject to enrichment along all the avenues of personality, and especially liable to loss by trespass, incursion or surrender of its least outposts. She was not understood. Her words were simple enough; but, without being told, she knew that they were unintelligible. She sat and gazed at Io, and Io gazed back with a troubled little frown, and whispered over and over again, "Yes, mother."

Eunice attempted the specific only once. "Io, you have never let Jimmy kiss you, have you?"

Io stared at her, completely at a loss, but from what cause Eunice was never to learn.

Comforted by the look alone, she cried out, "Never mind, dear. Forgive me. Only I wanted you to know——"

Behold Io, the arrow, in winged flight, escaped without a spoken word. Quick! Out to the stable and hitch up Kentucky, worthy son of a horse-famed state. Out! Out along the highway to just beyond the last tollgate left in the three counties, meeting motor cars all the way. Swing to the left along the track which leads to the forked roads, and then take the center one of three.

This rough road which on a memorable day had led the judge to the endless discovery of Rattling Run Fields, was emblematic. Within itself it comprised negation in gigantic terms. At one end of the Sherborne property, the Rattling Run Company, whose Rattler brand of cement had already been used in an experiment at New Brunswick in the form of a concrete pavement, first realization in New Jersey of Tryer's fantastic dream. At the other end of the same property, this road—this rutted and inhospitable evidence that the youthful proprietor of Rattling Run Fields, either through an embedded aversion or a love of solitude, hankered for no metaled highway across his front doorstep.

At Io's shout Tom came rolling out hatless from the kitchen. His hair and beard had turned quite white, while his bushy brows remained startlingly dark. As a result, he now gave the impression not only of a barrel but of a barrel stenciled and ready for shipment.

"Hello, Tom," she cried, leaped from the cart and tossed him the reins.

236

She went in search of Drake and found him in the living room, which, in spite of its great size, was made cozy by its low ceiling barred with rough-hewn timbers. Along the walls were bookcases and such few trophies as a man who has won his university letter is apt to preserve; also, there was a division of which Robert Colter, uninvited, had taken charge.

In rummaging through the lumber of ancient trunks and old boxes which had accumulated in the small peaked garret at Rattling Run Fields, Colter had come upon certain documents which appealed to his antiquarian interest. He purchased an easel and such a folio as is used for rare prints. In it he was mounting in chronological order such papers as the original deed of Rattling Run Fields; the commission of one Isaiah Hancock Sherborne, captain in the Revolutionary Army; certain letters in faded brown ink; the discharge of Warner Truesdale Sherborne from a regiment which had never reached the front in 1812; a quaint collection of the wedding lines which had tied the Sherborne women so tightly; the commissions or discharges of various other male Sherbornes in the Civil and in the Mexican and Spanish wars. Warner Sherborne, Drake's father, had gone no farther than Tampa.

Only today Colter had discovered among the papers a small leather purse, almost brittle with age. In it was a packet done up in many folds of oiled paper, dried together so that they had to be pried apart with a knife, disclosing finally a seal ring so tarnished that it was not easily distinguishable for gold. He took it to the kitchen, rubbed it in ashes until it shone, and looked for the crest. There was none; only an emblematic plow with a lantern hanging from one of its shafts. He was disappointed, but went in search of Drake and laid the ring on the table before him.

"Found it with the junk," he explained.

Drake glanced up and was about to suggest that the ring be added to Colter's chronological file; but perceiving that it was a seal ring, curiosity got the better of him. He picked it up, glanced at it, and immediately his careless bearing changed. He stared unbelievingly at the graved emblem and finally slipped the ring on his middle finger, for it was much too large for his little one.

"We Sherbornes," he remarked, "seem to have been bigger men a few generations ago." Colter turned to go back to his self-appointed task, but Drake stopped him. "Bob," he asked, "did you ever hear what they used to call my father?"

"No."

"They called him the man who plowed by lantern light." He stared again at the ring. "Queer things happen, don't they?"

When Io entered the room Colter glanced at her absorbed expression, saw that she had something on her mind and promptly slipped out through a door which opened to the rear. Drake was sitting in a low chair surrounded by a heap of books treating of fertilizers, their composition and correct application. He looked up to see Io standing before him, very erect, her brows drawn in a tiny frown.

"Hello!" he said. "What's up? What's the matter?"

"Sometimes," said Io, "you have to tell a lie to tell the truth."

"That is a deep saying," said Drake. "Do you want me to think it out?"

"No," said Io. "I've thought it out myself. If mother should ask me if a boy has ever kissed me, and I should say yes, it would be a lie even if they have kissed me, because it would mean something to her that it doesn't mean to me—what she calls the Point of Danger, with capital letters."

"That's very complicated," said Drake with mock solemnity, "but I think I know what you mean. Who has been kissing you, young lady!"

Genuinely serious and without hesitation, Io began to recite the names of almost every one of Drake's classmates who had visited Rattling Run Fields. When she finished, he added for her, "And Jimmy Mattis."

"Oh, yes," admitted Io, "and Jimmy."

Drake in his turn became serious.

"Just when did you begin," he asked, "and how and why?"

"Well," said Io, meeting his gaze without flinching, "when they say good-by, I would rather kiss them than shake hands—especially if it's hot."

Drake threw back his head and laughed.

"If it's that way I guess it's all right, Io. Anyhow, I've got too much to learn even to pretend to teach. Go your own way. Do you know what I mean by that?"

"No," said Io; "not unless you mean just what you say."

"I mean your way—Io's way," replied Drake. "Follow that as high and as far as you like."

"Drake," said Io, "I want to tell mother the truth. Do you understand? Not—well, not make her think I'm horrible. You know. Yet sometimes I think and think, but I just don't know the words she knows. Oh, that's awful. It doesn't mean anything at all."

"Oh, yes, it does," said Drake, taking up his book again. "It means the whole works to me, Io. Run away and don't worry any more."

If Eunice could have heard this conversation in which so little was said and so much expressed it is possible that she would have worried less but puzzled more. She had watched Io's hasty departure with a little catch in her heartbeats which was growing to be a frequent and familiar sensation. She did not have to ask where Io was going; she knew. She was going to Rattling Run Fields.

It might be expected that the spectacle of a single family living in a double establishment in an environment famed for its simplicity would have aroused comment; but the condition had come about so naturally that it passed unnoted, even by the most avid scavengers of gossip. It was as though the subtle power of Rattling Run Fields over all those who sprang from its loins imposed even upon outsiders to the extent of forcing the acceptance of its domination as a matter of course.

Thus Drake, from the moment of his first return from boarding school, aided by the timely advent of William Alder, Jr., had reassumed with no spoken arrangement his lifelong home; and thus Io, from spending a few hours with him, had grown tacitly

239

into a surprising independence of residence, staying a night or a week at the farm with a naïve casualness which made comment seem absurd. The judge, who, next to Eunice, might be thought most liable to a sense of injury, did more than anyone else to establish the anomalous situation by accepting it whole-heartedly. In her innermost thoughts Eunice even credited him with being a champion of the homestead as a concreted force against which it was futile to battle. Whenever he thought of Rattling Run Fields he seemed to live within the undying impression bequeathed by Warner Sherborne, adamant to his last breath.

"Son, the land's yourn; you ain't got no call to sell it."

Eunice was not a meek woman, nor was she wholly without her father's strain of sardonic humor. Her lips could curve and her eyes smile quizzically at the perplexing impulses of the younger generation, devouring latitude and longitude with its beanstalk tendrils; but when she thought of Rattling Run Fields an opaqueness like a cessation of vision seemed to film her gaze. It was as if Rattling Run Fields had all the terminal qualities of a blackboard built solidly into a wall; on it and not beyond it were mortal eyes to read all sums and all subtractions.

Chapter 34

Of all those who frequented Drake's domain at different times in the year, but especially during the summer months, there were two who seemed freer from the house, in the sense of being disjointed, than any of the others. But the paths of these two, in fact all their ways, were diametrically divergent. Jimmy Mattis pulled away from the homestead through a persistent desire to draw Io from the midst of friends among whom he never ceased to feel awkward. In the case of Robert Colter, motive and manner were as different from Jimmy's conduct as the open sea is from swamp water.

Colter made himself a man of mystery to others for his own comfort. He came to Rattling Run Fields when he felt like it and left without a word even to Drake. While there, he was always busy, but never with anybody else's business.

He seldom danced, though he would play for hours for others to dance, waiting until they were exhausted to drift off into fantasies of music for which they had ears only when their feet were tired. Aside from this limited association, he took little part in the activities of Drake's classmates or of Io and her friends.

In a certain way he possessed the whole farm more broadly than did Drake, for there was one section to which its owner never wandered—the cliff where great blasts of dynamite from time to time were blowing away the core of Rattling Run Fields. In fact Drake was almost a stranger even to the pasture, sentineled with cedars, where the continuous thunder of the mills throbbed its undertone to every sound and scene, by night as well as by day.

Colter, however, was not averse to this mighty rumble which suggested to his thoughts and feelings gigantic chords. To him the blot of shade thrown by the upland cedar, which permits few familiarities from other trees, was the coolest of all shadows, because it was wind-swept by every moving air. Lying beneath such a tree, he would fasten his eyes on its distant mate, his head propped on a hummock, with his back to the quarry, and keep his gaze fixed interminably.

To the youth who could find fun in watching an oak grow, there were depths in the blackness of a cedar thrown against an empty sky as profound as the depths beyond the stars on a moonless night. Soon vision would become confused as to whether it was gazing at a plume of inky smoke, magically static, or was lost in the stillness of a century, compressed within the compact veins of a single tree.

From the far boundary of the pasture down past the swimming hole, and along the brook to the point where Rattling Run crept beneath the bridge and away toward the Cohansey, there was no spot which Colter did not love and frequent, searching not only for a solution of Drake Sherborne, the unreadable, but for the answer to the question of himself. So many questions that, it seemed to him, were being more forcibly pressed by the passing day than ever before—what to do and what to believe; what to take and what to leave untouched; whither to go amid the myriad pathways of life and come out eventually among the upland cedars. And here was Drake, knowing for himself all answers!

Through these thoughts, almost against his will, played a flashing intermittent vision of Io, not objectively, but as a restive beam plays amid moving shadows. Her actual relations with him were casual; limited for the most part to a wave of the hand and calls of " 'Lo, Bob!" and "Hello, Io!" when she ran across him during her wanderings, bringing a half-rueful, half-amused twist to his lips. He believed, rightly, that she never really saw him. Perhaps this was due to the seniority of eight years, which makes such a vast difference to a girl still in her teens, or perhaps merely to his habit of keeping out of the way of other people's minds. Then there was the possibility that the constant intrusion of Jimmy's bulky body obstructed her view.

Dismissed by Drake from the living room, Io went out to talk to Tom for lack of anything else to do. There had been a time when the old man could be loquacious on a variety of subjects; but ever since Alexander had died his talk was limited to one of two lines. He would discuss plans for the improvement of Rattling Run Fields from sunrise to sunset; failing that, he fell back on tales of Alexander, all of which Io had heard many times, ending up invariably and inevitably with the historical account of the only animal to die standing up and keep his feet thereafter. Drake, some time since, had begun experiments with such fruit as flourishes in a light soil, and Tom's subject on this day was a pessimistic discourse on the plantation of a group of fig trees.

"Figs in Jersey, Io!" he concluded at last. "What do you think of that?"

"I don't think anything about it," replied Io listlessly. "But if Drake plants them they will grow."

She left him, went to her room and put on a wisp of a bathing suit, to wander barefoot through the orchard and the woods toward the swimming hole. In a scallop of the rise to the left she saw Colter lying with his back against the log where the judge had imparted memorable advice, the same log where, years later, he learned from the lips of Colter the result of his counsel to Drake.

" 'Lo Robert," called Io with a wave of her hand.

"Hello, Io," he replied.

She continued for a few paces, then her steps slackened; she paused, turned, and with head dropped in thought, came to sit down cross-legged in front of him.

"Do you mind?" she asked.

"Mind!" exclaimed Colter. "I should say not! Why should I mind?"

"Oh, I don't know. You always seem to want to be alone."

"I'm never alone. I can't stand it."

"You must mean something by that," said Io, throwing up her head and smiling. "I give it up. Tell me."

"I'm always with something or someone every minute," complied Colter, smiling back at her. "I get a lot of fun out of listening to trees; I take walks on my back that I took long ago on my feet, and revisit the friends I made. I spend hours with Drake when he isn't around, and hours with you."

"With me?" cried Io, her eyes suddenly alight to the eternal lure of any particle of oneself in the eyes of another. "What do you see?" she asked. "What do we talk about?"

"Ah, what do we talk about? Well, so far you haven't said a great deal, Io. I just watch you and think: 'Here's a straight young tree out for a walk; let's see what she'll do.'"

"And what do I do?"

"Never the same thing twice."

A slow flush mounted to his cheeks. He was wondering why she had stopped to speak to him, but he would not ask. He did not even wish to know, for he was being assailed by the temptation to break through her unconscious wall of impersonality. He had summed her up in talking to the judge as being all question. Why should he, Robert Colter, remain forever outside the range of her demanding mind? In the pause their eyes met and held until he became aware of a peculiar sense of immersion.

"I could tell you," he said recklessly, "something you did once which you will never remember and I shall never forget."

"Tell me," begged Io gravely.

"I don't think I could, after all," said Colter, "because you've never seen a field of California yellow daisies."

"Don't you mean poppies?"

"No, I don't," he replied almost gruffly. "I mean daisies. Not orange; yellow—solid and even—laid on like golden butter on a fresh slice of the earth."

"You make my mouth water," murmured Io. "Please tell me,

Bob. Please."

"Shall I?"

"Yes."

"Listen:

> *"Said Io's mother to her girl's sweetheart,*
> *One lovely March-blown day,*
> *Just pick the daisies from Ridgefold Acre,*
> *And then you may go and play.'"*

Colter's eyes sparkled into hers; his lips were half laughing, half serious before the absorption in her eager face, solemnly intent.

"More?" he asked.

"Of course," said Io impatiently; "and please don't stop again."

He continued:

> *"The boy climbed up to the high hilltop,*
> *Alas for his day of play!*
> *Like a yellow carpet, a thick yellow carpet,*
> *The flood of daisies lay.*

> *"'Oh, Io dear, so far, so near,*
> *Across the daisies fey,*
> *Wait but a moment or wait but a year;*
> *I'll pluck the field away!'*

> *"He kneeled him down on the soft lush ground*
> *And reached forth fingers two;*
> *Each flower cried out as his hand drew near*
> *'I'm Io; I live for you.'*

> *"The sun climbed up, the sun went down,*
> *And still the daft boy kneeled,*
> *Till a soft air swept the day quite out*
> *And rustled the bright gold field.*

245

"The lips of the wind were on his mouth,
The stars were in his eyes,
When the maiden moon tossed up her horns
And stepped from the sloping skies.

"Like a snow-white heifer, a milk-white heifer,
She walked on the cloth of gold;
The flowers cried out at the kiss of her feet,
'Up, lad, and pluck her; be bold!'

"But Io's mother snatched his cap from his head
And threw it far away;
'With never a flower for my dear girl's dower,
Alone you shall go and play.'"

There was a tense, smiling moment of silence, and then Io cried sharply, "Bob, how did you know?"

"How did I know?"

"Ah, of course," she said, with a falling gesture of her hands. "Everyone may know about Io and the crescent moon without my telling. They can read it in books."

"Only part of it, Io."

"Is there more, Bob?" she asked eagerly.

"You mean of the Ballad of Yellow Daisies? No; there isn't any more to that—at present. Did you like it?"

"You know without my saying," she replied. "Only mother would never have snatched the boy's cap and thrown it away—not that boy's."

"Perhaps not," said Colter; "but, just the same, I'm never going to wear a cap."

Io glanced up as if she had been startled into seeing him, and a faint color glowed for an instant deep beneath the surface of her cheeks. She was truly aware of him for the first time in her life and it made her restless. She arose, stood for a moment, still wholly unconscious of her body so frankly displayed, and then started toward the swimming hole. Halfway down the slope she paused to turn and look at him as one looks at an interesting stranger.

The Lantern on the Plow

Chapter 35

On the day following Io's visit to explain when a lie is not a lie, Colter came to the window of the living room and called to Drake.

"Come out," he said; "there's something in the pasture I wish you to see."

"I never go to the pasture," replied Drake.

"You'd better come today, Drake," persisted Colter. "You needn't come all the way in. Just stand at the fence and look across. I'll tell you. The Statue of Liberty has wandered from Bedloe's Island."

Drake was persuaded. He tossed aside his book and went with Colter along the edge of the wood, pausing from time to time to examine his fruit trees and make mental notes of how they were doing and of what they seemed to require.

Three years, all but a few weeks, had slipped by since he had come into his patrimony, and a glance was enough to show how he had been spending his money and time. In the triangle formed by the irregular line of the wood, the easterly fence of the pasture and the private road which bifurcated the farm, he had erected stretches of high brick wall set at varying angles to establish the merits of different exposures. Against these walls were trellised peach, apple, nectarine and pear trees. In one corner was a plot given over to experimenting with different varieties of fig trees.

These had been recently released from winter coverings and the columns of their brown branches, freshly in leaf, were loaded with weights to pull them open.

"I'll say you are thorough," remarked Colter, following the direction of Drake's eyes and thoughts. "How many years before you'll quit experimenting and plant, you tortoise?"

"I don't know," said Drake. "There's no hurry."

He stood stock-still, gazing at the hand-groomed trees, until Colter joggled his elbow and nodded toward the pasture. They went on, but not until he reached the zigzag of the split-rail fence did Drake turn questioningly toward his companion and suddenly abandon the idea of speech, his eyes fastened on an incongruous vision. Silhouetted against the black cloud of Colter's favorite cedar overlooking the quarry was the figure of a woman.

Those were the days when the daily press was given over to the inanity of Fluffy Ruffles competitions, but the figure at the edge of the cliff was decked in no furbelows. There was something poised in its pose as though it felt the eyes of the world to be watching. One hand rested on the knob of a parasol and the other at the hip; one knee was slightly bent, the other straight. The head, beneath a drooping picture hat, was dropped forward, and one could imagine a gaze, intent and calculating, directed toward the busy scene below. A tan dress of some clinging material floated in the breeze, wrapping itself around long limbs so closely that an impression of molded nakedness was produced. Even at such a distance, however, and in spite of Colter's insinuation, the woman did not appear statuesque; one knew that she lived and breathed.

As they watched she turned abruptly and walked straight toward them. Colter was for running to the shelter of the wood; but Drake stood firm, his eyes staring, his lips parted in a half smile. As with an easy, languorous stride, her head still bowed, the stranger came nearer and nearer, picking her way, Colter uttered a startled exclamation.

"Drake," he whispered, "do you know who it is?"

"Yes," said Drake, "I think so." He paused, and presently added, "Yes, I know her."

"You know her?" cried Colter, puzzled by Drake's composure. Receiving no answer he turned and walked away along the fence. He heard Drake say "Hello, Lessie," and could not resist a backward glance over his shoulder. The woman stopped and threw back her head.

"Hello," she replied very slowly, questioning eyes fixed intently on Drake.

He stared back at her. It was as if her puzzled pause had given him what he most wished for—a chance to study her brazenly. He began with her hair, drawn in two smooth amber bands from the center of her forehead down over her ears with a severity which no commonplace features would have dared. Her brows were sharply penciled, and beneath them were long almond-shaped eyes, brown, at the moment rather glaring, but presently growing cynically humorous. Her nose was straight; her lips were irregular, full in repose, twisted to a quirk at one side when she smiled. As he persisted with his downward inventory she spoke, awakening him from his trance.

Holding out her hand across the fence, she said, "You have gone far enough, Drake. It is Drake Sherborne, isn't it? How are you? For a minute I couldn't think where I was or who you were."

He took her fingers, which closed over his with a firm grasp.

"I'm all right, Lessie. How are you?"

I'm very well," she answered; "just as well from the neck down as I am from the neck up, and you ought to know by this time how well that is."

He laughed nervously.

"All right," he said, "I won't look any more. Do you want to get across the fence?"

"I do, unless there's some way for the hired automobile I told to drive around from the quarry to get into the pasture."

"No, there isn't," said Drake, and started to work out the top rail.

"What's the need of that?" asked Lessie. "Don't you suppose I know how long it takes to pull down a snake fence and put it up again? Give me your hands."

He took her hands. The rings on one and the agate head of the parasol in the other bit into his fingers, but Lessie did not seem to feel the pressure or to flinch. Her hands were strong. She walked up the rails as easily as if she were climbing a stair, stood for a moment at the top and jumped. As she came down her body brushed against his.

What happened during the next five seconds was so astonishingly unexpected to Drake as well as to Lessie that one is tempted to pause and flounder in explanations of the inexplicable. Under command of an irresistible impulse, he released her hands only to take her in his arms, hold her tightly and kiss her gasping lips. Instantly her face became contorted; she writhed her body free, drew back and slapped him with all the strength of her swinging arm.

There was something tremendous about Lessie at this moment, something greater than the ordinary reactions of manhandled virtue, something which declared her equally above prudery and innocence, something individually splendid and flaming.

"Low!" she cried. "Low down! Beast! Just because you think— just because I am on the stage—just for no reason at all in this dirty world of Christians——"

She stopped, arrested against her will by the frozen immobility of Drake's face. Save for the blotch of vivid red where she had struck him, it was white as paper, empty of expression; no shade of triumph in it, nor yet any dismay. His steady gaze met her angry eyes without a tremor. He stood very still; so still that she could not help but wonder if he heard her.

All fury wears the tragic mask; the most mobile features become fixed in anger. But rage may admit of no questions, for once it does, the mask breaks and tears threaten. Lessie's face suddenly began to crumple, her dilated nostrils quivered and her lips twitched spasmodically; but she was not yet through with anger. Her eyes, seeking something within reach, something vulnerable, fell upon the parasol still held in her left hand. She stared at it. Another moment and she had broken it across her knee.

"That's you!" she gasped at Drake. Then, as she tore its silk to shreds, scattered the tatters about her and tossed the wreckage aside, "That's you—and that, and that, and that!"

Colter arrived, panting, upon the scene. He laid his hand on Drake's shoulder and whirled him around.

"Drake," he cried, "in the name of heaven what came over you?"

As if he had touched some powerful hidden spring, Drake struck him with his closed fist. Colter, a look of childish amazement spreading on his face, threw up his hand instinctively, but only partially warded off the blow. The seal ring which he himself had unearthed only the day before gashed his cheek from jaw to temple. He raised his arm to stanch the flow of blood with the sleeve of his shirt.

"What did you do that for?" demanded Lessie, her own troubles instantly wiped from mind.

"Because," said Drake, "he meddled in our business."

"Our business!" she cried. "Did you say our business?" Her sense of humor began to return, and with it some measure of that level-headedness which had made her one too much for her father, Tryer Mattis. "That's interesting," she continued. "You'd think I'd be overjoyed, coming across stock in a company I never heard of; but I'm not particularly happy about it. No; I'm sorry— sorry for you, Drake. Because the truth is, you don't know what you're talking about. You don't even belong here. You belong in a lunatic asylum."

"I do belong here," said Drake quietly. "We both belong here."

Lessie's long eyes narrowed and her face hardened.

"That's right," she said, her moment of banter passed, "cast it up to me that I started from here." She threw out one supple arm in a sudden wide gesture. "Look around you!" she cried. "Look at this parasol," giving the wreckage a kick. "Look at my brute of a father when you see him, and then look at your own beastly face in the glass, and remember as long as you live that Lessie Mattis was through with all kinds of dirt and her own name at seventeen. Bah!"

She made a triple snap of her fingers under his nose, turned and started toward the automobile, which had come around the cliff and was waiting at some distance on the road that ran past the homestead. While she spoke a flush had mounted from Drake's neck to his face, almost obliterating the red mark of her slap. He gulped and tried to speak.

"Lessie!" he called at last. "Wait!"

Without looking around, she threw one hand up above her head, the fingers slanted backward in a gesture eloquent of conclusion and denial. Drake, as if petrified, followed her only with his eyes. The free movement of her body added to his intoxication. No one, looking upon her with attention, would have called her a large woman; but she was nobly proportioned, with a breadth of shoulder, a depth of bosom and a length of limb which seemed the outward symbols of a fundamental generosity.

He did not stop to give a name to what had overcome him; he only knew that as far as he was concerned the great die of life had been irrevocably cast. This woman or none other. He watched until she entered the waiting car and saw it start. Then, turning, he started for the house at a run.

Colter, mopping his cheek, followed more slowly, his face still wearing the look of childish amazement induced by Drake's unexpected blow; but oddly superimposed upon it was a puzzled frown. Reaching the stables, he found Tom hastily hitching up a rig with nervously trembling fingers.

"What's come over Drake, Bob?" called the old man.

"I don't know," replied Colter.

He went into the house in search of Drake and found him in his room, packing a large bag with haste aided by method. All the drawers of the dresser had been pulled to the floor in a semicircle. On the bed were suits, ties, shoes, a light overcoat and an extra hat.

Drake's face looked as though he were in a trance, but his fingers and hands moved with incredible rapidity, picking out six of this and a dozen of that, sorting clothes and ties, choosing one article, discarding another, until he had gathered in a single large heap all the objects which he purposed taking with him.

"Drake," asked Colter, "what are you doing? Where do you think you are going?"

"I don't know. Don't bother me, Bob. I haven't time just yet even to tell you I'm sorry. If your face doesn't hurt too much pack those things into the bag while I wash and change my clothes. You'd better go into town with me to have your cheek plastered."

Half an hour later they left Rattling Run Fields at a furious pace, the buggy caroming from one rut to another along the rough going of the private road. When they reached the smooth surface of the highway Drake longed for the speed of a motor car for the first time in his life. Nevertheless, they covered half the distance to town before he spoke.

"Bob, I've got time now. I'm sorry about your cheek. I mean, I'm sorry I had to do it."

"Oh, that's all right, Drake," replied Colter. "I suppose I'll never get over my habit of sitting on your log at the wrong time."

"What do you mean by that?" asked Drake, half absently.

"Nothing, nothing at all—to you. But let that go. I'll forgive you the blow if you'll only tell me what you think you're doing and where you're going. This isn't butting into your business again. Believe it or not, I'd like to help you if you'll let me."

"I have told you the truth," said Drake quite gravely. "I don't know where I'm going or what I'm going to do." His lips closed tightly, and then opened to add, "But I'll know when I get there."

At the station he had no time to lose. He turned over the horse to Colter, dragged his bag from the back of the buggy and started straight for the train without stopping to purchase a ticket.

"Drake," said Colter loudly, delivering a parting shot, "I believe you don't even know who she is. She isn't known as Lessie where you're going."

He called out a name which lately had become familiar to the theatergoers of the metropolis with that suddenness which makes the star of an hour seem to have belonged to all time. Drake paused in his stride and half turned around. Two belated travelers, in spite of their haste, threw up their heads and smiled. One of them, an elderly man, laughed good-naturedly:

"Go to it, kid! But you're flying high."

No sooner had Drake gained the platform than the train started, but before it had reached the first station he had ascertained that his surmise was correct and that Lessie was on board. He placed himself at the back of the car in which she sat and sank low in the seat so that she would not notice him if she chanced to glance around.

Chapter 36

Just as each arriving moment, for the length of its insignificant existence, is a culmination of eternity, so is life a distillation, drunk blindly, of all that has gone before. Thus is it made evident that while Drake stared out of the car window with aching eyes and brain, asking over and over again what had happened inside of himself, the gods could look on and laugh, remembering Vic Teller and her electric blood. Here was irony on a broad scale—Tryer's daughter and Eunice's son joined in battle; and that no less incongruous couple, Jimmy and Io, left behind to linger in the gloom of the gumberries.

Strange, hazy summer; drowsy, yet importunate; to Io Sherborne, so full and withal so empty. Drake gone from Rattling Run Fields. Jimmy forever at hand. Bob Colter, more solitary than ever after his extraordinary half revealment, wandering around in shirt and flannel trousers, here today, away tomorrow, like a white ghost with irregular habits, haunting the outskirts of her consciousness. She watched him out of the corner of her eye, not ready to see him fully, and he seemed to know it.

Boys and men began to take on form to her as differing in substance as well as in outline. She perceived Tryer Mattis, stalking up and down through the land, eyes now perpetually round with staring at an accomplished vision. He had added unto himself a

257

new nickname—they called him the cement king of South Jersey. Strange individual, pompous and harmless, whose touch as a child she could never abide. She wondered why.

How different was his urbane partner, the judge, grown wealthier than his ambition or his dreams, benevolent to all with whom he came in contact, a pillar of the church and in the state, a sort of deep reservoir of strength. He was a silent and contented man, occupied and preoccupied, but never too absorbed to give her a kindly understanding glance. She loved him deeply, and yet with an affection quite different from the love she accorded her mother. That was another thing to ponder over, for the relations between Io and Eunice had come to a peculiar impasse. They cast fond, puzzled looks at each other over a wall, one woman looking at another.

It requires a wider vision, however, than that of Io to perceive Eunice at the close of the most somnolent and perhaps the happiest period of her existence. Let us choose a moment at church when she sits with William Alder, Jr., trapped in a corner, Io at her right, and the judge exercising the male prerogative of the seat on the aisle. Her expression is not that of one who is engaged in a perfunctory duty, even though it lacks the concentration of the ardent and unquestioning believer.

Her face seems rather to mirror a profound peace born of the understanding that controversy is among the most negligible factors of existence, and that all the varied sources of eternal life spring from outside the limits of the inquiring cynicism of the world's Abraham Tellers, however intrinsically lovable the skeptic may be in moments of aberration from the sturdy philosophy of doubt.

She had grown almost subconsciously to feel that church was worth while to the spirit; she knew it irrespective of whys and wherefores in the realization that an act of worship is essentially indefinable, bounded by neither walls nor creeds. Even so, gazing at her trim figure in its setting of the variegated yet dominant personalities of her family, one felt no need to abjure Vic Teller as the antecedent of this quiescent woman. Something vibrant within her, as within all those with whom she came in contact, still marked the division between the quick and the dead, drew and satisfied the eye.

Sitting erect in the pew, Eunice was not intent on the preacher or his sermon, but on preparing herself to abandon the idea of peace as an end in itself. She was thinking that William Alder, Jr., had been and still was a source of illimitable comfort owing to his understandable simplicity, and that when she turned from the open book of her younger son to meet the mystery in her daughter's gaze, pellucid and yet unfathomable, the violence of the contrast filled her with dismay. She had begun to ask, not what was Io thinking, but how did she think?

One evening she came in from a chance encounter with Tryer Mattis, her face white and her eyes flashing; but nevertheless a little frightened. She was up in arms, angry, angrier than she remembered ever being before. She stepped into the library and glanced at the judge, but did not speak to him. She entered the loneliness of the cool drawing-room and stood for a while in thought; then she went upstairs to her own sitting room and sent for Io.

"Io," she said, "sit down. I want to have a talk with you. I met Mr. Mattis on the street a while ago. He stopped me. Would you like to know what he said?"

"Yes," answered Io, perched on the extreme edge of a chair.

"He said he was getting ready to give Jimmy the thrashing of his life for your sake."

"What did he mean?" asked Io.

She felt a catch in her breath and in the beating of her heart. Her mother seemed very near, lovable, beautiful; but like a picture which is tangible and yet remains in its essence intangible. Was it possible that all of us, each one of us, is imprisoned in a frame? Was her mother trying, as she herself was trying, to step for a moment down from her frame?

"I don't know, if you don't," replied Eunice, and waited.

How tell her? thought Io confusedly. How put into words feelings, thoughts, vague speculations which had no form even

259

to oneself? Jimmy? What was Jimmy anyway? A hitching post, a car track, in rare moments perhaps a gondolier upon a sea of dreams? Almost; but never quite. How tell that? What did he matter? There were things infinitely more important than Jimmy; things she herself would like to ask, if only she knew how. She began to feel awkward, empty, hopeless. A lump rose into her throat.

"Everything you ask," she murmured, "when you speak and even when you look at me these days, I have asked of myself over and over."

"Io!" exclaimed Eunice, throwing out her hand in an impulsive gesture of acceptance.

"Oh," cried Io, springing to her feet and intertwining her fingers, "I wish Drake were here! I wish he hadn't gone away!"

Eunice's eyes contracted suddenly as if something within her winced.

"Why, dear? Why do you wish for Drake just now?"

"I don't know," replied Io; "but I do, with all my heart. Bob Colter says not to worry—that he's only traveling. Why should he travel? Five weeks! More than a month away from Rattling Run Fields—and in summer! Do you remember when he ran away from school and left me behind? Do you?"

"I'll never forget it," replied Eunice.

Her eyes widened and turned soft as if she abandoned deliberately all thought of further inquisition.

"Well, he's done it again," said Io over the lump in her throat. "He's gone away and left me behind. Mother, may I go now, please?"

"Yes, dear," said Eunice, half absently.

On the stairs Io met the judge.

"Jimmy's out front," he said.

"I know," she murmured, not trusting herself to speak aloud.

He drew aside to let her pass, but stopped her as she came even with his eyes, one step above him.

"Are you going out with him?" he asked, fumbling with his fob as if his watch were in some way mixed with his thoughts.

"Yes," said Io. "It isn't very late."

A faint flush mounted to his cheeks and a sudden fire of allegiance lighted up his eyes.

"Io," he said, "you have the straightest figure and the straightest eyes I ever saw. Shouldn't wonder if you were the straightest little person in the world."

Without waiting to measure the effect of his words he hurried past her. She stood for a moment with the long fingers of one hand opened spiderlike against the wall. What had he meant? She went slowly down the remaining stairs and out to Jimmy.

"Where shall we go?" he asked.

"I don't care. Anywhere; but quickly."

"Not too quick. I got to stop for some calcium carbide."

"Nasty, smelly stuff," said Io. "Can't you do without it?"

"Sure; if you'll go for a canoe ride instead, I can."

"No; not the canoe," she decided promptly. "Go get the carbide. I'll wait. If I'm not out here when you come back it means I'm not going for a ride at all. Hurry!"

While he was gone she walked up and down the path between the horse block and the dignified portal of the house. Within her was a turmoil, not of weaknesses but of swirling forces which demanded intelligent arrangement. She was furious with herself at not having been able to say just this one thing to her mother: "I am full of things I don't know anything about; but since I'm not afraid, why should you be frightened? How can I tell you? How can I? Listen! If I could fly, everything would be all right. Does that mean anything? No? Well, there you are! It means everything!"

For no reason that she could fathom, a memory of the deep, controlled rumble of the cement works assailed her ears. When Jimmy came back she sprang in while the machine was still moving and told him to drive straight on.

Presently she said, "Go out to the plant. I've never seen it at night—only from far away, I mean. And I've never been over it since the day you took me. Do you remember?"

261

"Sure I remember. I wouldn't call it going over the plant, though. The old gyratory crusher was all the further you got. 'Member how you hung on and Tony Mazaro didn't dare pull you off or let you go?"

Io nodded her head.

"Yes, I remember."

"And then dad come along," continued Jimmy, "and said he'd hold you for a spell. The minute he put his hands on you, why you fought like a cat. Got away, too, and when I wanted to know what was the matter you just said he touched you. Remember?" He laughed.

She glanced at his snub-nosed profile curiously. As if he felt her eyes upon him, his face sobered and assumed an expression she knew well. He was going to ask her for the hundredth time to marry him. Well, let him. While he talked she settled back in the seat, narrowed her eyes, and set out deliberately upon an orgy of random thinking. Her mother, worrying, who never used to; the judge giving out riddles on the stairway; Jimmy laughing—what was there to laugh at? Oh, that she should ever have minded being touched. Was that it? Had he found it irresistibly amusing that she should ever have minded? Drake. "I wish—I wish with all my heart Drake were here." Tom—poor Tom—so old, but not so old as Alexander, because Alexander was dead. Tryer Mattis. He had come to the funeral too. No; not Alexander's funeral—her own father's. Tom and Tryer—they had both come that day. Tryer had brought his girl with him, just as old and as big as Drake—bigger, almost. She had refused to play, and her name was Lessie Mattis, the same Lessie who had run away. Tom had known her well.

Jimmy was saying, "Will you, Io? Will you marry me? Listen——"

"Jimmy," she interrupted without compunction, "what's ever become of your sister Lessie?"

"Lessie!" he exclaimed, startled, and then asked, "What do you know about Lessie?"

"Nothing; only that she ran away. I was just wondering."

"She came back for a day four or five weeks ago," said Jimmy after a pause. "Wouldn't go to our house. Come out here to size up what she thought the old man ought to give her, I guess."

"Four or five weeks ago?" repeated Io absently. "Did she? And did you see her, Jimmy? What does she look like?"

Jimmy frowned.

"Well, it's like this," he said: "She ain't pretty exactly—you know she ain't pretty; but she makes you think she's one of the best-looking women you ever seen."

"You didn't think that out, Jimmy," declared Io promptly.

"No," admitted Jimmy. "Tom saw her drive by and he said all that and some more."

"Tom!" exclaimed Io. "Drive by where?"

"Why, Rattling Run Fields. Didn't I say she come out to get a line on how big the works was?"

"Five weeks ago," thought Io to herself. "Drake has been gone five weeks."

263

Chapter 37

Over ten years of operation had brought about a noticeable enlargement of the cement plant, as well as of the gaping hole in the side of the hill whence the rock was now being rived at the rate of something over a quarter of a million tons a year. During the same period the power of a single blast had been increased to a hundred and fifty times that first explosion which had so disturbed Drake. Needless to say, the new works were erected much farther away from the quarry than the old, and also the face of the cliff had steadily receded until one looked across acres of splintered shale, level as a floor, and connected with the foot of the hoist by a fanlike system of tracks.

Io made Jimmy stop the car while she gazed at a scene quite familiar to her from the level of the pasture, but utterly strange when approached from below. Everything seemed now tremendously enlarged except the distant cliff itself, which appeared diminished, especially at that northeastern extremity where blasting had been early abandoned owing to a seepage from some buried spring which had given forth enough water to form a considerable pool. Rather than increase the flow so that it would inundate the quarry, requiring the installation of a pump, the center of activities had been moved to the south and west. All else seemed fantastically magnified, even the men, even the idea that for half her life save for the week of the annual winter shutdown for repairs, and one only holiday, the Fourth of July, the devouring rumble of the mills had been going on night and day. Half her life! Night and day! Clatter and bang!

"Half your life! Night and day!"

There was a moon, and everything in sight was silvered with the white powder from the works. Jimmy insisted that she put on a dust coat and an old cap before he led her along the top of the new hoist to where a powerful roll crusher had supplanted the ancient gyratory one which she had found so entrancingly rapacious. There was still a rail facing the tipple, and over it she leaned as on that long-ago day, except that Jimmy's arm was around her now, holding her more closely though perhaps less safely than had Tony Mazaro's rough and reverential hands. What ages since she had seen Tony, she thought. Why didn't he come for a chat with Tom any more? It was she who had made them friends.

Passing along the covered way leading from the crusher to the huge milling shed, their feet sank to the ankles in dust so fine as to be almost impalpable. It was dark gray; it looked like city snow, only it sifted stingingly into their nostrils. Jimmy was trying to speak to her through the roar. She leaned toward him. Again he put his arm around her as if to steady her, holding her close and shouted, "The dust doesn't hurt! Good for you! Never goes to lungs. Stops on way."

She nodded; they went on.

"Know what this is?" shouted Jimmy. "You don't remember the old ball mills. This here's a Goliath. Does—work—thirteen ball mills. We got three of 'em on the raw side alone, and that's the comminuter. Boosts—output—one-third."

"What do you mean by the raw side?" asked Io without shouting.

Her voice slipped between the key of the rumble and the pitch of the roar, making itself clearly heard.

"Before you cook the rock it's raw," shouted Jimmy; "but after it's been through the kilns it's clinker. You have to grind the clinker same

266

as you do the raw. Everything in the whole works divides on whether it's on the raw side or on the clinker side, see? Want to go down?"

He pointed to the battery of giant kilns below, six of them, each nine feet high and a hundred and forty long. She nodded. He climbed down the narrow iron steps and motioned to the fireman for his smoked glasses. The man handed them not to Jimmy, but to Io. She stooped down to look into the incandescence of the vast revolving furnace. How strange! The entering coal looked like crude oil, sprayed from a nozzle, so finely had it been powdered. Black, red—then white, instantly—white-hot.

"Three thousand degrees, miss, at the mouth of the kiln," growled the fireman; "but a lot of the heat still goes up the stack. Too much—ye-ah. Some day some guy will figure out how to cut it down, and perhaps they'll give him a ten per cent raise."

She heard him perfectly, and liked him. She lingered; stayed until she felt her face would peel; then they went on.

"That's the last of the raw side," she heard Jimmy's voice say presently in the comparative quiet of a staging flanked on each side by conveyors.

The one on the right was carrying clinker to the tube mills. The burned rock looked like ashes, dark gray, cool; and then, as each bucket struck its tipple, there was a flash of garnet red, sudden, unexpected, vicious; cool gray on top, raging heat beneath.

More mills—tube mills—revolving, pulverizing. Where there had been eight on the raw side, there were twelve for the clinker. Everything was vast, everything incessant. So few men. One here, one there, like visitors paying calls. They came to call on the huge mills, but the mills had not time to bother with any man. They were ponderously continuous. They never stopped for anyone, night or day—only for Christmas and the Fourth of July.

"Look," said Jimmy, laying his hand on her arm, "that's where it goes into the coolers. See? Better let me go ahead now."

He led the way along a trestle, bringing her out on a high gang-way which bifurcated the top of the stock house. It was ankle-deep in soft powder, but the powder was no longer gray—the gray of sooty snow. It was of the palest yellow, almost like ground amber. On either side of the gangway were huge square bins, forty feet deep and wide and long. One or two of them were empty, some were half full, others brimmed with the pale-yellow powder. That powder, fine as flour, was Portland cement of the Rattler Brand. Beneath the bins were shoots, and beneath the shoots were the new Baker packing machines.

Jimmy wished especially to show Io these machines in operation and watch her face when she saw that the bags were completely sewed and tied before they were filled from the bottom. Funny how few people knew that. He would explain it to her. He would show her how, just by a turn of the cloth, they made a valve in the lower corner which closed when the bag was packed full. But first he had another surprise for her. He knelt and thrust his hand into the rippled mass in the bin.

Looking up at Io over his shoulder he said, "Dare you."

"Dare me what?"

"Do what I'm doing. Put your hand in."

She did not hesitate, and in her haste thrust half her forearm into the cement, only to snatch it out. Tears of anger and pain filled her eyes. Her hand was scarlet. He pulled his own out hastily; it, too, was red, but not so red as hers.

"You went too deep, Io. This stuff's been here for a week, and it's as hot as that; but it doesn't really burn. Just grinding anything hard into powder makes it mighty hot. Come on down and see them fill the bags."

Turning, Io was in the lead going back along the gangway. She had scarcely heard what Jimmy said; she certainly had no intention of watching a machine fill bags. The hugeness of everything about her, the insignificance of herself and of the men who waited hand and foot on all this iron-jawed, stone-devouring Moloch of a mill, the very revenge taken on her slender arm by the soft finished powder and, above all, the incessant, unmodified roar—all these things made her feel a subtle exhilaration, a stirring up and confounding of her emotions, so that it became difficult to say what was safety and what danger. Was death, for instance, danger? Say one were ground into a hundred billion particles—what would become of danger then?

Suddenly a sense of well-being swept over her. Without being able to formulate her thought, she knew now why she had had the impulse to come to the works. Here were terrific forces which, were it in their power to run amuck, contained ghastly potentialities of destruction; and yet they destroyed only in an orderly manner, and to create. There was an abrupt reversal in the cry of her heart for Drake; now her longing was that, instead of Jimmy, her mother might be standing there with her—just the two of them; thinking together, saying nothing.

She smiled at herself and looked up to see lounging at the head of the gangway no other than Tony Mazaro. At the sight of him her smile deepened and her pace quickened; only suddenly to slacken. There was no answering smile on Mazaro's face. Save for his beady eyes, his whole expression seemed purposefully apathetic, intentionally inscrutable. In his eyes was a look of inquiry, profoundly eager; under complete subjection, however, to a stare of insolence. His pose was that of a man who debates how much of the right of way he will yield to the talk of the town.

Chapter 38

Never was gage more quickly taken up. With a single ripping movement Io tore off the borrowed dust coat and cap she wore. Nothing could have surpassed the effect of her instant transformation from something grotesque into the essence of grace and the spirit of dominance. As she came within a stride of Tony—a stunned, staring and confused Tony—she tossed him the discarded garments. One moment he had been a free man through the talisman of democracy, a great man of muscle and delegated authority, a veritable sledge hammer in the Rattling Run Cement Company's employ; the next he was a slave, a lackey, catching coat and cap, getting out of the way to let her pass, bowing, scraping, following.

Following Io in a simple frock of blue; Io, hatless, dark hair powdering swiftly to white, blue dress turning to silver beneath the invisible shower of the dust; Io, incomparably slight, threading high-headed through gigantic shapes with a mien that made him, Tony Mazaro, tremble lest she hold out her hand and command the huge mills to cease their rumble or call upon the heavens to fall.

He caught up with her, groaning and stammering through the roar, "Please, Miss Io, what you want me to do with them? Give them Jimmy, eh?"

She paid no attention to him. Moving swiftly, she gradually distanced him, so that finally he gave up the chase and stood hold-

271

ing cap and duster, afraid to let them go, much as he had held Io in person over the crusher so many years ago.

Ah, these Americans! They were too much for him; he was not one of them, after all! Not yet! Fool! How had he dared look at her like that? Never would she speak to him again.

Escaped from the works, she did not go to the automobile, but toward the path around the quarry to the pasture. Her eyes were wide, the red flecks within them glowing. She moved so swiftly that Jimmy had to exert himself to keep up.

"Io," he panted, "let me brush you off, and you got to shake out your hair. If your dress gets wet with the dust on it, it will be spoiled for good. Just let me——"

She came to a stop by a cedar, high up, at the edge of the quarry, put her back to it and looked down. Her hair and her dress were white, but she knew that her face was whiter still. She shook her skirt free of the dust, took down her hair and plowed her fingers through it; then she threw up her head. Now let Tony lookup, or any man, or the whole roaring mill. What would they see? Her face, a white star against the smoky blackness of the cedar; she herself, all of her, a star, a point of silver in the gloom, æons, millions of miles away, higher, greater——

Jimmy slipped off his coat and spread it beside the tree. He knelt on it and tugged at Io's skirts. She sank beside him, settling to earth with folded knees, supple as an ash, light as thistledown. He drew her back slowly to pillow her head against his arm. Thus she had permitted him to hold her before, the back of her neck in the crook of his elbow, herself face to face with the sky, never allowing him to bend over her, only to babble, sometimes refusing him even the poor solace of monologue. Tonight, instinctively, he strove to be impersonal.

"They're all laughing at old Laning Pearson down to Alloway on account of selling Three Roads Farm to Bob Colter."

She did not move. Presently Jimmy went on: "The old man took Bob, in his shirt and trousers, for a tramp trying to be funny. The more serious Bob got the doggeder was Lan, thinking it was a joke. The two of them kept on and on, trading and dickering and finally signing papers and things, the old man winking to his friends all day and laughing to himself all night."

Jimmy paused, giving Io a chance to stop him or urge him on; she did neither.

"Well," he continued listlessly, "I guess it was the only sale of its size ever took place in the county without mention of time or mortgage. Just a check for three hundred acres' worth of land with a house thrown in, but no stock, and when the old Pearson found that it was drawn on his own bank in Salem he laughed himself sick. He'd never seen or heard of a certified check before he saw that one; but he knows now what it is. He took to bed wondering how much more he could of got, and tomorrow they're moving him to the hospital."

Did Io hear? She gave no sign. What had she made of him, Jimmy Mattis? The stolid pedestal to her sundial? The wooden frame upon which to weave the warp and woof of her fancy? The pillow of her enchanted dreams? Almost a gondolier? The magic carpet of her journeys to and fro amid the worlds? A doormat upon which to wipe her returning feet? Was that all he was to her as she lay, relaxed and floating, in his aching yet ecstatic arms? Well, what of it? Wasn't that little much? These were not Jimmy's thoughts; nevertheless, he had the intuition to sense a difference tonight—the difference of a great loss subtracted from nothing. For tonight she did not relax, nor did she float. She was less than indifferent; she was inimical.

She put her fingers over her eyes and pressed them there. Myrtle Manor. Jennie. Her own mother. The judge. Tony. Jimmy. Near things—too near; you couldn't shut them out. Still keeping her eyes tightly closed, she threw out her arms. Her head fell back, making a bow of the column of her throat. She stirred, moved; her body quivered from head to heel. It was too much for such human flesh as Jimmy's to bear. Where was she gone? What flight held her?

How to bring her back? He leaned over and kissed her throat.

He never remembered how she gained her feet, so suddenly had she become erect before him, standing like an intaglio cut within the blackness of the tree. She was quiet, apparently not at all angry.

She looked at him calmly as she said, "Go home, Jimmy. Stop to tell mother I'm at Rattling Run Fields. And Jimmy, listen! Don't ever come back!"

Chapter 39

He did not leave her; she left him, though he stumbled after her with one hand out, almost blubbering, round-eyed, staring. She crossed the full length of the pasture, climbed lightly up the fence, stood upon its top rail, threw out her arms and leaped. Just so had Lessie Mattis climbed that fence with the aid of Drake's hands; just so had she leaped. How wide would Io's eyes have opened did scenes leave behind them pictures in the grass! What would her troubled soul have said if she could have witnessed under the drifting moonlight the reconstruction of Drake's unpardonable assault?

Without even a backward glance to see whether Jimmy was following, she ran along the path which first bordered the wood, then dipped into it, issued presently to cross the orchard, and finally debouched on the growing seclusion of what had been the backyard of Rattling Run Fields. Here, where once had been baked clay, scattered chicken coops, warped lean-to, weathered outhouses and gnarled trees, were the same gnarled trees, only springing from a mat of freshly mowed lawn. Trim bushes. A lusty private hedge set within the little one of box. Slow-growing vines creeping hopefully up the face of new stone walls; and, drifting from the west, the heavy, clinging odor of fig trees in full leaf.

She looked, expecting to find all of Rattling Run Fields a dark bulk; but to her astonishment there was a light showing from the great living room. She flew to its rear door, which gave upon the garden, knocked lightly, waited, and then beat upon it with her fist. No one came. She went back to the garden, stood on tiptoe and glanced through the window. Drake was sitting at his desk, eyes wide open and fixed before him, lips parted; face thin, gaunt, almost emaciated.

"Drake!" called Io, and then more loudly, "Drake!"

He did not move. She went around to the front and began to throw clots of earth at old Tom's open window, arousing him at last. He came stumbling and grumbling down the stairs to open the kitchen door.

"What's this now?" he said. "What's this, I say?"

She paid no attention to him, brushed by, passed through the ancient parlor and into Drake's presence. Guided by a profound instinct, she threw herself upon him, flung her arms around his neck and embedded her face against his shoulder.

"Oh, Drake, you've come back! Hold me! How could you go away? How could you?"

Thus aroused from his trance, he took her on his knees, rocked her, petted her. What was it his mother had said? "Drake, go up to your room; don't come down until you have made Io laugh." How tiny she had been and still was, and yet how completely formed. Io grown! Io a woman!

Still holding her in his arms, he arose, carried her to her own room, laid her on the bed and tried to leave her. Her arms tightened about his neck; he knelt; presently he sank to one side, sitting on his hip, holding her hands until she slept.

In the morning came Eunice, frightened.

"Drake! You here! Where's Io? What's happened to her?"

Io, curled up in the end of the enormous couch of the living room called, "Here I am, mother. What is it?"

"Oh!" breathed Eunice, sinking into a chair.

"That Jimmy Mattis! Why couldn't he have said Drake was here?"

"He didn't know," said Io.

Eunice clasped her hands tightly and looked at one and then the other of her children with puzzled eyes.

"Io——" She stopped and turned toward Drake. "I can't tell you what I've gone through with Io this summer. Not she herself—not that, Drake. But what she does—what people say. Miss Drew wouldn't have taken her back at Myrtle Manor, and now—last night—Jimmy Mattis, coming at two o'clock in the morning like a madman, waking the servants, the judge, everybody; insisting on seeing me——"

She stopped and forced her lips to smile; but they twitched straight in spite of her, and a frightened look crept into her eyes. To herself she repeated monotonously, "If you only love enough, everything is all right—always. Io," she went on aloud, "can't you understand? I'm your mother—your own mother. You can tell me anything in the world. Nothing can stop my love for you—nothing. I mean it. You come to Drake, but never to me. I mean—not like this. Do you think he loves you more than I—more broadly, I mean? Try me! See if I don't understand too. Don't hold back! Please! Tell me!"

"Tell what?" asked Io, white of cheek, her eyes wide.

"What happened," said Eunice desperately.

"Something must have happened. If you could have heard him—at two o'clock in the morning shouting—shouting you'd never see him again two o'clock! Why, where were you all that time? What were you doing?"

"In the works—roll crusher—Goliath mills——" began Io, and ceased.

Amid the thunder of the works she could have told; here, in the quiet room, how futile were her meaningless words. She looked wilted, like a bent reed; there was no longer any fire in her eyes or strength in the fullness of her lips; she even hung her head.

"Nothing at all has happened; nothing ever happens," she murmured. "I'm just through with Jimmy, because—well, because he called me back. He's always calling me back."

"Back?" asked Eunice. "Back from where?" What language was this? Had she once talked it herself?

Io turned her head slowly and looked at Drake. He arose, came forward, knelt and slipped an arm around her.

"Mother," he said, "Io's all right. What business is it of ours where she goes? How do you know but what Jimmy dragged her back from making the rounds of a million stars? To the devil with Miss Drew and what she thinks! Send Nora out here to look after Io and to cook. I'm tired, anyway, of all the things Tom knows how to make. And by the way, if it comforts you any to know it, Io was in her own bed and asleep by eleven o'clock." His smile deepened as he looked steadily at his mother. "Try it, won't you?" he pleaded. "Just let Rattling Fields have an innings all by itself. Will you?"

Eunice sat for a moment in silence, regarding her two children, who looked back with a soft quality in their gaze which seemed gradually to envelop her in a nameless warmth. She remembered that day and hour when, elated and happily victorious, holding them each by a hand, she had taken a single symbolic step forward. She had possessed them at that moment in a nobler sense than ever before or since—until now. Now she possessed them again. Knowing it, she smiled on them with no rebellious twitching of her lips.

"You two!" she murmured. "Have it your own way. Since there's nothing the matter with either of you, it must be with me—and someday I'll see it."

"No!" they cried in unison, half rising, but she stopped them with a gesture.

She went outside, but did not immediately join the judge, who was driving a restive successor to Gypsy mincingly up and down the road. She waved to him, a little movement of one hand which said among other things, "Everything is alright, Will. Don't hurry. Leave me alone for a moment."

She walked slowly down the steps and to the corner of the house. There she paused. How worn Drake had looked, drained, nothing left but bone and sinew. Not a word as to where he himself had been, or why. What had happened to him? Never mind; some day she would know that too. The important thing was that he had come back. She looked all about her deliberately, and drew a quivering breath at what her awakened eyes beheld.

All of Rattling Run Fields seemed to have emerged from a century of niggardliness into a burst of fruitful liberality. Whether from the quaking of the earth produced by the gigantic blasts or from the disintegration after many years of the marl hauled by Warner Sherborne or from the intensive tilling aided by overhead irrigation introduced by Drake, or perhaps from the sum of all these causes, the hard face of the farm had changed more than its forbidding expression, defying memory to recall its sterile and malicious past. Here, as far as the eye could reach, was a translucent tenderness found only in the texture of living and growing things.

Eunice's eyes opened wide with inner amazement at the fantastic vision which suddenly beset her—a vision of herself, of anyone, lying down to press face against the ground. Still gropingly, but with a definite reaching forth of the spirit, she glimpsed the origin of the endearing phrase "Mother Earth" as springing from some such visualization as now confronted her of the lifegiving breast of the soil, not in combat, but in alliance with all womankind.

Chapter 40

Something was preying on Drake's mind, gnawing it day and night; but whatever it was, he kept it to himself. After his mother, Tom; after Tom, the judge; after the judge, Colter, reluctantly, each in turn, gave him a chance to speak out; but he ignored all overtures. Bob was puzzled—more puzzled than the rest, even though he had more to go on than all the others together. What had happened? He wondered. Had Lessie Mattis, in that world where she was not Lessie Mattis, turned Drake down? If he felt as badly about it as all this, why wasn't he going after her? Was it conceivable that Drake was a quitter? The answer to that last question was at hand; one had only to look out of the window at his all-conquering handiwork.

But if something preyed on Drake's mind in spite of his entrancing absorption with his hedges, plants and trees, what of Io? Behold her, one slumberous, startled morning, fleeing through the wood with a darting flash of gray wings, rushing up to Bob, seizing both his wrists, casting a glance backward over her shoulder to where Jimmy comes lumbering along, hat off, mopping the sweat from his brow. Io, shaking Bob's wrists: "Please, Bob, make him understand. He must keep his feet off Rattling Run Fields or I'll lock myself in my room and throw the key away. I'll get a dog—a dozen dogs——"

"Hush, Io, now! Quietly! Go anywhere you please, and he'll not bother you again. Don't give it another thought. Do you understand? Don't worry. Just leave it to me."

"Thank you, Bob."

She gave him just such a smile as had subjugated Tom Bodley a dozen years before. Bob felt something bulge within him, but laid the phenomenon to pity for the unusual emptied pallor of her face and the nervous twitching of her lower lip. He watched her go; then dealt wisely and effectively with Jimmy Mattis, persuading him that his method would gain him nothing.

But for the rest of that day Robert Colter, who prided himself on looking upon all worlds, all tribulations, all vicissitudes of emotion and fortune from without, found himself subtly entangled within a web. Its mesh was unfelt, unseen, yet as present as a surrounding mist; so that he trembled when, late that afternoon, as he lay with his back against a hummock and his head caught in his hands, he saw Io coming toward him, not by chance but by intent. She stood for an instant directly before him, and what the judge had seen he also perceived—that she was an arrow incarnate, direct symbol of ambition and a goal, subject only to the Master Archer's hand.

"Hello, Io," he said, making no move to rise. "Lo," she replied shortly, without interest in formalities; then her face became alive and intent; yet apart from him, from Robert Colter, the individual. Of him as a person, as of her own body, she seemed totally unconscious. She sank cross-legged before him.

"Bob," she began with an uncertain smile in her eyes, "what is the answer to this? I'm Io. I get up, I do this, I do that; the day begins, the day goes on, the day grows old and dies. It's gone. I say, 'Good-by, day.' But I'm still Io just the same, am I not?"

"Go on," said Colter. "One day you smile," she continued more gravely, "and people love you. They don't say so, but you just feel it. Then, while you are exactly the same you, a day comes when you smile and all of a sudden you know here"—laying her hand on her breast—"that they don't love you any more, not in the same way. What is that, Bob. Am I somebody else?"

282

"Go on," said Colter, drawing himself up to sit erect, his arms wrapped around his knees, his eyes fixed on her face. "Go on. I'll tell you when I know."

"Mother says 'Danger!' like that, with a big D," continued Io, frowning and trying to smile at the same time. "You meet the judge on the stairs, and he stops and fumbles with his watch, then he turns red and mumbles 'Straight figure, straight eye, straightest little person in the world!' But somehow it doesn't make you happy; it makes you choke. Then I got into Jimmy's car. When he asked where to go I told him the works." She threw out her hand toward the quarry. "Down there," she continued. "I wanted something tremendous in my eyes. Do you understand wanting a funny thing like that? Something big, inside my eyes, so I couldn't see anything else but just that big thing. We went into the works and there I found it. Everything prodigious; everything rumbling and roaring. You know. You can hear it down there now. Only bigger, nearer, a thousand times; then——

"Listen, Bob." She held out her two hands, closed tightly into fists, white across the knuckles. "Everything terribly wicked, terribly powerful, but held in its place like that. Yes! Like that! I loved to breathe the dust. I loved to hear the roar. I loved the great grumbling mills; and then I turned, and there was Tony."

She relaxed her hands and threw back her head.

"You know Tony. You think you do, Bob, but not this Tony, looking like a dog that's made up his mind not to get out of the way. Well, I took off the coat and cap I had on, and walked at him; through him; I made him carry them as if he were a servant.

"So!" She motioned Tony out of sight and out of mind with a backward thrust of her hand. "Then we came out of the mill and climbed up here, into this pasture. I sat on Jimmy's coat, against his knees, my head thrown back in the crook of his arm, like many a time before, not looking at him, just looking up, tired—tired of asking 'Why? What is it? Why?' Do you see? Just looking up, floating, going away, thinking that somehow I'd found an answer down there in the works, an answer to mother, to all of them, perhaps even to myself. Only I didn't quite yet know what."

She drew erect from the hips, straight as a quivering sapling, and placed her hands against her throat.

"Just then it occurred to Jimmy," she continued in a voice with a thread of steel running through it, "to kiss me here, on my throat. Who cares about lips? People take them as they take your hand. But here! Something turned over inside of me and said distinctly, 'You're not the same Io any more.' What do you think, Bob?"

"Now I can answer you," said Colter, his eyes intently fixed in hers. "I suppose every girl passes through the mill of herself, but never two of them along exactly the same path. If I were you, I'd stop worrying. Be just yourself. Remember only one thing and stick to it—that you are Io, the same Io, undying, eternal; in the meadows a milk-white heifer; in the skies the crescent moon. Never forget it."

"You mean it, Bob, don't you?"

"With all my heart."

She threw out her arms and let them fall; the frown cleared from her brows and her eyes sparkled.

"Let's look for it," she said, arising. "The baby moon, I mean."

She walked to the edge of the quarry and gazed over the gap at her feet toward the west into the paling heavens.

"Oh, it's there!" she cried. "It really is. How faint! It's like a white eyebrow fallen against the sky. I'd like to slap it—not hard—then blow, and make a wish."

Colter laughed, but his eyes were gravely intent on her straight figure, etched vividly like a spire against the void.

"Shall I dance for you, Bob, and for the moon?"

"No," he answered. "Don't move. Stay just as you are, and listen. I've simply got to quote something:

> *"As a young beech tree on the edge of a forest*
> *Stands still in the evening,*
> *Then shudders through all its leaves in the light air*
> *And seems to fear the stars—*
> *So are you still and so tremble."*

284

"Lovely!" said Io over her shoulder. "Am I like——" Her words ceased with an absolute suddenness.

"Jump!" cried Colter, seeing with horror what she had already felt. "Jump back—straight back!"

A tall spar of the rock upon which she stood, loosened by the seepage of the buried spring, leaned slowly outward, leaving a widening gap behind it. With her head twisted sharply on her shoulders, she saw that she was already too late. For an instant her eyes met Colter's.

"Bob," she gulped, "I fear no stars."

She faced the quarry, spread her arms wide and launched herself free of the toppling rock; floated, fell—like an arrow lying flat against the wind.

Even as he rushed at top speed along the edge of the cliff, Colter felt a surge of consuming admiration for the cool nerve which could see so quickly what to do and for the courage that could then do it. When the descending bank became too steep for him to run, he cast himself down, rolled sideways, relaxed all his muscles, and fell heavily down a short drop to the level of the quarry floor. Scratched and bruised, but with no bones broken, he scrambled to his feet and dashed back toward the base of the sheer wall of stone, never pausing until he reached the verge of the pool formed by the treacherous spring.

In its center was Io; just behind her, the fallen spear of rock broke in three sections. She was holding herself up on her arms, her chin just above the level of the water. Except that her head was slowly sinking forward, threatening to immerse her face, she did not move. He waded toward her with long, stumbling strides, seized her, and dragged her upright, but she could not stand.

"What's the matter?" she asked between chattering teeth. "What happened, Bob?"

"Lock your hands around my neck," he ordered, perceiving that her body was helpless from the waist down. She obeyed, and at the tightening of her arms, so purposeful and yet so pitifully light in their pressure, his heart began to thump with battering beats which were to remain forever unforgettable as marking the very pinnacle of all the combined emotions of affection. He had been entranced by her as a child, he had worshiped her girlhood whimsically from afar; but now, in this instant, he loved her overwhelmingly, and knew it.

Chapter 41

No other single event in the tragic history of the Sherborne homestead had quite the galvanizing effect of the accident to Io, which statement leads one by indirection to the surprising discovery that to the community at large Rattling Run Fields had no more tragic a record than any one of a dozen other farms in the three counties. In the Spartan rural mind it takes one or more murders to make a tragedy.

But there was something so gripping to the most untrained imaginations in Io's leap from the forty-foot cliff into the quarry pool that the spectacular startled these people, who took deep waters for granted, into making of her act a nine day wonder, and of herself an object of interest and solicitude. Excursions of those who were merely curious to the works to view the scene of the catastrophe became a nuisance, and the pilgrimages of kindlier persons to the house itself a revelation.

The occupants of the buggies and cars which threaded the rough road to Rattling Run Fields did not knock at the front door or leave cards to inquire; they lined up their vehicles by the way-side and waited patiently until someone happened to come out to them. At first it was Tom, wondering what they wanted; and then Drake or the judge who issued from the house to satisfy the silent appeal for news. The judge felt a glow of gratification at the thought that out of the infinite complexities which went to make up Io Sherborne, all that these neighborly folk seemed now able to remember was her unforgettable smile.

Drake, astonished at the range of her casual acquaintance, and watching its crystallization overnight into friendship, felt a swelling of the heart, an increase of his love of Io and of gratitude toward the undiscovered world in which they lived. His gray eyes turned dark as he faced neighbors and strangers to make his frank statements: Io's life was not in danger. Evidently there had been a dislocation, for she had no control over her body from the waist down. The doctors did not despair of restoring her completely, but it would take time. A famous specialist was on his way to the farm.

Upon first being summoned, Eunice hastened, white-lipped but unshaken, to Io's bedside and did all that it was possible to do for her comfort. Fortunately, there was no physical pain to combat, only the mental torment which might come at any moment as a reaction to one who had been all her life straight and swift as the arrow which was her symbol. Awaiting that moment, Eunice was outwardly calm; inwardly, however, remembering their last interview, she was a prey to an agonizing fear. She asked no questions of Io, but at the first opportunity drew Colter aside.

"Robert," she said, "tell me exactly what happened. Don't be afraid."

Colter's eyes opened slowly and unusually wide.

"Afraid?" he repeated. "What do you mean?" Without waiting for her answer, he called Drake and the judge. "Listen, you three people," he said. "Anyone else in Io's place would be dead today, mashed up with the rock that fell with her. No one else could have thought quickly enough and had the nerve to do what she did. She jumped, and she fell clear and in the deepest water there was to fall in, and—and I'm in love with her."

He flushed with unreasonable anger and embarrassment, turned and left them abruptly.

Fully advised by the colleagues who called him in consultation, the specialist brought with him an assistant and all appliances

288

necessary for a thorough examination. The X-ray disclosing nothing specific, he agreed with the diagnosis already made, advised
quiet awaiting of developments, and suggested that Io be moved
forthwith to the city, where she could remain indefinitely under
his surveillance. At being informed of this recommendation, she
gave Eunice and Drake a look which neither of them could mis-
read or ignore.

It was scarcely necessary for her to supplement her glance by
adding aloud, "I won't leave Rattling Run Fields for anyone or
anything."

The specialist heard her; he smiled, looked around the room
and then through the windows, first toward the sombrous ravine
of Rattling Run, and then out over the garden and the orchard
to the high bank of the long line of woods.

"Is this," he asked with a flick of his hand, Rattling Run Fields?"

Drake answered "Yes" in a full voice, and Io nodded, her eyes
directed pleadingly at the physician and still giving an impression
of rebellion held merely in abeyance.

"My dear child," he responded, "I don't blame you; and just
your wanting anything as badly as you want to remain here is an
encouraging symptom. Stay, by all means. I'll make it my business
to drive down for Sunday lunch once in a while."

Thus it transpired that the homestead gradually settled into a
new routine. Eunice remained in attendance for three weeks and then
returned to town. Nora was installed as sole nurse, and found the
burden light. The family physician came in from time to time, watch-
ful for the first signs of curvature or any other radical development.

Drake visited Io regularly three times a day in much the same
spirit as he visited his plants and trees. His faith never wavered;
and watching him through long, understanding silences, Io was
comforted, remembering what she had said to Tom in regard to
the fig-tree venture: "If Drake plants them they will grow."

It was Colter, however, who did most to lighten Nora's duties.
Individualistic to the last, he had abandoned his casual residence at
Rattling Run Fields on the very day he had made open confession

of his love for Io. He took definite possession of Three Roads Farm, got out his riding togs, bought himself an excellent saddle horse, had dinner promptly at twelve, and immediately thereafter mounted to ride the ten miles which separated him from Io. He stayed with her for three hours of every afternoon.

He had asked no one's permission for this extraordinary procedure and there was none to say him nay; partly through sympathy and largely because of a general feeling that any interference, however well intended, would lead directly to the murder so far lacking in the annals of Rattling Run Fields. When he arrived for the first time Nora lingered in the room, uncertain what to do. She was so thoroughly ignored that she soon knew herself to be less than the least of the unoccupied chairs and learned to be her own furniture over. Even Eunice bowed to the inevitable and made her visits in the mornings.

None but a bold man or a fool would have undertaken to spend three hours a day with a bedridden girl in whom he wished to awaken love; but Colter had the faith which transcends courage and an insight which was uncanny. He watched Io's moods with a keenness that bordered on the feral, and, alone among those who attended her, acquired the power to make her sleep almost at will. But it was when she was gay and eager for companionship that the depths of his nature and the variety of his resources came into play.

He told her of his lonely childhood spent with governesses and tutors, of his boyhood under the guardianship of an uncle and a trust company, the only father and mother he could remember, and of his discovery that freedom cannot be handed over even with a large checking account. What had helped him most, what had brought him to Rattling Run Fields, and held him there, was something said to him by Drake, and to Drake by the judge many years ago, as far back as boarding-school days.

That foundation laid, he took to reading to her, or writing her a poem, or making her write one, filling in the alternate riming lines with a facility which aroused either her gasping admiration or peals of mirth. At such times Drake would come in, his eyes shining, and demand a reading; while Tom and Nora, dropping whatever they might be doing, would fill the door and their ears. This proved the favorite of all games; but there was many another which ran it close, and finally there were hours of talk and silence.

One day—the first of snow—she said to him, "Bob, why do you do all this for me? Just because you were there when it happened?" "I'm glad you asked that," he answered, swinging in his chair and leaning toward her. "I do it because I love you with all my heart and soul."

"But, Bob," she stammered, "what—what's the use?"

Suddenly the courage which had never yet faltered began to break visibly in her face; her eyes became suffused and her mouth contorted.

"Don't!" she cried, flinging her arms around his neck and burying her head against his shoulder. "Don't look!"

He held her quivering body tightly.

"Of course I won't look," he murmured; "but why shouldn't I? You don't understand, Io. I love you, crying or laughing, every least bit of you."

"Half of me is dead," she sobbed. "Why play it isn't true? I can never marry you."

"In the spring, on the first day of June. Are you listening?"

She shook her head in affirmation, and then violently in denial.

"No! No! Please, Bob, I can't stand it. You're hurting me."

"In the spring, on the first day of June," he repeated evenly, "you and I are going to be married. Now, darling, don't let's talk about that any more; just get accustomed to thinking about it. Tell me instead, do you love me—a little?"

She threw back her head and held her tear-stained face openly before his eyes.

"I do," she said gravely. "I love you a great, great deal. I shall always love you, and never marry you—while I'm like this."

"Kiss me," he begged.

She studied his face for a long moment, then closed her eyes, touched her lips to his and threw herself back on the pillows.

Chapter 42

It was part of the wisdom of Colter that he could wait for the lift of spring to start the sap of the world about its business before he made a second attempt to shake Io's determination. Neither the snows of winter nor the mud of March succeeded in making him miss a day, but during three months he never attempted to take Io in his arms or to kiss her. The very fact that he never stooped to the casual good-by salutes she had granted to others made her wonder whether he knew that in touching his lips so lightly she had given, though infinitesimally, something of herself never before surrendered. She began to wish that he would kiss her again.

As this desire grew she became supersensitive to all that was going on about her, within and without the room. She felt not only the poignant ache of the nameless longings which bud with crocus and pussy willow, but divined the growing purpose behind Colter's waiting eyes. A lump came into her throat when she looked at him, and a weakness into her heart and arms. Afraid to put herself to the test, and knowing that an attack on her fortitude could be forestalled in only one way, she wrote him a letter and gave it to Drake for delivery.

"Dearest," she wrote, "this letter has no date. It is for you to read whenever you are lonely. Let these written words be my own voice in the silence, my hand in the dark. I put myself in these words. I need you, my own dear. Every night I take your heart in my hands and hold it close—close against my heart. This letter is for every day 'Good morning,' and for every night 'Sweet dreams.' It is as if I came to you when you call 'Io.' I come to you across the yellow daisies and touch your arm, and say 'Yes, Bob.' But, Bob, my own dear, it's the only way I can come to you, or you to me."

Colter was handed the note in the great living room. When he turned from reading it to rush to Io, Drake barred his way.

"Bob," he said, "I'm for you; you know I'm for you; but when it comes to a choice between standing by you or by Io there is no choice. Whatever she says goes. What's more, you've got to give her her chance in the way she asks for it. You simply can't do anything else. There's just one thing I can tell you out of fairness to yourself, and you may think it's a miserable straw. She's demanded a string of doctors, one after another, and the first of them is on his way. If anything happens you'll get the news as fast as I can bring it."

Six days later, long after nightfall, Drake hammered on the door at Three Roads Farm, and jumped back in surprise when it was flung open almost immediately. His face was enough to show that he was the bearer of no happy tidings. He asked Bob if he might come in, and was shown through an empty hall, past open and echoing doors, to the only apartment which seemed furnished. It was comprised of two large rooms thrown into one, and took up the full depth of the house. Here Colter had installed himself in great comfort and with excellent taste. He motioned Drake to one of the two big chairs flanking the fire.

"Bob," said Drake, staring frowningly at Colter's unkempt appearance, "there's no good news, but I've got to talk. The specialist came and stood pat that there was nothing to do at present. When I told him straight out that she was going to have an osteopath he just threw up his hands and went. We had another man in between, and then came this bonesetter. The things they've done to that kid's body—the things she made them do——"

Colter sprang to his feet.

294

"What the devil did you come here for? To tell me you've been standing by watching a brute pull your sister apart?"

Drake's eyes darkened.

"No, Bob," he replied quietly; "I came here to tell you that Io has been going through hell, not on her own account but on yours, putting up with torture no human body would stand for its own sake alone, because she longs to be with you. The worst of it is, they've all told her it's because her injury is so slight that it's so hard to locate and to cure. She made them do things, Bob. The last man, the bonesetter, sweated blood and begged her to let him off. Ever since he went she hasn't slept. Staring awake. Mother and I thought perhaps if you'd come over you could put her to sleep."

Colter leaped into the air, gesticulating and shouting incoherently. His words became intelligible only as he left the room, closely followed by Drake.

"Why didn't you tell me what you wanted when you came in? We've lost time—hours."

"Oh, no, we haven't," replied Drake as they left the house for the stables; "I've been here only five minutes." He started to tell Colter he would do well to brush his hair and shave, but changed his mind. Instead he said, "It wasn't part of the plan to take a wild man to Io. Fortunately, you have ten miles in which to steady down."

His words had a sobering effect, and they came just in time to prevent Bob from starting out on the long ride at a foundering pace. The two rode for over half an hour in silence, coming into closer sympathy with each other moment by moment. Colter succeeded not only in calming himself but in remembering that he was not the only unhappy individual in the world.

Without warning even to himself he turned toward Drake in the dark and asked, "What's your trouble, Drake? What happened between you and Miss Mattis?"

There was a long pause before Drake answered, and yet it was not an awkward pause. Both men knew themselves to be at bed rock and each accepted the sincerity of the other without question.

"I married Lessie," said Drake finally, "while I was away ten months ago. We quarreled the next day over something that I can't tell you about because I know you wouldn't understand."

"How do you know that?" demanded Colter.

"Because of you and Io," replied Drake. "I might as well tell you frankly, Bob, that I can understand your wanting to marry Io, but I can't understand your doing it. To me it would be a wrong thing to do."

"Wrong?" cried Colter. "What has right or wrong to do with marrying the one woman you love? What have conditions or disabilities to do with it? You've got to take your chance as it comes, haven't you? If you love her that's all there is to it. It's beyond you. You simply can't help yourself. Now tell me why you left Lessie and see if I don't understand and perhaps help you to understand that there are times when half a woman can be the whole world."

"Tell you now!" exclaimed Drake with a short laugh. "Never!"

He put heels to his horse and they plunged forward at a gallop through the splattering mud. Arrived at Rattling Run Fields, Eunice came out to meet them. She drew Colter aside, and, shocked by his appearance, her first impulse was to send him to a bathroom and a borrowed razor; but like Drake she changed her mind. Without saying ·a word beyond a soft-voiced greeting, she accompanied him to Io's door and left him. The talk with Drake had sobered him as no discussion of his own affairs could have done. He stood quietly waiting for Io to realize his presence. Head back upon a single pillow, she was lying with arms outthrown and eyes staring at the ceiling. Presently, as though he had called her name, she raised herself on her hands and looked directly at him, taking in only slowly his disheveled hair, apparently unbrushed for a week, his unshaven cheeks and bloodshot eyes.

"Robert!" she whispered. He went forward to kneel beside the bed. "I have been thinking about you," she continued, "every hour. Worrying about you. I was right to worry, because I have hurt you terribly."

"You, worrying about me!" exclaimed Colter. "What do I matter? Nothing! They have done things to you that no one will ever do again—not while I live. Lie back."

She obeyed with a long, quivering sigh. He put his right arm under her neck and settled her head comfortably against his shoulder; his other hand he laid on her side, pressing her lightly to him in an intuitive action of protection.

"Sweet dreams," he whispered, "and remember that I love you."

Toward morning Eunice looked in to see Colter apparently asleep at his post; but it did not matter, for Io was plunged in profound and unmistakable slumber. She was breathing deeply, easily; her hands, however, seemed awake. They held tightly to Colter's arms and occasionally her fingers moved as if to reassure themselves of his nearness. Eunice tiptoed away, but her silent presence appeared to have created a disturbance. Io stirred and awoke. She lay still for an instant with caught breath, and then resolutely freed herself from Robert's arm.

"Unfair!" she murmured, looking into his tired eyes. "Who told you you might come here?"

At the hurt look in his face she suddenly became fully matured, grown, packed with all the experience of all the ages of woman.

She threw her arms around his neck, clung to him, raised her lips and with half-closed eyes kissed him passionately.

"That is how I love you, Robert. Remember it; but please go."

"Io," said Colter, holding her erect and forcing her to meet his gaze, "you don't understand. You don't know that you are trying to do the impossible. You can't give me up. We just haven't anything to do with it. It's the clearest thing to me and I'm amazed that you can't see it. Sooner or later you are going to get well, but even that has nothing to do with you and me as we are. Just what are you trying to do? Do you think you could give me anything by taking yourself away? Listen. I am alive, body and soul, only when I am near you. I live only as you live. If that is true before God, true in letter and in spirit, do you dare give me up? Do you?"

"Is it true, Robert? True not just for today but for always? Are you sure?"

"I am sure."

"Then I'll marry you, even if it breaks my heart."

Chapter 43

Strange was the list of guests whom Io invited to her wedding; she explained to Colter that she had known so few people that she must have them all. How easy for her to go back in memory, checking all the landmarks of acquaintance—of persons whom she had actually known by name! First of all came the Sunday-school superintendent, whose face had burst open like an overbaked potato, but she could not recall his name. Leave him out. Next was the group that had gathered for Warner Sherborne's burial. She included the judge, her mother, Drake, old Tom and Nora under the general heading of her immediate family; then she named Tryer Mattis and—yes, Jimmy. She looked shyly up at Colter.

"You don't know Lessie Mattis," she added; "you never saw her; but I want Lessie too."

"Are you sure you want her?" he asked quickly, stalling for time, wondering how Drake would react to the sound of that name.

"Well," said Io, "I'm quite sure. Yes; I know I want her."

"Why?"

"Because of something Tom said about her," replied Io promptly.

"Old Tom?"

"Yes. He said she isn't pretty; you know she isn't pretty, yet when she passes by, you can't help but think she's the handsomest woman that ever walked. Something like that."

"Where did you get it? Where on earth did you hear that?"

"Tom said it," repeated Io. "He said it last year to Jimmy Mattis. He said it on the day Lessie came here, the same day that Drake went away."

Colter's eyes narrowed, and he studied her face, seeking in vain for some hidden current beneath the surface of her words.

"Will you get her yourself, Robert?" she continued. "Promise you will see that she comes to my wedding."

"I'll tell you what I'll do," agreed Colter. "If you'll write her a note I'll see that she gets it."

Next upon her list were Tony Mazaro, Jake Werten, whom she had seen but once and never forgotten, and a few of the hands at the works who had been wont to call to her when she passed, or merely to doff their caps. Then came Jennie, her roommate; Miss Drew too; and all the girls she had known at Myrtle Manor. Perhaps none might come, but she wished them all to be invited.

"That's all," she finished, and drew a long breath. "And now you, Robert. Whom do you want to ask?"

"Only my uncle," replied Robert gloomily, "and I hope he won't come."

"Why?" asked Io quickly. "Why do you say that?"

"Oh, nothing to do with you or the wedding. Just a matter between him and myself. We agree on nothing except a whole-hearted disagreement."

"Leave his address with me," said Io. "I shall write to him too.

What she wrote to James Fordyce Colter, Esq., is a matter of record, but closely guarded by a gentleman who prided himself on his appreciation of the fine points of privacy. Her other note, read by at least two persons to whom it was not addressed, may be quoted:

Dear Lessie: I would like so much to have you come to my wedding on the first of June. I remember you very well, and of course I know that you ran away from home—so won't you come straight to Rattling Run Fields and stay with us? Come a day ahead. I am the little girl whom you thought too young to play with.

Io SHERBORNE.

Colter read the note at her request; then folded it and put it in his pocket, wondering if he dared send it without consulting Drake. While he was still anxiously mulling the point of honor in his mind, Drake entered Io,'s room according to his custom.

"Drake," said Io, "I've written a letter I wish you to read. Show it to him, Robert."

Colter drew out the slip of paper rather hastily, handed it to Drake, and then watched his face as he read. Scarcely a flicker of betrayal; only a faint straightening of his lips and a deeper shade of gray in his eyes.

"Is it all right, Drake?" asked Io. "You don't mind, do you? On that night we can have a bed put in my sitting room, and Nora can go back to her room upstairs."

"Quite all right," said Drake. As if he challenged Colter's eyes, he added with a white smile, "Why should I mind?"

It has been indicated that Lessie Mattis, on and off the stage, had not only a sense of humor but the rare faculty of measuring the dramatic interest against the passing moment. It appealed to her to appear at Rattling Run Fields on the eve of Io's wedding day, but when she was ushered by Nora into Io's sitting room, patently transformed into a bedroom by the addition of a bed and dressing table, her pride felt a little hurt, as was professionally inevitable. When, however, she passed into Io's room and saw Io's dark head against the pillows and Io's great consuming eyes staring from the appealing white shadow of her face; when she saw that she whom she remembered as a vivid, darting little girl was terribly stricken, Lessie forgot her fame, her pride and every unkind jab she had had of fortune. For an instant she stood resplendent in

301

the doorway, then swept forward and sank on her knees with her cheek against Io's hand.

"Darling Io! Lovely name! What has happened?"

Io looked at her.

"You don't know? No one has told you?"

"No," said Lessie, "no one."

"I was standing on the edge of the cliff over the quarry," said Io. "The rock broke away and I jumped. It did something to my back."

Lessie burst into tears. She wept as Io had never before heard anyone weep. She sobbed as if all the pain in the world had found an echo in her heart; but when the storm passed, it passed utterly, leaving her face tear-stained, unashamed, serene. Io reached out and touched her cheek lightly.

"Lessie," she whispered, "you have made me love you." Someone entered the room. "Here is Drake. You know—you remember him, don't you?"

Lessie arose with a quick straightening of her shoulders, stood erect, and turned. Io strained her eyes and saw nothing save that these two faced each other without a tremor; she strained her ears, but heard only Drake's formal greeting: "Welcome to Rattling Run Fields."

Chapter 44

Io lay on her bed, suddenly wide awake. She looked at the little clock placed within the glow of the night lamp, and saw that it was past midnight. What had awakened her? Voices. The silence of the night makes a funnel for murmuring voices, especially if it be in a house where such a sound is seldom heard. Drake's voice, coming through the window, across the angle of the yard, coming from the living room; Drake's voice, and another's. Not Robert's. A woman's voice. Lessie! Then afterwards, Robert's voice too.

Io listened. She could make out no words as yet, but the murmuring was growing steadily louder. There was a rhythm to it, and a throb. It billowed, and with each billow came nearer to her ears. Presently she would know what they were talking about; but even before she could quite hear she was startled into calling out for Nora. Then she remembered; Nora was upstairs. People did not speak so rapidly as that unless they were angry, she thought. What was happening?

She raised her hands, caught her arms around the corner post of the bed and dragged herself high on the pillows. One voice triumphed over the others and became clearly audible; a voice of astonishing power and range of expression—Lessie's voice. Now it was modulated, like a muted string; now it swelled evenly to a climbing rush of words; and now it broke with the crack and sting of a whiplash. Io's eyes grew wide. How terrible! To whom was Lessie talking? Not to Drake. To Robert, then? Where had she learned to talk like that?

"Every night, every performance—always there; and no woman ever showed a man a colder shoulder. Ask him. He won't lie. And he knew that I meant it. Why, I've never meant anything in my life more than when I said back here in the pasture that I was through with all kinds of dirt at seventeen, and added Drake Sherborne for good measure!" There was the sound of a fist striking a table. "Through!"

A pause, and then she began again.

"All the old tricks, though he hated to do them; I'll say that for him. Notes by the ushers; then when that got him nowhere, notes by the door man. Look at him. Can you imagine him standing at the stage entrance? Can you? He did it!"

The trained voice lowered, but still Io could hear each word, sharply clipped from the next, clear without resounding.

"He could have kept up that sort of thing for all time, and I would never have known he was alive; but he did something else which had never been done before. He took the same seat night after night; not the first row—the third, on the aisle. Well, you think, that's been done before, thousands of times. Yes; but not this. Wait till I tell you." A break; then, "Have you seen me act?"

She must have addressed that question straight at Robert, for Io heard him reply fervently, "I have."

The voice opened again on a fuller tone:

"I don't know when I looked at him first; but I'll remember until I die the night it swept over me that he saw me alone, not what I was doing. You don't realize what I'm saying. I mean he never saw me act the part! Think! You remember it, don't you? Ha! Well, ask him. Twenty-forty times, and he can't tell you what I did or said." Snap of the whiplash; "Can you?" and Drake's low, strong voice, answering "No."

"Oh, Drake! Poor boy!" gasped Io as she dragged on the bed-post in an impulsive movement to go to him. Then Lessie's rising

304

voice halted her and she sank back limply, her ears straining to catch every inflection.

"How could I act in the face of that? A man's hungry eyes on me every moment, seeing just me, nothing but me, without voice, without anything—without my clothes even—crying out so I alone could hear him: 'Don't fool yourself. You're only Lessie Mattis, the woman I kissed on the mouth without so much as a by your leave! Remember? In the pasture.'"

Her voice fell to a still lower key, but was yet winged, pitched to carry.

"I sent for him. I couldn't help it, of course. I'm not a fool. I knew I had to give in or quit acting. But there was something else—something above and beyond my pocketbook. There was the thought that it's something with a sort of price of its own to have a man see you, only you, just for yourself. So I sent for him and asked him what he wanted.

"I wish you could have seen him standing there in my sitting room, looking like something caught that might break down a wall or two to get out. He called me Lessie, and I almost looked around to see whom he meant! He said, like this: 'Lessie, I've waited all these weeks because I must tell you how it happened'; and I asked 'How what happened?' and he said 'In the pasture. It was this way: I just had to do it; I couldn't help it. So please forgive me, please marry me, and let's go back.'" Sharply: "Is that what you said? Is it?"

"Yes," came Drake's voice. "Bob has a right to know."

"Bob has a right to know!" repeated Lessie. "Well, has he a right to hear this? Listen! These are his words: 'Lessie, you alone, no other woman; do you understand? None other. Since the world began, Lessie, and while it lasts, here in my arms, here against my heart! You see, it couldn't be helped. Your mouth, your eyes, my face against your throat. No other, ever. No——'"

"Stop!" from Drake. A hoarse cry like a groan, one word, cutting across her speech, stanching it, damming it.

"No, Drake, no!" sobbed Io beneath her breath, and writhed

until she hung on the verge of the bed, one nerveless leg oddly bent and hanging to the floor.

"For hours," continued the voice, more quietly. "For days. Like that. Saying the things I'd heard all my life—and yet never heard before. Ramming them into my ears, making me believe them. He was real. Everything about him was real. There wasn't any asking of questions. No need. None. You knew it; and I used to wish some other woman might see him, hear him talk to me, to just Lessie Mattis without her jewels or her fame or her fine dresses. Building a wall, each word a stone between me and everything that had gone before. No eyes over his shoulders—not a glance. No. Just fixed on me, in me, so that in the end—I forgot my sense of humor and married him."

Robert's voice: "Drake! Steady, old man!"

"Yes! Steady!" cried Lessie, loud, like the peal of a clarion. Crash of her chair to the floor as she arose, hurling it backward. Hearing that cry, that sound, walls were no bar to sight. Io could see her taking the stage—long eyes, long limbs, deep bosom—inscrutable face flung open, uncovered to anybody's gaze. "Yes, steady! You men! Fist against the heartstrings! One minute, 'Have a cup of tea'; and the next, 'Have a baby!' Yes; like that—like that! Get to work and have a baby!"

Snap of her fingers like a pistol shot.

"No, and no! And you turned white to the gills, went, and never came back! Just because I said I didn't believe in it. Just because I said I thought there were enough unhappy babies in the world already. Just because you couldn't wait until I knew I wasn't living a dream. Just because you couldn't see that in a day, a month, perhaps in another hour, I would have torn myself to pieces for you, and laughed."

"Robert!" screamed Io with all the strength of her lungs.

She freed her arms, writhed, pushed herself violently from the bed and fell jarringly to the floor. Above the dull thud sounded from within her body a sharp, infinitesimal crack, like the explosion of a minute percussion cap. She lay quite still on her back, arms

306

outthrown, so that her limbs formed a cross, and listened to that tiny sound, as if it lived on in her ears, as if it were a great shout, bidding her arise and walk.

Colter entered almost before the echo of her scream had died. He cast his eyes at the bed, which looked as if a whirlwind had struck it, and then wildly about the room.

"Here, Bob! On the floor!"

He leaned over, slipped his hands beneath her and lifted her. How slight, how incredibly warm and alive! She laid her face against his shoulder; her hands crept around his neck.

"Take me in there," she whispered. "Take me to Drake quickly."

Halfway through the house, he staggered and stopped. The featherweight burden he carried had suddenly grown heavier than his strength could bear. He felt the veins in his temples distending and his head began to reel.

"Robert! What is it? Don't stop."

"Your knees!" he gasped. "They moved!"

She half turned in his arms and raised a radiant face to his.

"I believe it is so," she murmured. "Something happened when I twisted off the bed and fell on the floor. I can move, Bob. Look down. I can move my toes. Hold me so I can see too."

She straightened one leg weakly and moved her toes. Neither she nor Colter laughed or smiled; they stared reverently, beholding for themselves all the miracle of resurrection in the absurd, faint wriggling of five pink toes. From the living room near by the long silence, electrically charged, reached out its waves, included, and drew them. Colter moved on, as one who walks in a half sleep.

When he reached the door Io whispered to him, "Put me down. Let me stand on my own feet."

She looked in and saw Lessie, long bare arms outflung across the table, face down, her amber head fallen between her shoulders. Beyond her was Drake, sitting in a high, square chair, gripping its arms, staring before him with just such a dumb look as his father, Warner Sherborne, had often worn.

"Drake!" called Io.

He changed the direction of his eyes gradually; then his head snapped back and his lips parted to a low cry. Lessie also raised her head and turned toward Io. They stared at the vision framed in the shadowy doorway; a slight, straight figure in a white nightdress, with hands resting against the doorposts on either side, and Robert Colter on guard close behind. Immediately Lessie's face went through one of its remarkable transfigurations. All its trouble faded from sight. It became illumined, generous, radiant with another's joy. Looking upon it, one knew that here was no actress, but a woman who wore her heart on her sleeve only because it was too big for her breast.

Drake leaned forward, his grip on the arms of the chair tightening spasmodically.

"Io!" he cried, arose and walked slowly toward her, staring fixedly as if he did not yet dare credit his eyes.

As he drew near she spoke to him in a whisper.

"Don't touch me, Drake. Don't dare to touch me tonight." He stopped in his tracks, and waited. "There's only one thing in the world that matters," she continued in a whisper. "Only one thing, Drake. Look around and you will see it in the face of the woman who loves you."

He turned obediently, and remained tensely immobile for an instant; then his shoulders braced and he strode swiftly forward. Without looking at him, Lessie arose and stood with one knee slightly bent and one hand resting lightly on the table, her head down, her face still flooded as if with an afterglow of happiness.

"Lessie," said Drake, "can you forgive what I did to you?"

She raised her head and looked at him squarely. Her eyes crinkled at the corners and her lips twitched into a smile.

"Until you did it, Drake," she answered, "I wasn't sure that I loved you."

Chapter 45

The curious may find in the files for May, 1901, of the *Bridgeton Daily Statesman*, established 1886, a boldface announcement which reads thus:

To Whom It May Concern: J. J. (Tryer) Mattis Hereby Gives Notice That Today He Will Drive His Automobile Out The Buckshutem Road, Returning Via The Millville Pike.

Turning to the news columns of the issue of July 17, 1923, of the same journal, the following appears:

For more than a half hour the automobiles filed slowly east and west on Commerce Street. Scores of them, hundreds of them—it seemed thousands. For nearly the entire half hour there was a continuous procession of the machines, and the traffic officers at Bank, Pearl and Laurel Streets had their hands full in regulating and guiding them over the intersections.

Thus has Tryer Mattis been vindicated within the quarter century; thus has the prescience of Judge Alder been overwhelmed.

For the honor of the three counties, however, put on your seven-league boots. Take half a step to the north, and you may straddle forty thousand peach trees and a hundred-thousand-dollar crop of strawberries as the by-products of a single farm. One step to the south, and you may stand knee-deep in the swale of the Cohansey meadows, more shades of green than in a million dollars' worth of emeralds. Drop statistics. Take one more step to the west and lose yourself amid a network, a web, a maze, of the loveliest gravel pikes, lanes and wood roads left in all this Lincoln-Highwayed land for the comfort of horses' feet and the lifting of the heart of man to the throb of a thudding gallop. A rolling country, gentle and soft-spoken in its beauty; but once heard, holding the lingering note of a bell of bronze.

Where else may one find an equal diversity in trees, flowers and grasses; in structures of red brick, clapboard and stone, or in the beat of everyday hearts? All the varieties of oak, including the masquerading chestnut and the finger-leafed willow. Along the runs, broad catalpas; within the woods, the ghostly shadbush, dogwood and magnolia, in seasonal white procession; in the open, astonishing holly trees with trunks four feet in circumferences and berries enough for a carload of Christmas red; on the uplands, the towering plumes of solitary cedars. Of flowers, a legion, from the gold-hearted, immaculate mandrake of April through joe-pye weed to the purple asters of autumn. Of grasses, all the steps from matweed to meadow beauty, and from meadow beauty to the spiked blood of carnation clover.

It is difficult to credit that even as late as Io's wedding on the first of June, 1913, old Uncle Jim, and older Uncle Harry, each with a white chin beard, a fat horse and a ramshackle cab, used still to meet every train, take folks to any address in town for a dime and, in between fares, cart a load of children around for nothing but the pleasure it gave their worn yet unwithered hearts. On the other hand, 1911 had already seen the rocketing of the demand for cement predicted by Tryer Mattis, and the succeeding two years had clinched his reputation as a prophet forever.

Macadam with its ineffectual wet binder was on the wane; asphalt was at the apex of its short preeminence; concrete was coming into its own, and the highway of cement as king of metaled roads was on the eve of its reign. Therefore it is highly fitting, all things considered, that Tryer Mattis, who died in 1916, should have taken it upon himself to pronounce a valedictory on the occasion of the midday breakfast which followed the wedding of Io Sherborne to Robert Colter, of Three Roads Farm, Pedigreed Stock, Alloway.

Ah, yes! Io's marriage. Well, she managed to stand for a moment, to kneel at the silk padded altar for another; but for the most part let it be recorded that she was married against all rules, cradled in Robert's arms, blob of foam in a dress of satin; dark eyes shining through the mist of the bridal veil; a coronet of orange blossoms vying with the fragrance of her hair. Oh, milk-white heifer in the meadows of the gods! Crescent moon against a lover's breast! Arrow to pierce the heart and make it whole! Oh, Io, dear girl, point your feet, lift up your wings, and fly!

Scarcely a single invited guest failed to appear for the ceremony, which constituted in itself the only announcement to the public at large that the bride had miraculously regained the use of all her limbs and was on the highroad to complete recovery. But of all those present none drank in the loveliness of flowers and setting, and of Io herself, more avidly or with deeper emotion than did Eunice—Eunice who had twice been married before a justice of the peace. Happiness thrilled through her veins, setting her aglow, so that hair, face and eyes all seemed to become sources of light. Joy made of her an ageless woman, charged with a distillation of elusive beauty which challenged and then defeated the wondering gaze of the beholder.

Owing to the fragile condition of the bride's health, the reception was of short duration. Guests ate, drank, made merry in moderation for an hour, and went, leaving behind a small gathering for the set wedding breakfast. Most noticeable among this group at first glance was James Fordyce Colter, Esq. Upon arrival he had been received by Io in her sitting room.

She had said, "Bob didn't think you would come," and smiled.

Holding her slender fingers, he had answered, to his nephew's amazement, "My dear, I would have crossed the continent to take the hand that wrote to me. I have been in love with you since the hour your letter came."

Mr. Colter was noticeable by reason of his meticulously groomed appearance. He was not a sartorial exquisite, but his clothes were beautifully made according to a conservative pattern. He held them in great regard and had a theory that wherever they seemed to feel at home he himself was bound to be in his natural element, however contrary the external evidence might appear.

At the moment of crossing the threshold of Rattling Run Fields he had perceived that his clothes entered as though to their own, and when he took his place at table on Io's left he was still absorbed in an effort to discover the reason.

He leaned forward and his brilliant eyes swept the length of the board, pausing to do homage to Lessie's peculiar beauty. "Diva!" he had exclaimed in his surprise at finding her in these surroundings, and she had promptly turned her shoulder on him. Leaving her out, and the rest of the younger generation, he classed the others as having arrived at the static age without accumulating any of the intrinsic values which could lift them from the category of ordinary small-town folk and justify their ready acceptance by his clothes. He was puzzled, but not annoyed; the answer would surely develop in its own time.

Eunice sat on his left; he might look at her, but he could not read her thoughts. She was happier than she had been for many a day, more alive, more at one with Io and Drake than since the hour of their first going away to school. Gazing about her at the changes which had come to Rattling Run Fields, she could scarcely reconstruct those days when she and her children had been draft horses in the fields, or that long night, when, released by the death of Warner Sherborne, she had reviewed her whole life for the judge.

While the others talked she was silent; while they ate and drank she was thinking—thinking with the compact swiftness of a dream, of her father, old Abraham Teller, the cobbler. Of Tryer Mattis, young, frank, too frank; open-faced but shrewd-eyed, free with his money and with his love. Thinking of her own other self, Vic Teller, pride of the hamlet of Greenwich. Of Warner Sherborne. Of this house. These walls. Her first-born. Warner's accusing echo of her cry, "Unhallowed! Unconsecrated!" The snow! The blizzard which had clamped its ice upon the body of her unseen babe! Ah, how terrible! No, she would not think of that. Skip it. Leap. Freedom at last. Her children, fully possessed, then slipping for a time almost beyond the grasp of understanding, now creeping back to the inner places of her love.

With that thought, she linked the judge and William Alder, Jr., in a double glance. Peace filled her eyes, and a smile played with the corners of her lips. Save for his white hair, the judge had scarcely changed; he still shaved with an old-fashioned razor and shaved close, so that his pink cheeks were smooth, pleasant to the touch. The blue in his eyes had paled a little, but not the humor; it twinkled, watching for a chance to blaze.

Opposite him sat his own son, William Alder, Jr., nine years old, freckled, legs badly scratched, and a split toe that was just beginning to itch, showing it was on the mend. The judge never wearied of observing this offshoot of himself. He was more lucky than Eunice in that the boyhood of any man is more or less of a constant; not only does he retain it, fetch it out, dust it off, and reassume it from time to time successfully, but he is more than apt to discover it fundamentally unchanged in his male offspring. As for Eunice, Io was her own daughter; but she could not relive her own life in Io. She had learned that.

Drake, at the head of the table, had Lessie at his right. Eunice wondered why. She had seen Tryer's daughter only once before and had noticed her so little that today she had had to ask who she was. Now she studied her by the little stolen glances with which women size up their own kind apparently without looking, and found her the source of a varied mixture of reactions. She liked her, and she did not like her; there were moments when her face seemed hard, and others when it melted, and melting, softened one's heart.

As for Drake, he scarcely spoke, but his mother needed only to look at him to know that for some reason his melancholy had passed. The set of his jaw was changed, the brooding in his eyes had gone. The more she thought of these things, the more frequently did her eyes go back to the strange face of Lessie Mattis, hauntingly familiar, long-nosed and crowned with amber—a strong face. Yes; admit it—a man's woman, complete. More than that. A woman who might love with something of the broad sweep of her arms and of the depth of her bosom. Drake Sherborne—Lessie Mattis! She looked deliberately at Lessie's hand and was relieved to see that she wore a wedding ring.

Mr. Colter glanced at the youth sitting beside Tom Bodley and wondered what catastrophe had befallen him, for Jimmy Mattis, defiantly unkempt, with wrinkled clothing, bloodshot eyes and badly shaven cheeks, was shaking as if with an ague. He was staring straight ahead, seeing over and over again the marriage of Io Sherborne to another, wondering where he himself had first gone wrong, and cursing the impulse to kiss the bent bow of a white throat which had brought a black period to long years of happy servitude.

Next to him was Tom, once a hogshead of a man, today a half-deflated pigskin; old, very old, too old to worry about more than one thing at a time. During the meal he took a little wine for his stomach's sake rather frequently, and gradually his tongue became loosened. Some driving thought in the abandoned recesses of his mind forced sonorous words from his lips, deeply guttural at first, but presently intelligible.

"'For the Lord thy God bringeth thee into a good land,'" he quoted with roving eyes, "'a land of brooks of water, of fountains and depths that spring out of valleys and hills; A land of wheat, and barley, and vines, and fig trees, and pomegranates; a land of oil olive, and honey; A land wherein thou shalt eat bread without scarceness, thou shalt not lack any thing in it; a land whose stones are iron, and out of whose hills thou mayest dig brass.'"

314

In the thirty seconds it took him to enunciate the pastoral panegyric a subtle change befell the atmosphere of the room. It had not been hilarious at any time, owing to the marked diversity in the persons and attitudes of those present; on the other hand, except for the detached mournfulness depicted in Jimmy's countenance, there had been no doleful note. The change induced by old Tom's words had none of the violence of a shock; it was more as if these people, no less than Mr. James Colter, had been awaiting an eventuality which now made itself manifest.

Through the poetic, rock-ribbed phrases of the apt quotation, through the open windows and through the very stones of the ancient house, Rattling Run Fields, the farm, seemed to enter arrogantly and as by sovereign right to a place amid the company. Rattling Run Fields, not as the murderer of love and Warner Sherborne, not as enemy or friend, but as a crag set within the limits of eternity, changed by human hands, and yet unchanging. Into the minds of all save William Alder, Jr., it came as no mere nebulous presence, but rather as an embodied giant ready to give battle should any accept the challenge.

As though he heard the call, Tryer Mattis stirred in his chair, coupled up his limbs and arose. Well on in his sixtieth year, he was still so massive a figure that he seemed too big for indoors. Caved bulk of a frame, like a looming rock deeply eroded by wind and weather. Leonine head; sandy, irrepressible hair, splotched with white patches. Round eyes, full of the empty insolence of material success. Sagging mouth and scarred face. Yet through it all, not glossing or shining, but rather butting a way against all reason, came the confounding likableness of the man to stare James Fordyce Colter out of countenance and make his clothes feel too small for the occasion.

315

The Lantern on the Plow

Chapter 46

Thus Tryer Mattis: "Folks, in a manner of speaking, all on us here is one family, sons and daughters and connections by marriage of a mother lode of cement rock carrying 75 per cent carbonate of lime. But before we come around to that, there's a thing I want to get off my chest, and this is it: The way people and things feeds on each other and themselves, head eat tail the year round." His shrewd eyes fell on Tom Bodley and narrowed. "Here's Connecticut Tom, now, pensioner on Rattling Run Fields for twelve years. What's Tom? I'll tell you. A lump of education on the road to turning into nothing but fertilizer, and the longer he lives the less top dressing he'll make."

Consternation. A scraping of chairs. Vapid dismay in Tom's face. Tryer's great hand lifted to push protest back down the throats of all, and Tryer's voice rising to a shout:

"Hold fast for the turn! Where's the harm, I say? Where's the harm in Tom, or ever was to God, beast or man? Is there anybody ever knew him wasn't glad to have him around, and can't a plot of ground five feet eight by four feel the same about his carcass without us making a fuss about it? Huh!

"Look at me and the judge, now. I took his woman and he took mine; dog eat dog, and turn about is fair play—only you had ought to have sense enough to pick the right turn. Well, here we are, him and me, and if you ask me to name us, he's all the horse sense in three counties walking on two legs, and me's a load of hay.

"Vic, now."

"Blood of my heart," thought James Colter, "who called these people static?"

Bodley, the judge and Eunice, unresentful, hearts thick in throat, all a-quiver, looked up at Tryer with a uniform rapt expression which, far from bidding him cease, seemed to urge him on, as if they welcomed the thrill of a quickened pulse and the sensation of a last trembling on the verge of life's eternal precipice. Stop him? Never! Let him go on.

"Vic," he continued in a voice which ignored the world at large, "let them as never knowed you when you was sixteen call you Eunice. Girl and woman, you was never really angry with me but once, and that was when I told you I loved you. 'Love!' you says, dynamite in your eye. 'How dare you say that to me?' Them was your words, but I want all here to know, dare or not dare, I never took it back."

"Don't, Tryer," whispered Eunice. "Please don't. It isn't fair."

"Not fair?" repeated Mattis, understanding her, staring at Lessie and then at his son. "Well, perhaps it ain't, but I never was one to lie about them things."

He dropped his eyes as though he had been thrown off his subject, but presently raised them to look at Io.

"As for you, Io, half as big as a minute, skinful of mortal nerve, I'll say no word against you only this: You ate up my son Jimmy without thinking, like a pretty snake swallowing of a toad. Look at him!"

He faced squarely toward Jimmy and roared, "By the living Harry and the blazing Zenith, if you don't go to work tomorrow I'll take you up and throw you off where she had the guts to jump!"

He turned slowly and his gaze met that of Lessie. A tremor shot through him and his shoulders braced. Lion to lion's whelp; no cringing on either side. She sat, elbow on table; chin in hand, cool and smiling in the face of battle. One could read the glimmer of a thought, a cry, in Tryer's eye as he looked at her: "Ah, Lessie, all that was best in your dad, why weren't you a boy?" But he did not say the words aloud.

His face hardened and his lips opened, but before he could speak——

"Say it if you dare, you old thingumabob," murmured Lessie.

"Thing what?" shouted Tryer, instantly enraged.

If she had called him anything else—hypocrite, bag of wind, scoundrel—But no. She wouldn't; not her! She had to pick the one word that no man ever yet found a grip on!

"You!" he shouted. "Ever since you could talk you've been spitting me back in my face!"

Last flare of the genius for imagery. Everybody knew instantly what he meant, and saw that it was true, like at war with like. Up went his hands in his familiar gesture of a man fighting off bees.

"I don't want to fight you or anybody else! I want to be friends, even to you. Didn't I say that all on us here is one family in a manner of speaking, and didn't I mean it?"

He shook his shoulders, calmed himself and faced Drake.

"This here is what I wanted to say: We're all sons and daughters of the same mother lode; but you, Drake, is the master of Rattling Run Fields. Eleven years ago the judge fitted out a legal straitjacket in the way of a contract and I put it on. Why? Because I seen what was coming. We opened in 1901 at one dollar twenty cents a barrel and dropped to eighty cents three years later. Was I scared? No! Because I'd told the judge about cement roads when he was still wondering whether motor cars would die out. Huh! And now we seen it come, them roads people thought I was crazy on, and what else? What else have we seen? I ask you. Cement touching the roof, jumping from a piddling eight million barrels for the whole country thirteen years ago to over ninety millions in this last twelvemonth.

"But that's neither here nor there. This is what I say: The contract that bears the names of me and Warner Sherborne is the charter of the Rattling Run Cement Company, and it's got only four years more to go. It's high time all on us knowed where we stand. Drake, listen to me. Do I wear that straitjacket for another fifteen years, or do we get something that cuts even, both ways?"

There was a long pause before Drake, frowning, asked, "How many acres have you blasted away, Tryer? I mean, how far has the floor of the quarry spread? How many acres?"

"That's the queerest question a quarryman ever heard," commented Tryer. "Put it in tons and I can tell you. Two million, nine hundred and thirty thousand, and next week we pass the three-million mark."

"Tons?" cried Drake, startled, half rising from his chair.

"Yes, sir, tons."

"Well, Tryer, listen to this: From the day that contract expires, there'll be no more blasting on Rattling Run Fields, tearing its heart to pieces. Never another blast. Make your plans accordingly."

For a moment the room was absolutely still. Tryer swayed forward and leaned with his knuckles on the table.

"Say that last again, will you, and say it slow."

Drake repeated his words.

"Never another blast," whispered Tryer, and then rocked his head from side to side and roared. Not laughter. He roared like the king of beasts with a javelin in his side, a terrible sound, an awe-inspiring bellow that only gradually became intelligible.

"Never another blast! No more blasting! You can't stop me— Tryer Mattis! Perhaps I can't split a rock, but I can try. Ask Vic! Ask her! Two cases of dynamite, one in the corner yonder and the other is me. By the living rock of Rattling Run, I'll bore a hole in it three feet wide and a hundred! I'll drop myself into it and I'll blow your—your damn—your God damn———"

Purple in the face, bloated, gasping for breath, knees suddenly slumping, he crashed backward into his chair. They leaned forward and watched him, prayed for him, every one. Air; air for his lungs, and he got it. He breathed, at first gaspingly, and then with a slow, steady heave of his chest. Head bowed, hands laid loosely on the table, he looked vacantly around until his eyes fell on his daughter.

"Lessie, my lass, come on out of this."

"Where to, father?"

"Where do you think? Home to your bed and board. Home, where you belong."

"This is my home, father. Here's where I belong, and nothing and no one will ever throw me out."

Drake arose and she with him. He put his arm around her and looked first at Eunice and then into Io's shining eyes. A smile twisted the corners of his lips and lifted them; a smile which the judge, for one, remembered across the years; such a smile as can die from a face, but never from the eyes which have seen it.

"Today a mistress goes out from this house," said Drake simply, "and another enters—Lessie Sherborne, who has been my wife for almost a year."

There was silence, a long silence.

Toy balloons, ordinary people, nothing much to look at, gathered for a space around Drake Sherborne's board: Farewell.

You pass, and yet you do not pass. Spring cannot always reign. Flakes of snow, like great white tears, will drive against the panes, yet surely the branch will bud, the leaf sprout, and the vine send forth its shoots. Thus Rattling Run Fields across the measured cycles of the years; and thus you also may endure.

THE END.

Drawings by Ernest Fuhr

Drawings on the following pages illustrated the serialized, first publication of *The Lantern on the Plow* in the *Saturday Evening Post*.

Ernest Fuhr (1874–1933), born in New York City, was a successful magazine illustrator during the first third of the twentieth century. He served as illustrator for the *New York Herald* and the *New York World* newspapers as well as for magazines such as the *Saturday Evening Post*. Fuhr studied at the National Academy of Design in New York and in Paris at the Academie Colarossi. William Merritt Chase and Thomas Eakins were among his teachers.

Repository: Library of Congress Prints and Photographs Division Washington, D.C. 20540 USA http://hdl.loc.gov/loc.pnp/pp.print
Medium: Charcoal and wash.
Gift; Ernest Fuhr estate.
Forms part of: Cabinet of American illustration (Library of Congress).

The Cabinet of American Illustration contains more than four thousand original drawings by American book, magazine, and newspaper illustrators, made primarily between 1880 and 1910. It includes illustrations for magazines, novels, and children's books; cartoons; cover designs; and sketches for posters. More than two hundred artists are represented, including Charles Dana Gibson, Elizabeth Shippen Green, Oliver Herford, and Jessie Wilcox Smith.

The collection was the brainchild of William Patten, art editor for *Harper's Magazine* during the 1880s and 1890s, who established the Cabinet of American Illustration in 1932, in cooperation with the Library of Congress, in order to create a national collection of original works of art documenting what he and others considered the golden age of American illustration that took place from the 1880s through the 1920s. Donations by artists, publishers, and their families have fostered the growth of the collection.

Are you the man of the lantern on the plow? (page 13)

The judge knew she had heard him. (page 23)

He stood profoundly still. (page 51)

"That man," she whispered. (page 63)

He tried to remember that only a few weeks before. (page 129)

At sight of her, Tryer caught his breath and gulped. (page 161)

At that moment the morsel of human woe in his arms . . . (page 166)

For a long time neither of them spoke. (page 229)

George Agnew Chamberlain

Colophon

The text of this edition of *The Lantern on the Plow* is based on the 1924 edition. Several talented editing interns helped to established the initial text, to create the design and layout, and to proofread. They include Mariah Ayala, Olivia Harris, Zophia Krause, Nyzira Lynn, Isabella Monacchio, Cassius Navarro, Katharyn Sagusti, Rose Shaw, Lindsay Wilson, Rachel Wronko. Cassius Navarro drew the lantern used throughout the text. Cynthia Anstey completed the final proofreading. Tom Kinsella supervised all aspects of book production. A hearty thanks goes to Jim Bergmann, the South Jersey resident expert on George Agnew Chamberlain. This book would not have come about without his encouragement and advice.

The text is set in 12-point Baskerville. Chapter divisions, signaled in the original text by small lantern glyphs, have been regularized. Gary Schenck completed the cover design.

This is a publication of the South Jersey Culture & History Center at Stockton University. Our mission is to foster awareness within local communities of the rich cultural and historical heritage of southern New Jersey, to promote the study of this heritage, especially among area students, and to produce publishable materials that provide a lasting and deepened understanding of this heritage.

stockton.edu/sjchc/

Other Literary Titles
Published by SJCHC

Dallas Lore Sharp. *Seasons.*
"Nature appears at her best when Dallas Lore Sharp introduces it." So wrote an anonymous book reviewer in the *Journal of Education* in August 1912 about the author of *Seasons.* Born in 1870 in Haleyville, New Jersey, Sharp spent his childhood roaming the woods beside the Cohansey and Maurice Rivers, and went on to become one of the most popular nature writers of his day. A "rare and honest soul," he sought to inspire young people to share his appreciation for the glories of the natural world, available in their own backyards. *Seasons* presents a selection of essays first published in Sharp's *The Whole Year Round.* 158 pages, paperback.
ISBN: 978-0-9888731-1-7. $14.95

Dallas Lore Sharp. *The Nature of Things.*
Our second volume of engaging nature essays from Sharp's *The Whole Year Round,* originally published in 1915. Dallas Lore Sharp, born in 1870 in Haleyville, Cumberland County, New Jersey, was an outstanding essayist writing for young adults in the early twentieth century.
179 pages, paperback.
ISBN: 978-1-947889-00-2. $14.95

Samuel Scoville Jr. *Everyday Adventures.*
Twelve essays that describe Samuel Scoville Jr.'s jaunts into nature with arresting detail and introduce readers to hibernating mammals, snakes, orchids, and other flora, but especially to birds. Whether listening to birdsong, searching for hidden nests (which remain undisturbed), or quietly observing avian daily routines, Scoville describes his surroundings vividly and often with considerable wit. He recounts expeditions in Connecticut, the Berkshires, Pennsylvania, Delaware, the Pine Barrens, and the far north of Canada. Quickly, readers find that they have stepped into everyday adventures of their own.
252 pages, paperback.
ISBN: 978-0-9976699-9-2. $14.95

Samuel Scoville Jr. *The Out of Doors Club.*

A collection of essays that follows the adventures of the "Band," a group of siblings led on imagination-filled hikes by their father. In twenty brief essays, many set in the Pine Barrens, Samuel Scoville Jr. reminds readers of simpler times, when the world held fewer cares and nature walks with a parent could be the highlight of a day. Trekking through fields, bogs and forests, canoing down rivers, the Band learn amusing lessons about nature and life. Readers will appreciate the gentle and loving relationship depicted between father, mother and children.

147 pages, paperback.
ISBN: 978-1-947889-90-3. $14.95

Charles K. Landis. *A Trip to Mars.*

Charles K. Landis, prominent real estate developer and founder of Vineland and Sea Isle City, New Jersey, wrote this foray into science fiction on an early typewriter c. 1876. The title alternates between thrilling storytelling and thinly veiled commentary on the social ills of Earth. A pair of intrepid travelers journey to Mars, explore its geography, confront terrifying monsters, and encounter the ancient culture and philosophy of the Martians, from whom the Earthlings may learn much. Never before published. With an introduction by Patricia Martinelli.

136 pages, paperback.
ISBN: 978-0-9888731-5-5. $14.95

Gary B. Giberson. *Swan Bay Jim & Gasoline Seventeen Cents a Gallon; Moonshine a Dollar a Quart.*

The mayor of Port Republic for over three decades, Gary B. Giberson is a master decoy-carver, entrepreneur, and author. This volume pairs two short stories with illustrations from distinguished artist Kathy Anne English. Follow a poignant hunt through the cedar swamps of the Mullica River and join an adventurous chase to capture rum runners during Prohibition.

40 pages, paperback.
ISBN: 978-0-9976699-4-7. $5.00

George Agnew Chamberlain. *Highboy Rings Down the Curtain.*

George Agnew Chamberlain's 1923 story about a proud, high-stepping horse and its aging owner. The story pivots around a high-spirited gelding named Highboy, who has been given up as too recalcitrant to ever be a show horse. Bimbo, Kindly Crewe's resident horse trainer, believes that Highboy has great potential and needs someone like Kindly to give him a reason to show off his abilities. The story goes on to tell just how that happens.

xii + 45 pages, paperback
ISBN: 978-1-947889-17-0. $8.95.